At the *Point of the Bay*

At the

Point
of the **Bay**

KENNETH TYE

ARCHWAY
PUBLISHING

Archway Publishing books may be ordered through booksellers or by contacting:

Archway Publishing
1663 Liberty Drive
Bloomington, IN 47403
www.archwaypublishing.com
1-(888)-242-5904

ISBN: 978-1-4808-0071-7 (sc)
ISBN: 978-1-4808-0069-4 (hc)
ISBN: 978-1-4808-0070-0 (e)

Library of Congress Control Number: 2013908589

Printed in the United States of America

Archway Publishing rev. date: 5/22/2013

DEDICATION

This book is dedicated to Barbara, my wife, colleague, and best friend, who helped and supported me through the process of writing this book

It is also dedicated to my daughter Debbie, who read the drafts, made comments, and also learned some things about her ancestors

CONTENTS

LIST OF MAIN
CHARACTERS

PART ONE: THE VILLAGE AT
THE POINT OF THE BAY

Notaku – first village chief

Helki – Notaku's first wife

Litonya – Helki's younger sister and Notaku's second wife

Lokni – Notaku's first son and second chief

Elsu – Notaku's second son and village elder

Sitala I – shaman

Malila – Elsu's wife

Kolenya – Lokni's wife

Manipi – shaman

Langundo – Lokni's grandson and village chief

Sitala II – shaman

Captain Pedro Fages – first Spanish explorer to reach the village (1772)

Father Juan Crespi – accompanies Fages, writes diary

Juan Manuel Ayala – captain of the *San Carlos*, which sailed past the point of the bay (1775)

Don Jose Canizarers, Juan Batista Aquilar – first and second mates on the *San Carlos*

Captain Juan Bautista de Anza – second Spanish explorer to reach the village (1776)

Father Pedro Font – accompanies de Anza

Telutci – Langundo's son and village chief

Lieutenant Gabriel Moraga – led attack on Suisuns, Carquins, and Chupcans (1810)

PART TWO: THE MISSION AT THE POINT OF THE BAY

Father Lasuen – founder of Mission San Jose

Magdalena – Native American convert (neophyte) with measles

Father Duran – Franciscan head of Mission San Jose

Lilia – young girl who is raped

Anselmo (Molimo) – rebellious neophyte

Salvino (Sewati) – rebellious neophyte

Cucunuchi – young Yokut Indian who converts and becomes Estanislao and leads resistance movement against Spanish

Jedediah Smith – American trapper who helps Indians organize against the Spanish

Antonio Soto – Indian fighter who leads first attack against Estanislao and his Indians

Ensign Jose Sanchez – leader of the second attack against Estanislao's forces

Ensign Mariano Vallejo – leader of the third and successful attack of Estanislao's forces

Juanita – Estanislao's daughter and Sebastiano Perez's wife

Sebastiano Perez – Spanish soldier who gets land grant and marries Juanita, owner of Rancho Santa Maria

Luz – Estanislao's wife and Juanita's mother

Elvira – Juanita's sister

Orencio – brother of Estanislao and Juanita's uncle

Enzo – trusted neophyte worker for Sebastiano and Juanita and carreta driver

Linda Consuela – first child of Sebastiano and Juanita

PART THREE: THE RANCHOS AT THE POINT OF THE BAY

Don Salvio Pacheco – founder of Rancho Monte del Diablo

Don Fernando Pacheco – son of Don Salvio, sent to manage Rancho Monte del Diablo

Colleta – Juanita's maid

Doña Maria Pacheco – Fernando Pacheco's wife

Doña Juana Flores Pacheco – Don Salvio Pacheco's wife

Harold Marsh – nephew of John Marsh, suitor of Elvira at Rancho Santa Maria

Jorge Perez – second child of Sebastiano and Juanita

Dr. John Marsh – owner of Rancho Los Meganos

Hipolito – carpenter at Ranch Santa Maria

Ruben Perez – third child of Sebastiano and Juanita

PART FOUR: THE COMING OF THE AMERICANS TO THE POINT OF THE BAY

John Sutter – gold discovered on his land

Elena Perez – fourth child of Sebastiano and Juanita

William Simms – visitor to Rancho Santa Maria, later partner of Sebastiano and husband of Linda Perez

David Broderick – San Francisco businessman

Yan Wo – chairman of the Chinese Benevolent Association

Sam Brannan – gold country businessman

Levi Strauss – San Francisco businessman

Abigale Marsh – wife of Dr. John Marsh

Alice Marsh – daughter of Dr. John and Abigale Marsh

Jose Olivas and Felipe Moreno – vaqueros who murdered Dr. John Marsh

Charles Earl Bowles (Black Bart) – gold country holdup man and versifier

Notaku – descendent of original Notaku and worker for William Simms

PART FIVE: THE TOWN OF BAY POINT

Daniel Cunningham – early settler at Bay Point

Addison Neely – partner with Daniel Cunningham

Daniel Finnegan – foreman of construction of the San Pablo–Tulare Railroad Company at the point of the bay

Samuel Bacon – partner of Sebastiano Perez

William Patterson, Charles Patterson, David Jones – train robbers

Aaron Birk – railroad detective

Frank L. Gardiner – founder of Copper King Mines at the point of the bay

Charles Axel Smith – owner of C. A. Smith Lumber Company

Arno Mereen – C. A. Smith's friend and colleague

Simon Cunningham – Daniel Cunningham's son and Bay Point businessman

Dan Desmond – C. A. Smith foreman

Betty Palawski – midwife, bootlegger, and mother of Martha Palawski

Albert Chapman – foreman at C. A. Smith Lumber Company and head of the Chapman family

Gustav Hansson, Knut Svenson, Icarus Petridis, Jacob Kaminski – employees of C. A. Smith Lumber Company and visitors to a brothel

PART SIX: PORT CHICAGO

Robert (Robbie) Chapman – son of Albert Chapman, husband of Martha Palawski, father of John (Johnny) Chapman

Martha Palawski – Betty Palawski's daughter, Robert Chapman's wife, Walter Rankin's wife, Johnny Chapman's mother

Jeff Palawski – Martha's older brother

Lillian Chapman – Albert Chapman's wife, Robert Chapman's mother

John (Johnny) Chapman – son of Martha and Robert Chapman, later adopted by Walter Rankin and took the name Johnny Rankin

Owen Van Horn – owner of utilities and other property in Port Chicago, responsible for the name change from Bay Point to Port Chicago

Wilma Miller – became Wilma Chapman, Johnny Rankin's aunt

Hugh Rankin – Johnny Rankin's younger brother

Frank Chapman – younger brother of Robert Chapman and husband of Wilma Miller

Marni Chapman – oldest daughter of Frank and Wilma Chapman, later married to Fred Cabrita

Mrs. Crane – the Rankin neighbor who served with Johnny Rankin in the Aircraft Warning System

Gloria Grumman – neighbor girl of the Rankins

Elisa Mercurio – Johnny Rankin's first love

Tina Bianci – Elisa Mercurio's cousin, later the wife of Aldo Contavalli

Margaret Charles – Johnny Rankin's second love

Kent Grumman – the Rankins' neighbor

Nikos Kostupolous, Eric Johnson, Bart Cox, Marco Contavalli, and Guilio Contavalli – Johnny Rankin's boyhood friends

Bob Newman and Ed Freire – high school friends of Johnny Rankin

Jethro Ross Smith, Earl Thomas Hughes, and Willie Lee Battle – surviving sailors of the Port Chicago explosion and participants in the Port Chicago Mutiny

Rear Admiral Carleton "Bosco" Wright – commander of the Twelfth Naval District, with the Port Chicago Naval Base under his command

Thurgood Marshall – chief counsel of the National Association for the Advancement of Colored People

Carlos Lopez – Johnny Rankin's butcher shop boss

PART SEVEN: THE TOWN IS DEMOLISHED

Greg Davis – Port Chicago rancher, leader of the pro-navy buyout plan

Aldo Contavalli, Andy Zaworski, Judge Oscar Litchfield, Eric Johnson, Bart Cox, and Kent Grumman – early leaders of the anti-navy buyout plan

Luigi Amato, Harold Martinson – pro-navy buyout plan supporters

Eugenia Van Horn – wife of Owen Van Horn, owner of all his properties after his death, major opponent of the navy buyout plan

Judge Litchfield – justice of the peace, leader of the opposition to the navy takeover

Ramona Cabrita – president of the Royal Neighbors, mother of Fred Cabrita

Nancy Caudell, Betty Johnson – other members of the Royal Neighbors

JoAnne Rankin – Hugh Rankin's wife

Congressman John Baldwin, Congressman Jerome Waldie – opposed the navy buyout plan, proposed that the navy move the base

Captain T. R. Eddy – commanding officer of the Concord Naval Weapons Station

Jim Edwards , David Hansen – flew with Aldo Contavalli to Washington, DC, to plead the town's case

Governor Ronald Reagan

Wanda Sykes – waitress at Humphrey's Inn

Marsha Humphrey – owner of Humphrey's Inn, supporter of the navy buyout plan

Fred Cabrita – San Francisco Giants first baseman, leader of opposition to the navy buyout plan, stood his ground against US marshals delivering eviction notice

PART EIGHT: UNCERTAINTY ABOUT THE FUTURE

PREFACE

This is a historical novel. The setting is the point of the bay, earlier called Seal Bluff, on the southern shore of Suisun Bay, halfway between San Francisco on the west and the Sacramento–San Joaquin River Delta on the east. It is the story of the people who have inhabited the area, beginning with the Chupcan Indians in the early eighteenth century. They are said to have lived there for over five thousand years in what historians have often referred to as Eden because of the harmony between humans and the environment.

Many of the characters in the story are fictional. Some are real. The historical context is as accurate as possible, based on a good deal of research, with a few adjustments to aid the narrative.

The location of the Chupcan Indian village is thought to be close to accurate. The description and the activities that take place there are made up, but based upon fact. The same is true of the arrival of the Spanish; the founding and life at Mission San Jose; the story of Estanislao, the Indian rebel; life at Rancho Monte del Diablo and the towns of Bay Point and Port Chicago; the story of the naval ammunition depot with the explosion of two ammunition ships in 1944 and the subsequent mutiny trial of black sailors who refuse to return to the loading of ammunition; and the destruction of the town of Port Chicago by the navy. The story of Rancho Santa Maria and the Perez family is fictional and serves as a bridge from one period to another. Other historical events such as the gold rush, the growth of San Francisco, the building of the railroads, prohibition, bootlegging, and prostitution are historically accurate but told mostly by fictional characters and through fictional events.

The recurring theme of the book is the cycle of the building and dreams of one group of people after another on the one hand, and the destruction of those dreams on the other, followed by the rise of the next group. The book ends with up-to-date events at the point of the bay and speculation about the future.

ACKNOWLEDGMENTS

I wish to thank Dean McLeod, a historian of Chupcan Indian life as well as the history of Port Chicago and surrounding areas. He generously gave of his time and materials to make my task easier.

Patricia Harriman patiently and thoroughly edited my copy. More importantly, she made suggestions that helped to make the story more readable and interesting.

The Contra Costa Historical Society made available to me any number of historical documents that helped to make the descriptions of events as accurate as possible.

Others I wish to thank are Paul Apodaca, an anthropologist of Native American descent and a professional colleague who gave me insights into the lives of early California Indians. My brother-in-law, Ian Benham, my son Steven Tye, as well as friends William Norin, William James, and Robert Leon, all read drafts and gave me good feedback. Finally, I wish to thank my brother, Bill, for sharing with me his memories of our town, and my cousin Nancy Colchico, who gave me valuable information about our family tree.

PART ONE

THE VILLAGE AT THE POINT OF THE BAY

FAMILY TREE
— 1 —

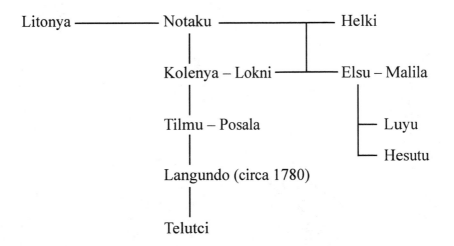

Litonya ———————— Notaku ——————┐———— Helki

Kolenya – Lokni ——┴—— Elsu – Malila

Tilmu – Posala ├— Luyu

Langundo (circa 1780) └— Hesutu

Telutci

MAP ONE: BAY MIWOK PEOPLE

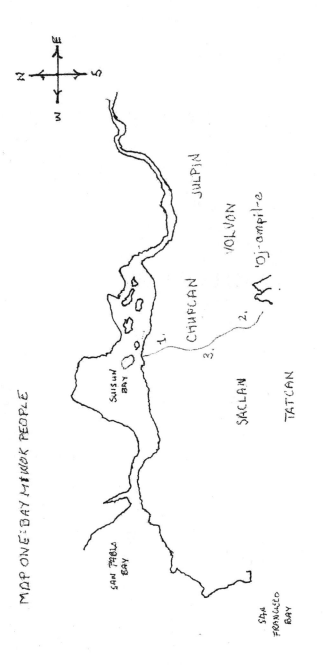

N E
W S

SAN PABLO BAY

SAN FRANCISCO BAY

SUISUN BAY

CHUPCAN

SACLAN

TATCAN

VOLVON

JULPIN

'Oj-ampil-e

1.

2.

3.

CHAPTER 1

THE EXPEDITION

The baby was restless in his cradle. He was nearly two and no longer suckled at his mother's breast. According to tradition, it was time for him to receive his name and to leave the confines of the cradle.

A large brown bear had entered the village and was feasting on a stash of honey gathered from the wild beehives in a nearby grove of trees. The villagers were alerted to the bear's presence by the growling and snuffling noises it made as it next tried to reach the deer, elk, and rabbit meat that was hanging to dry. Men, women, and children began to shout at the bear, and many of the men began to poke at him with spears. "Get back!" they shouted.

The bear continued growling and moved toward the baby in the cradle, but instead of attacking its tormentors or the baby, it lumbered away to look for food elsewhere. Thus, soon after the event, the baby boy was named Notaku, "Growling Bear."

Now in his early thirties, Notaku was the chief of his village, as his father had been before him. He was an important member of his extended clan and subject only to Enyeto, the chief of the main Chupcan tribe, who lived in a larger village about five miles away. It was near the foothills of the local mountain, Oj-ompil-e, which the Spanish later called Monte del Diablo. The people of this larger village did not depend on the bay for food and the tule reeds used for building materials and clothes, although they did trade for these items. Rather, the villagers fished for trout and salmon in the streams and hunted for the deer, rabbits, elk, and other animals that were plentiful near their own village. As with all villages in the Chupcan area, the nearby oak trees and their acorns provided a large part of their sustenance.

As was the custom in the summer, Notaku wore no clothes. He was muscular, about five foot six, and his long hair hung down over his shoulders nearly to his waist. His hair was tied in a knot at the top of his head with a band he had made from animal sinew. He wore no sandals, and the bottoms of his feet were hardened from walking barefoot. Scraggly hair covered his cheeks, above his mouth, and down his chin. His skin was dark, and tattoos spread across his chin and cheeks. A small bone pierced the lobe of his left ear. He smiled often and was known as a pleasant and approachable leader.

Notaku made the rounds of the village each evening. This particular evening was special because the next day there was to be an expedition to the bay, and it was his job to tell the villagers what game, fish, birds, and tules they might look forward to sharing. Old people, widows, orphans, and others understood that he would take care of them from both the community stores and his own wealth, which as chief he was obliged to give away. As he made the rounds, he would get questions from different people. "Will you bring me some tules so that I can make new mats and baskets?" "I hope you can bring back some salmon from the bay, since we have not had fresh fish for a while." "We would really like some ducks, such a delicacy." To all of the comments and requests, Notaku would always answer, "We will do our best for you."

In the morning, Notaku stepped out of his large wickiup next to a smaller one, both of which housed his family—his two wives and five children. He looked east into the rising sun and called to his second son. "This is your eighth summer, Elsu. Now it is your time to go with me and your older brother, Lokni, to the bay to help catch fish, gather tules, and hunt for any game we might find.

Some of our neighbors will go with us to do the same for their families and for coming celebrations."

The skies over the village and the surrounding area bristled with the soaring and sounds of a rich variety of birds. The most revered of these were the falcons. When he finished his suckling, Elsu had received his name, "Soaring Falcon." His older brother was born in the first wickiup during the rainy season. The wickiup in which he was born was made from birch and covered with tules. During a storm, the roof would leak. The name given to this baby was Lokni, "Rain Falls through the Roof." Each child carried the name of his early life throughout his years.

Elsu felt honored to be invited to go to the bay. "Thank you, Father. I will try hard to do my share and make you proud. I have been practicing with the spear I made and with one of the nets in the village."

Looking down at his growing son, Notaku smiled warmly. "Good. With you and Lokni able to fish, and then later hunt, we all will provide well for the family and maybe even increase our trade for other things we need." He went on, "Soon you will be able to choose if you want to continue to work with the women making acorn mush and gathering grasses, insects, and honey or to hunt and fish and be with the men."

Elsu eagerly responded, "I will choose to hunt and fish and to be with the men!"

The day of the expedition began with the hunters and fishermen going to the men's sweathouse two hours before sunrise. About eighteen feet in diameter and dug about three feet belowground, the sweathouse was made of bark and tules, covered with dirt and grasses, and had a deerskin door. In the middle of the house was a large fire filling the dwelling with smoke and intense heat.

One of the men threw sage into the fire, remarking, "The odor will help to cover our smells so the animals will not notice us."

Elsu was excited to be in the sweathouse. He had been there before, but never with a group of hunters and fishermen. Anxious to join and not be a bother, he told his father, "I hope the animals will not know my smell."

Notaku looked at his son. "Even though you are still growing, I don't think they will smell you. You do need to keep yourself cleaner as you get older."

Elsu nodded to his father and vowed to himself to follow his advice.

The time in the sweathouse was followed by a meal of acorn mush, roasted grasshoppers, strips of dried deer meat, and berries and grapes. During the meal, Elsu looked admiringly at his older brother. "Lokni, I want to stay close to you and learn all the things I will need to know about fishing and hunting."

Lokni smiled with pride. "I will be happy for you to be with me during the expedition, and I will try to teach you what I know."

After the meal, Notaku, his sons, and other men and boys from the village set off for the bay, a walk of about three miles. Some of the men and older boys carried canoes made from tules, paddles made from local birch trees tied together with animal tendons, and long poles—all for catching fish and game in the marshes and sloughs. Others carried birch bows and arrows. Some of the group would go out in the tule canoes a short way into the bay to catch salmon, sturgeon, and bass with their throw nets and spears. Even though there were other kinds of fish in the bay, as well as many catfish in the sloughs, these three were their favorites.

Notaku and his sons walked together and talked about the day. The father noticed his youngest son struggling with the weight he was carrying. "Are you enjoying yourself? The poles you are carrying seem like a very heavy load for you."

Elsu, who was small-boned and thin but strong for his age, did his best to stand taller. "I am really glad to be with you and the other men on the way to hunting and fishing. The poles are no problem. I could carry many more."

Lokni jumped into the conversation. "Ha! You are bent like a willow branch. You could not carry more poles. Should I take some from you, little brother?"

"No!" shouted Elsu. He made a point of walking past his brother, and then he mumbled without turning around, "Take care of your own load."

During the short journey to the marshes and the bay, all of the men were quite animated as they laughed, told stories, and sang hunting songs. The boys in the group listened and participated when they could. However, as they approached their destination, Notaku spoke firmly. "It is time to be quiet. Otherwise, we will scare off the birds, fish, and other game."

The group began to communicate silently with head, hand, and arm movements.

Notaku motioned to a small group of the men and boys to set up poles and nets to capture ducks, geese, and other birds. Another group was assigned the task of canoeing into the bay to use other nets and spears in the hope of catching a bounty of fish to eat now or dry for later use. A third group was sent with spears and bows and arrows to hunt deer, elk, and other animals. The final small group had the task of cutting the better tules and cattails. The tules would be used for construction and clothing, their sprouts and roots for food. The pollen from the cattails was mixed with water and made into cakes, mush, or bread. Fluff from the spike was used to line cradle boards and as diapers for babies in the cradles. The young roots were considered a delicacy. The roots also could be peeled, dried, pounded, and used for flour.

Luckily, the villagers had been able to trade for the obsidian used for spear points, scrapers, fish hooks, and other tools. It came from people far to the north, who took it from the lava of the numerous volcanoes of that area. By the time the obsidian reached the Chupcans, after it was traded through several tribes, it was very expensive. But they didn't mind trading furs and baskets for the valuable rock.

The group worked efficiently for the rest of the day. They encountered only one problem, their natural nemesis: four brown bears intent upon their own fishing. Instead of trying to scare the bears off, Notaku said, "Let us see if we can kill a couple of these bears. If we can, then we can skin them here and take the meat and pelts back to the village."

Elsu timidly asked his father, "I thought that the brown bears were revered by our people. You are named after the bear. Are we really supposed to kill them?"

His father, smiling gently, answered, "Yes, I am named Notaku, and brown bears are very special to our people. We do honor them and usually do not kill them. However, the skins and the meat are needed by our people and for trading; and that is most important right now."

Killing the bears was not easy. They were agitated and growled, stood on their hind feet, and swatted at the villagers with their sharp claws. The men shouted and fought back with spears, poles, and bows and arrows. Above the din, Notaku could be heard yelling directions. "Over here … attack the small bear first … work in fours or fives … be careful of the claws." The men were successful in killing three of the bears, while the last one loped away.

The bad news was that one of the boys had been clawed. His right thigh had been slashed. Blood was pouring down his leg. After staunching the blood flow with tules and mud from the marshes, Notaku directed, "Because of his wounds, Wilu will remain here on solid ground while we continue our fishing and hunting. Kono, you will stay with him and also begin the process of gutting and skinning the three bears with obsidian and abalone shell scrapers."

As a team, the group had succeeded and survived. Once they knew that Wilu would be taken care of, each group of men set about completing its assigned task. They worked hard for a long time, stopping only to walk back to the village before the sun went down. In addition to the bears, they had killed a number of deer and elk and had caught a lot of fish and several birds, mainly ducks and geese. They also managed to cut a large number of tules and cattails and to dig out their roots with obsidian stones and abalone shells.

Before they began the trip back to the village, Notaku walked to the point of the bay with Elsu and Lokni. They looked to the east and west, and then out into the bay to see the islands that were visible from their vantage point. He said to his sons, "We are fortunate to have such a beautiful and bountiful place. We can provide a good life for our families."

Wilu was placed in a canoe to be carried back to the village, along with many of the ducks and geese that had been captured in nets and killed. Notaku gave directions to the group. "Tie the fish and other birds together with tules so that long strings of them can be carried over the shoulders of some of the boys. Some of you tie tules together in bundles to be carried back to the village. Those who have been hunting, lash the deer and elk to poles, so that each pole can be carried by two men."

The bears presented a special problem. They had been gutted, and two of them had been skinned and quartered so the meat could be carried. The one that still needed to be treated was lashed on two poles that could be dragged back to the village by two men.

The walk back was not easy, because of the size of the catch, but the group was happy. It had been a successful day. They laughed, told stories and sang, although they were quieter than they had been in the morning, because they were tired, and because of their care for the wounded boy. When they returned to the village, they stored the deer, all the birds and fish, the tules and cattails, the bears, and two snakes in the large, central ceremonial round house, the *hangi*, where tomorrow everything would be divided among the villagers.

Wilu was brought to the village shaman, Sitala, an elderly woman. Although it was uncommon to have a woman as a shaman, Sitala commanded respect from the villagers because of her connections with the spirit world. Often she had a glazed look that was caused by the use of special hallucinogenic herbs.

Notaku approached Sitala as the others brought Wilu to her. "I hope you can help him. He is a fine young man and always takes part in what needs to be done. Unfortunately, that's how he got injured."

Sitala looked over at Wilu and then turned back and nodded to Notaku. "I will appeal to the spirit gods for assistance and use special plants and stones to cure Wilu. I will also suck the pain from his body."

Sitala was also able to predict the future, start the rains, and see to the religious needs of the village. In very serious cases of illness, she resorted to singing and the use of a cocoon rattle. In return for her services, Sitala was provided with a hut, food, and other necessities by the villagers, and she was paid for her services with various kinds of shell money, hides, and other types of rewards.

The evening ended with a village celebration in the hangi. Dug four feet into the ground and covered with earth, the frame of the structure consisted of four crotched poles, with numerous rafters holding up the roof. The largest structure in the village, the hangi could hold up to one hundred people. Unlike major celebrations planned long in advance—such as the acorn harvest celebration, or those having to do with marriage, passage to adulthood, birth, death, or the spirit world—this celebration was spontaneous, in honor of the bountiful nature of these lands and the success of the expedition.

The event involved looking over and dividing up the catch of the day, as well as feasting on the plethora of foods to be found nearby: deer, rabbits, fish, nuts, berries, wild grasses and plants, and the ever-present acorn mush and bread. It also involved games, dancing, music, and storytelling.

A favorite game of the village was *Hi'nuwa* (The Hand Game), a guessing game. Two pairs of deer bones about the size of a man's index finger were grooved and wrapped together with sinew. Ten sticks of willow, about eight inches long, were used as counters. Two players on each side hid the bones, and anyone could bet on the game by choosing one of the pairs. One pair of the players had the first turn. They hid the bones somewhere nearby, rolled them around, and sang a gambling song in order to confuse their opponents. One of the men who was watching became very excited and began to shout, "Look under the mat. They are hidden there! No, look under her blanket; that is better!"

When the time came for guessing, the players held their hands in front of their chests and circled each other, in time to the song, until the guess was made. If the guess was incorrect, the holders kept the bones for the next round and received one or two counters from the guessing team, depending upon the number of mistaken guesses.

The game went on until one team had won all of the counters. Often there was more than one game going on at the same time, with people going back and forth gambling on who would win. Lokni often won this game, his favorite. He would look at Elsu to see if he was watching, and then he would beam with pride. Elsu thought to himself, *I will be old enough one day to play these games and make him proud of me!* And he would.

Another popular game, *Chatatuu* (The Dice Game), usually was played by women, but sometimes, like this night of celebration, it also involved the men. Halves of acorns were used as dice, cast from the hand upon a sifting tray. Two pairs of partners sat on the ground side by side. The first team cast the dice. If the dice all fell alike, the count was two; if they were evenly divided, the count was one. Other combinations meant the loss of the dice. As with Hi'nuwa, there was much shouting and giving of suggestions.

The Chupcans, like other Native Americans, worshipped animals as ancestors and imitated them in dance. The Chupcans danced to celebrate; they also danced for religious ceremonies: to give thanks for a good acorn harvest, for good weather, for marriages, to cure the sick, to pray for the dead. Tonight they celebrated a successful hunting and fishing journey that had brought food and other rewards to the village. Both men and women wore special regalia while they danced. They painted their faces and bodies red and black and wore headdresses woven of beads, grass, shells, and feathers—the latter the most important part of the costume.

The dancing on this occasion was only for the one night. For more important ceremonies, the dancing might go on for days. But even for this night of celebration, both men and women wore costumes and painted themselves. Many of the dancers were dressed in animal skins, beads, feather plumes, and moccasins tied up to their ankles.

Notaku was an especially good dancer, and so was his first wife, Helki, "To Touch." Notaku smiled at his wife. "To have such a beautiful wife who can dance so well is a blessing."

Helki beamed back at her husband. "Dancing with you, Notaku, is one of the things I most like to do." They both put their greatest energy into the dance on this important evening, which inspired the other dancers to also do their best.

Partway through the dancing, Notaku drew Helki out of the circle. They sat together a little way from the dancers. "My feather plume is beginning to wear. I think I will take Lokni and Elsu with me to find new feathers for my plume and some for them so they can put together their own plumes. We probably will use turkey feathers. I know eagle feathers are the most beautiful, but they are very hard to get. You must climb to the eagle's nest and wait patiently to take a feather. The eagle is the mediator of the creator and is very important." Notaku paused, deep in thought. Finally, he spoke again. "This will be a good time to teach both Lokni and Elsu how to get the prized red tail feathers of the hawk. For this they must dig a shallow hole and place a rabbit skin in the hole to make it look like a live rabbit. When the hawk dives to get the rabbit, one of them must quickly grab the red feathers from the rear of the bird without hurting it."

Helki placed her hand on her husband's. "These are good ideas, but our oldest daughter, Papina, 'Vine Growing around an Oak Tree,' also needs feathers so that she can have a plume."

Notaku nodded in agreement. "Yes, all of our children will need plumes with feathers of different colors tied upon strong pieces of birch or oak wood."

Helki paused for a moment. "We'll need a number of costume pieces as the children grow older: feather plumes, feather crowns made from the tails of magpies, and feather cloaks or shirts made with wing and tail feathers using crow, turkey vulture, magpie, owl, and hawk feathers. Both Lokni and Elsu will have to help you capture the birds, remove the feathers, and put together the costumes. And you know that eventually this will include costumes for little Awanata, 'Turtle,' the baby of your second wife, Litonya, 'Hummingbird Darting.'" Notaku and Helki nodded to each other and returned to the dance.

Litonya was Helki's younger sister and was not able to dance, because she was still nursing the baby, and she could not have sex with her husband or dance with him until her milk dried up. She sat against the wall, watching the baby in front of her and the dancers in the center of the room.

The music pulsed with strong and repetitive beats. Flutes of various sizes made from elderberry were played at celebrations like these, and also at other times by young men as a favorite pastime, sometimes during courtship. A second instrument was the rawhide rattle bound onto willow handles about ten inches long. Another rattle was made from several deer toes, each attached to a separate buckskin thong, secured to a wooden handle by wrapped sinew. A third popular instrument was the musical bow, which was made in different sizes. And, of course, there were a variety of drums made by binding various kinds and sizes of animal skins across the top of baskets. It was the drums that created the driving beat for the dancers.

While the adults were dancing, the children gathered around Wapi, "Lucky," the old man who was the best storyteller in the village. The children chorused, "Tell us a story about Coyote!" Stories were memorized and told over and over again in order to pass on the history, folklore, and traditions from one generation to the next. Some of the favorite types were the creation stories that included animals. Arranging a thin blanket over his shoulders, Wapi began:

One day Coyote saw a feather floating on the water. As it reached the island, it turned into an Eagle, which then spread its wings. The Eagle then flew over to Coyote. Later Coyote and Eagle were joined by Hummingbird. This then became the trinity of gods who created the race of people. Eagle told Coyote that he should find a wife and have children so they could populate the world. But Coyote did not know the facts of life, so he had many problems with this situation.

"How do you make children?" asked Coyote. Eagle did not reply. He wanted to see what Coyote would do. Coyote considered trying to make children in the knee. Eagle sat back and laughed at him. Next, Coyote tried to make children in the elbow, then in the eyebrow, and finally in the back

of the neck. Eagle could not keep quiet anymore. He was laughing so hard that Coyote looked at him with anger.

Hummingbird was watching Coyote's attempts at making children and could not refrain from laughing also. Finally, he told Coyote, "This place will be good. Try the belly."

Then Coyote went off with the woman and said, "Louse me." The girl found a wood tick on him. She was afraid and threw it away. Then Coyote made her look for the louse. "Look for it, and then eat it!"

Then the girl put it into her mouth. "Swallow it," Coyote said. She swallowed the louse and became pregnant. Coyote did not like his first wife, so he later found another wife and had five children by her. These children became the five tribes. He told them to go out and populate the world. They did and founded the five languages.

Now Coyote gave the people nets to carry. He also gave them bows and arrows to kill the rabbits. He said, "You will have acorn mush for your food. You will gather acorns, and you will have acorn bread to eat. Go down to the bay and gather seaweed so that you may eat it with your acorn mush and acorn bread. When there is low tide, you can gather shellfish to eat. When there is nothing else to eat, you can gather buckeyes for food. If the acorns are bitter, wash them out. Gather grass seeds for pinole, carrying them on your back in a basket. Look for these things of which I have told you. I have shown you how to gather food, and though it rains a long time, people will not die of hunger. Now I am getting old, and I cannot walk. Alas for me."

As the time became late, first the children and then the adults fell asleep upon the floor of the hangi. This had been a very fine celebration, but tomorrow would be a busy workday for them all.

CHAPTER 2

LIFE AND DEATH IN
THE VILLAGE

After Notaku's death, the chiefdom of the village passed to Lokni, his oldest son. He, too, was a good chief—generous and kind. Elsu, although not chief, was a respected member of the community and often served as an advisor to his brother.

As on most mornings, Elsu was at the sweathouse with other men of the village. They sat breathing in the sweet smell of herbs and scraping themselves with shells and curved deer rib bones to remove their smells and the dirt brought out by the heat of the fire. The ten men had come to the structure before dawn, stayed a few hours, and then gone to the nearby stream to cleanse themselves.

The men who were not going to hunt were sitting in the sun outside the sweathouse, talking and smoking their soapstone pipes. The tobacco that grew wild in the washes near the village was cut and put in the dew in the early morning and then hung in the sweathouse to dry. After several of these cycles over several weeks, when the harvested leaves were dry, they were rubbed between the palms of the hand and then broken into a rough powder and stored in baskets that hung in the wikiup. Enough for daily use was carried around the neck in a buckskin bag.

The village recently had been moved to a new location near the old one, because the midden, a pile of discarded shells, husks, and other waste, had become very large, and because the village had become infested with fleas. Such moves were made short distances every so often, up or down the nearby stream so that water was always available.

Most of the villagers stayed close to home. Except for trading, the acorn harvest, and some celebrations, outsiders were viewed with suspicion by many of the older villagers. However, the young people looked forward to times with their neighbors because they could meet other young people, and this often led to marriage.

For the Chupcans, land was not considered personal property. The land belonged to everyone, and enough was claimed to provide food for all. They enjoyed fruits and other foods from the trees and plants, and access to hunting and fishing areas. Individuals had their own bows and arrows, musical instruments, costumes, and other personal possessions. The village had wikiups built by families. A sweathouse for the men; storage granaries, mostly for acorns; and a hangi for meetings were built by the men working together. However, most of village life took place outside of the buildings. Women prepared food, made baskets, ground acorns, and completed other tasks in open structures that provided shade. The men used these structures for tasks such as skinning, cutting, repairing nets, and drying the fish and game they had killed and brought back to the village. As with all Chupcan villages, there was a large area for playing games and holding ceremonies.

After he left the sweathouse, Elsu decided to walk to the stream and take a dip in the cool water. He then lay on a rock to dry. He could feel the early afternoon sun warming his chest, his arms, and his legs while the rock below cooled his back. While lying there he began to think back to the time of his marriage.

He recalled how he and Malila had noticed each other a number of times at acorn harvests. At the last harvest, they finally had shyly flirted with each other. He had found out that she was of the Kiku'u moiety (waters) while he was of the Tunuka moiety (lands). This meant that they could marry.

The marriage of a chief's son usually was arranged for political reasons. That had been the case with Lokni, but not with Elsu. However, when Elsu approached his parents about the possibility of marriage to Malila, they were receptive to the idea. His father had said, "Let's send my cousin Helaku to visit Malila's parents to see if they will agree to the marriage."

Several days later, Helaku made the trip to Malila's village to speak to her parents. At first he talked with them about their crops and about a celebration that was being planned in a few weeks. Finally, after patiently engaging in this small talk, Helaku brought up what he had come for. "I am here to find out if you might be interested in a marriage between your daughter, Malila, and Elsu, the second son of our chief."

The parents had known of their daughter's interest in Elsu, and they were proud to agree to her marriage to a chief's son. They knew the marriage would include a bounty of gifts from the chief and that they would have to provide gifts to him in return. Malila's mother looked at her husband, who, as was the custom, responded formally to Helaku. "Thank you for coming to visit us. We would like to talk with Elsu's family about such a marriage."

A few weeks after Helaku's visit, Elsu and his family paid a visit to Malila's family to present a formal proposal of marriage. They brought beads, furs, baskets, and, most important, obsidian arrowheads and scraping tools with them as gifts to Malila's family. For their part, Malila's family prepared a sumptuous feast that lasted several days.

After the feast, Elsu's family returned to their village, but he remained with Malila's family to consummate the marriage and to provide hunting and other services to them for a few months. After Elsu had proved himself to Malila's family, the newlyweds returned to his village.

Malila was a stranger to the women in Elsu's village, and she often thought of her family and her own village. When Elsu was in the sweathouse with the men, or hunting and fishing, she spent her time alone. Gradually, though, she made friends as she became involved in gathering, cooking, basket making, and paying attention to the children of the village. The women also invited her to play games with them. The rest of her time she spent with her new husband, and they went about building a life together.

Within a year, Malila became pregnant. For the next several months she followed the many restrictions that Chupcan custom decreed for women in her condition. Late in her pregnancy she was sitting with other women who were making coiled baskets. She gave out a tiny squeal. "Oh, the skin on my tight belly itches. I don't know if I can stand it."

Two of the older women looked at each other. The one closest to her cautioned, "Malila, you know that you cannot scratch your belly now. It is one of the many things you mustn't do if you want the baby to come easy and be well. You also must avoid fish, meat, and salt. You are not to look at the sky at night, in case you see a shooting star, which would be bad luck. Most of all, you must be thoughtful of all people and of the animals."

Malila sighed. "I know! I am trying hard to do all things expected of me, just as Elsu is doing for his part." As she said these words, the other women nodded.

One of them smiled and said, "It will not be long now."

When the baby came, a boy, Malila was attended by the village midwife, Taipa. Following the birth, the afterbirth was buried and the young mother was led to the nearby stream to cleanse herself and the baby. As she walked along the trail toward the stream, villagers warmly smiled, nodded, and spoke kind words of acceptance and congratulations to the new mother.

By custom, Elsu had to avoid contact with Malila and maintain his celibacy until she finished nursing the baby. During this time, he often could be seen at the sweathouse and he frequently hunted, fished, and gathered wood.

At the appropriate time, the baby was named Luyu. As he grew, his parents treated him lovingly, but they also worked hard to train him in the values and ways of his people. When he asked questions, they would tell him a story or give him an experience to educate him.

In his early years, Luyu played with both the boys and the girls of the village. By the age of six, he began to work as was expected. Often, he would follow older boys to watch them hunt small animals such as squirrels, rabbits, and rats. He also would go with the older girls to gather grapes and berries.

By the time he was eight, Luyu began the gradual transition from adolescence to manhood. This stage centered at the sweat-house and involved learning about hunting and fishing, making tools, and cultural practices shared by the men of the village. As he reached puberty, he began to participate in the songs and dances of the men. By this time, too, he had become a skilled player of the favorite village game, *Shinny*. In this game, players hit a three-inch ball with a long club. Each team would try to hit the ball between the parallel "field stakes" of the opposing team set at their end of the field.

Three years after Luyu's birth, a girl was born to Malila and Elsu. She was named after Elsu's grandmother, Hesutu. She, too, was in a cradle for about two years. After that she played with the boys and girls, and she followed the older girls to gather grapes, berries, grasses, seeds, and other foods.

Her passage into womanhood was not gradual as it was for Luyu's passage into manhood. It came at her first menstruation, which ranked with birth, marriage, and death as an important part of the life cycle. At this time, the women of the village visited her and told her what her womanly duties were. From this time on, at the onset of each menstrua-tion, Hesutu would isolate herself in the wikiup to be in contact with the spirit world. Here she fasted, abstaining from meat, fish, salt, and cold water. As was required, she bathed regularly and did not touch herself. For this first time, in her early menstrual periods, the women of the village visited her and lectured her on the duties of women. Each night male and female members of her family came before her to perform the sacred first menstrual dances. Between the visits she was left alone with the mystery of her change from child to woman.

At the end of her first menstruation, her parents prepared a feast in her honor. She was bathed carefully and dressed in her best costume. The whole village participated in the coming-of-age feast and dance. A common song was,

> *Thou art a girl no more,*
> *Thou art a girl no more;*
> *The chief, the chief,*
> *The chief, the chief,*
> *Honors thee*
> *In the dance, in the dance,*
> *In the long and double line*
> *Of the dance.*
> *Dance, dance, dance, dance.*

As puberty began, Hesutu received tattoos on her face, shoulders, and breasts. The ones around her mouth were of special significance because they showed her lineage, which, in turn, told boys whether they would be able flirt with her or needed to avoid contact.

☙

Oak trees were a vital part of the life of the village. After the acorns were shelled, leached, and ground with a stone mortar and pestle, the flour was used in Chupcan meals. As with all families in the village, the steps in the preparation of the various acorn dishes were passed down from mother to daughter.

When Hesutu was a small child, her mother, Malila, taught her how to cook. When the acorn flour was ready for cooking, Malila told Hesutu, "Now you put the flour in this watertight basket. You must be careful with the next step because the stones in the fire are very hot. Lift them out of the fire with these sticks, brush them off, and put them in the basket."

Hesutu was anxious to help. She hovered near her mother and struggled to keep her hands out of the way until she was give permission. "Let me try, let me try!" Finally, Malila stepped back and let Hesutu lift the stones out of the fire. On her first try, she dropped one of the stones on the ground. On her third try, she got a good-sized stone into the basket.

"Now stir it with this wooden paddle." This was easy to do, and soon Malila asked Hesutu, "What would you prefer to do, make soup or porridge? Later we can make acorn bread together, because that takes extra steps. You need to cook the mush a long time and put it into our oven until it gets firm. Your father likes to take the bread with him when he hunts or visits nearby villages."

"I like the porridge best!" Hesutu not only liked the porridge, but had often watched her mother make it, and she was excited to learn how to do it herself.

Her mother continued, "You first must cook it longer than the mush to make it thicker. Then you can add some berries, mushrooms, herbs, or dried meat or fish to make it taste better."

Hesutu smiled up at her mother. She felt grown-up and excited to be given the task of creating a meal. "I will add more stones and stir it until it gets thicker, and I will add some berries. May I put some honey into the porridge, also?"

"What a good idea," said Malila. "We haven't done that before.

I think your father will like it very much. Put in both the berries and the honey!"

In addition to providing acorns, the oak trees were important to the people in other ways. They helped them to mark the seasons of the year. The appearance of the oak flowers meant that spring had arrived. The ripening green nuts signified summer. The harvest of the acorns was in the fall. Winter came after the harvest. The entire village turned out for the harvest in the nearby oak forest, and they were joined by people from other villages. It was the biggest event of the year and lasted for two or three weeks. People danced, laughed, and told stories. Young men and girls flirted with each other. The days and nights were filled with feasts, gambling, trading, and games. At night the dancers dressed in their finest feathers and body paint and danced the ancient steps of celebration.

Each morning after breakfast the people gathered acorns. Everyone was expected to work hard. Elsu instructed the twelve-year-old Luyu to "join the other boys and climb the trees, and shake the branches so the acorns will fall."

Luyu was proud to do this, and proud that his father had asked him. "You can count on me. I will shake the branches harder than any of the other boys!" And he did.

Elsu and the other men used long sticks to knock the acorns down. The men sang songs and egged each other on to see who could knock down the most. Luyu tried to keep up with the older boys. Malila and the other women and children, along with the men, picked up the good acorns from the ground, snapped off the caps, and dropped them into large baskets. When a basket was full, it would be brought into a clearing and set out to dry. During the early years, when Hesutu was still in the cradle, Malila would either carry the cradle on her back or put it on the ground in a safe place. As Hesutu got older, she too joined in the work.

When the harvest was over, the people returned to their villages.

The storage baskets were relined with herbs to keep the insects away and to prevent the acorns from molding. As winter came on, it was time to repair bows, arrows, spears, other tools, and the wickiup. It was also time to make new baskets, nets, traps, knives, beads, and all the other things needed for hunting, fishing, and trading. Women made sure that the granaries were in good shape. They also made brushes from local soap roots and crushed and cooked the bulbs to make a kind of glue used to attach feathers to arrow shafts. The crushed bulbs were also used as food, and some was saved to put into the stream to stupefy the fish so they could easily be caught.

Daily life for the Chupcans meant preparing meals, gathering, and hunting for nearby animals and fish. But it was not all work. There were songs, dancing, games, the telling of myths, and, for the men, the daily ritual of the sweathouse.

The villagers were wary of strangers. When strangers did arrive to trade or otherwise interact, the villagers tended to be hospitable, but on guard. In fact, the local shaman, Manipi, was very outspoken, and he often talked of the evil of the people in nearby villages.

One evening a young stranger came to the village and asked to be allowed to stay the night. Because of the distrust of strangers, Lokni, the chief, was reluctant to allow this to happen. He consulted with Elsu and other elders, letting them know of his concerns. "We don't know this man. We don't know his intentions." However, Elsu and a few of the elders asked Lokni to reconsider, giving the stranger the chance to present himself. Lokni finally agreed that the young man could stay.

But it turned out that Lokni was right to be cautious. The young stranger had come with four other young men from his village, with the goal of killing Manipi. They believed that he had cast an evil spell upon their chief. The other four young men stayed hidden outside of the village. Late in the night, all five of the visitors gathered outside Manipi's wickiup with the intent of sneaking in and performing the deed.

What they were not aware of was that, after letting the stranger into their village, Lokni had begun to suspect the young man of doing evil to the shaman for the things he had said. He gathered Elsu and a group of eight other men from the village to talk about what they should do. "Our shaman has said bad things about the people of this young man's village, but he has not cast a spell."

One of the younger village men, Kono, became excited and said, "We should kill this stranger and then attack his village to avenge this attempt upon our shaman's life."

This bothered Lokni. He excused himself from the group and then motioned to Elsu to talk with him away from the other men. "Elsu, Kono wants to kill the stranger. What do you think we should do?"

Elsu hesitated for several minutes and then answered, "Our village does not make war. Neither does the chief of the other village, Apenimon. He is a peaceful man just as you are. His people are water people, and we have married some of their women, and they have married some of ours. This is a misunderstanding. They mistakenly believe that Manipi has cast a spell on their chief. I believe that I have a better idea. Let's capture the young man and return him to his chief for a ransom." Lokni agreed that this would solve the problem without raising the prospect of enmity between the villages.

When the five strangers entered to kill the shaman, they were met by Elsu, Lokni, and the eight village guards. After a brief struggle, the strangers were subdued and taken prisoner. The next day they were taken to their own village by the eight guards and turned over to Apenimon. He was very embarrassed and apologized profusely on behalf of his village. He also sent the guards back to the village with many gifts for both Manipi and his chief, Lokni. The event was never discussed again.

Two months later, a different kind of visit to the village occurred. A runner approached from the south. He was from the larger village near the great mountain and was well known to the villagers. He was first seen by young boys who gave the news of his arrival to Lokni. He, in turn, found Elsu, and the two of them went to greet the runner and invite him to the chief's house. The runner delivered a message: "A group of six men who wish to trade are on their way to your village. They have left our village and will be here soon."

Lokni responded to the runner by giving him an invitation stick wrapped in fine deerskin and saying, "Please tell the traders that they are welcome."

When the runner departed, Lokni asked his wife Kolenya to get some other women to assist her in preparing a feast for the visitors. This was an important event, and the visitors needed to be welcomed warmly.

As the traders neared the village, many of the people gathered to welcome them. However, these visitors wished to deal first with the chief and his advisors. The villagers saw that the traders were carrying large nets full of items for trade.

The prominent men of the village put paint on their bodies and feathers in their hair to greet these strange men, who spoke a different language. Lokni stepped forward and gave a long welcoming speech, which the visitors did not understand, but they could tell from his tone that he was friendly.

The leader of the trading group responded with his speech. He told his hosts where his group was from and what they had to trade. Much of what he communicated was expressed through body movements and showing of their wares.

The group was seated on tule mats outside Lokni's wikiup. Kolenya and her companions served them a feast of acorn porridge and bread, deer and duck meats, and a variety of other tasty foods.

After dinner, the men got down to business. Lokni asked and motioned to the leader of the travelers, "What do you have to trade?" To his surprise and pleasure the traders showed him a variety of obsidian arrowheads and cutting tools. He was surprised because these usually came from the Mono people to the east. The traders also had pine nuts, stone figures, mortars and pestles, and even bowls that came from the quarries in the eastern mountains. From the west came clam disc beads, other shells, dried mollusk meat, and salt. From the south came the valuable but highly toxic cinnabar used for jewelry. The village was indeed fortunate to be at a crossroads for trade.

From their side, Lokni presented goods that his village could exchange: animal hides, baskets, bows and arrows, dried fish and meat, seeds, many tule products, and of course, a horde of shell money. It was a successful day. As usual, they had avoided haggling and kept their discussions friendly and businesslike.

◌〰〰◌

Lokni lived to be a relatively old man of forty-seven years of age. When he was a young man of twenty, and because he was in line to be chief, his marriage had been arranged although Kolenya was just eight years old at the time. She was from a nearby village and, as expected, was of the water moiety. There was no sex in the marriage until she had experienced her first menstruation. Kolenya had first given birth to a girl, Posala. Their first son, Tilmu, was born nearly three years later, and when Lokni died, the boy was only fourteen years old. For this reason, the elders had decided that Tilmu would become chief, but that his mother, Kolenya, and his uncle, Elsu, would be his advisors until he reached the age of twenty.

Immediately after Lokni's death, the female relatives of the water people prepared his body by washing it. With some help from men of the same moiety, the body was adorned with all of the ornaments he had owned, as well as with feathers, flowers, and beads. Meanwhile, runners were sent to nearby villages and those across the bay to tell of his death. The body was kept for three days until the most distant relatives arrived. When all were present, the family selected a man of the water people to build the funeral pyre with the assistance of men of his family.

These men carried Lokni's body to the pyre, laid it on the wood, and placed a basket beneath his head and another over his face. The body was positioned so that his knees could be tied under his chin and his hands were against his chin. They then started the fire, and the entire group of villagers and visitors stood around the pyre giving out a high-pitched, shrill wailing. Relatives and friends cast valuable possessions onto the flames, and all of Lokni's personal property was burned.

Kolenya was so distraught during the ceremony that, in addition to wailing loudly and singeing her hair, she tore at her face and breasts with her fingernails until she was covered with blood. Posala also wailed loudly and felt so much grief that she attempted to throw herself onto the fire. Tilmu cried out to her, "You are my sister. Please save yourself so you can help me when I am chief!" Posala was beside herself and got so near the fire that her hair was also singed. Finally, she was restrained by Tilmu, Elsu, and some of the men from the water people.

The Chupcan people did not believe in an afterlife. The villagers were members of the Kuksu cult. They believed in elaborate acting and dancing ceremonies in their traditional costumes to ensure good health, bountiful harvests and hunts, and good weather. Ceremonies were held for mourning, rites of passage, and shamanistic intervention with the spirit world. At times, as at Lokni's funeral, the men danced in disguises so as not to offend the spirits. At the conclusion of the funeral rites the men in charge symbolically cleansed themselves and the people by formal washing with water in which crushed leaves and twigs of wormwood were mixed. The moieties acted reciprocally, men of the land people washing the water people, and vice versa.

This cleansing did not end the ceremonial rituals. A few months later the people of the neighboring villages were invited back for a very large feast, which took the village women several days to prepare, followed by the nightly *Yalka*, crying, which lasted for four days. The visitors camped around the hangi in temporary brush shelters. All of the meals were served in the hangi, but the cooking took place outside. For this somber occasion there was dancing and singing and many words of tribute for Lokni. The people sang:

My heart is lost, lost.
My heart sets, sets.
My heart goes to the other world.
My heart goes to the other world.
My heart goes to the bay waters.
My heart goes to the bay waters.

Kolenya remained in seclusion until the following spring. However, Elsu did not. After the funeral, he gathered his nephew—Tilmu, the future chief—and a few of his closest friends and took them on a short journey to the marshes and sloughs. He ended the journey by taking them to the point of the bay, where he had them look to the west, then to the east, and finally to the islands in the bay—which was named for the tribe to the north, the Suisun. They were impressed, and Tilmu exclaimed, "What a bountiful place this is!"

MAP TWO: SPANISH EXPLORATION

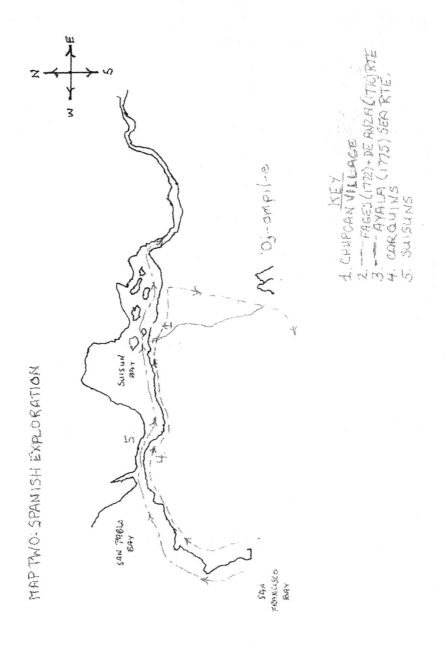

SAN PABLO
BAY

SUISUN
BAY

SAN
FRANCISCO
BAY

Mt. 'Oj-ompil-e

KEY
1. CHUPCAN VILLAGE
2. ---- FAGES (1772) + DE ANZA (1776) RTE
3. —— AYALA (1775) SEA RTE.
4. CARQUINS
5. SUISUNS

CHAPTER 3

THE ARRIVAL OF THE SPANISH

Langundo, the grandson of Lokni and current chief of the small village near the bay, stood outside the hangi with his elders to discuss a number of important matters. First, they talked about where to move the village again, since it had become infested with fleas and the middens had grown quite high. Finally, they came to the rumors they had heard from the main Chupcan village to the northwest about the coming of strange beings. One of the elders who had first heard the rumors said, "These visitors are mysterious. They are giants with four legs and long tails. On their tops are strange hard and shiny things."

A second elder scratched his brow and added, "They also have fire sticks that make great noises and are said to be able to kill animals and even humans."

The female shaman, Sitala, named after the famous shaman of four generations ago, became agitated. She cried out, "These are evil spirits sent to do us harm. We must gather all of our people and those from the other villages and try to kill these spirits. I don't know if we can do this, but we must try."

A third elder asked, "Do we think they will come to our village? If they do, how will we greet them? We have heard rumors that the shiny things are humans who can get down off the monsters and talk to us in a strange language. Also, it is said that one of them is a native. We have heard that they are friendly and wish only to trade with us."

Then Langundo spoke up. "Let's send a scout on the path to the large village. If he sees the strange beings coming, he will run back to let us know. We will gather to greet these strangers and see what they might have to trade. Their visit may be good for us!"

At this point, Sitala, still agitated, gave a loud grunt and stormed away from the group. "You will remember my words!" she shouted.

The Spaniards arrived in the village two days later, in the spring of 1772. The group consisted of their leader, Captain Pedro Fages; Father Juan Crespi; twelve soldiers; a muleteer; and an Ohlone Indian, probably recruited from a village near the Spanish capital of Alta California in Monterey. The chief and elders of the village who came to meet them were at first dumbfounded. These were very strange beings. The large brown things with four legs had tails that seemed to blow in the wind—even though there was no wind. One person they could recognize as a human was a man in a long robe. They did not understand why the Indian was with the strangers. The large beasts stopped, and the metallic things got down off the beasts and tied them to trees. Then they took off the metal things on their tops. Lo and behold, they were men, too!

Langundo stepped forward and drove a bow into the ground with arrows, animal skins, and other items attached to it. He signed for the Spanish to take the offering. At first there was no response. Langundo and his group fell back, now feeling like they should be afraid of these strangers. Finally, Captain Fages and one soldier went forward to gather the offered goods. He drove a pole into the ground with beads attached to it and signed for the natives to take them. Langundo took the beads and motioned to the Spaniards to go with them into the village, which they did.

The villagers timidly came out to meet the visitors. They, too, were fearful at first. Some stayed just outside their dwellings; others hid behind trees and peeked at the strangers. But soon, with Langundo's assurances, they began singing, dancing, and shouting in their traditional ways, and they were wearing feathers in their hair and marks on their faces, arms, and chests to welcome the visitors.

After the Spaniards left, there was a village meeting in the hangi to discuss the encounter. Most of the people, including Langundo, were still in awe of the strangers. However, they were generally positive and praised the opportunity for trade and other possible relationships. Only the shaman had a different view. She was an old woman, wrinkled and thin, with sagging breasts and marks all over her body. She held to her observation that no good would come of meeting with these people.

From the village, the Fages group proceeded eastward along the southern shore of Suisun Bay, stopping to visit with natives of the Volvon and Julpin tribes. They reached the delta formed by the convergence of what are now known as the Sacramento and San Joaquin Rivers. From there they turned south to return to Monterey. During this part of the trip they talked about their encounters with the natives. One of the soldiers began, "These people are so very primitive. They wear little or no clothes."

Another chimed in, "This is true, but worse than that, they are dirty, their hair is unkempt, and they have tattoos all over their bodies."

A third hit his forehead with the palm of his hand and added his opinion with a dismissive tone. "I saw evidence that suggests they burn their fields instead of working as real farmers who plow the soil and plant seeds."

With the consensus against the Chupcans growing, a fourth added, "Their houses and other buildings are poorly made. Most of the time they live outside in the open air." He went on to say, "It is going to be very difficult to bring these people to Christ. They seem very superstitious, and the sorceress seems to focus upon evil spirits. They are a barbarous people."

Father Crespi was uneasy about this kind of talk. He said, "They certainly are different, that is true. However, not everything is so bad.

They were very generous to us. Also, did any of you see the baskets they had? I found them as beautiful as any I have ever seen."

That night Crespi wrote in his diary,

We found a good village of heathen, very fair and bearded, who did not know what to do—they were so happy to see us in their village. They gave us many cacomites (root bulbs used for food), amoles (root bulbs used for soap), and two dead geese, dried and stuffed with grass. We returned the gifts with beads, for which they were very grateful, and some of them went with us to another village nearby.

Despite Crespi's words, the other men grumbled, and one other soldier concluded, "I have served in other parts of this new world, and I have seen many Indians. Some are very savage, but none are as dark or as ugly as the Indians of this part of the world."

The conversation turned to other topics, but the attitudes of the Spanish invaders toward the Chupcans and other Indians of Alta California had started to form.

Another important event associated with the arrival of the Spanish in this area was the voyage of the *San Carlos* in September 1775. It was captained by Juan Manuel de Ayala, who was commissioned to explore the waters associated with San Francisco Bay. The ship made four exploratory journeys into Suisun Bay, one as far as the delta, where it ran aground several times trying to travel up the rivers.

The Chupcans noted the four passages of the *San Carlos* during the summer of 1775, adding to their puzzlement about these mysterious beings and their boats, which had large white things at their tops that flapped in the wind. However, there were no direct contacts with the strangers.

Captain Ayala was ill for much of the journey in Suisun Bay, so his first mate, Don Jose Canizares, went to his cabin and reported to him the things he saw. As the ship passed by the point of the bay, he said, "I saw the smoke of a village about one league to the southwest of the shore."

Second mate Juan Batista Aguilar, who had used a spyglass, added, "I saw about twenty of the heathens, without clothes, who apparently were hunting and fishing in the marshes. They had nets, spears, and bows and arrows, and the game seemed to be plentiful. In addition, some of them were out in the bay, near the shore in small boats that seemed to be made from reeds of some kind. They move faster than the *San Carlos*."

The captain asked, "What else do you see?"

Both men, excited, spoke at once.

Captain Ayala said, "Wait, wait, one at a time. Canizares, you go first."

Canizares caught his breath and began once again to describe what he had seen. "We have measured the depth of the water here, and it is deep enough for ships to dock if a port is built. In addition, this seems to be the place where the salt and sweet waters ebb and flow together, allowing for different kinds of game and fish to be taken."

Aguilar spoke again. "We just passed an island with a large number of seals on it. We can use them for food, and their fat can be used to make oil for burning in lamps. I imagine the heathens kill them for food, but I doubt that they use the oil for light."

Ayala digested this information. "I would like you to write down all of this about this point of the bay. It may be important for the development of this land at some time in the future," he added prophetically.

The following year, Captain Juan Bautista de Anza arrived in Monterey with orders to establish a mission and presidio in San Francisco. Because of differences of opinion with the military commander of Alta California, his work was delayed. With time on his hands, he decided to explore the lands on the eastern side of San Francisco Bay. He organized a twenty-man group, which included Joseph Joaquin as his second in command, and chaplain and cartographer Father Pedro Font. The expedition followed the same route that Captain Fages and Father Juan Crespi had chosen, using the latter's diary as a guide. The company arrived at the village in mid-April. The villagers knew well in advance of the coming of the strangers, thanks to a system of smoke signals that passed information from tribe to tribe across the region. In fact, there was a well-developed mythology of these strange beings dating back to the arrival of Sir Francis Drake in San Francisco Bay in 1579, which brought fear to the people. Despite these fears, Langundo ordered the planting of the bow with skins and feather work as a welcome sign.

When the Spaniards arrived, they recognized the peaceful gesture from Crespi's notes, and they responded in kind with their gifts. The Spaniards offered the much-sought-after glass beads, but they also left items of clothing that were highly valued by the Indians.

In a report of the encounter, De Anza wrote, "After going a short distance, we came upon the village. The Indians welcomed us with indescribable hullabaloo. Three of them came to the edge of the village with some long poles with feathers on the end, and some long and narrow strips of skin with the hair on, which looked like rabbit skin, hanging like a pennant, this being their sign of peace. They led us to the middle of the village where there was a level spot like a plaza, and then began to dance with other Indians of the place with much clatter and yelling."

On the next day some of the villagers accompanied Langundo on a visit to the camp of the strangers. The visit started out to be very friendly. However, the villagers were very interested in the clothing hanging from tree branches and poles in the camp. With their view that things belonged to all villagers, they began to grab clothes to take with them. The Spanish, seeing property as belonging to individuals, began to cry out, "Stop, that is mine. Give it back to me!" They grabbed the items from the natives. However, as soon as a Spaniard would take a piece back from a villager, he would take another piece. The Spaniards were not able to keep up with them. The villagers were too quick. So De Anza motioned for them to leave the camp and said good-bye to them in a pleasant manner.

At this, one of the villagers raised his voice in protest. "What are we doing wrong? You are making no sense to us." He swept his arms to indicate all the villagers.

De Anza became angry and took a stick away from the native, struck him lightly with it, and threw it away, saying, "No, leave. We will have no more of this." There was no mistaking this gesture.

The villagers left, talking rapidly and shouting loudly. The Spanish were somewhat alarmed because they took this to be threatening. Font said to the captain, "Good riddance to these savages. They are nothing but thieves. We should not invite them to our camps in the future. This shall be known as The Village of Thieves."

For their part, the villagers were confused. One of them said to Langundo, "They are very selfish beings. I don't think we should trust them again." This news traveled quickly from village to village and set a new tone for the relationships between the Spanish and the Chupcans and other tribes.

Once again, Sitala was resolute in her view of these beings. She said, "These are evil spirits, and they have come to take everything that is ours. You will see. They bring bad times for our people."

Langundo was worried about her predictions, but he saw no reason as yet to completely distrust the strangers. After all, they brought good things to trade, and they seemed friendly. He did wonder about how many others would come. Time would tell.

After this encounter, the Spaniards continued their journey eastward toward the delta. On the way they climbed some hills that gave them a view of the Sierra Nevada mountains in the distance. De Anza remarked, "I have never seen such a majestic view. We shall make Alta California a wonderful place for our people to live. The native people shall provide us with the labor to build this land for Spain."

Father Font responded, "And we will bring them to Christ. That will be our greatest reward." With this he began to chant the Alabado as a sign of things to come.

The next several years saw very little change in the lives of the Chupcans. Langundo died and was succeeded as chief by his oldest son, Telutci. The villagers heard of the many encounters between neighboring natives and the Spaniards. In 1776, the Presidio of San Francisco and the Mission of Our Father San Francisco de Asis were built, and the Spaniards' search for native converts and labor began in earnest.

The first baptism of a Chupcan at the San Francisco Mission took place in 1779. Although the child was not of their village, this event was a not taken as a good omen of things to come. Telutci and the new male shaman, Knoton, were in agreement that the villagers should resist the efforts of the Spanish to make Christians of their people.

Telutci gathered his people in the hangi. "Each of you must make your own decision about joining these new people at their missions. However, you must know that the life we now know will be gone if many of you do so. The shaman and I believe that our ancestors would not approve of this. Also, we have heard that evil things happen to those people who do join the missions. These are difficult days for us. Beware."

It was not until 1795 that the first few villagers gave in to the temptation to go to the San Francisco Mission. They had heard of a number of rewards that awaited them there. However, in this same year a typhus epidemic at the mission caused most of them to die. Those who managed to survive escaped. A few returned to the village with stories of the illness and how the Spaniards had mistreated them and would not allow them to leave of their own free will.

Two years later Mission San Jose was built, and the efforts of the Spanish to convert the natives of the Chupcan area became a major endeavor. In this same year, the Saclans, neighbors of the Chupcans to the southwest, resisted an attack on one of their villages by soldiers from San Jose. Most of the tribe's members escaped, and some of them fled to Chupcan territory, specifically to the village near the point of the bay. One of the Saclan leaders told Telutci and some of his elders, "The Spaniards are terrible people. They demand that our people go to the missions, and if our people refuse, the Spanish kill them." The tide was turning. The Chupcans were now recognizing that they were in danger from the Spaniards.

In 1804, the Spanish carried out a punitive raid on a Chupcan village to the west of the village near the point of the bay. This attack resulted in the abandonment of that village and began a new trend: moving across the bay to take up residence with the Suisuns. Raids by the Spaniards upon Chupcan territories continued for the next few years. One raid was a total failure. During a search of the entire length of what is now the Diablo Valley, no Indians were found. They had temporarily abandoned their villages and hidden from the Spanish.

After this raid, Telutci and the shaman met with the remaining villagers in the hangi and once again began a discussion of what to do. Telutci opened by saying, "The Spaniards are trying to force us all to go to their missions, to be converted to their religion, and to work for them. That will destroy our way of life."

One of the elders asked, "What can we do? We cannot meet them in battle, because they are too strong for us."

The shaman replied, "We can fight and die for our way of life."

But Telutci proposed an alternative. "We can leave our village and join with the Carquins to our west."

Another elder spoke. "But we sometimes have had bad blood with the Carquins. They may not welcome us."

Telutci responded, "We are land people, and the Carquins are water people. We have married some of their women, and they have married some of ours. They also know of the danger that all of our peoples face. They will welcome us. As time goes on, it may be necessary for both of our peoples to cross the bay and go to the Suisuns. At this point, they are the strongest of all of our peoples. In the end, if we all work together, perhaps we may be able to outlast the Spaniards."

So it came to pass. The villagers moved to be with the Carquins, and by 1806 both of these groups did cross the bay and join with the Suisuns. However, their hopes for outlasting the Spanish did not come to pass. In May 1810, Lieutenant Gabriel Moraga, with seventeen soldiers and a large auxiliary force of mission Indians from San Francisco, attacked the Suisuns and their Carquin and Chupcan allies. The natives knew of the coming of the Spanish army, and they prepared themselves with paint, feathers, and a war dance and song:

> *From the south they come,*
> *The birds, the warlike birds,*
> *With sounding wings.*
> *I wish to change myself*
> *To the body of that swift bird.*
> *I throw my body into the strife.*

Indians fought hard, but in the end it was a massacre that ended the organized resistance of the Indians of the area. Their worst fears had come true. Almost all who survived were sent to the missions. The governor of Alta California wrote a letter to the viceroy in Mexico telling of the final battle:

Toward the end of the action the surviving Indians sealed themselves in three brush houses, from which they made their defense, wounding the corporals and two soldiers. After having killed the pagans in two of the grass houses, the Christians set fire to the third grass house, as a means to take the pagans prisoner. But they did not achieve that result, since the valiant Indians died enveloped in flames before they could be taken into custody. We could not reason with the pagans, who died fighting or by burning. There was no room for compassion in this disaster wrought upon them by our troops, because of their resistance.

PART TWO

THE MISSION AT THE POINT OF THE BAY

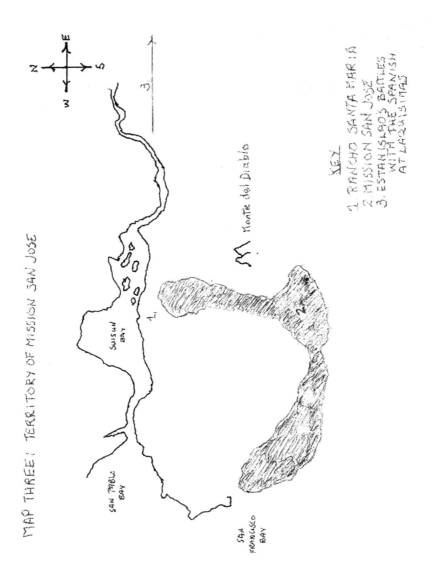

MAP THREE: TERRITORY OF MISSION SAN JOSE

SAN PABLO
BAY

SAN
FRANCISCO
BAY

SUISUN
BAY

Monte del Diablo

KEY
1. RANCHO SANTA MARIA
2. MISSION SAN JOSE
3. ESTANISLAO'S BATTLES
   WITH THE SPANISH
   AT LAGUNISIMAS

CHAPTER 4

THE BEGINNING OF
THE MISSION

At midday Father Lasuen pulled back on the reins of the mule he was riding and dismounted. He and the mule drank from the stream, and he filled the goatskin canteen, which usually hung from his saddle. The other two men who accompanied Father Lasuen—Father Diego Garcia with his mule and Sergeant Pedro Amador with his horse—did likewise. They also led their pack mule to the stream to drink.

At sixty-one, Father Lasuen was the oldest member of the group. The other two were younger, Sergeant Amador in his thirties and Father Garcia in his early twenties.

As they stood at the stream looking around at the beautiful scenery, Father Garcia asked Lasuen, "Why are we looking for a site for a new mission that is away from the coast? No other missions are inland."

Lasuen's eyes scanned the landscape and then returned to meet Garcia's. "Our most important job is to bring the natives of Alta California to Christ. There are many of them that we have not been able to reach, since they are far to the east. Founding at least one mission on the east side of the great bay will allow us to better reach these natives."

"There is another reason," Amador chimed in. "We must protect Alta California for Spain, since other countries are interested in the wealth of this place, particularly Britain and Russia."

Lasuen spoke again. "That is true, Sergeant. We do not have

enough people here to carry out all of the work that is needed. Because of this, our Holy Father Serra has set forth a plan for the missions, which is that once a mission is built, the natives can tend the crops and animals. Also, fewer soldiers will have to be sent into Alta California to control the natives, because many of the *neophytes*, baptized Indians, can serve as soldiers." He continued, "The plan suggests that a mission will be needed for only ten years or so, and then the missionaries can go to other areas. After that, the natives will be civilized enough to run a pueblo on their own. In Mexico and Peru this plan has worked well."

Climbing back onto his mule, Padre Lasuen said, "The pueblo of San Jose is only an hour or so from here. Let us resume our journey and see what promise it holds for a mission site. Fourteen new Spanish families have been sent there from Mexico to develop farming and ranching to serve the Santa Cruz and San Francisco Missions. When we get there, we are to contact Señor Jose Herrera, one of the leaders of the group, to see what progress is being made."

The other two remounted, and the trio set off for San Jose. When they arrived, their first reaction was one of discouragement. Father Garcia spoke softly. "This is not much of a place. There are only a few adobe buildings and a few made of wood. The rest all seem to be temporary shelters."

Lasuen nodded. "Understand, this pueblo is not quite two years old. The Spanish families live outside the town on their small ranchos. They agreed to come here from Mexico because they received land plots for farming and planting of fruit trees, enough for cattle, oxen, sheep, and goats to graze freely, and also for chicken coops. The plan is for these families to use the local natives to develop the farmland and tend the animals."

Lasuen changed the subject and spoke directly to the sergeant. "Why don't you ride down this main street and stop and find out what each of the buildings has to offer? Father Garcia and I will try to find out if there is a church in the pueblo."

The two fathers found a small building at the river's edge that had a cross on its roof. By questioning some of the people they met in the pueblo, they found that a priest came from Mission Santa Clara every Sunday to hold mass. They also were able to find out who acted as the local *alcalde*, a baptized Indian who spoke Spanish and acted much like a mayor for the Spanish. They met with him to see what he thought of the progress at the pueblo. Before they left his small office, they asked him how to get to Señor Herrera's rancho. The alcalde agreed to have a native take them to the rancho after they had finished looking over the pueblo.

He told them that the pueblo had problems, but that it was growing and that nearby ranching was a success. After this meeting, the fathers met Sergeant Amador at the end of the street, where the river flowed into San Francisco Bay. Lasuen asked the sergeant, "What did you find?"

"I'm not so sure you will be pleased," answered Amador. "One of the adobes is a bar where drinks are served. I observed several natives who were quite drunk. There also was gambling in the bar."

"And what else did you find?" asked Lasuen, obviously upset by what he had heard.

"In the two-story adobe," continued Amador, "I found a bordello where some native women were prostituting themselves for many of the men of the pueblo. Like the bar, it is filthy. The only decent place I found was a store that sells goods to both the Spanish ranchos and the native people, although the prices seem high to me. There also is a restaurant in one of the buildings that has rooms for rent. The menu looks good enough, but, like the other buildings, things are not clean."

The trio returned to the alcalde's office. They found their native guide and were taken to the Herrera rancho, where they were greeted by Señor Herrera, his wife, Isabella, and his oldest son, Manuel. Herrera smiled warmly at his guests. "Welcome! We seldom have visitors, and we wish to make this a special occasion. We'll have a fine dinner for you this evening when we can talk. We don't have a big house yet, but there is room for you to spend the night in our stable, where you can also find food for your animals. There is water from our well that you can use to cleanse yourself as you wish."

After some small talk, the trio went to the stable to pray, rest, feed their animals, and clean themselves for dinner. After the sun had gone down, they went to the house.

The visitors were shown to the parlor and served small glasses of sherry. "This is very fine sherry," said Father Lasuen. "It's been a long time since I have tasted any as good as this."

Herrera smiled. "It comes all the way from Spain via Mexico. We are very proud to be able to serve it to distinguished guests such as you."

After more discussion, mostly about news from the Santa Clara Mission and people they knew in common, the travelers and the Herreras moved to the dining room for their evening meal. They were served by two young native girls, and they also learned that the cook was a native woman. Father Lasuen asked, "Do you have many natives working for you? If so, what do they do?"

Herrera answered, "We have the three women who cook and serve. We also have a woman who cleans the house and does laundry for us, and another who takes care of our three youngest children. Plus we have two men who work here at the rancho, tending the gardens and doing whatever work is assigned to them. All of these are neophytes and are baptized. Then, of course, there are the *gentiles*, who are not baptized and who live in their own village, which is not far from here. They work for us tending the crops and the animals."

Lasuen continued his questioning. "And how does this work for you? Does everything get done well?"

Señora Herrera paused a moment before answering. "The neophytes who work for us are loyal and hardworking. In return, we treat them well. However, the gentiles from the local village are hard to understand. They seem lazy, resist the civilization we bring to them, reject our religious ideals, and, worst for us at this moment, they are thieves. Recently, they have been known to kill some of our animals and take the meat to their village."

Manuel spoke up. "This is becoming a growing problem. We must do something about it. Perhaps we should ask that soldiers come here from Santa Clara and San Francisco and punish some of these thieves as an example to the others."

The conversation went on long into the night. The Herreras excitedly related a number of similar tales about the natives. Father Lasuen had to acknowledge that he had heard the same story in other settlements throughout Alta California.

Early the next morning, the two priests and Amador went back into the pueblo to speak with the alcalde. When confronted with the story of the butchering of the animals on the ranchos, he nodded, started to respond, listened more, and then finally answered, "It's true that the natives kill some of the animals. But there are reasons for such acts. The Spanish don't understand that these grazing lands are being ruined for the Indians who depend upon them for the grasses and seeds. Also, since the grasses are no longer abundant, wild animals no longer graze nearby. They go off into the hills, and it is almost impossible for the natives to find large animals as a source of food. So they kill the animals of the Spanish."

Lasuen took this information in and decided that sometime in the future he would look more thoroughly into the problem. He realized that if it were not dealt with soon, it could become very serious.

After the meeting with the alcalde, the travelers resumed their journey to the northeast. "This is not the place for the seventeenth mission envisioned by our Holy Father Serra," Padre Lasuen said as they rode. "We must go on and locate the place where four years ago Father Dante and his party found what they thought would be a good spot for a mission."

At approximately four in the afternoon, the trio found the rough cross Dante had planted. They were sure this was the correct cross because, as Dante had said, "There is a good view across the bay of the San Francisco Mission and Yerba Buena Island."

So on that very day—June 11, 1797, Trinity Sunday—Padre Lasuen raised and blessed a new cross, celebrated mass, and dedicated a mission to Saint Joseph, Miswion del Gloriosisimo Patriarca Señor San Jose de Guadalupe. Padre Lasuen smiled and took a deep breath. As he and Father Garcia looked out over the plateau below, he proclaimed, "These fields will be ideal for growing corn and grain. The areas toward the bay and north of the creek will be good pastureland for cattle, and the nearby hills to the east will support the grazing of many sheep."

The younger priest caught Lasuen's enthusiasm and added, "Grapes will grow well on the slopes beneath the mission peak, and the warm springs to the south will provide water for healing and washing."

The two fathers concluded the celebration with a chant:

Cleanse me, O Lord,
with hyssop, and I shall be made clean.
Wash me, and I shall be made whiter than snow.

Have mercy on me, O God,
according to Your great mercy.

Glory be to the Father, and to the Son,
and to the Holy Ghost.
As it was in the beginning,
Is now, and ever shall be,
World without end.

Amen.

The trio set out the next day to explore some of the surrounding area. Around midday they encountered a very large grizzly bear. Garcia called out to Sergeant Amador, "Shoot the bear, shoot the bear!" Finally, after several shots, the bear was killed. That night they roasted bear meat around a fire.

The presence of the two priests and the sergeant drew the attention of the natives. Many turned out to see what they were up to. Father Lasuen was glad to see this. He said to his companions, "Even though the natives seemed accustomed to our animals, clothes, and weapons, they seem especially interested in our ceremony. This gives me hope that we can convert many to the one faith."

A few weeks later Padres Isidore Barcenilla and Augustín Marina, who had recently graduated from San Fernando College in Mexico, plus Corporal Alejo Miranda and five soldiers, arrived to start the work of the mission.

During the next ten years the mission grew, attracting many natives who accepted the faith and learned the trades taught to them by the missionaries and local craftsmen. Little by little, however, a good deal of unrest was growing among the natives, including the neophytes as well as the gentiles.

꩜

After the defeat of the Suisuns, Carquins, and Chupcans by Moraga and his army in 1810, most of the natives who survived were taken to Mission Dolores in San Francisco. However, Telutci and his wife and two children were among the few lucky Chupcans to escape the slaughter. They were present when Father Jose Viader, Lieutenant Gabriel Moraga, and four other soldiers came from Mission San Jose to the remaining Chupcan village near the foothills of Monte del Diablo. Telutci had fought successfully against the Spaniards and had been a chief of his own village before the Spaniards destroyed it. When he saw the Spanish in his new village, he was furious. At a meeting in the hangi he expressed himself forcefully, looking each man in the eyes. "These Spanish are our enemies. They are trying to make us give up our land, our way of life, and our beliefs. They kill our people. We must not allow them to force us to go to their missions."

However, since he was no longer a chief, some of the younger men openly disagreed. One said, "The Spanish have valuable things that we can have if we go to the missions: strong axes, clothes, horses that obey them and take the miles with ease, carts that can be pulled by oxen to carry heavy loads, and many more wonderful things."

Another young man added, "The world has changed. The missions are the only way we can have a life that is good. The Spanish are stronger than we are and have reached out to us to join with them at the Missions San Francisco and San Jose. I think we should ask these men who have come if we can join one of their missions."

Telutci sighed heavily and could be seen clenching his fists at his sides. "That is foolish. Life at these missions is hard. They work our people until they are exhausted. Their food is not plentiful. They lock up our young women at night. Most important is that they have much disease and many of our people die."

Telutci could tell by the looks on the men's faces that they were not in agreement with him. The first young man spoke up again.

"They have strong medicine at their missions. Also, everything I have said is true. I wish to go to a mission, and I am going to ask these visitors if I can do that."

So several young men approached Father Viader and asked him if they could go to a mission. The father was visibly pleased. "Of course that is possible. You can go south until you get to Mission San Jose. Take this small cross with you, and when you get to the mission tell one of the fathers there that you have spoken with me and that you wish to become baptized. With this you will be very welcome."

The young men were not sure what "baptized" meant. Even so, they readily agreed to follow the father's directions. The next day they set off for the mission.

As the young men went south, Father Viader, and Lieutenant Moraga and his troops left the village and went in the opposite direction. They had heard of a place at the point of Suisun Bay that provided an abundance of food and offered a possible deepwater port. Two days later, when they reached the point, they were impressed. Father Viader said, "This is truly a valuable place. It's much richer in animal life and a much better deepwater port than the opening of Alameda Creek into San Francisco Bay. We shall report back at Missions San Jose and Santa Clara. Perhaps this can even become a site for another mission."

That never came to pass. There were too many other priorities for the church and the crown. Even so, the marshes along the southern coast of Suisun Bay soon were explored. Indians were sent on expeditions from Mission San Jose with oxcarts to bring back some of the plentiful food supplies that were found there.

CHAPTER 5

LIFE AT THE MISSION

Magdalena, formerly Nawat, attempted to roll over on her straw mattress, but she couldn't. She was too weak, her body ached, and she felt as if she was on fire. She had a cough and a runny nose. Yesterday she found that she had little red bumps all over her face, chest, legs, and arms. The infirmary was too full to admit more patients, so she had to remain in her own room. She was frightened—she knew what was wrong. Many other neophytes at the mission had the *Sarampion*, measles, and many had died.

Magdalena's husband, Mateo, had left their small two-bedroom apartment at sunrise to go to prayers and mass for an hour. After services he went to work at the tannery, where he was learning to make leather from animal skins. He had just begun the process, so he was working on rabbit skins, which were thinner than the skins of larger animals and were easier to work with. Fortunately, he would be able to return to see his wife at the siesta time in the midafternoon.

Before he left her in the morning, he had put a piece of bread and a bowl with a portion of *atole*, barley or corn meal and lime juice mixed into a paste, on the small box that served as a table next to her bed. He also put a small bowl of water on the table with a cloth beside it. These latter items were to be used to help cool her burning body. However, she just couldn't bring herself to move. To make matters worse, she had dysentery and could not get to the clay pot under her bed.

Magdalena prayed as she had been taught by the priests. She was very grateful that they had taken their son, Felipe, and placed him with an uninfected couple who occupied a nearby apartment built for the neophyte families.

Father Duran visited Magdalena in the afternoon and found Mateo cleaning her and applying the cool wet cloth to her forehead. The father administered the last rites for her before she passed away and he did his best to console Mateo, who had fallen into a deep depression. The loss of loved ones as well as their old way of life caused many of the Indians to sink into an unending state of gloom.

Magdalena was not alone in her death. Almost a third of the Indians at the mission died as a result of this epidemic. Measles was not the only disease that ravaged the native population at the mission. Cholera, smallpox, diphtheria, chickenpox, and syphilis caused untold suffering and death among the Indians, who, as a group, did not possess any natural immunity to the diseases introduced by the Spanish conquerors.

The most horrific aspect of this plague of diseases brought by the Spanish was how it killed so many of the native children. The following poem, "Chupcan Lament," captures the sadness associated with these deaths:

The child rasped
its final breath.

Her mother wailed
into the February storm.
It was her third child,
her third dead child.

Slowly, the laments
became shudders, and
then stone cold silence.

She was Silveria.
She was the last of her mother's.
She was the last of her nation.

Death began in the mission.
A hundred children born,
a hundred children dead.
The nation was no more.
All were dead.

Two thousand years of tribe.
Gone.
The heavens wept
that February.

ᏜᎦᎦᎤ

It was not until four years later that the two young men who had argued with Telutci came to Mission San Jose to be baptized. They were renamed Anselmo and Salvino. Their behavior was not as satisfactory as the fathers would have liked it to be. They often were sullen and disrespectful. They were also often late to or did not even attend religious rites, and they did not try hard to learn lessons taught to them. In addition, they frequently slipped away from the mission and joined the gentiles in the nearby villages.

Father Fortuni was responsible for the discipline of neophytes. Normally, he was an easygoing, friendly person. In reality, he did not like the discipline part of his duties; and, in fact, he was not as strict with his punishments as some others would have liked him to be. He did not believe in beating the Indians.

On one occasion, after Anselmo and Salvino had slipped away for two days, Father Fortuni ordered that they be brought to the chapel for a talk. When they arrived and were seated, the father addressed them. "Why have you not lived here peacefully by the rules that we have set down for you? They are not so hard for you to follow, are they?"

Neither young man answered. They both simply kept their heads down and maintained their sullen expressions. The father continued, "You know that you have to be punished for your actions. You cannot be allowed to set a bad example for the other neophytes."

There still was no answer. The priest went on, "Since you tend not to do your duties and you sometimes run away, we will have to put you in irons and confine you to your dormitory for a week. You will be taken to religious ceremonies. You will have bread and a small amount of water brought to you every day at midday, but that is all. There will be no *atole* in the morning or *pozole*, corn mush and beans with meat, in the evening. Perhaps after a week you will see that it is better to comport yourselves in more ideal ways."

With that decision made, the father called for two trusted Indians to place the irons on the legs of Anselmo and Salvino and to take them to their dormitory. As they were removed from the chapel, it was quite clear that the two young men were very unhappy. They certainly did not appear contrite.

The normal day for neophytes began at sunrise when they joined the missionaries for prayers and mass that lasted for an hour. They then had their morning atole and a small amount of meat, usually jerky. This meal was followed by a period of work until approximately noon, when they had a dinner consisting of pozole and perhaps another small portion of meat. They enjoyed a brief siesta and then returned to work until nearly sundown. In the evening there was a supper consisting of whatever might be available. After this meal, the natives again were taught religion and, in addition, Spanish. There also were times for the women to learn to sew clothes in the Spanish style and for the men and women to have lessons in Spanish art and music. Before they went to bed, they usually were given an hour to relax.

This routine was different for Anselmo and Salvino during their week of confinement. They were taken to mass and prayers at sunrise as usual, but then they were returned to their dormitory by an older Indian who was their guard. They had no breakfast and were not assigned tasks. They simply lay on their cots with the irons on.

The irons were a bother and a constant reminder of their shame. However, being confined to the dormitory was not such a bad punishment. They would not have to participate in some of the ordinary routines.

As they lay on their cots thinking about their plight, Salvino muttered, "Telutci was right; we never should have come here. There is so much illness, and worse than that, we no longer have the freedom we had in our village." Then, trying to contain his anger, he asked Anselmo, "What shall we do? I will *not* stay at the mission as a prisoner."

Anselmo responded, "I agree, but we must be very careful. After the irons are removed, we will be watched carefully. If we run away, where can we go? It is told that the alcaldes, traitors that they are, work in the towns for the Spaniards and report anyone who is suspected of being a runaway."

They both were silent for a while, deep in thought. Finally, Anselmo broke the silence. "Once we are out of the irons, we should wait at least two weeks before we do anything. During that time we should pretend to be reformed and work hard to do everything that is expected of us. After the two weeks, it should be easy for us to overpower the old man who watches over our dormitory. We can do that late at night and be off with a head start of a few hours." He continued, "We should head for the bay and follow the shoreline to the east to the Indians who are in the great valley. They are resisting the Spanish. We could join them. It would be better to die fighting these evil ones than to live like slaves. We will travel at night, so that we are not seen."

Salvino then queried, "What about food and water for such a journey?"

Anselmo responded, "I suppose we could put aside pieces of jerky and bread. Our water will come from streams or from the sweet water of the bay. If we could somehow get materials to make a bow and some arrows, we would be able to hunt. Let us see what we can do to get such materials after our week of punishment."

Thus, when they were released, the two young men became model neophytes. They were always prompt, always worked hard, were polite, and participated fully in their religious responsibilities. Inside, they were full of hate for their captors.

About two weeks after their confinement was over, Father Fortuni commented to the pair, "You seem to be doing so much better. Your punishment must have given you to time to think about changing your ways."

Salvino spoke. "Yes, Father, we have learned that we need to behave in better ways. You will have no more problems with us."

A week after this interchange Salvino and Anselmo put their plan into operation. A bow was built from a sturdy but flexible birch sapling and deer sinew. The arrows were made from saplings, feathers, and small pointed rocks tied with deer sinew. They also had saved a good amount of dried bread, jerky, and some porridge placed in a watertight basket that could be carried over their shoulders.

They overcame the guard in the middle of the night, tied him up, and put a gag in his mouth. They found it relatively easy to get over the mission wall and were well on their way before sunrise. Throughout their journey, and until they reached Suisun Bay, they slept during the day and walked at night. Once at the shoreline, they turned east and began to walk during the daytime. Along the way they caught fish, killed small animals, and picked whatever seeds and plants that could be used as food. There was plenty of sweet water to drink. Ultimately, they reached the Yokut village of Laquisimas, where a language similar to the Miwok language was spoken. For now, they were home.

When the two did not arrive at mass, a guard was sent to find them. He found the bound and gagged overseer and reported to Father Fortuni. It took two days to get approval for a group of soldiers to find the escapees. Word was also sent to the local alcaldes to be on the lookout for the pair. No word came back. Salvino and Anselmo truly had escaped. However, the missionaries were conscious of the fact that this successful escape might give ideas to other neophytes. The oversight of the native population was increased.

Married couples and their children received generous portions of atole and pozole, which they ate in their apartments. The single women, widows, and girls older than nine years of age ate their meals in the *monjeria*, women's dormitory, in which they were locked, except during church services, to protect their virtue. The single men were able to take their food and eat it in their dormitory or outside in the shade of a *ramada* or a tree. The missionaries, of course, had their own housing and servants. Each of these sites had at least one additional guard assigned to duty.

To add to the food at the mission, the Indian men often were permitted to hunt and fish for their own benefit, and upon their return they generally made a present to the missionaries of a part of their catch. The women raised some poultry around their huts, and they fed the eggs to their children.

The monjeria had no windows, and the women kept inside were engaged with spinning, weaving, and other useful crafts. When it was time for services, two older trustees, rather than the usual one, were responsible for herding the women and girls from the monjeria to the church and then back again when services were over.

The occupants of the monjeria became restless. They simply

were tired of being held prisoners without contact with the men at the mission. The only times they were allowed to be with the men were at carefully guarded events such as on All Saint's Day, when there was music and dancing.

⌇⌇⌇⌇

Father Duran declared a fiesta for the first Tuesday of the next month, June 29, 1815, in honor of Saints Peter and Paul. A chorus of young Indian boys would do choral verse and sing hymns and Spanish songs. Also, the thirty-piece native orchestra which he had begun would play their flutes, violins, trumpets, and drums. Father Duran required perfection of his musical groups. His musical skills were so precise that he could hear any note that was out of tune. He invented a method of writing the music so the Indians could read it.

The orchestra had become famous in the area. Often visitors from Missions Santa Clara and San Francisco would come to listen, as would the *gente de razon,* Mexican and Spanish citizens, from nearby pueblos.

When the day arrived for the fiesta, a large crowd gathered inside the walls of the mission. Even some of the local gentiles, the unbaptized natives, of the nearby village of Orisom joined the festivities. The mission Indians were dressed in their best costumes, with feathers in their hair and girdles ornamented with feathers and bits of shell. Their bodies were painted with regular lines of black, red, and white. As usual, the men were dancing six or eight together, all making the same movements, all armed with spears. To the priests' chagrin, some of the women joined with the men, in a kind of shuffling dance. The priests exchanged looks and tried to get the attention of the women to let them know of their displeasure, but the women did not notice. They were too engaged and enthralled to finally be able to dance with the men.

If there had not been a crowd, they would have been punished for being so brazen.

Soldiers had all of their buttons and shoes shined and their beards trimmed for this occasion. The missionaries were in clean robes, and most of the visitors from the pueblos were well dressed— the women with bonnets, long and colorful dresses, and fine leather shoes; the men with waistcoats, high collars, tall hats, and highly polished shoes.

A few of the male visitors were not so well dressed. In fact, some of them seemed to have just come from work in the fields. They were unkempt, dirty, and smelled of alcohol. The priests wanted them to leave but did not ask them to go for fear of creating a scene.

The dancing went on for a long time. A further vexation for the fathers was that some of the gentiles joined in. For these celebrants, it was so much fun and a release from the drudgery of daily life.

During the dancing, four of the unkempt men from Pueblo San Jose gathered together. The leader of the group, a tall, bearded man with ulcers on his lips, Piro Gonzales, spoke to his friends. "See that little one in the middle of the dancers. Look at those breasts and swinging hips! I wouldn't mind having her."

One of the other men agreed. "She's quite a tease. Why don't we take her later when we have a chance? Then we all can have some of her." The other men nodded, and they continued watching the dancing.

Finally, after the dancing was over and food and small amounts of wine were served, the high point of the day came. Father Duran stood in front of the crowd and raised his arms for silence. His steady look and fatherly manner, combined with his square-jawed countenance, caused the crowd to become silent as he spoke. "Today, in praise of our dearly beloved Christ and his saintly followers Peter and Paul, we offer you choral verse and song from our young men's choir, as well as both fiesta and holy music from our orchestra. Both groups have worked long and hard to make their performances fitting for this occasion."

With that introduction, he brought the choir to order. The young men began in perfect intonation a choral reading from the sacraments:

This divine sacrament supplies, not only great strength to turn away from evil but even hinders or lessens the very causes of evil.

Does the water extinguish fire? But the divine Eucharist extinguishes, much more effectively, the heat of the passions.

For it contains every virtue, and, therefore, it checks every passion.

What wonder, my child, if this heavenly mystery renders all vices and unlawful pleasures unpleasant and distasteful, since it gives to men to drink the wine whose fruit are virgins, and offers to them the delights of angels.

Am I not the bread of the life of bliss, the fountain of everlasting sweetness? He that cometh to me shall no longer hunger or thirst after the forbidden and dangerous ailments of the world: for him I satiate the good things of God, which, by their deliciousness, have the power of causing all that is prohibited, all that is of earth, to not appear bitter and distasteful.

The young men then began to sing "Veni Creator Spiritus." The orchestra joined with the chorus to play this favorite song of Father Junipero Serra, the founder of the missions of Alta California.

Following the holy music, the orchestra began to play a number of popular Spanish pieces. The music went on for over an hour. During that time, Gonzales and his buddies moved to where the girl was standing and watching. Gonzales took two strings of glass beads from his pocket and showed them to the girl, Lilia. At first, she stepped back because she did not know what to make of these strange men. However, Gonzales kept motioning to her to come and take the beads. But the more she came toward them, the more they backed away toward the gate of the complex. She followed them toward the gate just enough so that one of the men was able to grab her out of the sight of the crowd. He put his hand over her mouth, and the other men picked her up.

The men carried the struggling girl out of the quadrangle and into the nearby cornfield. The three friends of Gonzales held the girl down on the ground while he stripped her naked and then raped her.

Sobbing, she protested in what seemed to be good Spanish, "Please, I am only fifteen, and I am a virgin. Let me go."

At that point she tried to bite Gonzales. He slapped her hard across the face and breathed his rotten breath into her face. "You little heathen, you're just a savage, no good for anything except to do menial work and give yourself to real men such as us. Feel yourself lucky. If you try that again, we'll kill you." All four of the men raped the girl, with each taking two turns. When they were finished, they left her lying in the field and went back to the pueblo.

Lilia lay in the field, continuing to sob. Finally, she got up, straightened her hair and clothes, and tried to wipe the smudged black, white, and red lines from her body. She decided to stay hidden until the fiesta was over. When the sun went down, she made her way to the monjeria and knocked on the door. The old woman in charge let her in. Instead of sympathy, the girl found more abuse.

The old woman reported her to the missionaries. Lilia's head was shaved, and she was flogged. She then was forced to dress in sackcloth and cover herself with ashes, and she was put into stocks for all to see her shame. To add to the denigration, in about three weeks she too had ulcers on her mouth and genitals. The rapists had taken her virginity, caused her shame and humiliation, and given her syphilis.

Lilia was shunned by the other neophytes and by her family. However, her older brother, Charro, did not shun her. He understood quite well that she was a victim and not a sinner. He promised that he would have revenge on the four men who had dishonored her. Unfortunately, he never was able to keep his promise.

Father Duran was a very strict disciplinarian, but he felt sorry for the girl. Recognizing that she could not stay at the mission, he went to the Herrera rancho and spoke to the new owner, Manuel, about having Lilia work there in some capacity. Herrera agreed, giving her a place to stay and work until she became incapacitated and died from her disease.

The rape of young women and girls such as Lilia by soldiers and settlers had become epidemic at the missions. In response to this, Father Serra issued an edict that promoted intermarriage between these Spanish men and Indian women to encourage family life and to curb sexual attacks. Serra recommended that soldiers who married indigenous women be rewarded with bounties of a horse, farm animals, and land.

CHAPTER 6

NATIVE RESISTANCE

Anselmo, age seventeen, and Salvino, age eighteen, had escaped from Mission San Jose and arrived at the Yokut village of Laquisimas in the late summer of 1815. Laquisimas was in the great valley at the foot of what later would be called the Sierra Nevada mountains. The pair immediately took back their Miwok names, Molimo and Sewati. They were heartily welcomed by the many Miwoks who had earlier joined their Yokut cousins, and they were frequently asked questions about their life at the mission. They always answered with stories of how bad their experiences had been. They told how they had to work long hours, how they were frequently and harshly punished and deprived of food, and how they had no freedom at all.

After a few months they began to join other young men at one of the sweathouses, this one usually occupied by Miwoks. Yokuts had their own. The sweathouse still was used as a center for preparation for the hunt. However, more and more it became a center for young men, many of them like Molimo and Sewati, escapees from one mission or another. The conversation frequently turned to the topic of how to get even with the Spanish missionaries and soldiers.

One young Yokut, Cucunuchi, would sometimes join his Miwok cousins for these discussions. He was very popular and respected in the village, and he was welcomed by the Miwoks. Much of the time he simply listened. Often he was asked his opinion of the missions. He was bright, and he was aware that this was a time of major change in the lives of the Indians of the area, all the way to the sea. In fact, he was weighing the advantages and disadvantages of going to Mission San Jose with his wife, daughter, mother, and father. The family frequently discussed the possibility, and only the father disliked the idea.

In one particular discussion in the Miwok sweathouse, Cucunuchi was with Molimo and Sewati. As they told of their lack of freedom and punishment at the mission, he asked, "And why did the padres see fit to punish you so harshly and take away your freedoms?"

Their responses were vague, and, in fact, they did not tell the whole story.

Cucunuchi pressed on. "We of this village have many relatives and friends who are at the missions and are allowed to visit their families for long periods of time. None of them have ever been punished that I know of."

Molimo responded bitterly, "Those people are weak. They go to the missions because they think that the missionaries will take care of them, and that is not true. They make slaves of our people."

Sewati added, "Perhaps you ought to go yourself and see what it is like. You will be looking to escape in a very short time."

Cucunuchi paused. After a while he spoke softly. "I appreciate your advice. I will think about this for a long time before I make any decision." With that, the conversation ended.

It was not until six years later, in 1821, that Cucunuchi made his decision. His younger brother, Canocee, had gone to the San Jose mission a year earlier, had been baptized, and had taken the name Orencio. His reports of the mission were positive. With this information, Cucunuchi decided to take his family to the mission to join his brother and his family. The father did not go.

They were all baptized immediately upon their arrival, and Cucunuchi was called Estanislao, the name of a Polish saint. His first act was to ask for an appointment with Father Duran. The meeting went well for both of them. They met with a translator, and Father

Duran was impressed with Estanislao. The Indian was a striking figure, six feet tall, light skinned, and muscular, and, above all, he appeared to be very bright. He seemed eager to learn and told the father, "The times are changing, and I and my family must change as well. I wish to learn to speak Spanish and to read and write. I will work hard if I have those opportunities."

Father Duran, usually a very brusque and sometimes harsh man, was obviously impressed. He responded with obvious pleasure, "I believe you will. You can be very helpful to me." The father was at least a head shorter than Estanislao, yet he reached up and almost stood on his toes as he touched Estanislao on the shoulder and with a gleam in his eyes continued, "I propose that you work closely with me in my offices. In return, you will be taught how to speak, read, and write Spanish. In addition, we will teach you mathematics so you can help us keep our books; and, of course, we will teach you and your family about the true faith. We will always be close together."

Estanislao worked hard and in a very short time did master Spanish and many other things as well. He also made it a point to get out among the Indians and find out what their feelings and wishes were. Within two years, the natives at the mission recognized his leadership qualities, and he was so popular that he was elected by them to be alcalde. It was his job to represent his people to the missionaries and vice versa. Father Duran was very pleased with this development, for, as he often said, he had come to love Estanislao as a son.

As alcalde and a favorite of Duran, Estanislao had a good life. But he could not help but see that Molimo and Sewati were right about the hard life and harsh treatment that were the plight of most of the Indians at the mission. He observed many floggings, the use of stocks and irons, long and hard labor, and other mistreatments of the natives. This was all added to the intense efforts to convert the natives to Christianity and to stamp out any vestiges of Indian culture. Gradually, it came to Estanislao that he could not continue to support the ideas of the missionaries.

With a growing but well-disguised rage, he held clandestine meetings with those Indians of all tribal groups at the mission he felt he could trust to ascertain how many of them would work with him to resist the work of the missionaries and even fight them if necessary. His charisma and the harsh treatment by the missionaries caused many of the Indians to pledge themselves to take action.

In 1822, Mexico gained its freedom from Spain. However, this development did not immediately change the relationship between the missionaries and the Indians. Estanislao was free to travel out of the mission to nearby areas. He frequently was sent to Mission Santa Clara on business. On one trip, he met with Cipriano, an Indian who had led a rebellion some ten years before at the Santa Clara Mission. Cipriano was old now. He had long gray hair, and he wore deerskin pants and moccasins. His face was not marked with tattoos, and he gave the impression of having what was often referred to as the *Indian gloom*, a feeling of helplessness and despair.

Estanislao spoke to the older man. "Cipriano, you are a brave and honorable man. Many who do not like what the Spanish are doing to our people see you as a model because you have tried to resist their efforts. I would like to ask for your assistance. Will you work with me?"

Cipriano was quiet for several moments. He finally spoke. "I am an old man now. I have tried to go against the Spaniards, but have mostly failed. I am not sure what I can do for you or for the cause." A faint smile came to his face, and he continued, "I will help you if there is anything that you think I can do. I have been severely punished by the padres and soldiers in the past, but they do not watch me so closely anymore. They think I am pacified. I am willing to risk more punishment. In fact, I would rather die than live as a slave."

Estanislao spoke calmly. "For now what you can do is easy, but it can be dangerous. What we need is for you to enlist as many of the natives at Mission Santa Clara to join us when the time comes to take action. I am not yet sure what that will be, but I do think that we should act within a year."

Cipriano again was silent for a long time. Then he said, "You can count on me. I will do my best to help raise an army. We shall keep in contact, I hope."

The response came quickly from Estanislao. "I will come here every few weeks. Thank you for your offer to help."

Estanislao did not talk to native leaders from Mission Dolores in San Francisco, for he didn't totally trust them to keep his emerging plan a secret. However, as a result of the native grapevine and his own growing reputation, natives from many missions let it be known that they were interested in following him.

By 1827, Estanislao had raised a following of over one thousand Indians. Some came from as far away as Mission Santa Barbara. Gradually his plan began to focus on having this force join with the Yokuts and Eastern Miwoks at the village of Laquisimas, near present-day Modesto, to put a stop to the Spanish incursions into the great valley.

When Estanislao got to the village, he immediately contacted Molimo and Sewati. He spoke to them. "You have been right about the need to do something about the treatment of our people. What I now propose is to raise and train an army to withstand the Spanish when they come to put down our revolt and try to punish us. Are you with me?"

In unison they forcefully said, "Yes!"

Estanislao continued, "An American trapper named Jed Smith has been coming to this area for some time. He buys horses and then takes them over the mountains to sell. If we can steal horses from ranchos, farms, and other settlements, we can keep what we need and sell the rest to him. We can use the horses against the Spaniards. With the money we get perhaps we can purchase weapons. Also, Smith is willing to teach us how to build fortifications to use when the Spaniards come to attack us. Can you two organize raiding parties in order to get horses?"

"We will," they chorused.

Shortly after that, Smith arrived at the village and taught the natives how to build two strong log forts. To the Indians, he was a funny-looking man. He wore a beaver skin hat, had a long gray beard, and wore a rather dirty buckskin outfit and leather boots. There was always a pipe stuck in his mouth even when there was no tobacco in it.

The local Indians did as Smith told them and built the two forts. At Estanislao's direction, they also dug trenches outside the walls to keep the Spaniards from getting close on their horses.

Led by Molimo and Sewati, the Indians became quite good at stealing horses from farms, ranchos, and other settlements. They even took horses from the missions in the Bay Area, including San Jose. Estanislao was able to sell a number of horses to Smith as well as to keep a number to add to the cavalry, which already had been developed and was housed at the village and the forts. What he was not able to do was get guns to use against the Spanish. There just weren't any to be found. Even the Spaniards were short of guns and kept those they had under heavy guard.

The following year, in November 1828, at the request of Father Duran, the commandant of the San Francisco Presidio sent Antonio Soto, an experienced Indian fighter, to bring in Estanislao and other neophytes who had escaped from Bay Area missions and fled to Laquisimas. Soto was a pompous, overconfident man. He had had success in capturing and killing individuals and small groups of

Indians, but he never had taken on a group as organized as the one he was assigned to deal with this time. He took only fifteen lightly armed soldiers to accomplish the task.

Soto and his men stopped at Mission San Jose and were provisioned by Father Duran. From there the small group continued on to Laquisimas. He understood enough of the Miwok language to know what Estanislao and his forces said to him. He ordered the Indians to turn over their arms, line up, and march with him back to the presidio. The response was loud laughter and the shouting of obscene insults, particularly at Soto. They made it very clear that they were having none of his orders.

Soto realized that he was vastly outnumbered. There were about five hundred natives, many of them escapees from Missions San Jose, Santa Clara, Santa Cruz, and San Juan Bautista. They were well dug in and well armed with bows and arrows as well as spears. He ordered his men to retire into a nearby thicket.

That was a grave error. Estanislao spoke to his men. "These fools have gone into the thicket, and there are very few of them. I want twenty of you to get into the thicket and keep yourself unseen. Sneak up on them one at a time. Remember you must shoot your arrows at their heads because their bodies are covered with thick clothing."

Taking advantage of the numerous willow trees, vines, and bushes, the Indians were nearly invisible and were able to pick off the soldiers one by one. Several of the soldiers were killed, and others were wounded. Soto himself was shot in one eye with an arrow and died a few days later during the retreat to San Jose.

Again Father Duran requested help from the commander of the presidio. Because of the lack of soldiers and the winter weather, a second force led by Ensign Jose Sanchez, another seasoned Indian fighter, was not sent until six months later, in May 1829. This force consisted of forty cavalrymen, a small cannon with two artillerymen, forty civilian volunteer fighters, and forty Christian Indians. They also left from Mission San Jose and made their way to Laquisimas.

Sanchez was a much humbler man than Soto. He also was much more cautious. He could not speak or understand Miwok or any other Indian language, and so he was impervious to insults. When he and his troop reached their destination, they found the Indians well entrenched.

Sanchez first tried to negotiate with the Indians rather than engage them in battle. However, it seemed as if Estanislao and his followers would rather fight than return to the missions. The rebel leader shouted, "I have to defend myself. I will not hesitate to die here in this place if it is necessary."

These Spaniards stayed out of the thicket, but made no attempt to breach the defenses of the Indians. They settled for firing the cannon and guns from a distance, but the cannon malfunctioned. After two days, Sanchez ordered his army to retreat because the troops were exhausted and they were running out of ammunition.

The celebration of the Indians after this victory was much more extensive and wilder than the one after the first victory. There was a sense of overconfidence, as was demonstrated by a special rhythmic "ritual" that was intoned in loud voices by several of the warriors:

Harken! The leader and his men
Made there the vict'ry song, and set the mark
Ye must o'ertake, if ye would be like them!
Harken! And whence, think ye, was borne
Unto these men courage to dare,
Strength to endure hardship and war?
Mark ye well my words, as I reveal
How the gods help man's feebleness.
The leader of these warriors was a man

Given to prayer. Oft he went forth
Seeking a place no one could find.
There he would stand and lift his voice,
Fraught with desire that he might be
Invincible, a bulwark 'gainst all foes
Threat'ning his tribe, causing them fear.
Nighttime and day this cry sped on,
Traveling far, seeking to reach—
Harken! 'Twas thus it came to pass:
The leader grasped the help sent by the gods;
Henceforth he walked steadfast and strong,
Leading his men through dangers drear,
Knowing that naught could strike at him
To whom the gods had promised victory.
Harken! His act lifted him
Where all his tribe behold a man
Clothed in new fame, strong in new strength
Gained by his deeds, blessed by the gods.

A few days after this second battle, a new force of one hundred soldiers and fifty neophyte auxiliaries with a larger cannon was sent under the command of Ensign Mariano Vallejo, nephew of Gabriel Vallejo, who had defeated the Suisun, Carquin, and Chupcan force in 1810. At the age of twenty-one, Vallejo was a very proud man, set upon maintaining the honor of his family. In addition, he was quite bright and understood military operations well. The members of his troop were very loyal and proud to be under his command.

The first day of the battle went on until sundown. It consisted mostly of Vallejo's army firing shots at any Indians who exposed themselves when they stood on the walls of the forts, and, more importantly, of firing the cannon at the walls in order to make a breach. For the Indians' part, a few tried to get up onto the wall to fire single arrows at individual soldiers who were in the thicket.

Toward the end of the day, the cannon fire was successful in creating a breach in the wall of the fort. Vallejo ordered his men to retire from the battle after sundown. As soon as the sun came up the next morning, the troops once again were aligned to resume the battle. However, the forts were quiet. Vallejo sent a small scouting party to see what they could find. The Indians were gone. Estanislao had ordered his followers to leave and head north to the village of Tagualames, near present-day Knights Ferry.

Vallejo's force was able to track the Indians, and when they reached the new village, which was unprotected, they were able to do a great deal of harm to them. However, exhaustion and running out of ammunition once again required the attackers to call off the battle and return to San Jose. Even so, the battle was considered a victory for Vallejo and his army.

Weary of the fighting and tired of his outlaw standing, Estanislao decided to rejoin his family at Mission San Jose. He went humbly to Father Duran and asked for forgiveness and for permission to return to the mission. The father, with his great affection for Estanislao, requested a pardon for him from the Mexican governor. The pardon was granted, and many of the Laquisimas Indians returned to their missions. Estanislao lived for another ten years at the mission until he died during a cholera epidemic.

"Estanislao became a legend in his own time," an old man told a group of children five years later. "Even though he returned to the mission, he inspired many of us to resist the missionaries and Spanish and Mexican settlers. I rode with Yoscolo in 1831," he added, thumping his chest with pride. "There were several hundred of us. We raided missions and ranchos for over a year and were never defeated." The children listened wide-eyed.

Not all resistance was that successful, however. In late 1837, a large group of two hundred Indians, half former Christians and half gentiles, attacked and stole several cattle from a neophyte rancheria, a small Christian Indian ranch, not far from Monte del Diablo. A group of seventy Mexicans, including soldiers and civilians, as well as two hundred Indian auxiliaries, tracked the culprits until they finally caught up with them. The Mexican sergeant said to several of his Indians, "Go to the other side of the river and convince the attackers that they should cross the river to us and partake of food that we will offer them. Try to convince them that they should sell some of their arrows to the auxiliaries. Tell them they will be unharmed." The thieves crossed the river to get the food and sold many of their arrows. They were surrounded and captured. Ropes were put around their necks, and they were tied together and led toward the base camp of the Mexican and auxiliary army. The neck fetters of the one hundred former Christian captives were removed, and every half mile six of them were told to kneel and recite their Christian vows. Then four arrows were shot into each one of them, two from the front and two from the back. Those who lived were killed with lances. This went on until all were dead.

The march continued with the remaining one hundred gentile prisoners still fettered. An argument ensued among the captors about what should be done with the prisoners. In the end, because of fear the captives would escape, it was decided that they should all be shot.

These kinds of events increased the hatred between the Indians of Alta California and the Mexicans who occupied it. This hatred created what amounted to a stalemate between the two groups. If the Americans had not begun to enter California over the Sierra Nevada mountains and attack the Indians from the rear, the Indians might have caused the Spanish and the Mexicans who came after them to leave Alta California.

CHAPTER 7

SECULARIZATION: THE END OF THE MISSION PERIOD

At seventeen, in late 1838, Juanita was beautiful. Her long ebony hair was neatly combed and fell to her waist. She had smooth, light skin—lighter than that of most Indian girls. A shy woman, she kept her head down when the ceremony began. When she looked up, her bright white teeth shone as she smiled.

Juanita, the daughter of the famous Estanislao, was marrying twenty-five-year-old Mexican soldier Sebastiano Colon Perez. She was given away by her uncle, Orencio, and the ceremony was performed by Father Duran, who was now ending his time as presidente of all the missions of Alta California, which he had been administering from his headquarters at Mission San Jose.

Perez was a handsome man with dark hair pressed to his scalp, sideburns, a pointed beard, an immaculate uniform, and a broad smile that endeared him to many of the women at the mission and in the general area. However, he had eyes only for Juanita.

After the vows were taken, a small party for the couple began. Music was sung and played by what was left of Father Duran's famous chorus and orchestra. There was even some dancing, although it was of the Mexican variety and not Indian.

The missionaries, remaining neophytes, soldiers, and the *gente de razon*—the Spanish and Mexican citizens of good standing—all crowded around the couple, complimenting them and wishing them well. Some of the corporal's comrades, as well as gente de razon, were a bit jealous of his good luck in marrying such a beautiful young woman. They also were envious of his receipt of land and animals.

Juanita excused herself from the crowd and moved to be with her mother, Luz, who was elderly but still active. The only differences in the mother's dress and appearance from her native days was a lack of tattoos, the wearing of a cloth skirt and blouse that covered her body, the wearing of her hair in the Mexican style, and moccasins on her feet.

Luz spoke tenderly to Juanita. "I am very proud of you, daughter, and feel good about this marriage. Estanislao would have felt the same if he could still be with us. Sebastiano is a good man and will bring you much happiness. I look forward to many grandchildren in the years to come."

Juanita smiled at her mother. "I do feel fortunate, Mother. Sebastiano is honest, hardworking, and thoughtful; and, yes, he is handsome. But that is not what I want to talk with you about. We want you to come with us. As you know, there has been an order to close the mission in two years and send all of the natives away."

Luz spoke sadly. "I have loved it here, but I will try to find some work on a nearby rancho or in the pueblo. I do not want to be a bother to you and Sebastiano."

"On the contrary," said Juanita. "You can be of great assistance to us. We want children, and you can help with them sometimes. Also, you and I can cook, clean, and garden together until we are able to employ other natives to assist us. My sister, Elvira, is coming with us. We also are taking Migel, a lad of fourteen, and Uncle Orencio with us to help on the rancho. Once the mission closes and the padres leave, many of the neophytes will be looking for work, food, and shelter."

Luz sighed and then smiled. "Of course I will go with you and Sebastiano to help you get started on your rancho. To have Elvira with us, also, makes it even more wonderful. How large is the rancho? Where is it?"

"It is small, about twenty acres, but it does have a creek with good water. As I understand it, our place is next to a much larger rancho of about eighteen thousand acres that was just purchased by one of the gente de razon who has ties to the Mexican government. I believe his name is Juan Salvio Pacheco. He has sent his son Fernando to occupy the grant and begin the cattle operation. Their rancho is at the foot of Monte del Diablo, and ours is north and west of his land, only about three miles from the point of the bay. We will be able to hunt and fish in the marshes there as well as farm on our own land. I also have heard that there once was a Chupcan village where our land is."

Luz very shyly made a request of Juanita. "We will be living near the point of the bay, with its marshes and waters. Is it possible that we can cut some tules so that I can make myself skirts in the old-fashioned way? I would really like that."

Juanita smiled and said, "Of course we can. I also would like to wear tule skirts as you and our ancestors did before us. The marshes and the bay can be of value to us in many other ways, also."

Juanita could see that her mother was quite pleased. Luz became animated and continued, "We will have neighbors, and that may give us some protection from the Indian raiders who have been attacking the missions, pueblos, and ranchos."

Juanita smiled and pointed out, "I'm sure that most of the Indians who are doing the raiding will not bother us. They know that we are the family of your husband and my father, Estanislao. He is still revered by most of the Indians in the area."

In actuality, Juanita, Sebastiano, Elvira, and Luz would be quite fortunate if they had this protection. These were very dangerous and evil times. In fact, the missions were never intended to be permanent. The plan had called for converting each mission into a civil community for the neophytes after ten years. The Franciscans, however, kept extending the time because the missions had become very lucrative enterprises. They also felt that the natives were not ready to govern themselves, and that there was much more proselytizing to do.

Secularization had long intrigued California's administrators as the best way to satisfy the needs of their gente de razon and Indian constituents. Four different provincial governors had issued orders to seize mission lands. The first three efforts failed. Finally, in 1834, Governor Jose Figueroa succeeded and decreed that administrators would supervise the missions' secularization. In speaking of this issue, Figueroa said, "Secularization will provide that the missions will become parish churches, in which the missionaries can remain to perform religious duties because there are no suitable replacements available."

An unfortunate loophole for corruption was left by the decree's omission of any plan for disposing of mission properties. The missions had become exceedingly rich, and Mission San Jose was the richest of the twenty-one in Alta California. The pressure to loot the missions of their wealth grew quickly, and the weak Mexican government was unable to enforce the secularization laws. The secularization decree removed the administration of the missions from the padres. At San Jose, in 1836, Jose de Jesus Vallejo was appointed civil administrator and the mission lands were divided into ranchos. Vallejo did not last long. He resigned after an investigation found proof of maladministration, including reports of starving naked women and children caused by Vallejo taking their food and clothing and giving it to his own ranch hands. He had acquired his own rancho with rich land and animals taken from the mission.

The Indians did not fare well under secularization. Many eventually lost the small bits of property that they had received, despite the legal protections that they supposedly had been given. When land fell free from church control, those Californios who once sympathized with the Indians now had little cause to remember any bond with them, because they coveted the riches of the missions for themselves. A few gente de razon sincerely supported justice for the Indians, but by the late 1830s the prospect of gaining church land and other wealth obscured all other thoughts. After 1834, they saw the Indians only as laborers to be exploited.

Once they were free, many natives fell into arrears and sold their property to gente de razon creditors. Californios often enticed the Indians with alcohol or by drawing them into gambling debts, and enterprising gente de razon soon relieved the ex-neophytes of their land titles.

The negative reaction to secularization of the many Spanish-born Franciscan padres was based on their continued allegiance to Spain and their rejection of Mexican independence and the liberal reform measures of the 1820s and 1830s, which challenged the strong role of the Catholic Church in Mexico. In addition, the break-down of the social controls implemented by the Franciscans led to a massive exodus of hundreds of neophytes from the missions.

The sadness of this dramatic change for the Franciscans was captured in a letter sent by Father Soria at Mission San Jose in 1840 to Father Jose Gonzales Rubio, who presided over the secularization of the missions from 1836 to 1842:

> *What can I say to your Reverence that will not sadden your heart and break it as mine? Everything is destruction, every-thing misery, humiliation, and abandonment. The evil today is certainly irreparable. Our predecessors so entwined the spiritual and temporal interests of those neophytes that one sustained the other. Consequently, when the direction of the temporalitie was taken from our hands, everything crashed to the ground.*

Many other Mexican politicians used these times to fatten their own purses or those of their relatives. For example, in 1846, Governor

Pio Pico sold the Mission San Jose lands to his brother for $12,000. They were valued at $155,000. Mexican settlers were allowed to buy Indian land. Often, instead of buying it, they cheated the Indians out of it or just took it.

When the Indians left the missions, they were not able to function as they had before the mission days. Many died of disease and starvation. Others were sought after by Mexican rancheros who wished to exploit them as a valuable labor source because of the skills they had learned at the missions. This exploitation resulted in long hours of hard labor and poor living conditions. For most, the freedom they were promised never came to be. The only ones who, in a sense, were free were those who formed raiding parties that stole from the ranchos and pueblos.

Before the wedding, Corporal Perez had made a number of trips to his rancho, accompanied by Orencio, Migel, Hipolito (a neophyte skilled in carpentry), and two local Miwok gentiles for general labor. Using a cart and an ox borrowed from the mission, the men took tools, some furniture, and animals to the rancho. This crew was given the responsibility, under Orencio's supervision, to begin constructing a small adobe house, a barn, and other outbuildings for the animals and storage. They also were assigned to plant fruit trees, wheat, corn, oats, and a vegetable garden. The one assignment the crew enjoyed the most was going to the marshes to hunt and fish, after which they smoked much of the catch for use throughout the year. Nearness to the marshes at the point of the bay truly would be an advantage for those who were to live at the rancho.

When the rancho was ready, Juanita, Luz, Elvira, and Sebastiano packed their remaining belongings and loaded them into the cart. Their possessions included their clothes and other personal belongings, more household furniture, kitchen utensils, various tools, two matates for grinding, and additional animals given to them according to the decree by Father Serra. They followed old Indian trails to the shadow of Monte del Diablo and beyond to the rancho near the point of the bay.

On the slow journey, Sebastiano entertained his new wife, her sister, and their mother with songs he sang and played on his guitar. He had a strong, pleasant voice, and his singing made the time pass more quickly. He sang such songs as "El Capotin"; "Adios. Adios, Amores"; "Ay, Susana"; and "El Borrego." Of course, he played and sang their favorite, "El Fandango," many times:

Oh, my hopeless love!
How shall I forget you?
If I tell you good-bye,
I lose the glory of loving you.

Ay! Could it be a lie?
Ay! Could it be the truth?
These little dark-haired girls,
What a poor return they give!

Ay! Could it be a lie?
Ay! Could it be the truth?
Oh, my hopeless love!
How shall I remember you?
If I tell you hello,
I have the glory of loving you.

Ay! Could it be a lie?
Ay! Could it be the truth?
These little dark-haired girls,
What a poor return they give.

Ay! Could it be a lie?
Ay! Could it be the truth?

After five days of travel north into the Diablo Valley and then on toward the point of the bay, the party arrived at the rancho to begin a new life—one of hard work, but also one with great satisfaction because of its freedom, sense of accomplishment, and love of family. They arrived in the early afternoon and were greeted by Orencio and Migel. The other men were working at various tasks, and it was only after another hour that they, too, were able to come to greet the family.

Orencio raised his arms wide as he walked toward the group. "Welcome, Sebastiano, Juanita, Luz, and Elvira. I see that you had a good journey. I'm sure you would like an opportunity to freshen yourselves after your trip. After that, I can give you a tour of the house and grounds, which I hope will meet with your approval. There is clean, fresh water from the nearby creek that is filtered in the *destilador de aqua*, and there is a toilet behind the house."

Juanita, anxious to see the rancho, said, "Yes, we would like to freshen ourselves, but we will take only a few minutes because we want to see everything as soon as possible!"

"Of course," said Sebastiano. "Juanita, Luz, Elvira, please take the time necessary for your ablutions. I will go with Orencio to see the animals, and we will return for the tour in about ten minutes."

When Sebastiano and Orencio returned to the house, the women were waiting for them on the stone steps at the front door. Orencio immediately began to show and tell the group about the house and its surroundings. "You will notice that the buildings are on three sides of the patio, which has a ramada to protect against the sun in the summer when you are outside for meals or entertaining. The house is made of adobe and is whitewashed inside and out to keep the adobe from melting. Now the roof is made of oak, but later we will use tiles to make it more attractive."

Sebastiano was quick to respond. "We will use the patio much of the time, and it will be particularly important when we have visitors."

The group then entered the adobe through the wooden door, which also was framed in wood, as were the windows. Orencio waved his arms and said, "This is the *sala*, the sitting room."

The room was small, but Juanita could not hide her pleasure. She never had lived in a house with a sala. "Oh, this is lovely. Look at the fine chairs and wonderful fireplace. When my mother, sister, and I are able to put some flowers, a picture of the Madonna and Child, and some lace curtains and hangings around the room, it will be even more beautiful."

Orencio then led them to the two *dormitorios*, bedrooms. The first one was the largest and had a big, sturdy bed. "This is your room, Juanita and Sebastiano. The second dormitorio has two beds and is to be shared by Luz and Elvira. The beds, chairs, closet, and chest were built by our carpenter, Hipolito. He made all of the furniture for us, as well as many other things on the rancho. He still has a lot of work to do, building storage space and additional rooms, including a nursery for the children to come. We are lucky to have oak tress nearby to provide the wood we need."

Sebastiano added, "Perhaps sometime in the future when we have more money, we will be able to buy some fancy mahogany furniture made in South America or the Philippines."

Juanita answered immediately, "But this is so lovely. We don't need anything fancier."

Sebastiano smiled and said, "We shall see, my turtle dove. We shall see." He then motioned for them to move to the *cocina*, the kitchen. It was quite small, with only an open cooking area built of adobe, two chairs, a table, and a few shelves where kitchen utensils could be kept along with clay pots and baskets for storage.

Looking at the shelves, Luz said, "I know how to make pots and baskets. I can make them as we need them."

Juanita continued to be elated at what she saw. "This will be a wonderful place for me, Mother, and Elvira to prepare meals for the family."

Orencio spoke up. "There also is an adobe oven on the patio. A lot of the time we can eat outside under the ramada. Tonight, however, Migel and I will prepare the dinner for all of us. We have been to the bay and marshes and have brought home some fresh salmon and duck to go with the fresh corn and greens from our garden. We also are drying other fish and game for use at a later time. We are lucky to be so close to the bay."

They continued their tour, viewing the dining room with its table and chairs and a few decorations. After seeing the inside of the house, Orencio and Migel showed them the rest of the rancho, including the sleeping quarters for the men, the storage sheds, the garden, the new fruit trees, the chicken coop, the small corn and grain fields, and the ranges where the cattle and sheep would be after the herds grew. During this part of the tour, the family met the other two men who labored on the rancho. As gentiles, they still had their Indian names: Huslu and Iye.

As they viewed the front of the house, Luz asked Sebastiano, "What is that stripe that is about eighteen inches wide and runs around the house, and why is it there? It is quite pretty."

Sebastiano chuckled and explained, "That is simply a bit of vanity. It is made up of gravel from the nearby creek and is a mark of beauty not found at all ranchos. The gravel is put into the clay bricks as they are being formed and then carefully placed in line when the rows of bricks reach about three feet high." Once the tour was completed, everyone took time for a short siesta so that they would be ready for an evening of celebration.

After the siesta, Orencio and Migel began to prepare a sumptuous dinner for all of the family and the help. Luz could not simply stand by. She set the table on the patio with plates and flatware, she gathered and boiled eggs, and she picked greens and vegetables from the garden for a salad and the main dish.

While the meal was being prepared, Juanita and Elvira unpacked their belongings and made the beds in the two dormitorios. Sebastiano and Hipolito remained outside and did an accounting of what animals, plants, and tools were present on the rancho and what more they needed to gather. Orencio joined them when he could. The plan was for Sebastiano, Hipolito, and Huslu to return to Mission San Jose to see if there were things remaining that they might bring back to the rancho. Father Duran had left Mission San Jose to go to Santa Barbara, where he became the president of the Alta California Mission System. However, he was returning to San Jose in the next month for business connected with the distribution of mission properties.

The rancho already had two horses, two cows, two steers, one ewe, one ram, one female and one male goat, four chickens, and one rooster. Thus, they were provided in the short run with eggs, milk, and cheese. In addition, they were able to hunt and fish for additional meat. The garden provided them with vegetables. While they had ten or so fruit trees, it would be a couple of years before they would bear any fruit. They had seed for corn, wheat, and oats, but planting had to be done by hand with hoes. A crop of corn and one of wheat had been harvested and stored, and a crop of oats would be ready to harvest in the near future. It was clear that they would not go hungry, but they needed some additional animals, seeds, and plants from the mission if they could get them. Another horse or two, as well saddles, would be of value. Grapevines would add to the garden, and it also would be good if they could keep the ox and cart, as well as get a plow. Of most importance would be the acquisition of a bull so that a herd of cattle could be developed.

Everyone, including the workmen, gathered for dinner as the sun went down. Sebastiano said a prayer to begin the celebration.

Then he announced, "I have been able to bring four bottles of Father Duran's famous brandy. Tonight we will celebrate by having one with our dinner." With that said, he poured a small glass for each person, and they toasted the success of the rancho.

The dinner was served in several courses. First, there was salsa with tortillas made from ground corn. That was followed by a soup made with beans and rabbit meat in a tomato broth. The third course was a salad made from fresh vegetables from the garden. Next came large pieces of salmon baked in milk and herbs. The main course consisted of elk meat roasted on a spit and accompanied with boiled potatoes and fresh vegetables. For dessert there was a large flan. It was a feast. Following the dinner there was coffee, and the men smoked cigars while the women cleaned up and the laborers went off to their sleeping quarters.

During the dinner the conversation was light. After a while, Sebastiano asked Juanita and Elvira, "Is there anything you would like me to try to bring back from Mission San Jose?"

Juanita thought for a minute and answered, "If any linen is available, we can use it to make simple clothing, towels, sheets, and even decorations. We also could use a few blankets."

Elvira added, "I would like to have some wool if any is available. Perhaps Hipolito could make us a loom so that we can make our own cloth."

Sebastiano scanned the women's faces. "I will try. These are practical things you ask for, so perhaps they will be available." To end the evening Sebastiano and Orencio played their guitars for the others, and they all sang a number of songs. This was to become a regular pattern at the rancho.

Finally, the conversation turned to the particulars of the journey to the mission. Sebastiano said, "Soon Father Duran will be at the mission, but he'll be there for only a few days. We should return there immediately to meet with him and see what we might be able to bring back to the rancho. I suggest that we rise early with the sun, pack a few provisions, and begin our journey tomorrow right after we have our morning meal. If we hurry and continue to drive part of each night, we should be at the mission in just over two days. Allowing up to three days to meet with the good father and to pack, we should return home in just over one week."

And so it was that Sebastiano, Hipolito, and Huslu began their journey to Mission San Jose in early 1839. As they had estimated, they arrived at the mission in three days. They found Father Duran getting ready to leave. He welcomed them warmly and asked a number of questions. "How are things going at the rancho? Have you met your neighbors, the Pachecos? Are there things that I can provide for you that will help you make the rancho grow?"

Sebastiano answered each question in turn. "The rancho is fine. Orencio, Hipolito, Migel, and the other men have done very good work to build the adobe, storage rooms, and sleeping quarters for the men. They have planted a vegetable garden as well as corn, wheat, and oats; and they hunt and fish at the point of the bay. We are well provided for." He continued, "We have not met the Pachecos yet, but hope to in the near future after we have fully settled in. As for what we need, I have prepared a list. I do not know what is left at the mission, but anything on the list that is available would be of assistance."

The list Sebastiano handed to Father Duran was as follows: "We would like to keep the cart and ox. If there is another cart and ox, we could use that, also. A plow or two would be helpful. We can use more cattle and cows; ewes and a ram or two; chickens and a couple more roosters; a few more horses, including a stud and some saddles; and a few goats. As far as plants are concerned, we could use some seeds for vegetables and grain, fruit trees, some climbing ivy, and particularly grapevines."

He added, "Other things that the women have mentioned are linen to make clothes, household goods, and blankets. Hipolito will make us a loom that can be used to spin wool for clothing and other articles. As I said, this is a lot, but we will be happy to receive whatever is possible."

That evening, Sebastiano was invited to have dinner with the father. During this time, Duran reminisced about his time at the mission and, in particular, about his relationship with Estanislao. "Natives such as Estanislao are what are needed in Alta California. He was intelligent, a strong leader, and, in his way, a good Christian. I am so pleased to see you and his family able to carry on his tradition."

The padre turned to another topic. With deep sadness in his voice, he said, "We have just completed an inventory of the mission possessions. There is a very great quantity of grain and implements, as well as movable goods. There are forty thousand bushels of all kinds of grain in the granaries, sixteen thousand head of cattle, thirty thousand of sheep, three hundred service horses, five or six hundred mares, one hundred yoke of oxen, one hundred domesticated cows, besides the other goods, gardens, and so forth. My prediction is that all of this will be gone in a couple of years, taken by some of the gente de razon for their own use and none to go to our neophytes. That is another reason that I am happy to give you the items you have asked for."

In the morning Sebastiano, Hipolito, and Huslu were assisted by two neophytes in the loading of goods into the two carts, and in stringing the walking animals behind them. By midday they were ready to make the three-day return journey to the rancho. In addition, they added one of the neophytes to their little group. His name was Enzo, and he was very happy for this opportunity.

What Sebastiano did not know was that two days after he left the rancho, a group of Indian raiders had appeared, intent upon stealing whatever they could, and even perhaps taking the women off with them. As the raiding party approached the rancho, Orencio went out to meet them. He didn't carry a weapon. The party was headed by an older Indian. Orencio immediately recognized him, and he spoke to the leader. "You are Molimo. You fought with my nephew Estanislao. This is the rancho of his daughter Juanita. His wife and other daughter are here also. In his memory, I would expect you to not do them any harm."

Molimo recognized Orencio and responded gently, "You are correct. We raid only the Mexican ranchos, pueblos, and missions. We do not attack our own people. In fact, we are prepared to leave you some cattle and horses, if you would like them. We also would ask you to give our greetings to Estanislao's family. He was a great man, and we are sorry to know that he has passed. He is missed by all of us."

The group cut out about a dozen cattle and six horses to leave at the rancho. Orencio offered the men a meal, and they responded with pleasure. After they were fed and waited upon by Orencio and the women, they said their good-byes and rode off. The neophytes of the rancho stayed indoors and out of sight that day because there were many stories about Christian Indians being killed by non-Christian Indians in the lands south of the bay. Much of this happened because many of the neophytes had joined the Mexicans as auxiliaries to attack the unbaptized Indians living near the missions.

After Sebastiano, Hipolito, Huslu, and Enzo returned from the mission, the routines at the rancho were set. With the oxen and plows, more fields were planted with grains. The trees and grapevines were planted and cared for. Furniture was built. Hunting and fishing continued. More building was done, including two large granaries; an enlarged carpenter's room for Hipolito and his tools; additional rooms for workers; fencing to keep the cattle, horses, sheep, and goats from roaming off; and an enlarged henhouse for the chickens. Most important was the addition of a nursery to the house, for Juanita was to be a mother in six months.

These were happy times for all the residents at the rancho. All of the help was treated well, and in return they worked hard at their respective tasks. The family spent each evening eating together and listening to music and tales told of earlier times. On these pleasant evenings, Sebastiano often would play his guitar and sing songs such as "Arruru mi Niño" for the coming child:

With a little shirt
I will dress you
On your birthday
When the sun comes up.

Mrs. Saint Anne,
Mr. Saint Joaquin,
Hide the baby
From the weasel.

Mrs. Saint Anne,
Why is the baby crying
For an apple
That has been lost?

Don't cry, little baby,
Because I have two apples—
One for the Virgin and one for you.

The baby was born and christened Linda Consuela. She was much loved and fussed over, particularly by Luz and Sebastiano. He often carried her around and showed her various parts of the house, the garden, the orchard, and—what she seemed to like the most—the animals.

As the baby and the rancho grew, thoughts turned to other things to do. First, it was time to name the rancho. One evening, the family discussed possible names. Orencio suggested that they name it Rancho Estanislao. There was much nodding of heads at that suggestion. Then Sebastiano put forth the idea that it should be named Rancho Duran. This, too, received positive responses. Finally, Juanita announced firmly, "I wish the name to be Rancho Santa Maria, in honor of the sainted mother of Christ." This was the name that was chosen.

The second task was to get to know their neighbors, the Pachecos.

PART THREE

THE RANCHOS AT THE
POINT OF THE BAY

MAP FOUR: RANCHO MONTE DEL DIABLO

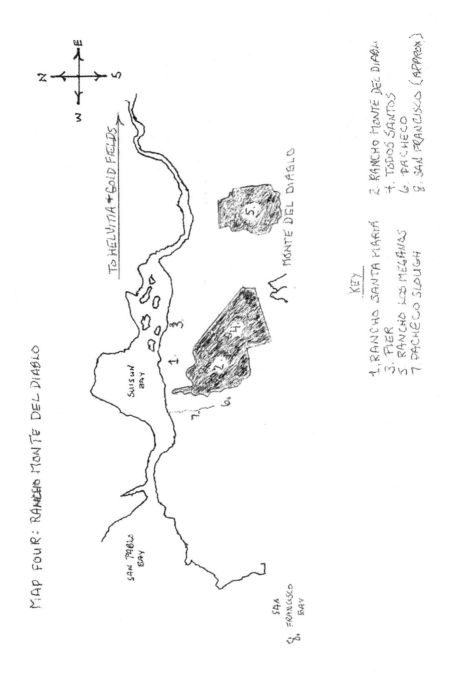

TO HELVETIA + GOLD FIELDS

SAN PABLO BAY

SUISUN BAY

SAN FRANCISCO BAY

MONTE DEL DIABLO

KEY

1. RANCHO SANTA MARIA   2. RANCHO MONTE DEL DIABLO
3. PIER   4. TODOS SANTOS
5. RANCHO LOS MEGANAS   6. PACHECO
7. PACHECO SLOUGH   8. SAN FRANCISCO (APPROX)

CHAPTER 8

LIFE AT THE RANCHOS

In 1784 Governor Fages, the same man who, as Captain Fages, had visited the Chupcan village in 1772, had begun the land-grant system. He first made small private grants, each to be beyond the limits of the existing pueblos and not conflicting with the property of missions or Indian villages. Some of these went to Spanish soldiers such as Sebastiano Perez, who had served their government well.

Most of the land grants were made after the establishment of the Mexican Republic. Any Mexican of good character, a member of the gente de razon, or any of a small number of foreigners who became naturalized and accepted the Catholic faith were able to petition for a grant. The largest of these grants were in the neighborhood of eighteen thousand acres. The smallest were in the range of twenty acres. Boundaries tended to be imprecise, which caused problems when the Americans began to take over much of this land.

⟨∞∞⟩

In 1828, Juan Salvio Pacheco, who had the title of Don, petitioned the Mexican government for lands in the Diablo Valley, and six years later he received a grant of 17,921 acres that began in the foothills of Monte del Diablo and extended to the point of the bay. Don Salvio's son, Fernando Pacheco, was immediately sent to occupy the grant and begin cattle operations.

Don Salvio remained in Pueblo San Jose as a senior civil servant while Fernando began the work of developing the large rancho. The adobe home had two large ground-floor rooms plus a dining room and kitchen, and six bedrooms were upstairs. On the north side there were servant quarters with several bedrooms. Farther to the north were the barn, corral, and a bull ring. A swimming pool and a dance floor were to the west just next to the artesian well.

While the workers on Sebastiano and Juanita's rancho and the vaqueros of the larger Rancho Monte del Diablo had interacted in their early years, there never had been a formal contact until the spring of 1840, when Sebastiano decided to visit Fernando Pacheco. He sent a messenger to Pacheco with a request for such a visit. A few days later, he received an invitation for himself, Juanita, and Elvira to come to the rancho in a fortnight for a three-day visit.

Upon hearing of the invitation, the women were at the same time gleeful and fearful. Juanita exclaimed, "Oh, this is wonderful. I am so interested in learning about the life at Rancho Monte del Diablo. I have heard that there is dancing, singing, wonderful entertainment, and great feasts."

Elvira was not so enthusiastic. "I don't know how to dress for such parties. Also, we need to learn how to behave at such affairs."

Sebastiano chuckled and said, "You need not worry. You both are very beautiful, and I can help you decide what clothes to bring."

Luz added, "I will help both of you by sewing some of the clothes you will need. We will have to buy some very fine materials to make your dresses and other clothes."

During the next several days, assisted by their maid, Colleta, they busied themselves with preparing the necessary clothes. They also pestered Sebastiano to tell them how they should behave. He was not totally sure himself about such matters, but he did his best to allay the fears of the women.

Finally, the day came for the trio to make the trip to the rancho. Sebastiano cut a fine figure. His hair and beard were trimmed to perfection. He was dressed in his finest clothes with tight pants, a silk shirt and scarf, and a broad-brimmed felt hat with fancy studs. He had his boots polished so well that he could see his own reflection in them. He was mounted on his best horse for the journey, wore fancy spurs, and had his guitar strung around his shoulders.

The women were dressed in newly-made linen dresses that reached to their ankles. They wore highly polished fancy laced shoes with raised heels. Their hair had the benefit of hours of brushing, and each wore a plain white bonnet. Around their shoulders they wore attractive multicolored shawls. They rode in a *carreta*, a cart, pulled by two oxen and driven by Enzo, which also contained their finest clothes packed in two chests. The maid, Colleta, accompanied them.

The caravan arrived at the rancho in midafternoon after a journey of just more than five miles. Sebastiano, Juanita, and Elvira were met by eighteen-year-old Don Fernando and his young wife, Maria. With a broad smile, Don Fernando welcomed the group. "We have wished to meet you for some time. We have heard so many things about the successful settlement and growth of your rancho, and your contacts with Father Duran before he left Mission San Jose. Most of all, we are curious about the accommodations that you have been able to make with our local Indian raiders. I would like to hear about that in great detail, because, like most ranchos, we face a problem with such raiders."

Doña Maria immediately spoke to Juanita. "You are such a beautiful woman. We look forward to knowing you better and to opportunities to share our common experiences. We do hope that you enjoy your first visit to our home and that you will come often in the future."

Juanita was very pleased with this welcome. However, she responded shyly to avoid making any mistakes at the beginning of their visit. She realized that she had been staring down at her own lap when Doña Maria had been speaking to her. She looked up and said only, "Yes, thank you."

Don Fernando spoke again. "Our staff will see you to your quarters and help you to unpack your belongings. After a siesta, we will meet again to tell you about the plans for the next few days. A number of other people will be arriving for the fiesta. Some will stay, and some will live nearby. Your quarters will be in the house. Other guests will stay in the servant quarters made up for them in an appropriate fashion. Your servants are to be lodged in the barn with our servants and those of other visitors. We perfected this routine as we began to hold such events for our friends and important visitors. We expect nearly thirty people here for our small fiesta, and we are very fortunate that my father, Don Salvio Pacheco, and my mother, La Doña Pacheco, will be with us, also."

After the siesta, Juanita and Elvira began to prepare themselves for the evening's festivities. They put aside their traveling clothes, and with the help of Colleta, combed their hair again so that long plaits fell to their waists. Juanita wore a pink linen chemise trimmed with lace, and a sheer darker pink muslin skirt over a rough muslin petticoat with a lace bottom that showed just below her skirt. These were secured at the waist by a scarlet silk band and satin shoes of the same color. She also wore a silver necklace and matching earrings.

Elvira's outfit was much the same as her sister's, except that she had chosen to bring clothes and shoes in light and dark blue shades. Her jewelry was made of sparkling glass rather than silver. In addition, she wore a white cotton *rebozo*, a shawl.

Sebastiano changed into soft shoes of deerskin that were embroidered with silver threads, satin breeches that reached to the knee, long white stockings that tucked into his breeches, and a cloth vest under a short black jacket likewise embroidered with silver threads, The finishing touch was a sash of bright red satin. He did not, however, change his dark wide-brimmed flat Spanish hat for an even wider-brimmed Mexican sombrero such as was commonly worn by the men of the ranchos.

When the trio arrived at the patio where the fiesta was to begin, they heard mariachi music and the voices of the assembled crowd. They were relieved to see that they were dressed appropriately. In fact, there was a wide range of clothing, some of it quite plain, and some of it more ornate than their own. A few were even dressed in the English style. Many of the people gathered there stopped talking for a moment while they looked over these new additions to Pacheco's guest list. It was clear that they admired the beauty of the two women, particularly Elvira, who was known by some to still be unmarried.

Don Fernando and his wife, Maria, accompanied by an older couple, moved to greet the new arrivals. Don Fernando said, "I hope you have found the accommodations to be satisfactory. We will soon be adding new rooms for our guests."

Sebastiano responded politely, "They are fine. We are very pleased to be invited to such a lovely hacienda, particularly for such an occasion as this."

Juanita added, "Everything is lovely. This will be a wonderful experience for us." Elvira shyly followed with her own expressions of awe and thanks.

Fernando then introduced the older couple. "I would like to present my father, Don Salvio Pacheco, and my mother, Doña Juana Flores Pacheco. Father and Mother, these are our new neighbors to the north, Sebastiano Perez, his lovely wife, Juanita, and her equally lovely sister, Elvira."

Don Pacheco took Juanita's hand first and then Elvira's and kissed each one. He then shook Sebastiano's hand and said, "You are welcome to our hacienda, and we hope you will enjoy your stay with us. We feel fortunate to have such fine neighbors and wish to develop a long and friendly relationship with you. I would like to meet with you and Fernando in the morning to discuss some possible business relationships we might consider. I hope that will be satisfactory for you."

Sebastiano responded, "That would be of much interest to me. I will be at your service, Don Pacheco."

With that, the group proceeded with light conversation until Don Salvio and Doña Juana Flores moved to greet other guests. Don Fernando and Doña Maria then led the trio first to where they could get cups of wine, and then to meet other guests. Among those they met were Don Bartolo Pacheco, owner of nearby Rancho San Ramon, and Don Candalerio Valencia, owner of nearby Rancho Acalanes. Each was accompanied by his wife and a young daughter. Sebastiano, Juanita, and Elvira also were introduced to a young American, Harold Marsh, the nephew of the famous doctor John Marsh, who had recently purchased the nearby Rancho Los Meganos from Don Jose Noriega. This was one of the first purchases of a Mexican rancho by an American.

The young Marsh was quite taken by Elvira. He stayed in her company for much of the evening and asked to see her again the next day. Since he had converted to Catholicism, this was acceptable to Sebastiano.

At exactly 9:00 p.m. a bell rang announcing that the feast was being served. Juanita was seated to the left of Don Salvio, who was at the end of the head table. To her left was Don Valencia. One could not help but notice that some of the other women looked at her with jealous expressions. After all, to them, she was an Indian and not their equal. Sebastiano was seated to the right of Doña Maria, who was at the other end of the table, and to his right was Don Bartolo Pacheco's daughter of about eighteen years of age. She was a cousin of Fernando Pacheco, the host.

The remainder of the group was seated at either the head table or at one of the two other large tables that filled the patio. Interestingly, the young Marsh was seated across from Elvira, who was seated between two other young men. Marsh ignored the two young women at his sides and spoke mostly to Elvira. He frequently interrupted the two men at Elvira's sides, much to their annoyance.

There were at least twenty Indian servants performing various duties as the dinner progressed. Only a few lived on the rancho. Most came from a nearby village and were hired for special events such as this one.

The feast was opened with welcomes by Don Fernando and Don Salvio. These greetings were followed by words of blessing by a priest from the small, relatively new local pueblo, Todos Santos, which the Pachecos would help to grow and prosper in the years to come.

The meal was sumptuous: *carne asada* from two steers roasted on spits over glistening coals, and treated with saltwater brought from the nearby bay and olive oil from pressed olives from trees grown in the rancho gardens. There were roasted chickens and turkeys, enchiladas and tamales, and beans and green vegetables grown in the rancho gardens. For dessert there were cakes, berries, and other fruits plentiful on the rancho. Throughout the meal a good amount of wine and cider was served.

Conversation was light, and laughter was plentiful. The mariachis played throughout the meal, and occasionally someone would stand and make a toast, usually to the hosts, but at times to other things, such as peace with the Indians or good weather for crops. As the night went on, the toasts became more and more verbose.

When the meal was finally concluded, the party moved to the dance floor next to the swimming pool. Tables and chairs had been set up around the dance floor, and servants continued to serve drinks.

The mariachi players also moved to the dance floor and began to play appropriate music. The first dance, which was the most popular at the ranchos of Alta California, was "La Jota." Sebastiano knew this dance and had taught it to Juanita and Elvira. Each man who wished to dance took a partner and placed her on his right, facing another couple, with as many couples as could fit into the available space. As soon as the music began, the mariachi players—who also were the singers—started with the lyrics, and the dancers moved arms and hands as the spirit took them, as long as the verse lasted. Then the singers took up the chorus, and the dancers joined hands in two circles, one of men and the other of women. The circles turned in opposite directions until each couple was again side by side and took their place in the line.

The steps for the dance included picking up one foot and then the other in time to the music, hopping as in a folk dance. "La Jota" was beautiful and graceful. One of the nice things about the dance was that the older people knew it better because of all of their practice. This gave a certain dignity to the dance. "La Jota" was danced a number of times during the evening, with people changing partners, except for Elvira and Harold and a few of the other young couples. Other dances included "La Zorritta," which was similar to "La Jota" except that the men performed some different movements and couples joined hands in a chain of four. It also included "La Contradanza." In this dance, two lines were formed, one of men and one of women. The music was a slow waltz in three-quarter time, which was danced more by the older couples in the group.

Perhaps the two most interesting dances were "El Fandango" and "La Bamba." "El Fandango" was danced by a single couple at a time. The man began with castanets and danced in place, and then did several complicated steps around the floor while the music played and the verse and refrain were sung. Then the music stopped, and the singer cried, "Bamba!" He then had to extemporaneously compliment his partner. The music played again, another verse and refrain were sung, and then it was the woman's turn to direct a verse to the man. When the couple was finished, another one took the floor. The dancing went on until every couple that wished to dance had a turn. During this dance, Sebastiano joined the mariachi band and played the music with them.

"La Bamba" was danced only by ladies who knew how, because the steps were complicated. The most expert could do it with a glass of water balanced on her head. The spectators might throw a knotted handkerchief on the dance floor as she danced. The lady would pick it up with her feet without missing a beat. She would then pick up one or two more and then deposit them all on the floor again. She would then return to her seat to the applause of the assembled crowd. Often one, two, or three other women would follow with their own performances in a kind of competitive challenge, much to the pleasure of the audience. Lyrics of this dance were as follows:

To dance La Bamba,
To dance La Bamba,
You need
A certain amount of gracefulness,
A certain amount of gracefulness
And something else,
And up and up
I will go.

Bamba, bamba, bamba!
Bamba, bamba, bamba!
Bamba, bamba, bamba!

The dancing went on until midnight, when people began to leave to go to their rooms. It had been a wonderful evening for all.

The morning began, as always, with mass, in this case led by the priest from Santa Cruz. Nearly all of the family and guests attended. Only a few young men who had drunk a great deal of wine the night before decided to sleep in rather than attend the service.

Following mass, Sebastiano joined Don Salvio and Don Fernando for a ride. They rode to a nearby knoll, from which they could see thousands of cattle and a large number of horses grazing in the fields to the north and west of the adobe. In one field, a group of vaqueros were branding some of the younger cattle. This was necessary because the land was not fenced and often cattle wandered onto the land of neighbors. Periodically, cattle and horses with neighbors' brands were rounded up and taken to their owners. Cattle could not be given a new brand without permission of the office of the governor. During this part of the ride the trio engaged in pleasant conversation, getting to know more about each other.

After looking over the stock, the riders moved to another knoll, to the south and east of the adobe, where they could view wheat, corn, and oat fields, as well as newly planted orchards of fruit trees. Most ranchos focused almost solely upon the raising of animals. Those ranchos that also involved a good deal of agriculture were more often called haciendas.

It was at this point in the ride that Don Salvio turned to more serious matters. He said to Sebastiano, "We have become impressed with what you have done with your rancho, and we also have come to admire your personal qualities. For these reasons, we would like to ask you if you would consider coming to the rancho to serve as *mayordomo*, foreman, and manage the operation. We would pay you a good salary, provide you and your growing family with more than adequate housing, and see that you have a number of servants to take care of your needs. You can bring all of your own people with you, and they, in turn, will be well taken care of. As far as your own rancho is concerned, you can keep it and have it run by your people, or you can sell it to us for a good price."

Sebastiano did not reply immediately. Finally, he said, "Next to deciding to marry Juanita, this is the biggest decision I have ever faced. I know that as the head of my family it is my decision to make. However, I would like to talk the matter over with my wife before I decide."

Don Salvio pressed on. "I believe it wise for you to consult your wife. I have two other matters to propose to you, and neither depends on your decision about coming to our rancho as mayordomo. The first matter is that of the Indians. I am told that you have been guaranteed safety from Indian raids because of something to do with your wife. Is that true?"

Sebastiano answered, "Yes, that is true. My wife is the daughter of Estanislao, the famous Indian rebel and also the favorite of Father Duran. When the leader of one of the raiding parties learned of this, he guaranteed us safety and provided us with a few cattle and horses."

Don Salvio, obviously impressed, continued. "As you know, the ranchos south of Suisun Bay suffer from many raids by Indians from the great valley to the east. Do you think you could make some arrangement to also gain protection for Rancho Monte del Diablo?"

Sebastiano carefully selected the words for his answer. "Many of the Indians feel strongly that they have been wronged by the Spanish and subsequently by the Mexicans. I am not sure I can persuade any of the raiders to move beyond their pledge to protect us because of Juanita's father. I can promise you one thing, and that is to ask Juanita's uncle Orencio to talk with his contact to see what can be done. I will have him attempt to tell how well you treat the Indians who work for you, including both Christians and non-Christians. That might carry some weight with the raiders. I do know that they will not simply stop raiding all of the ranchos and pueblos, for that has become their livelihood."

Don Salvio smiled and continued, "That sounds as if it might hold some promise, and I thank you, in advance, for your efforts on our behalf. Even if only some raiders decide not to bother us, we will gain some advantage."

After that exchange, the trio rode on. In a little while, Don
Fernando, glancing first at his father, spoke. "The other matter in
which we are interested should benefit us both greatly. Currently,
out of necessity we are forced to transport our hides and tallow to
the southern end of San Francisco Bay to have them put aboard the
Yankee ships that come into port at Alameda. Jose Jesus Vallejo is in
control of that port, and the charges for using it are extremely high.
In addition, it is a long way to haul our products by cart. What we
are thinking is that we should build our own port at the point of the
bay. That way, we can ship our hides and tallow from there. Between
us, we control the land, and the distance is not far. We would save
much money in our shipping. As our grain crops become larger, we
can begin to ship them, also. They could go both to San Francisco
and east to the pueblos that are springing up in the great valley.
Soon, also, our apple, pear, apricot, almond, walnut, pomegranate,
and other fruit trees, as well as our grapes and berries, will begin to
produce large crops that will be in great demand in the cities. Do
you see the advantages of building our own port?"

Sebastiano was very enthusiastic about this idea. "I certainly
can see its value, and I am willing to begin such a project almost
immediately. Please count me in."

Having made these agreements, the trio continued their ride
until the Pachecos had shown Sebastiano most of the rancho/ha-
cienda. He was truly impressed, and he could hardly wait to tell
Juanita about the three proposals made by the Pachecos.

While the men were riding, Doñas Juana and Maria Pacheco
gathered a number of the female visitors on the patio. Once they
were all assembled, the doñas led them on a tour of the beautiful
gardens. They walked along a wide, straight walk shaded by a trel-
lis knotted with grapevines. The walk led to steps that took them
through the middle of the garden and to a brook at the foot of it.
Beyond the brook there were almond, apple, and pear groves, which

were usually green and laden with blooms or fruit. The garden was never without a variety of colorful flowers, whatever the season. To the side were vineyards lush with the growth of both green and purple grapes.

As the women walked, Doña Juana spoke of how the rancho had begun. She also disclosed that she would prefer to live here permanently rather than in San Jose with only visits to the rancho. The talk among the women was light, mostly about family, new fashions, and various forms of entertainment. Juanita confided to Doña Maria that she was pregnant with a second child and hoped that it would be a boy.

At midday, the hosts and their guests once again gathered on the patio. This time the event that was about to occur was a *merienda*, a picnic. The young people rode their horses, while the older women and children rode in two-wheeled carretas pulled by the slower oxen. The group traveled out to a knoll that looked down upon the creek, orchards, and grapevines. The picnic featured carne asada cooked the night before, as well as cold chicken, enchiladas, tamales, tortillas, hard-boiled eggs, fruit, and cheeses. During the journey and throughout the picnic, the group found that they had a lot in common. The merienda, of course, was followed by singing and some dancing to the music of guitars, including that of Sebastiano. Once again, the young Harold Marsh paid much attention to Elvira.

The remainder of the day began with a siesta. This was when Sebastiano told Juanita of his conversation with the two Pacheco dons. He finished by asking her what she thought of the idea of moving to their rancho. She had listened attentively to his report and responded to his question by saying, "My dear love, it is your decision to make. I would be happy with either choice. I will say, though, that I like the freedom that we have on our rancho, and I enjoy watching you plan and carry out the duties necessary to make it a prosperous place for us." It was then that Juanita told him he was soon to be a father for the second time.

Sebastiano took her in his arms and whispered in her ear, "I love you so much, and I must say that your words match my own thoughts. A second child will be a blessing for us. I believe I would prefer to continue with our own little rancho. Of course, we can cooperate with the Pachecos. They are good people—honest and pleasant to be with. Tonight I will tell them of my decision."

The siesta was followed by an informal late meal, again featuring carne asada. There also was much to drink, and singing accompanied by guitars played by several of the guests. Seating was informal, with people choosing where to sit. Sebastiano, Juanita, and Elvira were at a table where they soon were joined by Harold Marsh and Don Fernando and his wife. For the most part, the conversation was light. Marsh and Elvira were flirting with each other. At one point in the evening, Sebastiano drew Don Fernando aside and told him, "Don Fernando, I am very flattered by your offer to become the mayordomo for Rancho Monte del Diablo. However, I have decided to remain at my rancho. I also have agreed to see what can be done about the Indian problem. Finally, I am very interested in the idea of developing a port at the point of the bay."

Sebastiano went on, "We will be able to take care of preparing the hides and rendering the tallow on our own properties. However, we will need to develop a packing house for the grains, fruits, and vegetables. Is that not true?"

Don Fernando nodded to his guest. "Yes, we will. It seems to me that in the long run the shipping of these goods will become more and more important to us. I also believe that we will be able to take care of the goods of other small ranchers and farmers in the area. Also, as the town of Todos Santos develops, there will be additional needs for a port."

Don Fernando added, "I will tell my father of your decision, and we will then have to draw up a plan for an official partnership. I think it is fair to suggest that the Pachecos should be the major partners, while you should have a somewhat smaller share. We can set forth the details over the next few weeks before we start any work on the port."

Sebastiano answered, "That sounds fair to me, and I look forward to our collaboration." Shortly after this conversation, the evening came to a happy conclusion. After the dancing, music, good food, wine, and conversation, everyone was ready for a night's sleep.

After mass on the third and final day of the fiesta, Don Fernando announced to the assembled guests that they were in for a special treat in the afternoon: bullfights in the newly completed arena. Shortly after midday, most of the guests and some of the employees gathered in a pavilion that was shaded by a number of trees. In front of them was a large ring fenced with tin sheets and heavy rails. A bull was lassoed and dragged into the ring by a number of vaqueros. Several of the younger male guests, as well as vaqueros, were waiting on horseback for the bull in the ring. An equal number of men were waiting outside the ring for a turn to participate. A few of the more skillful men, mostly members of the host family, caped the bull with their serapes. Then one pricked the beast with a lance.

When the bull became tired and lost spirit, the gate was opened and the bull was herded out at a run with all the mounted men chasing him. The object was to seize the bull's tail and upset him. In order to do that, each group of riders jostled and trampled each other, at great risk to their safety. Then another bull was brought in, and the process was repeated. All the while, the audience was shouting encouragement to the men as the various moves were made. The word *olé* was heard over and over again. Since the bull was not killed, even the most sensitive of viewers could enjoy the event. Usually, the bullfight would last about three hours or until six bulls had been fought. The worst news was that some horses and men were hurt in this sport.

A siesta followed the bullfights, and later in the evening a new banquet, the equal of the first night of the celebration, was attended by the host family and all of their guests. There was more music, dancing, and conversation. The wine and cider flowed, and young singles flirted with each other. The event ended slightly earlier on this night because people needed to get an early start in the morning on their homeward journeys.

On the way home, Juanita, Elvira, and Sebastiano were happy, singing and reliving the events of the fiesta. In addition, Juanita was particularly looking forward to talking to her mother about the second child, Elvira was thinking of ways to see more of Harold Marsh, and Sebastiano was deep in thought about his future as both a rancher and a businessman.

FAMILY TREE
— 2 —

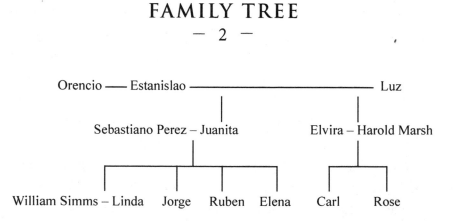

CHAPTER 9

THE END OF THE RANCHO PERIOD

During the rancho period, the family was central. It consisted of fifteen to twenty members, sometimes more. When in-laws and adopted children were added, families were even larger. Families shared a strong sense of affection, but at the same time there was strict discipline. All members of the rancho, including family, Indian servants, and sometimes even residents of the nearest village responded to the father's wishes. At times, he administered corporal punishment to his sons, even as adults of sixty years of age, and no son dared to smoke in his father's presence. Children even asked permission to sit down. Rancho Monte del Diablo was no exception, as Salvio Pacheco was in total command of everything that happened there, even though some responsibilities were delegated to his son Fernando. The blessing for his family members and servants was that he was a gentle and kind individual, not inclined to govern harshly.

At his rancho, Sebastiano, while not a don, also was given the respect owed to the head of the family, and he was expected to make all the important decisions. It was a busy place, with much hard work for everyone. Even so, it was a particularly harmonious and happy setting.

Five months after their return from the fiesta at Rancho Monte del Diablo, Juanita gave birth to a boy, who was soon christened by the traveling priest from Santa Clara, and named Jorge. He was an active baby and well spoiled by his father and grandmother. Because of the new family member and the addition of several more workers, there was more construction at Rancho Santa Maria. Another bedroom was added for Linda Consuela, leaving the nursery for Jorge.

Since there was no village close enough for natives to come to work, additional dormitories were built for the help, including one for the many women who attended to tasks in the house and the garden.

Luz and Orencio were getting older. She was in her midforties and still helped with the cooking and care of the children; but, in fact, servants now did most of the work. Orencio, now also in his midforties, had fallen and broken two ribs. As a result he was not able to do as much work as he had done in the past. Even so, at the request of Sebastiano, he searched out Molimo, who himself was in his midforties, to ask about not raiding the Pacheco rancho because of the good treatment of the Indian help there.

When asked, Molimo answered, "At this time, we raiders are under attack by more and more Americans who are coming into our area from across the great Sierra Nevada mountains. We are so busy defending ourselves that we have little time to raid rancherias, ranchos, what remains of the missions, or pueblos. Perhaps Sebastiano can ask the Pachecos if they have work for some of us. We are good horsemen and could work as vaqueros, or we could help to defend the rancho from other raiders."

Orencio was surprised by this answer and responded in turn. "I can ask Sebastiano to take your message to the Pachecos. I do believe that you will get a positive response that will be good for all."

When Sebastiano passed along this message to Don Fernando, he responded with questions. "Do you believe these Indians can be trusted? What is to stop them from working against us from within?"

Sebastiano replied, "I believe that these men are desperate and know that they have no future as bandits. I think they will be good workers and not be troublemakers. I plan to hire a few of them to work for me, including the old leader, Molimo."

Don Fernando did hire several of these men, and there was no more bother from the raiders. However, this was not a guarantee that there would be no further raids, for there were other groups who knew nothing of Estanislao and who had no desire to change their thieving habits. With some of Molimo's men working as guards, however, there was little raiding of Rancho Monte del Diablo.

In early 1842, Sebastiano, Juanita, and Elvira once again accepted an invitation to the Pacheco rancho. Sebastiano saw the visit as an opportunity to talk with the Pachecos about the port project, Juanita wished to know about new fashions and the happenings in the area, and Elvira hoped to see Harold Marsh again.

Enzo drove one caretta with the women and their new maid, Ariela; Migel drove the second caretta with the luggage; and Sebastiano, as usual, rode his best horse. Luz, Colleta, Orencio, and the other workers remained at the rancho to take care of the two children, the house, the garden, and the stock. When the group arrived at Rancho Monte del Diablo on Friday afternoon, Don Fernando and his wife, Maria, greeted them warmly. The guests then were shown to their quarters to unpack and have a siesta.

Almost everything was the same as it had been during the first visit two years before. There were sumptuous meals, dancing and singing, and time for everyone to get to see and talk to old friends. Elvira did spend a great deal of time with Marsh, usually chaperoned by Juanita. Salvio Pacheco did not attend this fiesta, so Sebastiano and Don Fernando met alone to talk about progress on the port project.

Don Fernando spoke first. "My father and I have discussed the port idea with a number of other rancho owners as well as with the growing number of merchants in the area, and everyone agrees that we should go ahead. We have drawn up an agreement for you to sign that spells out some of the tasks you might do and what percent of the income shall go to you. That amount is 15 percent. Is that agreeable to you?"

"I am sure it will be," answered Sebastiano. "Can you tell me what you expect of me and my people?"

Don Fernando explained, "For now, let us assume that since you are nearest to the bay, you will supervise the surveying that will be done to see exactly where the pier will be built and where the roads to your rancho, our rancho, and the planned community of Pacheco will be laid out. We have identified contractors from San Francisco to do the survey work. If this work is satisfactory, we can think of having them continue with further tasks." Don Fernando went on, "My father and I will bear most of the costs for the surveying, but we hope that you will be able to contribute a small amount."

Without hesitation, Sebastiano responded, "Our place is doing quite well now. We have begun to sell some hides and tallow, as well as meat and grains, to the Americans. I can afford to make a fair contribution."

Don Fernando added, "Once the area is surveyed, we can begin to think about actual construction. In the meantime, we will be seeking contracts from ranchers and merchants to use the port for transport of their goods. Our estimate is that the port will be in operation in about two years. How does that sound to you?"

Sebastiano smiled. "That sounds very good. I'm quite pleased with our agreement and with the plans you have developed. I want to thank you for involving me in this grand project. We shall help to make this one of the richest areas in Alta California." With the discussion completed, the two went on to talk of the general economy in the area, of family matters, and of the events planned for the fiesta.

There was one major difference at this year's fiesta. There was no bullfight. Instead, they focused on grizzly bears. On Saturday morning, the fattest cattle and sheep were driven into the rancho *calaveras*, the place of skulls. Indian butchers killed these animals, and by night the hides were all stretched out to dry. The meat was shared with all the people at the rancho. The grizzlies came at night to the ravines near the calaveras where the butchers had thrown the refuse. The young men at the fiesta rode out that night in the moonlight to lasso the bears. On this night, they successfully captured three bears and dragged them through the nearby Indian village, scattering the natives, and then to the rancho, where the bears were penned up and tied to stakes.

On Sunday morning after mass, many of the members of the family, including the children, the help, and guests, came to view the captured grizzlies. Elvira was walking with Harold Marsh, accompanied by Juanita, and they made it a point to join the viewers. Marsh commented, "Ugly beasts, aren't they? I wouldn't want to meet one of them in the forest while I was on a walk."

Elvira did not want to contradict Harold, but Juanita could not help herself. She replied, "I don't think they are ugly. In fact, to the contrary, I believe they are beautiful beasts. Furthermore, I think that hunting, capturing, and killing them is too cruel a thing to do. They should be left alone."

Marsh did not respond to this remark. Instead, he asked Elvira, "Will you accompany me this afternoon to the bullring to see the bears fight with bulls? I hear that it is a most thrilling spectacle."

Elvira was conflicted. She did not want to watch such a cruel sport. However, she did want to be with Marsh, and she certainly did not want to alienate him by declining his invitation. In the end, she agreed to accompany him. Juanita, on the other hand, was quite clear about her feelings. "I have no wish to see such a spectacle. I prefer to walk in the garden and perhaps read a book. I have one in English, and it will help me learn the language better. Perhaps, Harold, you can help me with my English also."

Harold was surprised by this request and responded, "I would be happy to do that. Perhaps the three of us can learn each other's language. I need to improve my Spanish, and I can help the two of you with your English." Both sisters agreed to the idea.

When the time came, a large crowd was assembled at the bull-ring. Three matches were scheduled. A tightly bound bull and an equally fettered grizzly were brought into the ring. Once the animals were there, one of the vaqueros tied the hind foot of the bear to the forefront of the bull, and all other restraints were cut off. Normally, a grizzly would be more than a match for a bull. However, with the feet tied together, they were equal. In addition, because they did not want to lose a prime bull, the rancheros tended to enter older, less ferocious bulls into the contests. The three contests involved a great deal of roaring by the bears and equally loud snorting by the bulls. Most of the spectators shouted in support of the bulls, while a few cheered the bears. A number of men gambled on the outcome, with odds in favor of the grizzlies. Many of the women didn't want to watch the cruel sport and hid their eyes. No children were allowed to attend the fights. In the end, all of the animals were badly wounded, and one bull was killed.

When the fights were over, Don Fernando proclaimed, "This sport is too cruel, and it is costly. We will have no more grizzly and bull fights at this rancho."

At the end of the three-day fiesta, Sebastiano, Juanita, Elvira, and their servants returned home. Harold Marsh had made it a point to seek permission from Sebastiano to visit Rancho Santa Maria to court Elvira. His wish was granted.

Harold visited three times after the second fiesta at Rancho Monte del Diablo. On the third visit, he asked for Elvira's hand in marriage. Everyone at the rancho was in favor, so a wedding was set for early 1844. Dr. John Marsh, who in 1836 had established his own rancho to the east of Rancho Monte del Diablo, was Harold's uncle. Because Dr. Marsh was the head of his family, his permission was also sought. He readily gave his consent and attended the ceremony. Don Fernando and his wife, along with other family members from Rancho Monte del Diablo, also attended.

The wedding was a gala affair. The priest from Santa Clara presided over the ceremony, and Sebastiano gave the bride away. Juanita served as Elvira's maid of honor and Linda Consuela as flower girl. The women and Linda Consuela were beautiful, all dressed in their best attire.

After the ceremony there was a reception with food and drinks prepared by the staff, supervised somewhat by Luz. There was dancing and singing and many toasts to the bride and groom.

Doctor Marsh turned out to be a most pleasant person. He was a cultivated French and Spanish scholar. In appearance, he was tall and commanding. He made a point of telling Sebastiano how much he appreciated the work that Sebastiano had done to establish the rancho. He also was quite interested in the possibility of a port at the point of the bay.

When the reception ended, the wedding participants either returned to their own homes or were made comfortable in accommodations at the rancho, for now there were enough rooms in the house and servant quarters, while the servants moved to the barn for the night.

Elvira and Harold spent their wedding night at the house. Early the next morning, Enzo drove a carreta loaded with Elvira's belongings to the Marsh rancho, where the young couple would live. Elvira rode next to Enzo, and Harold rode his horse. The journey was about thirty miles and took a full day.

The next year was both a happy and a sad one. Another boy, Ruben, was born and shared the nursery with Jorge. The sadness came with Orencio's death, by malaria. After his death, he was laid out on a table in the adobe and covered with a black cloth. A stone was placed at his head, and four wax candles were lit. The priest came and at intervals sang responses for the soul of the deceased. Since there was no church nearby, a low mass was said over the corpse. Then a procession of grievers followed the four pallbearers who carried the body to the place chosen to be the family cemetery, behind the adobe. At the cemetery the body was put into a coffin built by Hipolito and his helper. The coffin was lowered into the grave, and the priest said the final benediction. Luz seemed to grieve the hardest, but all were deeply stricken by the loss of Orencio.

Linda Consuela was now five years old. Sebastiano determined that it was time for her to learn the skills and duties that were necessary for her to become a refined lady: appropriate dress, manners, household management, conversation, and obedience. He also determined that she should learn to read, write, and be comfortable with numbers. Juanita was in charge of teaching her the duties and skills of womanhood. For academic matters, Sebastiano sought out an intelligent young man to serve as tutor. After interviewing several possible candidates, he chose one of the extended Pacheco family, Quiño, who came to the rancho twice a week to give Linda Consuelo her necessary lessons. In between his visits, Linda Consuela was expected to practice what he had taught her, and for this practice she was also supervised by her mother. The thought occurred to Sebastiano that as the number of his children and those of the servants of the rancho grew, he should consider the establishment of a formal school.

Unfortunately, the plans for a port at the point of the bay had languished. There were significant problems with the survey, and keeping a workforce going also was a difficult proposition. At the end of the two years predicted by Don Fernando for completion of the port, only the surveying had been done.

A pier was finally completed in early 1847, and roads were built. Hides, tallow, and crops from the local area could be sent to San Francisco and beyond. There also was the possibility that they could be brought from the great valley and shipped on to the coast. More and more, Sebastiano turned his attention to this business and left the running of the rancho to his trusted crew, including Hipolito, Enzo, Migel, Colleta, and others.

Sebastiano and Juanita still were able to maintain their idyllic family life. Almost always, except in winter, they ate their supper on the patio, where the two enjoyed time with the children. Sebastiano frequently asked Linda Consuelo, now seven, "How are your lessons going, my little beauty?"

She usually would answer, "I love what Mama is teaching me. I want to grow up and become a lady and have my own household. What Mr. Pacheco teaches me is harder to learn, but I am getting to be a good reader, and I also try hard to write my own stories. The numbers are more difficult, but they are like solving a puzzle."

Juanita, not wanting to leave the boys out of the conversation, said to Jorge, "Tell your father what you did today. I know you are pleased with yourself."

The boy responded loudly, "Enzo helped me ride the pony you gave me on my last birthday. Soon I will be able to help the vaqueros at the rodeo."

Sebastiano said, "That's wonderful, young man. However, it will be a while before you can ride in the rodeo. You need much more practice on your pony, and then you will need to learn to ride a horse. By the way, how are your lessons going now that you are working with Señor Quiño?"

This topic was not as exciting as talking about a rodeo, but he still wanted to make his father proud. "I like my numbers best, but I also am doing well with reading. I can't write yet, but I will try hard when my time comes."

Juanita pointed to the baby, Ruben, who was now a one-year-old. He had been fed in the kitchen and was now crawling around on the patio. Juanita spoke softly. "He is slower to walk and to speak than the older children were, but he is a beautiful child."

Sebastiano said, "I have noticed, but I am not worried about the matter yet. Let us see how he develops over the next year."

At the end of the meal, Sebastiano surprised the family by

saying, "While I was in San Francisco on business last week, I learned a new song that has quickly become popular among the Americans. It is what is called a minstrel, and it was written by a famous American songwriter named Stephen Foster. It is sung by Negroes or white men imitating Negroes." As he often did, he took out his guitar and began to play and sing, this time in English:

I come from Alabama with my banjo on my knee.
I'm goin' to Louisiana, my true love for to see.

It rained all night the day I left; the weather it was dry.
The sun so hot I froze to death; Susanna, don't you cry.

Chorus:

Oh, Susanna, oh don't you cry for me.
I'm goin' to Louisiana, my true love for to see.

I had a dream the other night, when everything was still.
I thought I saw Susanna a-comin' down the hill.
The buckwheat cake was in her mouth, the tear was in her eye.
Says I'm a comin' from the south; Susanna, don't you cry.

Chorus

I soon will be in New Orleans, and then I'll look all 'round,
And when I find Susanna, I'll fall upon the ground.
But if I don't find her, this darkie'll surely die,
And when I'm dead and buried, Susanna, don't you cry.

Even though the children didn't know English, they loved the rhythm and rocked back and forth while their father sang. He said to Juanita, "I would like you to ask Quiño to teach you this song so that we can all sing it together."

Later in the evening, after the children had been put to bed, Juanita and Sebastiano were having coffee and brandy. Juanita asked him, "Why do you wish to have the children learn English? Is it important for them?"

Sebastiano paused a moment before he answered her. "I always have been grateful that I learned English while serving in the army, because it has given me an advantage in my dealings with the Americans. Also, based upon what is happening between Mexico and the United States, it seems to me that this land may soon be taken away from Mexico by the Americans. On my trip to San Francisco last week, it seemed obvious to me that many of the prominent businesses there are owned by Americans and the city is growing rapidly. More and more, the language of business is English. It is important that our children learn it."

Juanita mused, "These will be difficult times, and you are right to think ahead. Perhaps we should ask Quiño to make English a regular part of his teaching. I know he speaks the language."

"That's a good idea. I also think that you should take English lessons with the children. You can tell him when he comes tomorrow. Also, you should say that we will pay him a bit more for these added lessons. This also means that we should try to speak English with the children ourselves."

⌇⌇⌇

From the middle 1820s to the outbreak of the US-Mexican War in 1846, many American traders had moved to California. Before 1824, most of the foreigners landing on the shores of California were visitors only. After a short period of trading, their ships raised anchor and sailed away. However, in 1824 the Mexican Congress passed an act that promised the security of person and property to foreigners settling in California and obeying its laws. Many traders took advantage of this invitation to conduct business regularly. Many settled in the region, married into Mexican families, and started families of their own. Over the next two decades, as a result of this act and of the migration of Americans over the Sierra Nevada mountains into California, the foreign population in Mexican Alta California increased dramatically.

There were a number of provocations against the Mexican government by Americans in California during this time. One of the most famous was in the winter of 1845 when John C. Fremont, a US Army officer, with his two longtime aides, Kit Carson and George Chapman, and a small force of "Pathfinders," entered California over the Sierra Nevada mountains via the Truckee Pass. The Fremont force joined with the main force commanded by Lieutenant Joseph W. Walker, which had entered California via the Owens Valley. Mexican authorities were concerned over the presence of a unit of the US Army in their territory and ordered Fremont to leave. Instead, Fremont's party built fortifications and raised the American flag on Hawk's Peak, some thirty miles from the Mexican capital in Monterey. When the Mexicans began to organize for an attack, Fremont abandoned this site and made his way northward toward the Oregon border.

The major event that dramatically altered the status of Alta California was the war between the United States and Mexico. Texans had revolted against Mexico in 1836 and declared Texas an independent republic. In February 1845, the US Congress passed a resolution making Texas part of the United States, to the delight of the Texans. Thus provoked, Mexico began the war on April 25, 1846, with an attack on American troops along the southern border of Texas.

In 1846, drastic changes occurred in California that had a pro-found impact on the region near the point of the bay. In the spring, a group of American farmers and mountain men who called them-selves the "Bears" decided to rebel against Mexico. Once again in the thick of things, Fremont advised the Bears on a plan to capture the pueblo of Sonoma, which was headquarters for some of the Mexican army in northern California. Mariano Vallejo was in charge of Sonoma. Though Mexican himself, he favored an ultimate take-over by the Americans. When Vallejo was surprised by the Bears, he turned over Sonoma to them. The Bears declared California free and claimed it was the Republic of California. They created a flag featuring a star and a grizzly bear, and the event became known as the Bear Flag Revolt.

The revolt lasted only twenty-six days, ending when the US Army arrived to occupy the area. Most of the people of Alta California never knew of the Bear Flag Revolt. Once the leaders of the revolt knew the United States was claiming the area, they disbanded their "republic" and supported the US federal effort to annex Alta California.

Events occurred rapidly. While the Bear Flag Revolt was in progress, preparations for the actual military conquest of California were being made. Commodore John Sloat, in command of the Pacific fleet of the United States, proceeded to Monterey in his flagship the USS *Savannah*. He took possession of the city, and a force of marines and seamen raised the US flag at the customhouse. Within days, the flag was raised at Yerba Buena, then Sonoma, and then Helvetia, Sutter's Fort. After the Americans won several battles throughout the state, the Mexican governor, Pio Pico, signed the Cahuenga Capitulation, which ended hostilities in California.

Inevitably, changes came to Rancho Monte del Diablo. Up to this date, Don Salvio had not moved permanently to the rancho, although he was a frequent visitor. He was too busy in San Jose serving as secretary to the town council and later as alcalde. When the Bear Flag Revolt occurred, a party of Americans demanded that he give them the keys to the hall of records. He protested, saying that he had to confer with the government at Monterey. The Americans repeated their demand and pointed their guns at him. He gave them the keys. He then decided to move to the rancho, where he felt secure because the Indian raiding also was under control.

Sebastiano's predictions about the Americans had been accurate, and because of the preparations made by his family for the transition, they suffered less than most of the rancheros, who had led an idyllic life without much thought given to the changing times.

PART FOUR

THE COMING OF THE AMERICANS TO THE POINT OF THE BAY

CHAPTER 10

THE GOLD RUSH

In June 1847, Don Fernando paid a visit to Rancho Santa Maria. He was greeted fondly by Sebastiano, Juanita, and others. After a brief siesta, he was invited to join Sebastiano on the patio for a round of talks.

Sebastiano had been expecting to hear some discussion of plans for the recently completed pier and roads. He was disappointed. Don Fernando spoke sadly. "The Bear Revolt has upset all of our plans. Things are uncertain. There is word that all of the rancho owners will have to reapply for their rights to ownership. This could take a good deal of time because, in many cases, boundaries have not been well marked. Also, many American squatters are putting pressure on the interim government to allow land to be sold for farming."

Sebastiano inquired, "Certainly they cannot contest your family's ownership of Rancho Monte del Diablo?"

Fernando responded, "We think there will be no problem, but we must be sure before we move on with many of our plans, including the pier at the point of the bay. We simply must wait to see how things work out before we make further commitments."

Sebastiano again asked, "How long do you think that will take?"

Fernando seemed exhausted but replied slowly, "Things are so uncertain now. We just don't know how fast we can move. We'll do our best to have our right of ownership settled as soon as possible. I wish I could give you assurances, but at this time I cannot."

Finally, Sebastiano asked, "I would like to use the pier at the point of the bay to ship hides and tallow, and perhaps even grains, fruit, and vegetables to San Francisco. It might even be possible to have the pier serve ships coming down the river from the great valley on their way to the coast. Would you and Don Salvio give me permission to do that for the next year or so until things settle down and the future becomes clearer?"

Don Fernando answered, "I will ask Don Salvio. I believe your use of the pier will be fine with him. I will get back to you within a few days."

Don Fernando remained at Rancho Santa Maria for the evening meal and breakfast in the morning, after which he rode back to Rancho Monte del Diablo. During supper and again in the morning, Don Fernando, Sebastiano, and Juanita talked about the events that were taking place in California and in the local region.

At supper, the conversation was about the hide and tallow business, which was important to both ranchos. Don Fernando noted, "To date, merchants from the eastern United States, Europe, and Latin America have been using our cattle hides for purposes such as bed mattresses, horse blankets, saddles, shoes, chair seats, and window and door coverings. Tallow, the fat of the cattle, has been used for cooking, candles, and soap. However, as you know, the business is declining because there now is a glut of hides and tallow on the market."

Juanita protested, "Surely, there is still some room to sell hides, tallow, and the meat from cattle?"

Don Fernando replied, "Certainly there is. However, prices have dropped so much that it almost is not worth raising the cattle. As I said, we will have to wait and see."

⁂

Don Fernando had been correct in thinking that changes were coming to California. However, he had underestimated the scope of those changes. On January 24, 1848, James W. Marshall discovered gold at Sutter's Mill in the foothills of the Sierra Nevada mountains at Coloma, California. The news of the find brought some three hundred thousand people to California from the rest of the United States and abroad. Of the three hundred thousand, approximately half arrived by sea and half came overland.

The news of gold being found spread rapidly. It came to Rancho Monte del Diablo and Rancho Santa Maria in March 1848 from travelers coming from San Francisco on their way to the gold fields. The first group consisted of four men and a woman. Two of the men appeared to be of good breeding. They were well dressed and neat, and they carried with them good supplies both for mining and for sustenance. The other two men obviously were not so well off. They wore common buckskin clothing and sported long hair and somewhat unkempt beards. The woman was plainly dressed and had a Cockney accent. It was obvious that she was not an American, but a recent immigrant from England.

The group was welcomed at Rancho Monte del Diablo, and was greeted by Don Salvio and Don Fernando. They were joined by Sebastiano and Juanita, who had ridden over from their rancho. Providing food and shelter was a common way to gather news from the outside world, and the people of both ranchos were eager to hear news of the discovery of gold.

The supper at the Rancho Monte del Diablo was well attended, and even some of the vaqueros stood nearby so that they could hear the news. Don Fernando, after saying grace and drawing out introductions from all present, addressed the visitors with a series of questions. First, he asked the well-dressed young men, "Is it really true that there is gold to be found in the foothills of the Sierra Nevada mountains?"

The older of the two, Percy Battle, responded, "That is what is said in San Francisco. The local newspapers report that the gold is literally 'swimming' in the American River, and is easily found. My friend Bradley and I were lucky to be able to buy picks, shovels, pans, and screens, as well as food supplies before we set out from San Francisco. These items were not cheap, but we believe we can make a fortune."

Bradley Wellington added, "It is a race now. Literally hundreds of people from all over California have come to San Francisco to begin the journey to the mining area. It is said that thousands will come via ships and overland from across the country. We believe that right now we are ahead in the race."

Sebastiano asked Bradley, "Tell us, please, what your employment has been to date and why you want to give up what you now do to hunt for gold."

Bradley enthusiastically answered, "I worked as a clerk for a merchant in San Francisco. The job provided steady employment, but what I could earn was limited. I believe it was worth the risk to resign my position and seek my fortune."

All of the members of the visiting group nodded their heads and spoke words of agreement. As the conversation continued, it was understood that Percy Battle had worked as a teller in a bank, and that the other two men were roustabouts at the port. They all had reasons to seek their fortunes in the streams of what was coming to be known as "The Gold Country."

Only the young woman did not offer information about herself. When asked what she did and why and how she believed she could make her fortune, she gave only vague answers having to do with her responsibility to earn money for her elderly mother and younger sisters in London. What seemed to be clear was that she hoped to find work near the gold fields that would provide her with good wages.

By the end of the meal, over glasses of brandy, the talk came around to the issue of transportation. Percy asked, "The overland route to the gold fields is long and at times treacherous, we are told.

Is there any way that we can find a ship that might take us the rest of the way?"

Sebastiano answered, "I have permission from my partner to provide a small sailing ship that can take you to a new landing near the gold fields that recently has been built by John Sutter at what now is known as New Helvetia. The small sailing vessel can leave from the point of the bay in two days and should take only two more days to reach New Helvetia. There will be a small fee for each of you for this service, of course."

The ship, which was docked at the pier at the point of the bay, was readied for the passengers and also packed with food provisions and whatever tools that could be spared from the ranchos to be sold at New Helvetia.

For a year or so other adventurers arrived to take advantage of the sailing ship from the point of the bay. However, the passenger business was short-lived, since enterprising businessmen in San Francisco soon developed their own fleets of ships to make the trip directly from their city to New Helvetia and back to San Francisco.

What did continue was the shipping of locally grown foods and other needed supplies to the miners, who were willing to pay high prices for such goods; despite the fact that New Helvetia had its own crops and stock to sell, there was need for more.

ᏮᏬᎧ

Early in 1849, John Augustus Sutter, Jr., traveling to San Francisco from New Helvetia, stopped at the point of the bay and visited Sebastiano. Sutter clearly had respect for Sebastiano, who was not afraid to compete with the big trading companies in San Francisco. He also respected Sebastiano because his produce and meat were always of the highest quality as well as reasonably priced. These reasons prompted Sutter to offer Sebastiano an exclusive contract for food and other goods from his rancho as well as from other local farmers and ranchers. The one condition was that he wanted a contract that lasted only two years.

With the limited knowledge that Sebastiano had of the gold mining in and around New Helvetia, he was puzzled by this request. In response to a direct question about the time limit, Sutter answered, "Ten years ago, in 1839, my father, John Augustus Sutter, Sr., received a grant of nearly fifty thousand acres from the Mexican government. He was authorized to act as a political authority and dispenser of justice in the region. He had Sutter's Fort built in 1841. In just a few years, he was a very successful landholder. He had acres of grains, several orchards, and a large herd of cattle."

"What happened to your father's claim to New Helvetia after the United States defeated Mexico?" Sebastiano asked.

"More and more Americans coming to California made it a point to stop at New Helvetia," Sutter continued. "Many of them were employed by my father. This flow of immigrants provided him with political protection when the United States seized control of California in 1846. The Treaty of Guadalupe Hidalgo gave California to the United States on February 2, 1848. As you know, less than one month before that, on January 24, James Marshall discovered gold at Sutter's Mill near Coloma."

Sebastiano once again spoke briefly. "You would think that the discovery of gold was good news for you and your father."

Sutter frowned. "Quite the contrary. First, many of our employees left New Helvetia and went to find gold on their own. Then squatters from all across the United States and from all around the world began to arrive to seek their fortunes. They are destroying our crops and butchering our herds. We don't know how we are going to protect what is ours. You can see why we don't wish to enter into any long-term agreements."

Once again, Sebastiano realized that his business ventures were to be influenced by the events of history. In the short term, he continued to look after the growing Rancho Santa Maria, as well as the small business of providing needed goods for New Helvetia. All the while, though, his thoughts were about future business opportunities.

⌒〰〜

Sebastiano also found himself thinking about his family and the future of its members. Now, in the fall of 1849, Linda Consuela was nine years old, Jorge was seven, Ruben was three, and the newest child, Elena, was six months old. Linda and Jorge were both fluent in English due to the tutoring of Quiño and the oversight of Juanita. Sebastiano was quite happy that Quiño had not run off to the gold fields like many of the vaqueros and young family members at Rancho Monte del Diablo. He also was grateful that none of his own employees had left for the gold fields. Only Ruben, at three years of age, presented a problem. He preferred crawling and did not try to walk. He also did not talk. No doctors were nearby to examine the child, so Colleta cared for him full time. His parents and older sister and brother also looked after him a great deal.

Juanita was concerned about her sister, Elvira. She was not sure what effect the discovery of gold would have on the rancho of Dr. Marsh, and thus on Elvira and her husband, Harold.

Nearing forty-eight years of age, Luz still tried to help around the house and in the garden; but in truth she had been relieved of all but the lightest of duties. She, too, was concerned about her younger daughter.

Both Juanita and Luz expressed their concerns to Sebastiano, who in turn took it upon himself to see what he could do to arrange a visit to the Marsh rancho. He began this surprise venture by purchasing and having delivered to the rancho a double Concord buggy, which was sturdy and safe for Juanita to handle, and also provided room to carry light luggage. It was only after he was sure that Juanita was comfortable handling the buggy that he surprised the women with the news. At supper on a warm fall evening in October 1849, Sebastiano poured three small glasses of wine made from grapes grown at the rancho. He then very quietly asked, "How would the two on you like to visit Elvira and Harold at Rancho Los Meganos? I have made contact with Dr. Marsh, and he is quite agreeable to such a visit."

The women were very pleased with this news, and they immediately began to speak of the arrangements they needed to make for the trip. Before long, Sebastiano broke into their conversation. "We will first go to Rancho Monte del Diablo and visit the Pachecos. From there we will continue on to Rancho Los Meganos. The whole trip should take us ten days: four for travel; three for our visit with Elvira, Harold, and Doctor Marsh; and another three for our stops at the Pachecos. For safety purposes we shall also have Migel and Enzo ride with us on their own horses. We will make up quite a caravan!"

By spring of 1850, the two ladies in the double buggy, accompanied by the three horsemen, set out upon their journey. The road to Rancho Monte del Diablo had been made quite usable two years earlier to connect the rancho and the pier at the point of the bay. The road from Rancho Monte del Diablo ran eastward around the northern slope of the mountain to Rancho Los Meganos, directly east of Monte del Diablo. Originally, it followed Indian footpaths, and then it was developed by the Spanish, Mexicans, and Americans as a trail for horses and carretas pulled by oxen. Both roads were easily traversed, with a few shallow creeks to ford and mostly flat land on which to travel. Much of the second trail was shaded by the many oak trees of the region.

Conversation at Rancho Monte del Diablo focused almost totally on the issue of land ownership. The 1848 Treaty of Guadalupe Hidalgo provided that land grants would be honored. On their last visit, Don Salvio had been quite sure that his title would be safe. When Sebastiano asked if he had heard anything about the matter, he responded, "As you know, Sebastiano, I was a senior civil servant in Pueblo San Jose before I came here to Rancho Monte del Diablo full time. While in San Jose, I came to know many Americans with influence. One of those was James Reed, a lawyer with knowledge about land ownership matters. He has proved himself to be a good and honest man, and I have engaged him to find out what it will take to confirm my grant. He assures me that we can do that as soon as California becomes a state. He estimates that statehood will become a reality in the very near future. He has found out from the Public Land Commission what it will take to file the necessary paperwork."

Sebastiano asked, "Will the process be costly for you?"

Don Salvio responded, "I believe so. However, I have the money to take care of the task, and because of the assurances of Mr. Reed, I am willing to make the necessary payments. I have heard from other rancho owners that they will have to sell stock and land to pay for their filings. Some may even have to give up their land because of the high costs. As I have said to you in the recent past, we will need to be careful about our investments until all of these matters are settled. What I did not tell you was that I always have believed that at some time in the future, I will want to sell or give away most of my holdings and more or less retire to a smaller rancho, while at the same time carry on my business interests. My life has been a good one, interesting and enjoyable, with family and friends such as you at the center of what I have been able to do."

There was no fiesta during this visit. Instead, there was a good deal of time for intimate meals, with many stories of the "good old days." There also was a good deal of speculation about the future of the area, including the point of the bay. While everyone seemed disappointed at the lack of quick progress in building a port, they all still believed that it would happen.

The trip from the Pacheco rancho to Rancho Los Meganos was very pleasant, with much singing and conversation. Juanita thoroughly enjoyed the opportunity to drive the buggy, and Luz was quite pleased to be making the journey. For some reason, the shade of the oak trees seemed to add a special pleasure to the trip.

The caravan arrived at the Marsh rancho in midafternoon, and the visitors received a very warm welcome. Harold was out working with the cattle, for Dr. Marsh owned a great number of them. Elvira and Dr. Marsh made up the welcoming committee, and the two-year- old boy, Carl, was a major focus of attention.

After a brief rest, Dr. Marsh, joined by Harold, led the group on a tour of the rancho. Dr. Marsh had purchased the land from Jose Noriega twelve years earlier, in 1837. The tract measured twelve by ten miles. He had built a small, one-story adobe house, divided into four large rooms and an attic where Indian helpers stayed. There was earthen flooring, and one room had a fireplace and kitchen, where Dr. Marsh, Elvira, and Harold gathered for meals and to converse and read in the evenings. Outside were benches where the trio sat with the baby in a cradle during the pleasant summer evenings.

Before coming to California, John Marsh had attended Harvard University. He received a bachelor's degree and then studied medicine under a Boston doctor. Upon his graduation, he moved to the Michigan Territory, where he opened a school and also was appointed a subagent for the Sioux Agency.

Marsh left Michigan and reached Pueblo de Los Angeles in 1836. He proclaimed himself a doctor and obtained a permit to practice medicine, and he immediately developed a large practice, exchanging his services for hides and tallow. His true wish was to become a rancher, so he sold his practice and, after exploring many sites in northern California, purchased the Noriega rancho.

His early days at the rancho were lonely ones. He took in his sister's son, Harold, in 1840 and was pleased also to have Harold

bring his wife to the rancho after their wedding in 1844. They occupied one of the four rooms and helped with the work around the
house and the ranch.

The rancho, along the creek that would later bear his name,
became quite prosperous. He and the Indians planted a vegetable
garden and orchard from cuttings he obtained at Mission San Jose,
much as Sebastiano had done for Rancho Santa Maria. Specifically,
Marsh and his Indian workers planted apples, plums, figs, almonds,
a vineyard, and a field of wheat.

The first "hospital" was Marsh's adobe, where he started to treat
wounded or sick gold explorers in 1849. His services were in great
demand, and his medical fees were paid in cattle, according to the
distance he had to travel. Consequently, his stock grew to nearly
six thousand head.

Much trading took place on his rancho, and he established Marsh's
Landing, present-day Antioch, on Suisun Bay near the mouth of the
San Joaquin River. Many gold seekers stopped en route to or from
the gold fields. Marsh did some mining of his own and returned to his
rancho with gold dust and nuggets worth nearly $40,000.

The visit to Rancho Los Meganos was quite pleasant for all
involved. Juanita, Luz, and Elvira spent long hours together talking about the children and their daily lives. Elvira was particularly
interested in talking about gardening and about entertaining visitors.
Since she arrived at Rancho Los Meganos, she had been responsible
for providing food for the many visitors, but she really had not
helped to plan any fiesta-like events. One particular conversation
had to do with planning a visit by Elvira and Carl to Rancho Santa
Maria, where Carl would be able to meet his cousins.

Marsh, for his part, truly enjoyed the company and was pleased
to spend time with people who spoke both Spanish and English. His
particular delight was that they read and were able to speak about
their books. In addition, his common-law wife, who had died years

earlier, was Indian, and he enjoyed the pleasure of being with literate Native American women such as Elvira and Juanita.

Juanita wanted to approach Dr. Marsh for advice about how to care for Ruben, because the family was not quite sure that the child was developing in a normal manner. However, she was reluctant to bother him with the problem. Finally, the opportunity presented itself one evening while the group was sitting outside the front door of the adobe. Doctor Marsh began to ask questions about the Perez children.

After telling him about the good qualities of the other children—Linda Consuela, age ten, Jorge, age eight, and the baby, Elena—she found the opportunity to ask the doctor questions about Ruben, now four years of age. She began by saying, "Our youngest son, now four years of age, does not seem to be able to do things that the other children can."

Dr. Marsh then asked, "What kinds of 'things' do you mean?"

Sebastiano intervened. "He is a sweet boy and loves to sit on my lap and give me hugs. However, he didn't walk until he was three years of age, and he still is not 'steady' on his feet. Also, he still has some difficulty feeding himself and is not yet totally toilet trained."

Juanita said, "As my husband says, he is a sweet boy, and he tries to please us."

Luz added, "He is a lovable child. I like to be with him, and so do the older children."

The doctor continued with his questioning. "Does he seem to understand you when you ask him a question?"

Juanita quickly responded, "Most of the time. Is that not true, Sebastiano?"

Sebastiano affirmed, "Yes, he does."

Dr. Marsh continued, "Does he have any unique physical conditions?"

Juanita thought for a moment and then said, "His eyes are shaped like almonds, his face is longer than that of most children, and his nose is quite wide. Can you tell us what causes his condition?"

The doctor answered, "No one seems to know what causes the things we've been discussing."

Juanita spoke sadly. "The priest once said that many children have problems that are due to the bad behavior of their parents, such as drinking too much or having loose morals. We do not think such things apply to us. Do you believe it is possible? I would feel so guilty."

Marsh exclaimed, "Madam, that is claptrap! Such views are very outdated. This is an age of science, and we are coming to understand that there are physical and emotional problems within the children themselves that account for such disorders."

Sebastiano asked, "What can be done to help Ruben?"

Doctor Marsh gave a fairly elaborate response. "There are no known cures for these conditions. Until now, in the United States, most children such as Ruben have been placed in almshouses, mental hospitals, or even abandoned or sold for their work. While I was studying at Harvard University, I met a man named Samuel Gridley Howe, who was studying medicine there. After he graduated from the medical school, he did serious work with the blind, oriented toward providing them with the most normal environment possible. Later he turned his attention to children with intellectual problems. About a year ago, Dr. Howe, working with Dorothea Dix, established the Massachusetts School for Idiotic Children. Thus far, his work has been successful."

"However," he continued, "it has led to problems. Some are arguing that disabled children do so well in schools like Dr. Howe's that they should remain permanently incarcerated there. Dr. Howe is opposed to this. He argues that people with disabilities, of whatever kind, have rights and that segregating them would be detrimental. There is some earlier history that seems to support his position. I have read about Geel, Belgium, which has developed into a town world famous since the twelfth century for its care of the mentally afflicted. There the action has been to place patients in homes with warm and supportive environments. In such environments, the mentally disabled lead a fairly normal life."

The doctor went on, "Given what I have heard of your family and the circumstances you provide for your son, I believe that the best thing for him is for you to keep him at home and do such things as showing him love and affection, maintaining regular routines for him, teaching him basic health and safety habits, talking with him in normal tones, and giving him some regular tasks to perform. By the way, you do have someone to help with Ruben, do you not?"

Juanita said, "Of course, my mother helps with him. We also have a young woman, Colleta, who has been with us for some time and whose main task is to help with all of the children. We could have her spend more time with Ruben and hire additional help for the other children. We also have a tutor for our two oldest children. Perhaps we could have him work with Ruben, also."

The doctor concluded, "I think that would be a good idea. One other thing occurs to me. I believe that you should talk with your older children and enlist their aid with their brother. In that way, he will feel that he is leading a normal life. Also, I believe that at some time in the relatively near future I should visit you at your rancho and have the opportunity to observe the young man myself."

Sebastiano responded, "It would be our pleasure to have you visit with us. Perhaps Elvira and Carl can come with you."

The homeward journey was pleasant enough. Juanita and Sebastiano were eager to follow up on Dr. Marsh's advice. They stayed one night at Rancho Monte del Diablo and then went home to Rancho Santa Maria.

Sebastiano and Juanita found everything in good order when they got home, and the next several months were devoted to work with the animals, crops, and the small amount of business carried out at the point of the bay.

ᏣᎳᎳᏬ

Dr. Marsh, with Elvira and Carl, arrived for a visit at the rancho in their own Concord buggy in April 1850. After observing Ruben for three days, he spoke to Juanita, Sebastiano, and Luz. "The boy seems happy, and you've done a good job of providing structure for him. I am particularly impressed that a five-year-old with his problems is able to hold an interesting conversation and do simple tasks. I observed him interact with his sisters and brother, as well as his cousin, Carl, for the first time. He seems to enjoy them all very much. My advice is to keep up the routines you have established for him."

Everyone was pleased with the visit. After the doctor, Elvira, and Carl left for home, life settled back into its usual pattern. The stock, grains, fruit, and vegetables did well. However, the contract with John Sutter, Jr., was not renewed. New Helvetia was overrun by squatters, and Sutter was in poor health. He eventually was able to sell some of his land and move his family to Acapulco, Mexico. These events required Sebastiano to find other buyers of his goods in Sacramento. After doing that, he added a second ship to the port and also obtained contracts from other farmers and ranchers to send their crops with his. His business faced strong competition, since ports were opening up all along the south shore of Suisun Bay.

In a small way, the rancho became a stopover for gold seekers who had come to San Francisco from all over the world. Many of those who did stop paid small amounts for food and lodging, and some even purchased goods that could be used for mining or panning in the gold fields. Many of these visitors had interesting stories to tell of their journeys to San Francisco by sea. The family often gathered in the evenings on the patio to hear these tales.

Of particular interest to the family was the story of a young man named William Simms, age seventeen, who had come to California from Boston to make his fortune in the gold fields. The story took two nights to tell. On the first night, Simms began, "I learned about the discovery of gold in California in the spring of 1848. I was working as an apprentice mason in Boston and immediately decided that I could do better by becoming a gold seeker. My father loaned me five hundred dollars, and I set out on my journey in the fall of the same year. I went to New York and took passage on the steamship *Crescent City*, which was overcrowded with gold seekers. Eighteen days later we arrived in New Orleans, where the ship was boarded by a hundred or so men intent on getting to California. The captain of the ship protested, but he backed down because some of these men threatened violence."

Jorge was fascinated. "Did anyone threaten you?"

Simms responded, "No, not directly, but these men with their guns took the best food and the best bunks. Some of us, including me, had to sleep on deck. The one advantage for us was that there were toilets on deck. That was important because many of us suffered from diarrhea."

"After two days in New Orleans we set off for the city of Chagres at the mouth of the Chagres River on the east coast of Panama. Fortunately, the weather was good, and it took us only ten days to make that part of our journey. However, when we got to the mouth of the river, there were reefs and sandbars that prevented our ship from entering the river. We had to anchor off the coast and had to pay native boatmen to shuttle us between the ship and the town. It was a very unpleasant time, and very expensive. There was a mad rush to cross the isthmus in order to board a ship to San Francisco, and many of those men could be violent."

Juanita asked, "What happened next? Were you able to easily cross the isthmus?"

Simms laughed gently and then replied, "It was anything but easy. While we were waiting for transport up the river to Las Cruces, several other ships unloaded their passengers. By then there were over one thousand angry gold seekers hoping for transport. There were not enough native *cayucas,* canoes, available to transport all of us up to the town of Las Cruces, forty-five miles upriver. Each cayuca was constructed from a large hollowed-out log about twenty-five feet long and three feet wide and covered with a palm leaf canopy to keep out the very hot tropical sun. Each cayuca was able to carry from four to six passengers, and a crew of three or four boatmen. When I got on a cayuca after two days' wait, I paid one dollar plus a tip for the journey."

He continued, "The journey took four days, so we stopped at towns along the way to eat and rest. These towns were not prepared for such large numbers of travelers. I had to pay to rent a hammock in each village to sleep in the yard of a *bohio,* bed and breakfast. Since I was one of the early arrivals, I found the food to be quite good."

Jorge eagerly speculated, "It must have been hard to sleep outside in a hammock. You were lucky that the food was good."

"I was lucky," responded Simms. "In Las Cruces, I stayed in a dirty, roach-ridden room for two nights at two dollars a night until I could rent a mule for the eighteen-mile, one-day trip over an old road to Panama City on the Pacific Coast. When my group arrived in Panama City, we once again had to wait, this time for four more days. In this case, I stayed in an aristocratic old home that had been converted to an inn. I paid two dollars for room and board. I was lucky, because many travelers had to rent a place in the city's slums for two dollars per night or sleep in the park in a tent carried in their backpacks."

The group was enthralled with the story. Simms went on, "Because I had booked my passage directly from New York to San Francisco, I was scheduled to board the *California,* which had only 250 berths for passengers. The hundreds of Americans were incensed because many berths had been given to Peruvians who were on their way to the gold fields. The Americans claimed that they should be given priority on an American ship. I was fortunate, because I was able to sell my ticket for $1,000 and purchase passage on the next ship, the *Philadelphia*, for only $75. Unfortunately, I had to wait two weeks before the Philadelphia left for San Francisco."

Sebastiano interrupted. "Colleta has put Elena to bed, and Ruben seems ready to go to sleep. Perhaps we should continue this fascinating story tomorrow."

Jorge, who knew better than to contradict his father, stated, "Please, father, can't we go on a bit longer? I have so many questions to ask Mr. Simms."

Sebastiano chuckled and retorted, "Even Mr. Simms seems a bit tired. We will stop tonight and continue tomorrow evening as a whole group. However, Jorge, if you have some special questions you would like to ask Mr. Simms in the morning, you may do that if he is willing." At that, the evening ended, and Jorge went off to bed to contemplate the questions he might ask.

Jorge was up early the next morning and soon sought out Simms. He found him after breakfast while he was looking over the vineyard. Jorge asked him, "May I ask you a few questions?"

Simms responded, "Certainly, but maybe only a few."

Jorge asked, "While you were in the jungle, did you see many snakes?"

Simms stated, "I didn't personally see snakes while we were riding the mules. However, I have heard that many men who were frustrated with the long wait for mules tried to walk from Las Cruces to Panama City. Several were bitten by snakes, and others fell ill to diseases such as malaria, cholera, or yellow fever. Many died."

Jorge said, "You were smart to wait for a mule. Are you in a hurry to get to the gold fields?"

Simms smiled. "Yes, I am. I suspect that the first people who get to the fields will be the lucky ones and more easily find gold. While I have waited a few days, I do believe that I will be in time to make my fortune. I find myself lucky to be able to spend a few days at Rancho Santa Maria to rest and add to my provisions for the fields."

Jorge added, "I think my father wants to talk with you about doing some work for him when you go to hunt for gold."

Jorge was allowed to ask a few more questions. Ultimately, Simms had other things to do, so he said, "We will be able to talk more tonight. I look forward to more questions, from your sister and brother, also."

In the evening, Simms resumed his story. "The trip from Panama City to San Francisco was terrible. The *Philadelphia* was extremely crowded, with many men sleeping on the floor below or on the deck above. Many were sick from diseases contracted in Panama. Others became ill because of contact with the already sick. Food ran out, and often the stronger would take from the weaker. Because I'd sold my ticket earlier, I had money to pay a bit more for food and water. This saved me from becoming ill, I believe."

"We arrived in San Francisco on April 2, 1849. The Yerba Buena harbor was full of ships from all over the world. In many cases, crews were abandoning their ships and going off to the gold fields. Some of the empty ships were turned into hotels; others simply began to rot. I spent three days trying to find passage to the gold fields. Fortunately, your father had docked in the Yerba Buena Cove and agreed to bring me here and then take me to the gold fields. I am so happy to be here."

Linda Consuela had the last question. "Mr. Simms, do you really believe that you will become rich?"

The young man laughed and answered, "I hope so. Even if I don't find much gold, there are other ways of making money when there are so many people who need things and there are so many things that need to be built. We shall see, miss."

Before the family left the patio for bed, Simms brought out a strange-looking instrument and said, "My voice is not terribly good, but on the journey I learned a song that's quite popular in the gold fields. The melody is from an old Spanish song, I believe, but the lyrics are truly American. Would you like to hear it?" Linda Consuela clapped her hands and said, "Oh, yes. Oh, yes, please."

With that, Simms took his banjo and began playing and singing:

In a cavern, in a canyon,
Excavating for a mine,
Dwelt a miner forty-niner,
And his daughter, Clementine.

Chorus:

Oh my darling, oh my darling,
Oh my darling Clementine!
Thou art lost and gone forever,
Dreadful sorry, Clementine.

Light she was and like a fairy,
And her shoes were number nine,
Herring boxes, without topses,
Sandals were for Clementine.

Drove she ducklings to the water
Ev'ry morning just at nine,
Hit her foot against a splinter,
Fell into the foaming brine.

Ruby lips above the water,
Blowing bubbles, soft and fine,
But, alas, I was no swimmer,
So I lost my Clementine.

When she slipped and hit the water,
'Felt my heart skip a time.
All had scattered; nothin' mattered,
'cept my darlin' Clementine.

Chorus

Linda Consuela applauded loudly and said, "That was pretty, but it was sad, too."

With that, everyone except Sebastiano went off to bed. Sebastiano asked William to stay for a bit so that they could speak privately. He made Simms an offer. "William, I am very impressed with you. You are yet very young, but you are smart and seem to see clearly the possible opportunities in the gold fields. What I would like to ask you is if, in addition to seeking gold, you would look for business opportunities for me and what I have come to think of as my company that can serve the people of the gold fields. I would be able to pay you a commission for whatever business you are able to come by."

Simms agreed to the idea, and a tentative contract was drawn up, which led to a number of unforeseen events that were to be both interesting and profitable.

CHAPTER 11

STATEHOOD

Despite his youth, or perhaps because of it, William Simms was very successful in the gold fields. Not only did he earn a small fortune from his own prospecting, but, in addition, he successfully found ways to sell equipment and food to the many miners who were in need of such goods. As a businessman he was soon earning more than he was as a prospector. Working on commission for Sebastiano, he received 15 percent of the profits.

In September 1850, Simms returned to Rancho Santa Maria to visit with Sebastiano and the family. One evening after dinner the two men strolled out to the young orchard behind the house. Sebastiano, who was becoming somewhat portly, loosened his belt and gave a sigh of relief. They sat on a bench to discuss plans for the future. Simms recommended that another sailing vessel temporarily be added to the company because business was so brisk. He also said, "There are many people now working claims, and there also are many who are giving up on the hunt for gold. They all need transportation to or from the gold fields."

He continued, "Methods of mining are changing. Now groups of miners are doing what is called 'placer mining.' That involves the use of 'cradles,' and 'rockers' called 'long-toms,' that process large volumes of gravel. At this point, we can still serve such groups. However, large companies are beginning to consider what is called hydraulic mining, where high-pressure hoses direct powerful streams of water at gold-bearing gravel beds. The loosened gravel and gold then pass over sluices, and the gold settles to the bottom, where it is collected. This is the thing of the future, and these companies are shipping their own provisions into the field for their workers to buy. In a few years our ships will not be as necessary."

Watching the barn sparrows circle the orchard and stroking his mustache, Sebastiano thought about this for a few minutes. "So what do you think this means for us?"

Simms answered quickly and easily. "Perhaps we should turn our attention to the west. San Francisco is growing rapidly, and it has no food or raw material sources of its own. It is becoming a business center. If we could become a center for shipping products from our region to the city, we might keep the business growing. I recommend that you devote a good deal of attention to this option. If you do arrange contracts such as the ones we are talking about, you might consider purchasing a steam-driven ship, which, while costly, would be much more efficient and could carry larger cargoes."

Sebastiano mused and then spoke. "Actually, William, I've been thinking the same thing. I will plan a trip for a fortnight from now and take Juanita with me to see the city. I will seek to meet with businessmen who are looking for food products that can be provided by the farmers and ranchers of this area. We can ship such products to the city."

Simms nodded. "I have one other thought. While the gold mining might slow down, some of the merchants who have built substantial businesses in the mining region might be interested in the goods from our area. In particular, I am thinking of Samuel Brannan, who now is perhaps the richest man in the gold fields because of his shops and other business ventures. I will speak with him when I return to the fields and let you know what he says."

One morning before Simms left the rancho, there was a celebration on the patio that, because of the interests of the children, featured stories from the gold country. After a pleasant meal and a few glasses of wine made at the rancho, Simms chose to talk about the difficulties faced by the people who were coming to California overland from the eastern part of the United States. He started with some figures. "Last year, it is said, as many as forty thousand people made the trip west. Some went to Oregon, but most came to California. Nearly five thousand of those died on the way, mostly from cholera."

Jorge could not contain himself. "How long does the trip take?"

"It depends upon where they start and which route they take. Most start from one of the towns on the Missouri River: Independence, Kansas City, or St. Joseph, Missouri; Council Bluffs, Iowa; or Omaha, Nebraska. From any of these beginning points the distance is about two thousand miles. As far as time is concerned, it depends upon weather, accidents, illness, and unforeseen events. It takes from four and a half to five months from the jumping-off place on the Missouri River to the gold fields. If they start from the East Coast, it takes an additional two weeks or so to get to the Missouri River, and then they often have to wait another two weeks until a wagon train can be put together."

Simms elaborated on the issue of weather. "The wagon trains have to start out sometime in the spring in order to take advantage of the grasses the animals graze on, and because there is still water in the streams they come to. The weather during the summer is very hot, and that's when many people become discouraged. Finally, they need to reach the Sierra Nevada mountains before the snows come. I'm sure you have heard the story of the Donner Party that was trapped by the snow in the Sierras. Almost all of them starved to death."

Ruben queried, "Do they walk *all* the way?"

The response came slowly. "There is a lot of walking, but they have wagons pulled by oxen just as we used to have. So those who can't walk can ride."

Jorge spoke again. "What are the wagons like?"

Simms answered, "Usually they have one or two small wagons

with canvas covers. In some cases, the travelers have what is called a Conestoga, a very large wagon with a large cover. The smaller wagons are usually pulled by four oxen or four to six horses or mules. The Conestoga wagons need to be pulled by six oxen." He continued, "They usually take extra animals along to pull the wagons in case they are needed."

Juanita asked, puzzled, "What do they take with them?"

Simms took a healthy drink of wine and went on. "First, they take cattle, sheep, and other animals to be slaughtered for food along the way. They also have salted meats, and when they can, they hunt or fish. Sometimes they hunt buffaloes. They pack such things as beans, rice, salt, dried vegetables, and spices. Some bring cows or goats with them in order to have fresh milk for the children. Wiser travelers bring dried fruit. Of course, they need to find water to cook the dried fruits and vegetables, and good water can be hard to find in some places along the trail. Other items include extra clothing, cooking utensils, tools, matches, blankets, and medicines. The rule is to pack as light as you can: don't bring anything that is not necessary."

Jorge had the last question. "Do the travelers have to fight Indians?"

"Occasionally, but not often. The biggest danger is that the Indians sometimes take their horses and other animals. Not many people are killed by Indians."

Linda Consuela interrupted. "I'm glad to hear that. *We* are Indians, and we don't want to harm anyone. I sometimes feel that the Americans look down on us."

Sebastiano, who had been listening, spoke forcefully. "My dear, you should never worry about what some foolish people might think or say. You can be proud of your Indian heritage."

Simms concluded his story. "Coming across the country is a very difficult thing to do. Many people don't finish the journey; they turn around and go home. One of the most discouraging things is seeing discarded wagons and other items where people have given up and died."

⁓

An American military government was established in 1846 after the Bear Flag Republic ended. This military government was sympathetic to the idea that civilian leadership should be allowed and developed, and in several locations, such as San Francisco, such governments were formed.

On September 3, 1849, a constitutional convention was convened in Monterey. After a serious debate over whether California should first become a territory or go directly to statehood, a constitution was framed that supported the idea of statehood. After a little more than one month, and after much discussion and even disagreement over such issues as slavery boundaries and the location of a state capital, a constitution was adopted. This was all done before the US Congress had taken action on the question of statehood. For Congress the issue of statehood for California was complex. The dispute was between those who wanted slavery outlawed in the state and those who wanted slavery. There even were those who wanted California divided into two states, the one in the south pro-slavery and the one in the north anti-slavery.

Finally, in September 1850, a package of five bills known as the "Missouri Compromise" defused the confrontation between the slave states of the South and the free states of the North regarding the status of all territories acquired as a result of the Mexican-American War of 1846–48 by deciding which states would be free and which would be slave. Although many people disliked specific parts of the compromise, there was a sense of relief that a conflict had been avoided. California was admitted to the Union on September 9, 1850, as the thirty-first state, a free state.

Soon after statehood for California became a reality, twenty-seven county governments were formed. Contra Costa County was one of those. Martinez, just seven miles from the point of the bay, was declared its capital. Towns grew all along the southern shore of Suisun Bay, and each one had businessmen who competed with Sebastiano Perez and William Simms.

⟨∞⟩

The next month, Sebastiano, Juanita, and Enzo sailed west from the point of the bay through the Carquinez Strait and San Pablo Bay to San Francisco. They arrived in the city to find it crowded and full of activity. They were able to dock their vessel only because one of their acquaintances, David Broderick, had a pier south of the city and provided them with a berth for the ship, as well as a buggy that they could drive to the city center. Broderick, who had been introduced to Sebastiano by Dr. Marsh, also had arranged accommodations for Sebastiano and Juanita at the fashionable Parker House Hotel, rebuilt after an earlier fire, and for Enzo at a much more modest inn.

Juanita was a bit overwhelmed upon entering their suite: "Oh, what a lovely set of rooms: a parlor and a bedroom. Can we afford such a palace?"

Sebastiano took her in his arms and whispered in her ear, "There is nothing that pleases me more than seeing you happy. We can afford it! In fact, the rooms weren't that expensive. The Parker House suffered two fires in the past year, and there have been a total of four fires in San Francisco in this year alone. They are keeping their prices low right now to bring back customers who have been frightened by the fires. You will also notice that much of the new construction is done with bricks instead of wood. In addition to having an inexpensive stay, we are also safe. Let's unpack now and have a brief rest. We are going to be very busy during the next few days."

After their rest, Sebastiano began to dress for the evening. While doing so, he spoke to Juanita of things to come during the visit to San Francisco. "Tomorrow I am to meet with David Broderick. Remember, we met him at John Marsh's rancho."

Juanita sat down at the vanity table and began brushing her hair. "Yes, I remember Mr. Broderick, a very pleasant man. Why are you meeting with him?"

Sebastiano replied, "He is an interesting man with many business contacts. He came to San Francisco last year because of the gold rush, and since then he has established a very profitable smelting and assaying business here in San Francisco. I've heard that he has begun minting gold coins, and that he has political ambitions as well. I plan to ask him to direct me to businessmen who might be interested in our ability to ship grains, fruit, vegetables, and meat products from our region to the gold fields as well as here to San Francisco. The city is growing fast. Today there are about twenty-one thousand people living here, and only a year ago that number was only a bit over one thousand. San Francisco is already the largest city in California."

As she arranged her hair in a fashionable style, Juanita asked about the business to be done while they were in the city. "How many people do you plan to visit?"

Sebastiano was not totally sure of his answer, but he replied, "I hope that Mr. Broderick will be able to direct me to some men he feels might be interested in what we have to offer. I do know that I want to speak with a representative of the banking-house of Palmer, Cook & Co., and land agents Stevenson & Parker, who are said to have a good deal of capital to spend. I have thought, too, of speaking with representatives of the Chinese Benevolent Association, which provides leadership for the growing Chinese community in

San Francisco. I look forward to Mr. Broderick's recommendations. I assume that these visits might take up to three or four days."

Putting on a clean shirt, Sebastiano smiled and added, "There also are a number of amusements that you and I can take in during our visit. For example, if we wish, we can attend the Jenny Lind Theater, which is housed in this very hotel. Perhaps while I am making my visits, you can see if something of interest is playing tomorrow night."

Juanita jumped up to help her husband with his cuff links. "I've never been to a theater, and I would love to see a performance. I'll see what's playing tonight *and* tomorrow night!"

Sebastiano adjusted his cravat and put on his jacket. He continued, "This also will be an opportunity for you to do some shopping. I understand that there already are several shops that sell fancy women's clothes. We have nothing like that near the rancho, so you shouldn't miss the opportunity to shop while you are here. In addition to clothes, you might look at other things; for example, the Still Bookshop and Stationer on the Square. You are doing so well with your English that you might want to purchase several books to take home, and perhaps you will find some that would be good for the children, as well. San Francisco has a reputation for crime, so I believe that Enzo should accompany you. I have asked him to check with you each morning at 10:00 a.m. to see what you would like to do that day. If you plan to stay in your room and read, he can be allowed to see the city on his own."

Juanita looked him over approvingly and gave him a kiss on the tip of his nose. She had one more question to ask. "Will you and I have time to do things together?"

Sebastiano laughed. "We will have the theater, and we will eat together every morning and evening, and we can walk together in the early evening around Portsmouth Square, or to the new wharves that recently have been completed. As we become familiar with the city, perhaps we will find other things to do together, and maybe even with new friends as well. We'll see. The most important thing is for you to enjoy yourself and be able to tell me each evening about your daytime adventures." After that, Juanita finished dressing, and the pair went down to dinner in the fine dining room on the first floor of the hotel.

The next morning, Sebastiano met with Broderick at his office. After thanking him for arranging the visit, Sebastiano posed his most important question. "David, whom do you recommend that I see about shipping goods to San Francisco from the area served by the pier at the point of the bay owned by Don Salvio Pacheco and me?"

Broderick responded, "Initially, I do believe that you should visit people such as Palmer & Cook, because they are quite open to the idea of investing in new businesses. They, of course, will need to see how they can profit from such an investment. I also believe that you should approach the owners of hotels, restaurants, and stores that sell foodstuffs. That could be very time-consuming for you, so I would propose that my company act as an agent for you, receiving a small share of whatever profits might accrue."

Sebastiano agreed. "That seems like sound advice, and I believe that using your company as an agent is a good idea. I will consult with the Pachecos before any written contract is drawn up, but I'm sure that they will agree."

Broderick added, "In addition, I think we should be aware of the many new businesses that are coming to San Francisco. For example, I hear that Wells Fargo Bank will be moving its headquarters to San Francisco by the end of next year. They might be interested in helping to finance such a business. Of course they, like any investors, will expect a return on their financing."

Sebastiano was quite satisfied with the conversation with Broderick and looked forward to speaking with the Pachecos about working with Broderick's firm. Broderick contacted an executive of Palmer & Cook, and an appointment was arranged for the next morning. Broderick also arranged for an appointment with another potential financier for the afternoon of the next day.

When Sebastiano returned to the Parker House in the late afternoon, he found Juanita very happy. Her words tumbled out. "I was able to get tickets for tonight's performance by Mr. Stephen Massett at the Jenny Lind Theater. He is a song and dance performer from England, and he composes some of his own songs. I know nothing about him, but the people in the hotel assure me that his show is outstanding."

"That sounds fine. And what else did you do today?" Sebastiano beamed at his wife's excitement.

Juanita continued rapidly. "Enzo came today at 10:00 a.m., and we walked to the Still Bookshop. I purchased several books written in English both for myself and for the children."

"What did you find to read?" asked Sebastiano.

"Oh, there was so much, it was hard to choose." Juanita frowned and then continued, "For myself I purchased *The Man in the Iron Mask*, *Queen Margot*, and *The Three Musketeers* by Alexandre Dumas; *Jane Eyre* by Charlotte Bronte; *Wuthering Heights* by Emily Bronte; *The Overcoat* and *Other Short Stories* by Nikolai Gogol translated from Russian; *A Christmas Carol* by Charles Dickens; and *Poems* by a new author, Robert Browning. I believe I can read all of these with the children, and I also believe that you and I might enjoy reading them to each other. I have made a list of several additional books that I would like to own. Perhaps when you return to the city, you can purchase a few each time."

Sebastiano agreed. "These sound very good. When I return to San Francisco, I can buy some from your list. What did you get for the children?"

Juanita answered, "I purchased only three for the children: *Brothers Grimm Household Tales*, and *Fairy Tales* by Hans Christian

Andersen, and *Children of the Near Forest* by Captain Marryat. However, an author named S. G. Goodrich has written many books for children that sound interesting. Most use the name Peter Paley. I wrote down the names of three books as examples: *Peter Paley's Tales about America, Peter Paley's Winter Evening Tales*, and *Peter Paley's Discovery of the Animal Kingdom*. I would like you to go to the bookshop with me to look at them and help me to choose the ones we would want for the children."

Sebastiano smiled. "It sounds as if the children can really benefit from such reading. I cannot go to the shop tomorrow, but let's go day after tomorrow."

That evening the couple went to the theater and thoroughly enjoyed Mr. Massett. When they returned to their rooms, Sebastiano commented, "Mr. Massett is a good performer. His voice is a bit squeaky, and he is a very little man. However, he makes up for these things by being very lively. I particularly enjoyed his rendition of 'The Bachelor's Song.'" With that said, Sebastiano began to sing the song, and Juanita, giggling a little, accompanied him with the chorus:

Oh, a bachelor's life is merry and gay;
He sips from each flower he meets in his way.
The nectar he quaffs while embracing the thorn,
He leaves the poor Benedick hanging forlorn.

Hush, brothers! That's the way,
Talking on day by day.
We'll thus deceive them
Then by our ready arts,
Of their fond honest hearts
We can relieve them.
As pleasantly o'er the bright world he goes.
Beloved by his friends, caring not for his foes.

Through each passing moment some happiness gleams,
Which night but recalleth in pleasanter dreams.

Then reckon the joys of a bachelor's life,
Ye recreant sons who are "seeking a wife,"
And ask yourselves then if there's aught can repay,
The wild joyous freedom ye thus throw away.
Go ask the poor henpeck'd unfortunate wight,
If aught in the wide world can give him delight;
He sadly reverts to the days of his bliss,
And sighs that his birthright was sold for a kiss!

Then brothers be firm, to the rescue advance,
A sign is perdition —there's death in a glance:
Yield no to the blast—be true to the last,
And revel in age o'er the joys of the past.

On the second evening, before dark and before dinner, Juanita and Sebastiano strolled around Portsmouth Plaza. The October evening was quite windy, and pieces of paper were flying everywhere. There also were many stray dogs wandering around the plaza. Even so, there were some interesting sights to be seen. When they left Parker House, they noticed that the whole east side of the square was lined with palatial buildings. The newest structure was the customs house in the northern portion of the square, which served to collect duties and taxes on imports and exports, control carriers of such goods, and combat smuggling. Also on the north side were several businesses, including the Palmer, Cook & Co. office that Sebastiano was to visit the next day. On the west side stood the post office; a few small coffee shops and mercantile shops, including Still's Bookshop and Stationer; and the justice's court. The city hall was on the south side. Next to that was Brown's Hotel, the most important of the gambling centers in the city.

As they passed Brown's Hotel, Sebastiano said, "Perhaps we should see this hotel, not to gamble, but just to see how such places work." He added, "Just off the plaza up Montgomery Street there are shops that sell fine clothing. Maybe you and Enzo should go there tomorrow to see what the latest fashions are and to purchase some for yourself." At the end of their stroll, the couple returned to Parker House.

The next few days were very busy. Juanita did her shopping and spent a good deal of time during the day reading one of her new books. She took Sebastiano to Still's Book and Stationer, where they purchased several books for the children. They also visited Brown's Hotel to view the gambling, and they had several sumptuous meals in the Parker House Restaurant.

Sebastiano went to Palmer, Cook & Co. and met with one of its executives. It was not a very successful visit, since the firm had little interest in helping to fund his business. He visited a few other businesses recommended by Broderick, but was equally discouraged. His most promising visit was one to Chinatown, where he met Yan Wo, who represented the Chinese Benevolent Association. Yan Wo expressed interest in Sebastiano's proposition and promised to bring it up at the next meeting of the association.

On the morning of the fourth day, having accomplished some of his business successfully and having made sure his wife had a good time, Sebastiano had Enzo take all of their valises to their sailing vessel for the journey home to the rancho near the point of the bay.

CHAPTER 12

TRANSITIONS

By April 1854, activities at Rancho Santa Maria, now called the Perez Farm, had settled into a recognizable routine. Sebastiano and Juanita, now forty-one and thirty-four, respectively, had increased in both wisdom and girth. Juanita was still beautiful and Sebastiano handsome. They both spent most of their free time reading contemporary literature and, consequently, were fluent in English. This, in turn, made them popular among the growing number of Americans in the area.

The only sadness at the farm resulted from the passing of Luz. At fifty-four, she had seemed to be well. However, in early April, she went to sleep and never woke up. No one could tell why she died. There was a funeral service and a wake after she was buried, and both of these events were well attended. In addition to the family and people of the farm, William Simms, the members of the Marsh family, and members of the Pacheco family were in attendance. With the abundance of love and friendship, it seemed more a festive occasion than one of sadness.

The children fared well during this time. Linda, having dropped her second name, was fifteen years old and as beautiful as her mother had been when she and Sebastiano were married. Her perfect features, long black hair, and blossoming figure made her attractive to many of the young men in the area. However, she was bright, well read, and articulate, and that caused many of them to be shy of her. That didn't matter to her at all, for she had eyes only for William Simms, who was now twenty-three. He had become quite important to Sebastiano as a business partner, and to the entire family as a loving friend. While he tried not to show it, it was obvious that he was in love with Linda. The two were together as often as possible.

The boys, Jorge and Ruben—thirteen and nine, respectively—were quite different from each other, but both were doing well and were the best of friends. Jorge was handsome and scholarly, read incessantly, and already had a strong sense for business, which gave his father a great deal of pride. Ruben, with the love and support of his family, had assumed several regular duties at the farm and was considered to be a fine helper.

Ruben had three regular tasks to perform, and he did them well. First, he was in charge of the small herd of milk cows and the half dozen female goats (Sebastiano favored goat cheese). He brought them in from the field and milked them every morning. He saw that they were fed and watered, and he kept them clean. His second job was to collect and store the cow and steer manure away from the house to be used as fertilizer for the gardens. His third task, his favorite, was to assist Hipolito in the carpentry shop. Over time, he had become quite good at wood carving. At first, Juanita had not cared for this, because she was afraid that he might cut himself, but he never did. His sculptures came to be quite good, and a few even had even been sold in San Francisco at Stills Book & Stationer.

The youngest child, Elena, at six years of age, also was a beautiful child and was learning to read and write in English. She was warm and loving, and it seemed that she would have a good and happy life.

Business at the pier also was good even though Simms had not been able to convince Sam Brannan, the successful businessman in the gold country, to enter into a contract with Sebastiano. Also, the New Helvetia contract no longer existed. In fact, there was very little business in the gold fields, because the large companies brought their own goods to sell to their employees and others.

The exceptions were the goods to be sold by a new arrival in San Francisco, Levi Strauss.

The Strauss family had emigrated from Germany and opened a wholesale dry goods store in New York City named J. Strauss Brothers, Inc. In 1853, Levi was chosen to go to San Francisco and open a dry goods store. He imported fine dry goods, such as clothing, bedding, combs, purses, and handkerchiefs, and planned to sell them to general stores and men's clothiers throughout California. He was willing to go head-to-head with the company stores in the gold country.

Other San Francisco initiatives also were successful. The collaboration with David Broderick provided the opportunity to bring many food products to restaurants, hotels, and markets in the city. In addition, the agreement with Yan Wo and the Chinese Benevolent Association opened a similar market in San Francisco's growing Chinatown.

Yan Wo was one of the early entrepreneurs in the Chinese community. He was wise in his investments and also was committed to the welfare of the growing Chinese population. He maintained his traditional dress, which consisted of a loose dark cotton blouse with long sleeves that could be used to hide his hands, and loose cotton pants that covered the tops of his soft sandals. His head was bald and topped with a pointed cap. His most distinguishing feature was the long braided "queue," which hung from the back of his head to halfway down his back.

By 1854, there were approximately twelve thousand Chinese mine workers. In the beginning of the gold rush, the Chinese workers were welcomed. These were men who would work hard at a reasonable wage when every other man wanted only to work at the streams and mines for gold. Here were cooks, laundrymen, servants, and laborers ready and willing.

However, the "Chinaman" was welcomed only as long as the

surface gold was plentiful. As thousands of Americans came flocking to the streams and mines, rich surface claims became exhausted. Miners became disappointed, and in their disappointment they began to turn upon the men of other races, in particular the Chinese. They accused them of stealing their wealth. The cry of "California for the Americans" was raised, and beginning in 1852 a special mining tax of twenty dollars per month aimed at the Chinese had been passed by the California legislature.

In addition, as rewards from mining became less available and economic times for many American miners turned bad, violence against the Chinese increased. It was these issues that prompted Yan Wo to travel to the gold country to assist the Chinese workers to organize their own Benevolent Association.

On his way he stopped at the Perez Farm. He was welcomed by Sebastiano and was a great curiosity to the young people, who had never seen a Chinaman. As usual, after a brief rest, Sebastiano gave Yan Wo a tour of the farm, and they were accompanied by the three older children, who were more interested in seeing the visitor than in touring the farm.

That evening, as usual when a visitor stayed the night, the family gathered for a fine dinner on the patio and took the opportunity to get to know Yan Wo better. Sebastiano began by thanking Yan Wo for his business. Yan Wo responded, "My friend, you are an honest man and always provide us with products of the highest quality. We are very satisfied with our relationship with you."

Sebastiano thanked him again and asked, "What is the purpose of your trip to the gold country, and may we be of any help to you?"

Yan Wo told them of the trouble his people were having in the gold fields. He then said, "I have three goals for this trip. First, I hope to persuade our miners to organize themselves in groups so that they can better protect themselves from attacks. Second, I wish to encourage them to seek out businesses other than mining.

For example, they should open restaurants, laundries, mercantile shops, and even hotels. Thus they will not be seen as competing, but rather as providing services for the miners. Finally, I wish to encourage them to work through the Benevolent Associations, since such organized groups can better protect their interests, and I'm sure that there will be other efforts to do harmful things to our people. I believe you can help us by continuing to provide quality goods for the Chinese-run businesses in the gold country."

Sebastiano replied, "You offer good advice to your people, and of course we will be happy to continue providing as many of the goods as we can for your merchants."

With the business discussion over, the conversation turned to more personal interests. Jorge asked Yan Wo, "Why have you and your countrymen come to California?"

Yan Wo chuckled. "Why have most men come to California? To earn money. While the life may be lonely, the work hard, and our treatment by the Americans unfair, we can earn a lot more here than at home. The times in our homeland are not good. In addition, we need to send money home to help our families."

This prompted Linda to add another question. "Why didn't you bring your wife with you?"

Yan Wo sighed. "I do wish to send for my family. When I first came, I thought that I would stay for only a short while and then return to my home a wealthy man. That proved not to be true. In addition, it has been my wife's responsibility to care for my aging parents. My father has passed away, and now I have enough money to bring my wife, two children, and mother to live with me here. Despite any problems, they will be better off here."

Juanita leaned forward. "I would like to meet your wife. I hope your family does come to San Francisco and that they can visit with us when they do."

Yan Wo smiled, but before he could respond, Ruben asked, "Why do you wear your hair in a long braid?"

Again Yan Wo smiled warmly. "It is a very old custom among the Han Chinese imposed upon us by the Manchu people when they conquered our land many years ago. It is a very strong custom now. Men don't have to wear what we call a 'queue,' but many do. Our prophet Confucius once declared, 'We are given our body, skin, and hair from our parents which we ought not to damage.' This idea is part of what is called filial duty, meaning that we must honor our ancestors."

Ruben then announced, "I'm going to grow my hair in a long braid, too. I think it looks very nice."

With that, everyone laughed and the evening was concluded. In the morning Yan Wo set off for the gold fields.

ᏇᎯᏇᏇᏇ

In June 1851, after a whirlwind courtship of two weeks, John Marsh, the owner of Rancho Los Meganos, married Abigale "Abby" Smith Tuck, a schoolteacher from New England who had moved to San Jose as the principal of a girl's high school. Abby moved into the adobe with Marsh and Harold's family, which now consisted of his wife, Elvira; son, Carl; and a baby girl named Rose.

Abby loved Rancho Los Meganos. She planted roses and other flowers outside the adobe and enjoyed the creek that ran deep near the kitchen door. She spent hours under the oaks that stood along the banks of the creek while she read many of the books in the library. She and Juanita soon became close friends, and when they had time together, they compared the books that they read. Abby also loved to ride her horse through the oak groves on the rancho.

Abby gave birth to a girl they named Alice in March 1852. She and John doted on the baby. They also cared very much for Carl and Rose. With the new family, John Marsh began construction of a beautiful home built entirely of stone quarried from the surrounding hills. Abby, with Elvira's help, chose the location of the house. It was next to the creek and had a great view of the surrounding valley and Mt. Diablo.

Unfortunately, Abby died before the stone house was completed. Marsh never moved into the house. Instead, he allowed his nephew, Harold, and his family to take control of it and to raise Alice along with their two children. He remained in the adobe and became quiet and withdrawn.

Marsh frequently had troubles with both squatters and cattle thieves. In addition, he had a major dispute with his vaqueros in 1856 over the issue of their salaries. On September 24 of that year, he decided to travel to Martinez, the capital of the new Contra Costa County, on business. He first headed to the Pacheco rancho to visit, and then he planned to continue the next seven or so miles to Martinez. He never reached the rancho. As he was riding in his buggy along the trail to Rancho Monte del Diablo, he was accosted by one of his young vaqueros, Jose Olivas, who asked for money that was due him as wages. The doctor replied, "I will pay you on my return from Martinez. I have no money with me now."

Marsh rode away, but Olivas, joined by two of his fellow vaqueros, followed him. When they overtook the older man, Olivas took his horse by the head, while one of the other vaqueros jumped into the buggy and the other stood guard on his horse. Marsh asked, "Do you want to kill me?"

Olivas answered "No," but his comrade in the buggy, Felipe Moreno, said, "Yes." He slashed the doctor in the face with his knife and dragged him out of the buggy, where he fell to the ground, now with a second wound on his hand. Olivas moved to help the doctor and yelled at Moreno to free him.

Moreno yelled back, "Why should I let go of this old *cabron,* this bastard?" and then stabbed his victim in the side.

Olivas pushed Moreno away and parried a thrust of the knife meant for him. Marsh attempted to rise, but he was able to crawl only a short distance before he died.

Moreno was tracked and killed by county sheriffs. Olivas and the third vaquero disappeared and were never heard of again. Marsh's body was taken back to his rancho by the sheriffs and it was at his funeral that the creek was named after him. Harold and Elvira, along with their two children and Alice, remained at the rancho and continued to raise the herds and tend to the crops.

⟨ɷɷɷ⟩

As was required by the Land Act of 1851, a claim for Rancho Monte del Diablo had been filed by Don Salvio Pacheco in 1852. It was finally granted in1859. In the meantime, business with Sebastiano had progressed as usual; that is, both partners had shared in the costs and profits of the shipping to and from the point of the bay and had worked with local ranchers and farmers to ship their goods.

However, in 1856 things changed. In July, Don Salvio invited Sebastiano to Rancho Monte del Diablo for a discussion about the business. Sebastiano rode to the rancho, received a warm greeting, and was allowed some time for a siesta. Following that, and since Juanita had not accompanied him this time, the meeting took place before supper.

Don Salvio began, "I have asked you to join me, Sebastiano, because there have been developments that will have a bearing upon our partnership."

Sebastiano was curious. "What kind of developments, Don Salvio?"

Pacheco answered, "Dr. J. H. Carothers is a city planner, and he is in the process of laying out a city just south of our rancho. The town is to be named Pacheco, in my honor."

"That's marvelous, Don Salvio," responded Sebastiano. "I would think such a town would only be helpful to our business."

Don Salvio frowned. "I do not believe that it will. The town will be built on a slough to be called the Pacheco Slough. It is deep enough to receive ocean-based vessels, and we will be developing it as a port where we can carry on our business."

Sebastiano was shocked. It had been his impression that Don Salvio was fully committed to the point of the bay project. His response carried with it his full sense of disappointment. "I really am speechless. I thought you truly believed in what we were doing."

Don Salvio responded in a soft voice. "Dr. Carothers has promised me that this will be a very wise move and that it will serve me well for years to come. What I propose, I believe, is to your benefit. I wish to give you all of the business at the point of the bay. It will be for you alone to develop and profit from. To a degree we will be competitors, but I also believe that we can continue to cooperate in many ways."

Sebastiano was discouraged, but also happy because he now would own the small business outright, which would benefit him greatly in the future.

The town and port of Pacheco were laid out in 1857, and deep-water ships were able to navigate the slough. However, a series of fires and floods and a major earthquake destroyed the town and filled the slough with silt, making it non-navigable by the early 1860s. Don Salvio made no attempt to restore his ownership claim at the point of the bay, now called Perez Landing. Instead, in 1868 Don Salvio, his son Fernando, and his son-in-law Francisco Galindo invested time and money to bring about the growth of the town in the center of their rancho. It was called Todos Santos, All Saints, and free lots were offered to the merchants and residents of the town of Pacheco. Don Salvio also gave land to Sebastiano, for both a business and a fine home. The town did not keep the name Todos Santos for long. Within a year, and despite protestations from Don Fernando, the town council changed its name to Concord.

By the time of Don Salvio's death in 1876, he had given away most of the original 17,921 acres of his Rancho Monte del Diablo. He had only 425 acres left, but did not seem to mind the breakup of his huge land grant. After his death, the 425 acres came under the control of Francisco Galindo, who had married Don Salvio's daughter Maria Dolores Manuela Pacheco.

༺ ༻

William Simms spent most of his time in Placerville, which boasted of being the gateway to the gold country. As a gateway, the town saw many famous people pass through. In the early 1850s Mark Hopkins, Jr., and Collis Potter Huntington got their start selling groceries in Placerville and later came to be railroad magnates and two of the big four responsible for building the Central Pacific Railroad. Ulysses S. Grant was briefly stationed there in 1858. Samuel Langhorne Clemens, better known as Mark Twain, went west with his brother Orion, and spent time in the Placerville area, where he wrote and became famous for *The Celebrated Jumping Frog of Calaveras County.* The book was published in 1867 and was an immediate success.

Perhaps the most notorious person in the region was Charles Earl Bowles, who specialized in holding up Wells Fargo stagecoaches during the mid- to late 1870s. He performed at least twenty-eight robberies. He did not ride a horse, but simply stepped out in the middle of the road carrying an unloaded double-barreled shotgun. He was always polite and on occasion left poems with those he had robbed. He came to be known as Black Bart. Two of his most famous "versifyings" were the following:

I've labored hard and long for bread,
For honor and for riches,
But on my corns too long you've trod,
You fair-haired sons-of-bitches.

and

Here I lay me down to sleep
To wait the coming morrow.
Perhaps success, perhaps defeat
And everlasting sorrow.

Let come what will, I'll try it on,
My condition can't be worse.
And if there's money in that box,
Tis munny in my purse.

From Placerville, Simms was able to travel throughout the region doing business. In his travels, he often observed the treatment of the Indians, which could be called genocide. Almost half of the miners were Indians, referred to as "diggers." Often, when they did strike gold, white miners moved in and took the gold and the claim away from them and killed anyone who protested. In addition, Indians often were cheated when they made an effort to trade gold for goods. Often miners and ranchers came together to kill Indians. Many massacres were recorded in the gold areas during the 1850s. In one case, following the killing of a white settler, more than 150 Indians were killed, and the remaining few were sold into slavery.

On one trip to Columbia, Simms came across a young Miwok Indian who was sitting in the shade of an oak tree somewhat removed from the main street. Simms asked the young man, "You seem not to be busy. Would you like a job for a few days? I need help moving crates of produce from Placerville to the many towns in the Sierra gold fields."

The young man agreed to the offer, which prompted Simms to say, "My name is William. What is yours?"

He responded, "My Indian name, which I prefer, is Notaku. It means 'Growling Bear.' It is the name of a famous ancestor of mine, who, I was told by my father, was chief of a Miwok village located down the great rivers where they become Suisun Bay."

Simms kept Notaku busy for many months. During that time they came to be good friends. Frequently in the evenings, they would sit around a campfire and exchange stories of their lives and families. On one such occasion, Notaku told William about what had happened to his mother, father, and sisters. "My father found gold near here and was on the verge of becoming a rich man. However, a group of white miners took his gold and then drove him away from his claim. When my father protested, the white men killed him. They then took my mother and sisters away, and I have never seen them since. Fortunately for me, I was on an errand, and when I returned to our camp I realized that I needed to get away from these men. That's when I came here, hoping to do odd jobs or beg for food. I didn't have much luck getting jobs until you came along."

Notaku told Simms many other stories of the Indians in the gold country. "I have heard that the white men receive twenty-five cents for Indian scalps and more than five dollars for a head. Also, I have heard that they sell captured children as slaves, and I fear that's what happened to my mother and sisters."

Simms looked aghast. "That is horrible. How can men be so inhumane?"

Notaku went on, "Many of my people have died from the white man's diseases. Also, the land and the animals are being poisoned by the chemicals used by the large mining companies. Because of these things, Indians are not able to live their traditional lives as hunters and gatherers. I feel that we are doomed as a people."

In the end, William Simms proposed to Notaku that they travel together to the Perez Farm, where there might be a job for him. Neither man realized that the farm was at the exact site where his ancestor had been a village chief.

⚬⚬⚬

As it turned out, Notaku was more than welcome at the Perez Farm. A new law had been passed in 1857 that required all ranchers and/ or farmers who raised stock to fence their land to keep the cattle from harming any nearby farmland. This was not too much of a problem for Sebastiano. He never had kept much stock, and when he surveyed his land he found that he could fence a relatively small amount for his purposes. He immediately put Notaku to this task. In addition, Notaku was directed to go to the marshes at the point of the bay to fish and hunt for the family. He really enjoyed this task, sensing that this was the way his ancestors had lived.

The family prospered. Since Sebastiano now had complete ownership of the shipping business to San Francisco and to the mining country, a significant income was made for both the Perez family and William Simms.

Linda was now eighteen, and she had continued to grow in beauty and learning from her books and tutorials. Simms, now twenty-six, was a handsome and successful man with a good sense of business. Their attraction for each other had grown over the years. In September 1857, Simms approached Sebastiano and asked him for approval to court Linda, with the intent of marriage. Sebastiano spoke to Juanita about the matter. She knew that Linda was attracted to Simms and agreed that it would be a good match.

The courtship lasted a year. Simms spent most of his time in the gold country, but he returned to the farm whenever he could. They had a simple wedding on September 12, 1858, and temporarily set up household at the farm.

Jorge, now sixteen, was restless. He, too, was well read, and he had paid full attention to the details of his father's business. In fact, he desired to take a more active part in it. While Sebastiano was very proud of his oldest son, he did not think it wise to have him involved in the business until he was older. This difference of opinion cast a shadow over the relationship between father and son that would have a major impact on future familial relations.

PART FIVE

THE TOWN OF BAY POINT

MAP FIVE: ORIGINAL BAY POINT & ENVIRONS

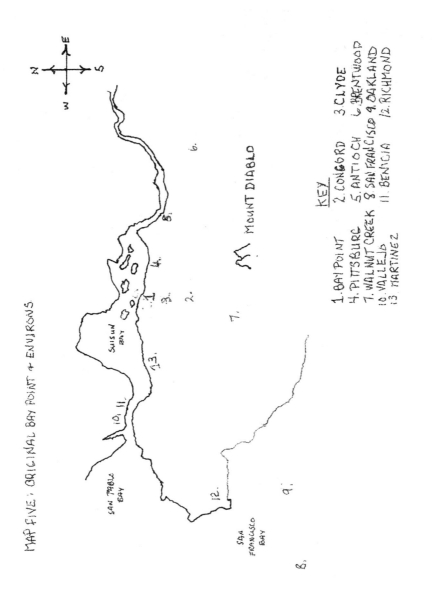

KEY

1. BAY POINT   2. CONCORD   3. CLYDE
4. PITTSBURG   5. ANTIOCH   6. BRENTWOOD
7. WALNUT CREEK   8. SAN FRANCISCO 9. OAKLAND
10. VALLEJO   11. BENICIA   12. RICHMOND
13. MARTINEZ

CHAPTER 13

MODERN BEGINNINGS

By 1870, the members of the Perez family had faced a number of important changes. At fifty-seven years of age, Sebastiano had gained a good deal of weight. The top of his head was bald, but long gray hair hung down on the sides and in the back. His full beard and mustache also were gray. He had maintained his sense of humor and pleasant manner and still read a great deal, rode his favorite horse, and played his guitar. As always, he showed a great deal of love for his wife and family.

Sebastiano had sold the farm eleven years before to an American named Daniel Cunningham, who had purchased the homestead rights to 640 adjoining acres in 1852 to use as a sheep farm. Cunningham wished to add acreage to his holdings, and the twenty acres of the Perez Farm seemed ideal to him. In addition, the fine adobe house and outbuildings were of great value. Sebastiano did keep the pier at the point of the bay, however.

After the sale, in 1860, Sebastiano took Juanita, Ruben, and Elena to live in a lavish new home in Concord, on the land deeded to him by Salvio Pacheco. In addition, he built an office in Concord, also on land deeded by Pacheco. The business continued to focus on selling locally grown agricultural products to businesses in San Francisco and other Bay Area cities, as well as to businesses in the Central Valley and Sierra Nevada foothills. In fact, Sebastiano was wealthy, and most of his time was spent in leisure activities and community service. Of course, Perez Landing at the point of the bay continued to be important to the business.

Juanita also had grown rather stout, but the gray streak in her hair only added to her beauty. She, too, enjoyed leisure time, when she could indulge in her favorite pastime, reading. Some of the servants also had moved to the new location. Most of the original ones, including Hipolito and Enzo, had passed away. Colleta, now old, was brought to the new home, more to retire gracefully than to work. She did small tasks for Juanita.

Linda and William Simms also moved to Concord and had their own home. He worked with Sebastiano in the business established there. In fact, he was in charge of the operation, to everyone's satisfaction.

Jorge, at twenty-nine, had left the family several years earlier and moved to San Francisco, where he used some of his father's contacts to find a place in the business world. At first there was tension between father and son, but after Jorge proved himself, the tension evaporated. In fact, Jorge was doing quite well, having gone to work for Wells Fargo, and having advanced rapidly to an important job helping to move the company from the stagecoach era to that of major banking on the West Coast. While his father had hoped he would stay with the family business, he had to admit that he was proud of his son, and they maintained a respectful relationship, visiting as often as possible. Jorge had taken a wife, Elizabeth Crabtree, three years earlier, and they lived in San Francisco with their new son, Emory.

Ruben was twenty-five and had become somewhat famous for his carvings. He had garnered several contracts for his work and was able to meet all of his deadlines. In fact, with his father's help, he established a business in Concord and was able to hire two assistants. William Simms was assigned the task of making sure that he was not cheated in his business ventures. The fact was that he proved not to need oversight. He did quite well for himself. His mother wondered if Ruben would ever marry, but since he was happy in his work, she decided not to ask him about it.

Elena at twenty-two, like all of the women of the family, was quite beautiful. Several young men wished to court her, but she didn't seem to warm to any of them. Instead, she found herself very busy working in a local bookshop and doing a bit of writing about life at the point of the bay. She also had formed a very close friendship with a young woman of her own age, Marianne Belmont. Elena wished only to spend time with her.

The family, now settled in Concord, was able to have many evenings together, and the holiday seasons were quite festive. The social life in Concord certainly was not as elaborate as it had been during the rancho years. Even so, there were many opportunities for parties and visits. The Perez family fit into this life quite easily, and their best friends were Francisco Galindo and his wife, Maria Dolores, the daughter of the deceased Salvio Pacheco.

✺

After the Treaty of Hidalgo in 1848, the land around the point of the bay not owned by Sebastiano or the Pachecos was owned by the federal government. As such, it was sold at a modest price to squatters who laid claim to it. Beginning in the early 1850s, a number of men made such claims. Most of them had failed in the gold fields and were looking for other ways to earn a living. The land at the point of the bay was not fertile, so these men tried to raise sheep and other stock. Many gave up after only a few years and moved on to other locations.

Upon purchasing the homestead rights to his 640 acres in 1852, Daniel Cunningham became the first permanent settler at the point of the bay. He and his wife, Fanny, came to the area with the first two of their eight children, and the ranch added horses and dairy cows to its holdings. After buying the twenty-acre Perez Farm in 1859, he contacted his friend Addison Neely, with whom he had worked on a sheep farm in Sonoma before moving to the point of the bay. He urged Neely to join him there and promised to assist him with the purchase of his own land. Neely decided to accept Cunningham's advice and, with his family in tow, arranged a visit to Cunningham and his family. When Neely and his family arrived, they were put up in the Perez adobe. After the visitors settled in, the two families met on the patio for a plain but hearty meal. No liquor was served. However, after the meal, the two men met for a glass of port wine and to talk business.

Cunningham, now thirty-four, was a handsome man, five foot ten, with square shoulders and a rather long face covered by a well-trimmed beard. He began, "I hope your journey here was pleasant."

Neely, two years younger, slightly shorter, and clean shaven, responded, "It was very pleasant, Daniel. The younger children particularly enjoyed riding the ferryboat from Benicia to Martinez. They hadn't been on the water before, and it was a thrill for them. The road from Martinez to here leaves something to be desired, but I am sure that will change in the years to come."

"It will," said Cunningham. "And there will be a railway, also." He continued, "I have decided to let you have this farm for a small price, if you want it. It has the adobe and a creek, and it is ideal for raising sheep, dairy cows, horses, and hogs. There also is an orchard and a vegetable garden. I am building a larger house closer to the point of the bay, where I believe there eventually will be a town. If you decide to purchase this place, we will be neighbors, and my family and I would like that very much. I can make the terms easy for you. In fact, you can take a year to stock your land before you begin to make payments."

This was a very good offer, and without hesitation Neely said, "I am ready to sign an agreement right now."

"A handshake will suffice," replied Cunningham. The two men

shook hands and became neighbors, and the families became even closer and tied together by friendship and business interests.

◠⚭◡

From 1852 until 1907, the area at the point of the bay was nothing but ranches and farms. To meet the educational needs of local families, the first Bay Point school was opened in 1858, serving ranch and farm families in a large area along Suisun Bay.

In 1862, Congress passed the Pacific Railroad Act, granting the Union Pacific and Central Pacific Railroads land for the construction of rail lines. This caused some settlers, whose land was given to the railroads, to move away. In fact, by 1870, there still were only a few families at the point of the bay. However, later in the decade the pace of growth quickened dramatically.

In 1878, the San Pablo–Tulare Railroad Company completed a road from Tracy that passed through the point of the bay and went past Martinez to connect with the Central Pacific line. The task was difficult because the land at the point was swampy and required bringing landfill to the bed and extra reinforcement for the tracks. The actual work was done by Mexican workers, who lived in a set of boxcars that were moved along as the work progressed from east to west.

The boxcars were hot in the summer and cold in the winter. There were no windows and no toilets. The men slept on thin straw mats, and each man had one thin blanket. Two meals a day were served. The breakfast consisted of beans, bread, and coffee. Dinner also featured beans, bread, and coffee, with small portions of meat added. The pay for a ten-hour day was two dollars.

The foreman of the work crew was Daniel Finnegan, an Irishman who had little respect for his Mexican workers. He drove them hard and had little sympathy for illness, accidents, or anything else that slowed the work.

When the crew came to the swampy area near the point of the bay, work slowed. Two of the men were seriously injured when railroad ties fell from a train bed and landed on them. One had a broken leg, and the other suffered from head trauma. Neither could continue working, and both asked Finnegan for paid leave. Finnegan, furious with the two men, let his feelings be known. "You damned fools, the injuries are your own fault. You will receive no pay. In fact, you're fired!" When word of Finnegan's actions reached the other men, there was a rebellion. They went on strike and demanded better working conditions, better food, and care for the two injured men. Finnegan's response was to fire the entire crew.

When news of the firing reached the headquarters of the railway, the immediate reaction was not what Finnegan had expected. The company had a tight construction timeline, and a work stoppage would cost a great deal of money. In the end, the company met the demands of the crew members and also replaced Finnegan with a Mexican foreman. Finnegan was reprimanded and reassigned to other duties. Shortly thereafter, with the completion of the railway, a station was built at the point of the bay.

⚬ᴍᴍᴏ

In June 1878, Samuel Bacon walked down the main street of Concord from his office to the office of Sebastiano Perez. Bacon was one of the businessmen who had set up his office in Pacheco, only to have it destroyed by floods. Fortunately, he had been able to relocate to Concord because of Salvio Pacheco's generous offer, which gave him land for both his business and his home for one dollar each. He reestablished his trading business and home there in 1860, the same year Perez did.

Bacon and Perez were competitors. They both bought the wheat, barley, oats, fruits, vegetables, and other products from the rich valleys of Contra Costa County and sold them to merchants in San Francisco, Oakland, and other cities of the Bay Area, as well as to merchants in Sacramento and Stockton in the Central Valley. The two men also were friends. Bacon walked with a decided limp that came from a wound he received during the Civil War. He had an extremely thin physique and a formal manner of speaking. While he was not as warm a person as Sebastiano, their common business interests drew them together, and their wives had become friends as well.

Sebastiano did not come to the office every day, and Bacon had been watching to see when he would arrive. When Bacon entered, he was greeted by William Simms, who asked if there was something he could do for him.

"Yes, I would like to speak with Sebastiano."

Simms pointed to the back of the office. "He's in the storage room. I'll fetch him."

Sebastiano made his way to the front of the office and greeted Bacon. "How are you, Samuel? It's been a while since we last spoke. To what do I owe this visit?"

"I often have thought about Seal Bluff with the idea that it would make a perfect place for a real port. You have a small pier there and use it well. I propose that we expand the pier, making a large dock and adding a substantial warehouse where we both can store the goods that we ship out of central Contra Costa County to the major cities to the west and east of us. I also propose that instead of competing with each other, we become partners in the enterprise. In addition to the dock and the warehouse, we also should also add a new steamship to our fleet, while still using the one you already own and the one I likewise possess."

Sebastiano listened intently, but did not answer immediately.

William Simms could not contain himself. "Sebastiano, I believe this to be a really good idea. We could expand our business, and by working with Mr. Bacon, together we can capture a larger share of the markets here and in the cities." Both he and Samuel Bacon looked at Sebastiano, who was gazing out the window at nothing in particular.

Sebastiano had two reasons for agreeing to the idea. First, he respected Bacon's business abilities, and, second, he was now sixty-three years old and felt that it was a good time to retire. Looking back at the two men, he answered, "I, too, think a partnership would be a good idea. I assume that you would agree to a 50-50 split of the profits. Also, I would insist that my son-in-law, William, continue to be employed in a leadership position in the larger company we create. He can be paid out of my 50 percent and ultimately will inherit my interest in the company."

Planning for the new enterprise began immediately, and two years later the dock and warehouse had been built, and a third steamboat had been added to the company. This was an important step forward for growth at the point of the bay, since it added jobs for people who came to live and work in the area.

Three years after Bacon made his proposition, almost to the day, Sebastiano, at sixty-seven years of age, fell from his horse and broke his neck while riding in the foothills of Mt. Diablo. The entire family gathered at the home in Concord for his funeral and a celebration of his life. The new priest in Concord presided over the funeral, and many friends, including Don Francisco Galindo and Samuel Bacon, testified to his outstanding character. William Simms, Jorge Perez, and his brother, Ruben, spoke of their love for him. As a testimony to the changing times with regard to the view of a woman's role in the family, Linda sang and played the guitar in his honor:

With friends on earth we meet in gladness,
While swift the moments fly.
Yet ever comes the thought of sadness,
That we must say good-bye.

Refrain:

May the choir of angels come to greet you.
May they speed you to paradise.
May the Lord enfold you in his mercy.
May you find eternal life.
We'll never say good-bye in heav'n,
We'll never say good-bye,
For in that land of joy and song,
We'll never say good-bye.
How joyful is the hope that lingers,
When loved ones cross death's sea,
That we, when all earth's toils are ended,
With Thee shall ever be.

:No parting words shall e'er be spoken,
In yonder home so fair,
But songs of joy, and peace, and gladness,
We'll sing forever more.

Refrain

William Simms, per Sebastiano's will, became half owner of the Seal Bluff Warehouse and its dock. Jorge received $50,000 and was a wealthy man in his own right. Juanita was well taken care of, and Ruben was still successful with his carving business and his new work at the warehouse dock.

⌀

In 1888, the San Pablo–Tulare Railroad Company and the Central Pacific line were incorporated into the Southern Pacific Railway system, and a station was built at the point of the bay. The following year the San Francisco and San Joaquin Railroad Company constructed a line parallel to the Southern Pacific tracks that went through the area. This line was taken over by the Atchison, Topeka, and Santa Fe Railway. The railroads increased the importance of the location as an outlet for the goods of Contra Costa County. However, other than the Seal Bluff Warehouse and dock, there was not much activity for a number of years. Nonetheless, the railroads often brought excitement to the area.

෬

William Patterson was, at best, described as "scraggly." His beard was full and untrimmed, and his hair was long and uncombed. He had a beaklike nose, his ears stuck out like a pair of wings, and he was missing three teeth. He wore dirty buckskin clothes with several holes in evidence. He had been a brakeman for the Southern Pacific, but in 1891 his knee was severely damaged when it was caught between two cars. After nearly two years of healing, in August 1893, he joined with his brother Charles and his friend David Jones, equally unkempt men, to form the Patterson gang. For five years they robbed Southern Pacific trains throughout the state.

Their last robbery occurred in 1898, five miles east of the point of the bay. The Patterson brothers were masked and able to get onto the train and climb over the tender. Heavily armed, they entered the engine and ordered the crew to bring the train to a stop. They then blew the doors off the mail car, seriously wounding the man inside. They took $20,000 and rode off on the horses that were waiting beside the train with Jones.

A posse, which included a number of railroad detectives, tracked Charles to a bar in New York of the West, later to be called Pittsburg. The lead detective, Aaron Birk, smashed through the front door and yelled at Charles, "Put your hands up, Patterson. You're under arrest. If you don't surrender, I'll shoot you dead."

The posse took him into custody, and Birk and another detective rode to the Jones ranch to find the other robbers. They entered the cabin on the ranch and found Jones. Birk asked, "Where can we find William Patterson?"

Jones responded, "I don't know." As he spoke, Patterson burst into the cabin and fired both barrels of his shotgun, badly wounding the two detectives

Deputies were nearby, and after hearing the gunfire they surrounded the cabin. Patterson and Jones were able to escape to the barn. One deputy kicked the barn door down, shot twice, and ordered the pair out. Patterson shot back and killed the deputy. Jones and Patterson were once again able to escape.

In May of the following year, the two men were sighted by a group of railroad detectives walking down the street in Antioch, formerly Marsh's Landing, twelve miles east of the point of the bay. A gunfight ensued, and Jones was killed. Patterson was captured and sentenced to life in prison.

ᏇᎲᎲᎤ

In early 1898, Copper King Mines, Ltd., built a smelter, the first major industrial plant at the point of the bay. The site was where the Seal Bluff Warehouse had been built in 1880 and abandoned five years later. Frank L. Gardiner was the person who had the major responsibility for raising the capital to put the deal together. However, the plant didn't last long, primarily because Gardiner did not realize that the smelting process of removing precious metals from ore requires that a great deal of ore be transported to the smelter. The source of the ore was mines near Fresno, California, a long way from what had come to be called

Seal Bluff. After the smelter was closed down in 1903, the site again lay abandoned.

ᏀᎷᎢᏖᎾ

Charles Axel Smith was born in 1852 in Sweden. He came to the United States with his parents when he was fourteen. Like many immigrants from Sweden, the family settled in Minnesota. In 1878 Charles opened a hardware store and lumber business, and he soon was able to include additional lumberyards in Minnesota. His businesses were very profitable, and because of the depletion of Minnesota forests, he decided to invest in forest land in Northern California and Oregon.

Like many other lumbermen of his time, Smith used both legal and illegal means to purchase stands of virgin northwestern forests. His agents filed fraudulent claims to 160-acre tracts of timber and then transferred them to the C. A. Smith Lumber Company. In the end, he had control of about thirty thousand acres of timberland.

In the beginning of operations in Oregon, there were 250 employees at what was called the "Big Mill" at Coos Bay. There were another 350 in seven logging camps. Eventually, the company boosted its production to more than 600,000 board feet daily. A lumber mill was soon needed to process the raw timber and ship it to markets.

CHAPTER 14

THE TOWN

In the summer of 1907, Charles Smith and his good friend and colleague Arno Mereen stood at the point of the bay. They were on a mission to find a location for a lumber mill and lumberyard. Smith, nearly six feet tall, was broad-shouldered and clean-shaven, and his hair was neatly trimmed. While he was dressed casually for the particular walk around the area, he gave the appearance of being well dressed. He seemed self-assured and was well-spoken, giving evidence of his college education. "Arno, what do you think of this area as a place for our lumber mill?"

Mereen, slightly shorter than Smith, was thin and had sharp features. He, too, was well-spoken and evidently self-confident. "We have talked before about what we need for a mill, and this place seems to have everything. There is deep water here, and ships can dock with raw lumber from our forests in Northern California and Oregon. There are railroads nearby so that we can ship finished products to markets. Finally, unlike the cold and wet weather in the south, the conditions here are such that our products can easily dry. The place is ideal for a mill."

They walked out along the old dock, being careful to avoid rotten sections, and inspected the building that had housed the old warehouse. Later, the pair headed south and crossed the railroad tracks, which were used by both the Southern Pacific and Santa Fe railway companies. Mereen commented on the tracks. "The railroads will be a big factor in making your decision, Charles. We can easily ship our products all over the country."

Smith nodded in agreement. While most of the land south of the tracks was used for farming and cattle ranching, there already was a grocery store, a post office, and a saloon. Smith and Mereen walked through what passed as a downtown.

As they continued south, Smith commented, "I think this will be a good site for a town. There is lots of room for houses and additional businesses. Highways will be coming through here in the near future to add to the railroad transportation. I think we should begin discussions with some of the local landowners to see whether or not we can buy what is necessary for our purposes."

"Yes," said Mereen. "What should we name the town, Charles? The area has been known as Seal Bluff."

"I don't think Seal Bluff is a good idea. The name has been associated with unsuccessful enterprises. I think we should give it a new name. Perhaps Bay Point would be a good name. We could make it a famous city."

"It's an exciting proposition, Charles. I feel very lucky to be part of this venture."

Smith patted Mereen on the shoulder. "Arno, you know I depend upon you. We are a team. Together we'll develop the mill and the town."

Then both of the men stopped in their tracks. Coming toward them was a man pointing a double-barreled shotgun. As he approached, he threatened, "What are you two doing on my land? You are trespassing, and if you don't get off, I'll have to shoot you."

Smith looked the man in the eye. "We mean you and your farm no harm. We are simply looking the area over to see if we would like to locate a lumber mill on the waterfront and build a town to serve our workers and others who live in the area. If you insist, we'll leave your property. Please, don't shoot." With that, the two men moved in the opposite direction from the farmhouse in the distance.

Smith grinned. "I suppose that we should make ourselves known so that we can move forward with our business without upsetting any of the people who live here!" The people living in the area soon would know quite well who Charles Axel Smith was.

⌒∞⌒

About three months later, Smith contacted Simon Cunningham, the son of Daniel and Fanny Cunningham, the original settlers of the area. After some negotiations, Simon and his brothers, along with the Neely family, sold the lumber company one thousand acres along the waterfront and up the sloping hills to the south of the railroad tracks.

The company included lumberyards, planing mills, a box factory, all types of woodworking manufacturers, an electric light plant, and a waterworks. It started with 950 employees, but ultimately the number grew to about 2,000.

The first structure built in the town was a boardinghouse in the southern part of the town just below the hills. It was meant to accommodate the office staff of the company and was adjacent to the old Cunningham ranch house. The Cunningham family brought eucalyptus seedlings from Australia and planted a row of them near the boardinghouse. Another larger stand of eucalypti was planted on the north side of town not far from the railroad tracks. Both stands of trees served as windbreaks for farming.

The company also built a bandstand in the center of the town. It was just off Main Street and was used for various kinds of concerts for the townspeople. The favorite music was that of John Philip Sousa, particularly "The Stars and Stripes Forever":

Hurrah for the flag of the free!
May it wave as our standard forever,
The gem of the land and the sea,
The banner of the right.

Let despots remember the day
When our fathers with mighty endeavor
Proclaimed as they marched to the fray
That by their might and by their right
It waves forever.

Of course, the children of the town had their own version:

Be kind to your web-footed friends,
For a duck may be somebody's mother.
Be kind to your friends in the swamp,
Where the weather is very, very damp [to be pronounced to
rhyme with "swamp"]
Now, you may think that this is the end ... well, it is!

The water supply for the town was provided by four wells, each one
a hundred feet deep, located in the foothills one and a half miles
south of the town. The water was pumped from the wells to two
large tanks. The bases of the tanks were about eighty feet higher
than the town, and the water was distributed by gravity

The town expanded rapidly. Businesses, including stores selling groceries, meats, hardware, men's furnishings, drugs, and other
goods, were opened on the main street of the town. An Odd Fellows
Hall and a movie theater were built in 1911. In that same year,
the Oakland, Antioch, and Eastern Electric Railway completed a
leg between Bay Point and Concord, allowing students to attend
Mt. Diablo High School. Ultimately, the line extended all the
way to Oakland, and passengers could connect with ferries to San
Francisco. There also was a new elementary school in Bay Point
with five teachers and 150 students in eight grades.

There were dances on Saturday nights at the lumber company
clubhouse. A small band or orchestra would provide music for fox-

trots, the two-step, waltzes, polkas, an occasional schottische, and even square dances. In the twenties, and primarily for the younger dancers, they played music for the Charleston:

Carolina, Carolina, at last they've got you on the map.
With a new tune, a funny blue tune, with a particular snap!
You may not be able to buck and wing, fox-trot, two-step, or even swing,
If you ain't got religion in your feet, you can do this prance and do it neat.
Charleston! Charleston! Made in Carolina.
Some dance, some prance, I'll say there's nothing finer.
Thank the Charleston, Charleston, Lord, how you can shuffle.
Ev'ry step you do leads to something new, man, I'm telling you it's a lapazoo.
Buck dance, wing dance, will be a buck number,
But the Charleston, the new Charleston, that dance is surely a comer.
Sometime you'll dance it one time, the dance called the Charleston,
Made in South Carolina.
Charleston! Charleston! Made in Carolina.

Entire families would attend the dances, and many of the older parents questioned the Charleston. Parents kept close watch over their daughters. There often were strong feelings about having daughters honor their own religious and national heritages. Thus, an Italian girl was expected to dance only with an Italian boy, a Swedish girl to dance only with a Swedish boy, and so forth. Before long, such boundaries would begin to break down.

⌒〤〤〤⌒

At 9:30 on the evening of August 26, 1913, the northern sky above the expansive C. A. Smith Lumberyards turned orange-red. Flames leaped high into the air, fanned by strong winds. The siren at the mills called the workers back to the yards to fight the fire.

Plant Superintendent Dan Desmond rushed to the plant to take charge of the battle, and calls for help were sent by phone to the fire departments of several nearby towns. Railroads sent crews to help fight the fire, and other companies in the area did likewise. Desmond decided to use dynamite to blow up the stacks of lumber in order to stop the fire from reaching the mill and the nearby box factory. The strategy did not work, so he gave an order: "Start a backfire. It may burn many feet of lumber, but it will save much more." It did save a good deal of lumber. More important, the backfire saved the mill and box factory. It took one thousand firefighters to control the fire, and by the time it was over, forty million feet of lumber were destroyed.

Reconstruction began the next day. Smith put most of his employees to work cleaning up and rebuilding. On September 26, a month after the fire, the steamer *Adeline Smith* arrived from Coos Bay with the first load of two million feet of lumber to get the mill going again. By 1914 the mill was once again thriving, and more immigrant employees were hired.

A number of changes were made at the rebuilt mill. One of the most important was suggested by a young engineer. Up until the time of the fire, teamsters would use horses to pull single flatbed railroad cars loaded with lumber. Giulio Bartolini, a recent immigrant from Calabria, Italy, developed an electric-powered vehicle that could pull several cars, thus increasing the amount of lumber that could be taken to the railroad station for shipment to Oakland or other destinations. The company and the town were blessed by the number of immigrants from many countries who brought needed skills with them.

⚬〰〰〰⚬

In 1916, the C. A. Smith Lumber Company was renamed the Coos Bay Lumber Company as a means of refinancing the business. That same year the California Hotel at the northern end of Main Street was opened and became a favorite place for lumber company employees to have lunch. By this time there also were Catholic, Congregational, and Lutheran churches. Within the next four years a foundry, bank, and lodges of the Odd Fellows, the Rebekahs, the Woodmen of the World, and the Royal Neighbors, as well as a Masonic Club, all had been established. The population had expanded to nearly one thousand people. At this point, it appeared as if Smith's vision of a thriving and growing town would become a reality

In building the town, Smith, a teetotaler, required that no alcohol be sold. This led to a proliferation of bootlegging, and a couple of "blind pigs," illegal bars.

Many of the employees of the lumber company were of Scandinavian descent, particularly Swedes, who had followed the company from Minnesota. Members of other ethnic groups also migrated from Minnesota. One of several Polish families, the Palawskis, made the move in 1914. The family consisted of Joseph, who worked at the lumber mill; his wife, Betty; and five children.

Betty was a midwife. She also was a bootlegger. She made what euphemistically was called "bathtub gin." It was not made in the bathtub. Rather, it was made in large bottles that were too tall to add the necessary water from the sink tap. It was necessary to add the water by holding the jar under the bathtub tap, thus the name.

The gin was easy to make, but one had to be careful in doing so because it was easily contaminated. Betty always was cautious and gained a reputation for mixing a strong, somewhat tasty, and safe brew. It consisted of grain alcohol and some berries and/or other fruit steeped together for forty-eight hours and stirred a few times. It cost about twenty cents to make a large bottle, which, in turn, was put into three smaller bottles that sold for fifty cents each. She usually made ten large bottles, and her profit was around thirteen dollars per week, a sizable sum.

Owing to the presence of the bootleggers and blind pigs, the liquor question became a serious one for the town. Smith and Mereen, along with other members of the lumber company management team, met several times to find some kind of solution. They grappled with the problem during the first three meetings without success. During their fourth meeting, a young yard foreman, Albert Chapman—the grandson of George Chapman, who rode with John C. Fremont—came up with a unique idea. Nervously he made a proposal. "People are going to drink. Why don't we try to control it somewhat and even make it profitable? What I suggest is that we open a saloon as part of a club for the citizens of the town. Once the club and the saloon pay for themselves, the profits can be used for town improvements such as streets, sidewalks, curbs, and sewers." The idea was put into action in early 1916 and became a model for other cities and towns.

Alcohol was not the only vice in Bay Point. From 1910 until 1920, prostitution was a big business that was basically ignored.

Gustav Hansson, Knut Svenson, Icarus Petridis, and Jakub Kaminski were all office workers for the lumber company. They lived at the Bayview Boarding House at the southern foothills of the town, and were immigrants from different countries: Sweden, Greece, and Poland. All had come with the company from Minnesota. They lived and worked together, and they were single and in their thirties; they frequently played cards, drank Betty's bootlegged gin, and otherwise spent time together.

Gustav was looked upon by the others as the leader of the group of friends. One summer evening in 1915, they were eating dinner together in the boarding house dining room when he said, "I've recently heard of the 'floating houses of ill repute.' They are boats that are offshore at Martinez. It is said that there are several of them, but that *Margaret's Scow* has the most beautiful girls. I think we should drive over there in my car tonight as soon as we finish dinner."

Jakub was the most dapper of the group, and also the most eager. A bit too loudly for the setting, he burst out, "I've heard of the scows, too. Let's go!"

Icarus was the most reserved. Glancing at the other diners, he whispered, "Is it too expensive? Are the girls clean? Can there be trouble with the law?"

Gustav responded, "I understand it costs one dollar to have a girl unless you want something special, and remember they're very pretty. I also hear that the girls are inspected by a nurse every week to make sure that none of them has any diseases. If they do, they are no longer allowed to work. Finally, I am told that the police are on the take. They get a cut of the profits. Also, some of the customers of these boats are local politicians and even judges who are protected from arrest. I think it's safe."

The four young men drove in Gustav's new Ford touring car the seven miles from Bay Point on the new highway that connected the two towns. When they got to the ferry dock, a ship's bell was rung to announce that the clients wished to be ferried to *Margaret's Scow*. Once aboard, they entered the red velvet lounge, where they were offered drinks. While they were enjoying their drinks, a number of girls entered the lounge. Gustav whistled and observed, "Look at those girls; they *are* beautiful! I like the redhead, but any of them would be okay."

Knut responded, "I'll take the blond. She looks just like your sister, Gustav. Ha, ha!"

After about a half hour, all of the young men except Icarus had chosen a girl. Jakub, anxious to get started, chided him, "Come on, Icarus, we don't have all night."

Finally, Icarus chose a mousy little girl who looked like any-thing but a whore. "I'll go with her," he said. With that they were all led to small rooms on the deck below. There they were given several options for sex. Icarus and Knut were the shyest and chose simple "missionary position," Gustav opted for "half and half," and the eager Jakub chose to "go around the world."

Before driving home to Bay Point, the men had more drinks and joined in song with some of the girls and other customers. When they finally left, they were quite intoxicated, and the drive was not easy. Twice they almost ran off the road and into one of the sloughs that ran along the side of the road.

By 1920, the "floating brothels" had been closed down. That was not a problem for the men of Bay Point, because by that time the town had its own establishments.

During Prohibition, from 1920 to 1933, bootlegging began again in earnest, and Betty Palawski again went into business. She was not the only bootlegger in town. The *Contra Costa Gazette* reported a story about a married Italian woman with six children who was jailed for bootlegging during Prohibition. Her youngest child was still nursing. Her husband brought the baby every day to be nursed, because they didn't have $400 for bail.

⧉

The Pacific Metals and Alloys Company built a plant to manufacture electrodes in 1916 just to the east of the lumber company. It did not last long and closed in 1920. During their operation, ten new homes were built on Park Avenue for their office workers and their families. Park Avenue, appropriately named, had some of the finest homes in the town.

Other companies that came to Bay Point during this period were the Pacific Chemical Company, H. O. Camm's Box Factory, and the Pacific Coast Shipbuilding Company.

The shipyard was located to the west of the lumber company and had about 450 employees. It created the company town of Clyde, three miles from Bay Point, and constructed 120 cottages for its employees. It also built a two-story hotel with 176 rooms and a seventeen-lane bowling alley in the basement.

The shipyard's task was to build ten transport ships for World War I. On November 30, 1918, nineteen days after the war ended, the Pacific Coast Shipbuilding Company left Bay Point, and the Clyde Hotel closed its doors.

The final blow for the town was the closure of the Coos Bay Lumber Company in 1932 when it moved to Oakland. Some of those who lost their jobs moved away. Many of the residents of the town stayed on, however. They found jobs at industries in nearby towns such as the Shell Oil and Associated Oil companies, located in Martinez and Avon, respectively; the U. S. Steel mill in Pittsburg; and the Shell Chemical plant in West Pittsburg. A few new businesses did come to town. One, the Bay Point Iron Works, employed men to cast iron, brass, bronze, and aluminum. Once again, dreams of success were met with a downturn in the prospects for the point of the bay.

PART SIX

PORT CHICAGO

FAMILY TREE
— 3 —

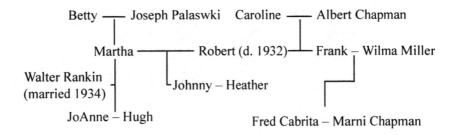

MAP SIX: PORT CHICAGO

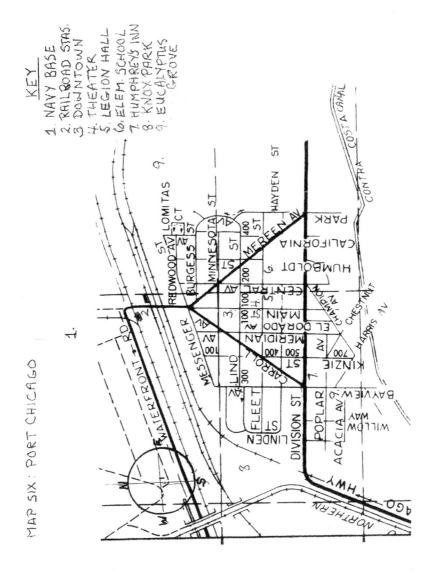

KEY

1. NAVY BASE
2. RAILROAD STAS.
3. DOWNTOWN
4. THEATER
5. LEGION HALL
6. ELEM. SCHOOL
7. HUMPHREY'S INN
8. KNOX PARK
9. EUCALYPTUS
   GROVE

CHAPTER 15

THE DEPRESSION YEARS

Robert Chapman graduated from Mt. Diablo High School in June 1927, and immediately took a job as a carpenter's apprentice with the Coos Bay Lumber Company. He lived at home with his parents and went to work each day with his father, Albert, who was a foreman at the lumber company.

Robbie was only five foot six, but he was a handsome young man. His hair was slicked down and parted in the middle in the style of Rudolph Valentino. Most of the young women of the town found him attractive, and he could not help but notice, which caused him to be somewhat vain.

Robbie liked the girls and the attention they gave him. He also liked to drink, and since it was the time of Prohibition, he would buy his alcohol from Betty Palawski, the bootlegger, who lived with her family in a small house on the hill side of the town, just behind the Bay View Inn. When he went to Betty's house for his transactions, he could not help but notice Betty's daughter Martha, who was two years his junior.

Martha was a pretty girl. Her smooth face was surrounded by bobbed brown hair, her brown eyes sparkled, and she usually had a broad smile.

During one visit Robbie spoke to Martha. "You're a very pretty thing. Do you, by chance, go to the Saturday night town dances? I don't recall ever seeing you there."

Shyly, Martha responded, "I do like to dance, but my mother is not too fond of the idea of my attending the dances. Also, I'm still in high school, and with travel on the train to and from school, homework, and helping around the house, I don't have much time for such things."

Robbie thought about this. "I think your mother likes me. Perhaps if I asked her, she would let you go to a dance with me. What do you think?"

Martha smiled. "I'm not sure my mother would agree."

Robbie did ask Betty, and after expressing some reservations she did agree, with conditions, that Martha could go to the next dance. The conditions were that there would be no drinking and that Martha would be home by 11:00 p.m.

Robbie arrived at Martha's house exactly at 7:30 p.m. to find that both Martha and her mother were ready to go to the dance. What could he do? He smiled and made it clear that he was pleased to accompany both women, despite the fact that he would have preferred that Martha was alone.

When they arrived at the clubhouse, they spent the first several minutes greeting friends and other townspeople. Finally, Robbie turned to Martha and said, "They're playing a fox-trot. Shall we dance?"

"I'd love to," she answered, and off they went. He was dressed in a white coat, dark tie, and dark pants. She was wearing an ecru blouse and a dark brown skirt cut just below her knees. They danced with grace and enthusiasm, and people stopped their own dancing to watch them.

Betty's husband, Joseph, her oldest son, Jeff, and her two oldest daughters, Victoria and Gertrude, arrived at the dance together shortly after the others. Immediately Betty and Joseph began to dance. When it came time for a polka, they gave a stellar performance. Jeff immediately joined a group of somewhat rowdy friends who were obviously stepping out of the hall frequently for a drink. Victoria and Gertrude were with other boys and were having a good time dancing.

As the evening wore on, some of Robbie's friends came over to him and asked if he would like to join them for a drink. He could see Betty watching him, and he made it clear that he was not interested. Betty knew that he was a drinker, because he did business with her. She was pleased that he was meeting the condition she had laid down.

At 10:45 p.m., Robert, holding Martha's hand, moved to Betty. "As you have said, it is time to go home." With that, he walked with Martha and her mother, father, and sisters to their house and said a formal good-night to them all. Only Jeff remained with his friends, and they headed tothe nearest blind pig for a late night of carousing.

On the way home, the group sang the lyrics and danced their way home to the "Beer Barrel Polka":

There's a garden, what a garden;
Only happy faces bloom there.
And there's never any room there
For a worry or a gloom there;
Oh, there's music and there's dancing
And a bit of sweet romancing.
When they play the polka,
They all get in the swing.
Every time they hear the oom-pa-pa,
Everybody feels so tra-la-la.
They want to throw their cares away;
They all go lah-de-lah-de-ay.

Then they hear a rumble on the floor, the floor.
It's the big surprise they're waiting for,
And all the couples form a ring;
For miles around you'll hear them sing.

Roll out the barrel; we'll have a barrel of fun.
Roll out the barrel; we've got the blues on the run.
Sing boom tararra; ring out a song of good cheer.
Now's the time to roll the barrel, for the gang's all here.

Robbie had charmed Betty, and he had behaved like a gentleman at the dance. Despite the fact that he was a customer and a known drinker, she allowed Martha to go to other dances with him.

For the next two years, Robbie Chapman and Martha Pawlaski saw a lot of each other. They danced. They went on picnics. They went to the local movie house, and when he was allowed to use the Chapman family car, they went on drives to nearby towns to see movies, have meals, and even roller-skate. Robbie did drink on these occasions. It was not too long before they found themselves having dinners at the homes of their parents, Albert and Lillian Chapman and Joseph and Betty Palawski. Things were getting serious.

A major problem was that Robbie was a womanizer. While he was dating Martha, he also chased after other young women, particularly if there was sex involved. It was not until a year into their relationship that Martha inadvertently found out about his behavior when one of her friends told her that she had seen Robbie in Martinez with a girl they both knew and who had a reputation as being easy.

When Martha confronted Robbie, at first he was angry and denied seeing the other girl. "You shouldn't listen to rumors spread about me. I love you, and I don't cheat on you!"

Ultimately, Robert admitted "seeing" the other girl, begged for forgiveness, and promised never to see her again. Martha, in love with Robert, believed him and told him so.

Robert and Martha were married at the courthouse in Martinez on July 17, 1929. Both families were in attendance at the civil ceremony, as were a number of relatives and friends.

The couple had a four-day honeymoon in San Francisco. Unlike Sebastiano and Juanita, who generations before also celebrated in "the City," they were able to get there on the Oakland, Antioch, and Eastern Electric Railway. This was the same railway that Martha, Robbie, and other high school students in Bay Point rode to Concord to attend Mt. Diablo High School, only this time they went all the way to Oakland. In Oakland, they transferred to a ferry that took them to San Francisco, now a thriving city of nearly 650,000 people. It had spread from the narrow harbor area known as Yerba Buena all the way west to the Pacific Ocean and from the Golden Gate south to San Mateo County—nearly forty-seven square miles. Martha and Robert had a room in a modest but pleasant hotel, the Barrington on Sutter Street. From there they were able to travel by streetcar to many of the sights in the city.

They ate most of their meals in the Barrington, where a steak cost them twenty cents apiece. They did have one lunch at the Cliff House overlooking the Pacific; and they visited Chinatown, the Steinhart Aquarium in Golden Gate Park, and the plush and ornate downtown Palace Hotel. What Martha liked the most was the newly opened Fleishhacker Zoo, with its exotic animals from all over the world. Robbie was attentive and loving throughout the entire stay in the city and did not have a single drink.

Things went well for the young couple for several months. In October, Martha told Robbie that she was pregnant. For a while he was very loving and frequently used words such as "darling," "I love you," and "sweetheart." They still went to the Saturday dances, where Robbie's drinking increased. In addition to the drinking, he spent more time with his friends and often danced with several other young ladies. At first, Martha didn't seem to be bothered by this behavior. However, after one dance where Robbie spent a great deal of time dancing with his sister-in-law, who was attractive and two years older than him, Martha challenged him about his behavior. "I'm tired of coming to the dance and having you go off with other girls. Tonight you had at least six dances with Edna while I was forced to talk with my friends and watch you make a fool of yourself!"

Robbie, somewhat inebriated, became angry and lashed out. "Don't be a nag. I'm just having a little fun. If you don't like my dancing with other women, find yourself someone else to dance with!" With that, he stomped off and danced with Edna again. He finally returned to Martha when it was time to go home.

Robbie's behavior worsened. He often came home late from work, and it was obvious that he had been drinking. He was sullen and critical of Martha. On many occasions he caused her to cry. Finally, she went across the street to Robbie's mother, Lillian, and told her about his behavior. Lillian listened quietly and was sympathetic to Martha's complaints because she was aware of Robbie's flaws. When sober, he was charming. When drinking, he often turned nasty.

Lillian talked to Robbie about his behavior, and he promised to be a better husband. As he crossed the street to his own house, his mood changed. By the time he walked in the door, he was furious. "How dare you complain about me to my mother—or anyone else, for that matter!" He stalked right out again and didn't return that night.

Martha's life was complicated by other events as well. Her mother's marriage to Joseph Palawski had been arranged by her parents. To them he seemed a good match since he was a success as a farmer. She was in love with another young man, but in those days arranged marriages were common, and she complied with her parents' wishes. However, and even after the birth of six children, she did not really love Joseph. In April 1929, she filed for divorce and took up with another man, a gambler named Bill Borden. Since all of the children except Jeff were grown and married, that was a simple answer. Joseph did not contest the divorce. Betty and Borden occupied the smallest but newest of the two houses built by Joseph and Jeff. The two men took up residence in the older house, which had no electricity or indoor plumbing. It did have gas for cooking and light, and there was an outhouse. The two men were quite content until Joseph passed away in the following spring.

In June 1930, a son called Johnny was born to Martha and Robert. At first, Robbie was a loving father and husband. He helped with the baby, even changing diapers and doing household chores. However, that lasted for only a couple of months, and then he returned to his previous habits. In addition, on occasion he would come home late after a night of drinking and "who knows what."

Robbie's drinking continued, as did his chasing after other women. Frequently Martha confronted him about his behavior, as did his mother. This often led to frequent fights, until one night in early 1932, the couple ended up screaming and throwing dishes at each other. Robert moved in with his parents across the street.

ᏩᎥᎥᏫ

With the closure of much of the manufacturing base in Bay Point, and exacerbated by the stock market crash in 1929, the town faced significant economic problems. Because of the railroads, roads, and deep port for shipping, the site had good potential for industry. What seemed necessary was a bold plan to get things going.

In early 1931, Owen Van Horn, the president of the Bay Point Chamber of Commerce and owner of the local light and power company, as well as a hardware store and other businesses throughout Northern California, conceived and put into action a plan to reenergize the town. At the January meeting of the chamber, Van Horn began by saying, "We need a plan that will bring the town back as a site for industry and business."

Other members of the chamber initially disagreed. "We are in an economic depression, and there is no money for risky ventures," stated one member.

Another member added, "The town is too far up the bay, and we cannot compete with the towns closer to San Francisco."

After several hours of debate the chamber did agree upon a plan that, at first, would require little funding. The first step was a cleanup program wherein volunteers moved loads of rubbish from city lots and backyards to the municipal dock and dumped them into the bay.

The second part of the plan, which involved discussions at open meetings of citizens, was the building of homes and industry. The rosy prediction was that the population would grow dramatically within three years.

The most consequential action arising from the plan was changing the name of the town from Bay Point to Chicago. However, when a petition was sent to the postmaster general in Washington, DC, to change the name to Chicago, it was denied. The name Port Chicago was selected instead and officially adopted on November 1, 1931.

On the night before, a "funeral" was carried out for Bay Point as a celebration of the name change to Port Chicago. There were great hopes for the development of the town into an industrial giant. The celebration included a torchlight parade led by a brass band. A coffin was carried by twenty pallbearers dressed in flowing white gowns. The parade moved through the streets of the town accompanied by a funeral dirge played by the band. The people were dressed in Halloween costumes. Ultimately, the coffin was cremated in a large bonfire, after which the crowd moved to the American Legion hall for dancing and refreshments.

Unfortunately for the town, predictions of industrial growth did not come to pass. The Great Depression did not allow for industrial expansion, and what growth did take place was, as predicted, farther to the west toward San Francisco, and also to the east in Pittsburg and

Antioch. Work for the men in the town was available in the nearby oil refineries, chemical plants, and steel mill. Robbie, for example, took a job just east of the town at the Shell Chemical Company.

〇vΩΩ9

In the 1930s, inoculations were not yet common. Children frequently fell ill with diseases such as measles, chicken pox, and whooping cough. In June 1932, two-year-old Johnny contracted scarlet fever, a very serious disease. He was taken to the county hospital in nearby Martinez and placed in the contagion ward with other children with a number of different diseases. In the ward, he also contracted whooping cough and mumps. The other problem caused by the scarlet fever was the development of a mastoid infection in his ear that had to be treated by surgery. He was a sick little boy.

Johnny's medical problems led to a truce between Robbie and Martha. Every night while the boy was in the hospital, they would drive the seven miles to visit him. Since they could not enter the contagion ward, they would come to the window and look in on him while a nurse or orderly would hold him up so he could see them. It was almost a month before Johnny was sent home, with all of his medical problems taken care of except the mastoid infection.

The truce didn't last long. Robbie returned to his earlier habits. Early in 1933, Martha took Johnny and moved to the home of a friend, Gizela Jaworski, who lived with her mother, Tekla, who was the best friend of Martha's mother, Betty. She enjoyed living with the Jaworskis. Gizela had two younger brothers and one younger sister, none of whom were married. There were always parties, and Martha learned to play poker quite well, a favorite pastime at this house. She also took a job as a waitress at the Bay View Inn. The inn had a life of its own: it served as a boardinghouse for some of the men who worked at the various industrial sites in and near Port

Chicago; it was a restaurant open to the public; it served illegal alcoholic beverages until the end of Prohibition in 1933; and then it sold them legally. There also were a few rooms set aside for three or four girls who came and went, working as prostitutes.

The food, drinks, and girls at the inn attracted a number of young men who were passing through town on business. One such fellow lived in Oakland and drove a gasoline truck that brought gasoline and other products to service stations. His route took him through Port Chicago, and he often stopped at the inn for drinks and dinner. He did not partake of the girls, but he was attracted to Martha and often sat a long time in the restaurant where he could talk and flirt with her.

This young man, Walter Rankin, was nearly six feet tall, often went several days without shaving, and was handsome in a rugged sort of way. Finally, one evening in June 1933, he asked Martha to sit down with him because he had something to ask her. She did, and he hesitantly said to her, "Martha, you are very pretty, and I really like the way you talk to me. You are always pleasant and thoughtful. I really enjoy being around you."

Martha was not sure where this conversation was headed, so she responded, "Thank you, Walter. I enjoy your company, too."

"What I was thinking was that perhaps you and I could go to a movie together some night after you get off work, or some evening when you are not working."

"Walter, I thank you for asking me, but I am married and also have a young child. I do not think you really want to go on a date with me."

He was surprised and stumbled a bit with his words. "I … didn't know. I'm so sorry. I never would have …"

"Please don't be embarrassed. My husband drinks a lot and sometimes hits me. I have left him and live with friends. But I haven't filed for divorce yet."

Walter paused, and after a while he said, "Does he hurt the

baby? If I was ever around when he mistreated you, I'd kick his butt." The conversation ended there. However, Walter kept having dinner at the inn.

One Sunday afternoon he arrived at the inn riding a motorcycle. Martha thought him very handsome in his riding garb: leather boots and jacket, riding hat buckled under his chin, flowing scarf, and goggles. When she served him his lunch, she told him, "I've been thinking about what you asked me, and I've come to the conclusion that since I'm leaving Robbie, it would be all right if we go out on a date. There just can't be any *funny business*." Martha and Walter continued to date. Occasionally, he stayed overnight either at the inn or at the Jaworski house, where he was welcomed by the family. The couple gradually came to feel close, and ultimately Walter asked Martha to marry him.

Martha filed for divorce in February 1934. Robbie slowed his drinking and promised Martha that he would change his behavior. He asked her to come back to him. Now in love with Walter, and tired of Robbie's habits and abuse, she refused.

Three months later Robbie came to the Jaworski home. He was drunk and shouting loudly for Martha to come to the door. Andy, the oldest boy, opened the door and told Robbie that Martha would not see him. Robbie responded by waving a small bottle in the air. "Thish is arsenic," he said, slurring his words. "If she doshen come out, I'll drink it and kill myshelf." Andy went into the house and told Martha what Robert had said. She still refused to go to the door. When Andy told this to Robbie, he staggered around in the yard, drank the arsenic, and fell to the ground, where he vomited, fouled himself, convulsed, and went into a coma. Within fifteen minutes he was dead.

Martha stood in the doorway and looked at Robbie's body. No tears came, but after a moment she had to grab the door to keep from falling. Though she wasn't sorry, it was still a shock. A month later, she and Walter drove to Reno, Nevada, and were married.

Unfortunately, almost at the same time they were getting married, Walter lost his job driving the gasoline truck. When they returned to Port Chicago after getting married, and with a not totally healthy four-year-old to take care of, they had to earn a living.

Walter and Martha decided to try their hands at running a restaurant. They approached Owen Van Horn for a small loan, and he made $1,000 available to them. There was a vacant space next to the town movie theater that they rented, along with the necessary furniture and equipment. Finally, a grand total of $200 worth of necessary foodstuffs was purchased to begin their experiment. A small living space behind the restaurant contained a double bed and bathroom with a basin, bathtub, toilet, two cabinets, and running water. There wasn't room to have Johnny live with them, so they found a couple in Martinez who would care for him during the week. Most weekends he came home.

Martha did all of the cooking, cleaning, and waiting on the customers. She also kept the books because Walter was no good with figures. Actually, what Walter did do, and he did it well, was talk with the customers and make them feel as if each one of them was special.

They had thought that being next to the theater would bring them a lot of business, but very few people had the money for both a movie and a meal. Occasionally, a couple would come in after the movie and have a piece of pie and milk, cocoa, or coffee. Since Walter often gave an extra piece of pie, this was not a terribly profitable bit of business, and Martha had to spend a good deal of time making extra pies. The business lasted only a few months, and they had to close.

Three things happened in early 1935 that made things work for Martha and Walter Rankin. First, just before they closed, they met with Van Horn and told him that they had to close the restaurant and would need more time to repay him. He was very generous and said, "Times are difficult. You are honest people, and I am confident that you will repay me when you can. Once you find other employment, we can work out a schedule of payment."

Second, Betty died of cancer, and they were able to move into her house with Johnny. The house was furnished, and there was no rent to pay. The only drawback was that there was no hot water in the house. Martha had to heat water on the stove in order to do the dishes. Walter had to bring two tubs of hot water in from the water heater in the combined detached garage and storage room on bath night. The system was simple. Walter took a bath first, Martha was second, and Johnny was last.

Third, Walter got a job at the Shell Oil refinery in nearby Martinez. Because they paid no rent, they were able to make payments to Van Horn, buy a new car for $650, and lead a fairly comfortable life by Depression standards.

Her mother's death was very stressful for Martha. They were a Catholic family, and their local church was served by a priest who came from Martinez on Fridays for catechism and on Sundays for mass. When Martha requested last rites for Betty, they were refused because of her divorce from Joseph. Martha never set foot in a Catholic church again.

Martha and Walter's main problem was Johnny's health. He contracted both measles and chicken pox, and he also had frequent colds. The surgery on his ear had not eliminated his mastoid infection, so Martha had to take him once every three months to the University of California Hospital in San Francisco for treatments. That meant riding the Oakland, Antioch, and Eastern Electric Railway to Oakland and then transferring to the ferry from Oakland to San Francisco, just as Martha and Robbie had done for their honeymoon. From there Martha and Johnny had to take a streetcar to the hospital, which was a good distance from the ferry building. For Johnny, it was a great adventure. To his mother it was a long, hard journey. Finally, at the age of six, the boy had another surgery that helped a great deal.

⟨∞⟩

In 1936, Johnny began to attend Bay Point Elementary School. Small for his age, and with tousled light brown hair, he usually was clad in bib overalls, as were most of the boys his age. He had a ready smile and was happy with his life, easily adapted to his schoolwork, and quickly learned to read, write, and do his numbers. He began to read the comics and other parts of the newspaper at home, and Martha often took him to the library, which was at the site of the bandstand built by the C. A. Smith Lumber Company in the early days of Bay Point. At school, his problem was that he was not a quiet boy. In fact, he was very active, talked a lot, and was frequently restless. He certainly was not a teacher's pet.

The best part of growing up in Port Chicago was the multicultural composition of its population. The early days of the lumber mill had brought Swedish and Polish families from Minnesota. In the 1920s, there was a large influx of Italian families. Residents of other nationalities included Greeks, Portuguese, and Mexicans. In the 1930s, added to the mixture were migrants escaping the "dust bowl" in Oklahoma, Arkansas, and Texas. Later, in the 1940s, significant numbers of Negroes came to the town to work at the navy base.

Walter Rankin was a bigoted man. He often talked negatively about the other ethnic groups, especially about the Negroes. Martha didn't speak evil of anyone, nor did she take a stand against Walter's rants. She did not try to influence Johnny one way or the other about other people. None of this made a difference to Johnny, because he spent time every day with his friends of every ethnicity in school and after school. In later years, even Walter mellowed and enjoyed the company of many of the different people of the town.

Port Chicago was a safe, comfortable, and fun place for children. During the summers and on weekends there were ball games for the boys that lasted all day long. Sides would be chosen and the game would start, be it baseball, football, or basketball, according to the season. If a player needed to go home for lunch, he would drop his mitt, bat, or ball, go home, eat, and then return to the game. While he was gone, someone else would take his place. The game was never interrupted. If a player had to go to the bathroom, all he had to do was go to one of the nearby houses and ask to use the toilet. When finished, he would return to the game. Games would finally end when it was time for everyone to go home for dinner.

Baseball games were played in a small field down the street from his house, in what amounted to an Italian neighborhood. Every evening Mrs. Contavalli would step out onto her front porch and yell at the top of her voice, "Aldo, Marco, Giulio, *va casa*, come home." Everyone knew it was time for dinner!

Games such as these would go on at various sites in the town. Occasionally, there would be competitions between teams called "hillside" and "bayside," designations referring to the main highway that ran from west to east through the town.

During the day in summer, girls would generally stay at home, perhaps helping their mothers, reading, or playing games with friends or sisters. Often in the evenings, boys and girls would play together such games as kick the can and hide-and-go-seek. Other coed activities included roller-skating and having "rubber gun wars." The latter involved making a gun out of wood, attaching a clothespin to the back of the gun with the clasp of the pin on top, and having narrow pieces of tire inner tubes to use as "bullets." The inner tube went around the front of the "gun" and stretched back to the clothespin, which when let go would propel the piece of tubing. One had to be accurate with shots because it took a while to reload.

One of the other things Johnny would do on occasion was go down to the marshes with his friend Nikos Kostupolous to hunt for ducks and mud hens. One time as they were walking in a marshy area, Nick said, "Stop, look at that." On the ground among the tules was a small black piece of obsidian. Johnny picked it up, cleaned it off, and observed, "It's black, but it looks like glass, and it is pointed."

Nikos responded, "I think it might be an old Indian arrowhead." He was correct. It was an ancient arrowhead somehow left there by a Chupcan hunter.

A favorite pastime for the children of the town was going to the local movie theater, particularly for the Saturday matinee. Favorite cowboy movies featuring such stars as Gene Autry, the singing cowboy; Hopalong Cassidy; Tom Mix; Buck Jones; Ken Maynard; Tim McCoy; and Johnny Mack Brown were very popular. Other movies, such as *The Hurricane*, starring Dorothy Lamour and John Hall (1937); *Snow White and the Seven Dwarfs* (1937); *The Wizard of Oz*, starring Judy Garland (1939); and *Gone with the Wind*, starring Clark Gable (1939), were also enjoyed.

In September 1938, Johnny was legally adopted by Walter Rankin. One month later, Martha gave birth to another boy, Hugh. The family home was quite small, about seven hundred square feet. Martha and Walter occupied the only tiny bedroom. Johnny slept in the front room. For the first six months of his life, Hugh slept in the bedroom with his parents. By the time Hugh was a year old, Walter had added a second small bedroom for him. As was tradition, Hugh was fourth in line on bath night.

The yard was fairly large. There was an apricot tree, an almond tree, and a small vegetable garden. There was always a dog; often a number of rabbits were being raised for meat, and chinchillas were being raised for their fur to be sold. In the front of the house there was a hedge and several poplar trees. On the side there were two pepper trees. Across the street there was a row of eucalyptus trees, the ones brought from Australia and planted in 1907 by the Cunninghams.

Some of the teachers at Bay Point Elementary School were "progressive" educators. That meant that they believed in "learning by doing," not learning by memorizing or simply reading a book and answering questions. In Miss Dalin's fourth-grade class, for example, Johnny learned math, writing, and reading skills while working with fellow students on projects such as planning, building sets, writing scripts, and acting roles in plays with topics such as "The Life of California Indians."

Another project involved teams of students going out into the community to conduct a census, gathering data about the number of people in a household, their ages, and their ethnicities. Johnny worked on the census with two other students. The group had responsibility for several houses in the southwest portion of town. They would first knock on the door of a house. When an occupant answered the door, Johnny would explain, "We are from Miss Dalin's fourth-grade class, and we're conducting a census so we know who the people are that live in Port Chicago. Would you be willing to answer a few questions for us?"

Almost all of the occupants would agree to participate. Johnny and his team would ask questions such as, "How many people live in the house? What are their ages? Where does the head of the household work? Does anyone else in the house have a job? What jobs do those people have? What church do the family members go to? Where does the family do most of its shopping for groceries?" Such data were brought back to the classroom; the data were aggregated and organized by adding, using fractions and decimals, and finding means, medians, and modes; and then reports were written and published to be made available to the community. This was a real education.

By the end of the 1930s, people wereback to work, community bonds were growing, and things appeared to be returning to normal. Unfortunately, however, once again the point of the bay was facing a new crisis—in this case, the coming of World War II.

CHAPTER 16

WORLD WAR II COMES
TO PORT CHICAGO

In the fall of 1940, Johnny moved on from the fourth grade with the progressive Miss Dalin, to a combination fifth- and sixth-grade class with an older, quite traditional Miss Brannigan. Johnny brought good skills with him and found the schoolwork rather easy. He often was restless. During his first week he was scolded twice for talking to fellow students, as well as for passing notes. Miss Brannigan finally had enough and walked over to him holding a ruler in her hand. "Johnny, you talk too much, and you bother other students. Put your hand out."

He did as he was told. "Thwack!" The sound of the ruler hitting his hand resonated throughout the room. "Ouch!" Tears began to roll down his cheeks, and other students snickered. The embarrassment was worse than the pain. After a number of similar episodes, Johnny learned to control his behavior a bit better.

However, he had another problem. The fifth-grade work was too easy. He usually was the first one to finish an assignment. He began to listen to the sixth-graders struggle with their work. Sometimes Miss Brannigan would ask sixth-graders a question that would go unanswered. For example, on one occasion she gave a word problem in math: "If a train went fifty-five miles an hour from town A to town B in three hours, how far was it from town A to town B?"

Silence. After a few minutes, Johnny blurted out, "One hundred sixty-five miles."

Another time, Miss Brannigan, in a history lesson, asked the sixth-graders, "There is a war going on in Europe. Germany leads the Axis powers. What are the Axis powers?"

Silence. Finally, Johnny, who regularly read the newspapers, spoke up. "I think Italy, Romania, and Hungary are on the side of the Germans. They also have captured Austria, Czechoslovakia, Belgium, the Netherlands, Poland, Denmark, and Norway." There was no snickering this time. Soon after, Johnny was moved to the sixth grade.

New students began to enroll at Bay Point Elementary School. Most had moved with their families to get away from the poverty of the so-called dust bowl of Arkansas, Oklahoma, and Texas. One such family was the Millers. Wilma Miller was twelve in 1931 when she, her mother, Ella, and her stepfather, Harry, left Hanna, Oklahoma, for California. They were very poor. A good meal had often consisted of bread, bacon grease, and a dollop of sugar. Their trip to California was typical of the journeys made by families at that time, the car piled high with all their worldly goods. They ended up in Port Chicago, where Harry found work in a nearby box factory. At this point, the family settled into a normal life.

Such families kept coming through the thirties, and Johnny made friends with several of these new students. He also continued to play ball, skate, and do other things with the children in his neighborhood.

At home, Johnny had regular duties to perform. One was to clean under the rabbit hutches by shoveling the droppings into a bucket and carrying it to a nearby empty lot. On occasion, he babysat Hugh. One time after he finished cleaning the hutches, he went to his mother and said to her, "I've finished my work, and I'm going to go and play ball."

Martha nodded. "Okay, but I have to do some shopping, so you'll have to take Hugh with you."

Johnny moaned, "Do I really *have* to? He's a pain."

"Yes, you do." And that ended the conversation.

The boys went down the street to where the game was being played. Johnny immediately got into the game. After a short while, one of the other boys let out a yell and said, "Johnny, your little brother smells! He pooped his pants!" Soon several other boys began to tease Johnny until he burst into tears, grabbed Hugh by the arm, and dragged him home, shouting all the way, "I'll never take you with me again." Of course he did, many times.

In the evenings, Johnny spent his time doing homework, reading books brought home from his trips with his mother to the little town library, reading the newspapers, and listening to the radio. Walter worked shift work, and the radio was in the living room just outside the parents' bedroom. When Walter was sleeping every third week before he went to work on the graveyard shift at midnight, Johnny had to keep the radio volume very low. This required him to sit in the lounge chair next to the radio with his good ear very close to the radio. His favorite programs were adventures such as *Jack Armstrong, the All-American Boy*, *The Green Hornet*, *The Shadow*, and *The Lone Ranger*. He also listened to comedies such as *Jack Benny, Fred Allen, The George Burns and Gracie Allen Show*, and *Fibber McGee and Mollie*. The advantage of listening to the radio was that it caused him to use his imagination to picture what was happening.

One other thing Johnny liked to do was visit his grandmother Chapman. Her youngest son, Jack, was only one year older than Johnny, and they enjoyed playing together. They often turned the kitchen chairs on their backs and pretended they were flying airplanes and having "dogfights." "Zoom, zoom, rat-a-tat-tat. Look out, here I come," could often be heard as the volume of play increased over time. The apartment was on the second floor, and underneath the apartment was a clothing store. Grandmother Chapman was constantly saying, "Keep it down, keep it down. They can hear you downstairs in the store." The boys responded by lowering their voices for at least a minute or two.

Johnny also liked to go to his uncle Wayne Chapman's house. Wayne was two years younger than Johnny's dad, Robbie, and he was somewhat of an inventor, especially of games. He created a football board game that allowed each player to decide what plays to call, what players to substitute, and what defenses to employ. He built a pitch-and-putt golf course in his backyard. Also, frequently there were card games at his house, particularly one called Pedro.

Martha and Walter also were card players, and they taught Johnny to play war, cribbage, and even poker, which they frequently played with family friends the Jaworskis.

Johnny was not allowed to swim, because of his bad ear. However, the family did go to public pools, and he was able to wade in the shallow water. On one occasion, the extended Chapman family held a picnic at Marsh Creek Park, at the site where the John Marsh ranch had once been. They swam or waded in the creek—which was dammed to make a pool—played baseball, and enjoyed a picnic with watermelon, hot dogs, and all of the trimmings.

Walter Rankin worked at being a good father for Johnny. He was a strict man, but he often did things with the boy. They played catch, and sometimes they went fishing in the local sloughs at the point of the bay. One evening Walter asked his stepson, "How would you like to drive with me to Oakland to watch the Oakland Oaks play the San Francisco Seals?" These were the favorite Pacific Coast League teams of all of the boys in the town.

Johnny beamed. "I would really like that! Can I get some popcorn, too?"

Walter was sitting in his favorite chair. He took his pipe out of his mouth and knocked the ashes into the nearby tray. He looked over the rim of his glasses, smiled, and said, "Of course you can, and a hot dog, too."

Walter also took Johnny to midget auto races and even once to a dog race. Johnny didn't hunt as much as many of the other young boys did. However, he did have a BB gun, which, by accident, he managed to use to put a hole in one of the windows of the Bengtsson house next door.

⚭

On the morning of December 7, 1941, Johnny Rankin was playing football with his friends on the lawn at the nearby home of Charles Morgan, the principal of Bay Point Elementary School. At approximately 11:00 a.m., Mrs. Morgan came out onto the porch in her bathrobe and with her hair in curlers and, with a terrified look on her face, told the boys gathered on her lawn that the Pearl Harbor Naval Base in Hawaii was under attack by the Japanese.

Johnny immediately ran the two blocks to his house and burst in yelling, "Mom, Dad, the Japanese have bombed Pearl Harbor!"

At first they didn't believe him. "Are you sure you weren't listening to a radio program?"

"No, it really happened. Mrs. Morgan heard it on the radio and came outside to tell us. Turn on our radio, and hear it for yourselves."

Once again, the lives of the people at the point of the bay were dramatically changed. The country was at war! Port Chicago was to become an important part of World War II. Almost immediately the US Navy purchased 1,200 shorefront acres to be used for loading ammunition for transport to the Pacific war theater and 6,300 inland acres for storing the ammunition. Also purchased on the western edge of the town was land for the construction of 250 low-cost houses for civilian employees at the naval base and their families. This housing was given the name Knox Park, after Secretary of the Navy Frank Knox.

Many of the young men of the town, like young men all across the country, enlisted in the service or signed on with the merchant marines. Only a few were classified as 4F and unable to serve. There were no conscientious objectors in the town. This made room for the youngsters and women of the town to fill work positions previously held by the young men. Johnny was no exception. He had spent a good amount of time before the war cutting weeds for many of the neighbors, including the Van Horns, who had been instrumental in changing the name of the town from Bay Point to Port Chicago and who had a large house and lot at the base of the hills. By the time he was twelve, Johnny had found jobs in a gasoline station, as a dishwasher and cleanup boy in a restaurant, and later when he was fourteen as a cleanup boy in a butcher shop.

Johnny's first real job was in the summer of 1942 at a gasoline station. He did a lot of cleaning up, but, although only twelve, he also waited on customers. He was not always successful at this. On one occasion, he was expected to wash the windows of a big car owned by one of the women of the town who was a somewhat fussy person. He was so small that in order to reach the windshield he had to climb up on the fenders. In doing so, he got grease on the fender. The woman howled at him, "Look what you've done to my fender. You've got grease all over it." She turned and faced the owner of the station. "Why don't you get an adult to do your work? This child doesn't know enough to keep off my fenders, and he has gotten them greasy by getting up on them. So what are you going to do about it?"

The owner, who was a pretty relaxed person, walked slowly over to the car, took a rag out of his back pocket, and wiped off the little bit of grease. To Johnny he said only, "Don't worry about her. She's a pain in the ass. Just try to be careful and not get the fenders.dirty."

Another time Johnny was supposed to change the oil in a car. He did everything correctly in the beginning. He took out the plug

in the oil pan, allowing the old oil to pour out into a receptacle. He
then put in four quarts of new oil. However, he forgot to put the
plug back in the bottom of the oil pan. The owner came running
out of the office and yelled at him, "The oil is running out onto the
ground." Although he was scolded, he was not made to pay for the
oil. "I'll never make such a dumb mistake again," Johnny vowed
to himself.

While not working for pay, Johnny and other boys were busy
helping the war effort by volunteering to do odd jobs for some of the
men who were building the navy base. For example, trucks would
drive into the hills, where they were loaded with dirt to be used to
fill in the marshland at the point of the bay where the loading docks
were being built. Some of the boys did odd jobs for the drivers, such
as getting sandwiches and soft drinks. What Johnny liked most was
helping to load the water trucks, which filled their tanks at fire hy-
drants and then drove to where the dirt was being spread. The water
trucks would spray the dirt as it was tamped down so that it would
ultimately make solid land. Johnny would climb up on the tank of
the truck and hold the hose so that the water went into the tank.

After the Pearl Harbor attack, it was feared that the Japanese
might try to attack targets on the mainland. In order to guard against
such an event, the Aircraft Warning Service was created. This service involved training civilian volunteers as airplane spotters. In
fact, some of the best spotters turned out to be young boys who
were teamed with adults. They were good spotters because they
were interested in airplanes and quickly learned the silhouettes of
the many planes that could be spotted.

When he was twelve, Johnny volunteered and was paired with a
neighbor, Mrs. Crane. She was in her midforties, a pleasant woman
who was a bit stout, wore glasses, and appeared to be distracted at
times. Johnny chalked that up to the fact that her son had just joined
the army and she was worried about him. She was an eager volunteer

and very patient with Johnny. In fact, he knew more about airplanes than she did. Training consisted of receiving a manual showing the silhouettes of American and enemy planes, and then taking a test at home and sending it in to the control center, where it was scored. Each team worked up to three times a week for six hours each time. The team would climb up to the roof of the legion hall, where a newly built platform was equipped with railings, necessary supplies, and a telephone. A typical shift involved recording and reporting as many planes as they could spot. On balance, the number was somewhere around twenty planes per shift. Most often individual planes would be spotted and reported by two or more posts, allowing the flight of the planes to be triangulated and tracked. It has been estimated that as many as 750,000 volunteers were involved in the work of the Aircraft Warning Service throughout the United States.

When Johnny and/or Mrs. Crane spotted a plane, they joined together to identify its make and report it to the center in charge of plotting flight patterns. They would spot both military and private planes. On one occasion, what appeared to be a private plane was identified by Mrs. Crane. "It's a private Beech AT-10 with a lower wing and two engines."

Johnny didn't agree. "It looks somewhat like the AT-10, but I think it is a Cessna AT-17, the Bobcat, and it's an army plane." They called in their different opinions to the center, and, lo and behold, found that Johnny was correct. "Well, well," said Mrs. Crane, polishing her glasses on the apron she always wore, "I'm glad you're my partner, young man."

Johnny tried to be diplomatic and not competitive with Mrs. Crane. Once, a dual-fuselage Lockheed P-38 fighter plane flew over. Johnny knew what it was, but he deferred to Mrs. Crane. She said, "It's a P-38." He agreed and pretended not to know. They were a good pair.

ᏫᎷᎩ

Early in the war, the Axis powers were successful in making a number of major advances. In Europe in 1941, the Germans, with their
Italian and Balkan allies, rapidly drove through the Soviet Union to
the outskirts of Moscow and Leningrad. They captured the Crimea
and laid siege to Stalingrad. The Japanese captured the Philippines,
seized Guam, and captured much of the Dutch East Indies. They
also made gains against the British, taking Burma and Singapore.
They were victorious in a number of sea battles, and they even
bombed Darwin in Australia.

Johnny followed the course of the war in the newspapers, on the
radio news reports, and in the movie theater, where the Pathé news
always played as part of the program. The school also sponsored
activities that were intended to help the war effort. Students were
encouraged to buy war savings stamps, which were available in ten-
cent and twenty-five-cent versions. They were collected in books,
and when they reached the sum of $18.75, they could be used to pur-
chase a war bond, which was redeemable in ten years for $25. There
was a kind of informal race among the schoolchildren to see who
could buy the most. Because of his part-time jobs, Johnny had extra
money and bought stamps; by the time he was twelve years old, he
had saved enough for three bonds. Elisa Mercurio was second. She
did part-time work for her father, who owned a local business, and
she had purchased enough for two bonds and another $10 in stamps.
Several other classmates had purchased more than one bond.

Sometimes students were released from classes to search their
neighborhoods and nearby empty fields for scrap metal. Johnny was
assigned to a team headed by an eighth grader, Aldo Contavalli. Two
other boys and two girls also were on the team. When it was time
to begin the search, the team came together on one of the school's
basketball courts. Aldo asked, "Where should we go? Where can
we find the most scrap metal?"

One of the girls spoke up. "I've collected a lot of tin foil from gum wrappers. I can donate it. Maybe other people in town would have some to give."

Aldo liked the idea. He made a sweeping movement to the two girls. "Why don't the two of you go from door to door to as many houses as possible south of the highway and see how much foil you can get. We'll meet back here at 4:00 p.m. It's now 9:30, so that will give you six and a half hours." The girls were very happy with the idea. Laughing and chattering, they went on their way. "We have our lunches with us. We'll see you at 4:00."

Aldo pressed on. "I've seen metal scraps down by the railroad tracks. I think we should go down there and look. The four of us may have to make more than one trip, because some pieces might be heavy."

There was much nodding of heads. Johnny added, "If we run out of metal from the tracks, maybe we can go to some of the businesses. They may have some pieces of metal they would give us. This should be fun. Let's ask the school janitor if we can store what we find in his closet. It's pretty big. I'll bet we can get more than any other group."

Off they went. The group finished and met back at the basketball court at 4:00 p.m. The girls had come back with thirty-three balls of tin foil of various sizes. They were pretty pleased with themselves. "I'll bet we can do even better if we try to work the north side of the highway. Also, several people told us they had other pieces of metal we could go back and get later this week."

Aldo again was pleased. "How many of you could meet tomorrow after school and go back to some of these houses and get their other metal?"

Everyone in the group responded in the affirmative.

The four boys had made five trips to the area by the tracks and had gathered a total of about three hundred pounds of metal, which was now in the janitor's closet. Aldo told the girls, "We also tried a few businesses, but no luck. We only got a few pieces of metal, and all of those came from the garage across the street from the theater. Even so, our group did a great job. I hope all the other groups did as well."

Some groups did, and some didn't. A few groups didn't even bother to look for metal. They simply played or just walked around town. On balance, the day was a successful one. Students knew that tomorrow the metal would be driven in several trucks owned by volunteers and turned in to a collection center in Martinez; it ultimately would be melted down and used to make essential products for the war. The most important part of the scrap drives was their ability to boost morale and promote patriotism.

Civilians made many sacrifices during World War II. A major one was complying with a complex system of rationing. Red stamps were used for meat, butter, fat, oils, and most cheeses. Blue stamps covered canned and bottled goods, frozen fruits and vegetables, juices, dry beans, and baby food. Each family was issued a war ration book. Each stamp authorized a certain quantity and time limit.

⬭⬭⬭

By 1936, the Millers were settled residents of Port Chicago and hadn't been thought of as "Okies" for a long time. In 1937, when she was seventeen, Wilma married Frank Chapman, a younger brother of Robert Chapman, Johnny's birth father.

In the early thirties, Frank had been enrolled in the Civilian Conservation Corps and had worked at clearing brush in the Marsh Creek area. For this he received room and board as well as a token salary. By 1936, he had been hired as a carpenter's apprentice at the Nichols Chemical plant just five miles from Port Chicago.

The couple's first daughter, Marni, was born in 1938. Four years later, after the war broke out, Wilma went to work as the cashier at the largest grocery store in the town. This put her in charge of collecting the ration stamps. Frequently, customers were confused about the stamps. Wilma could often be heard diplomatically saying things such as, "I'm sorry, Mrs. Smith, but you cannot use the blue stamps for cooking oil. That takes red stamps," or "I'm sorry, Mrs. Jones, but these red stamps are out-of-date. Perhaps you would like to exchange the butter for oleo, which doesn't need stamps."

Mrs. Jones became angry and shouted, "You can *keep* your damned stamps," leaving her groceries and stomping out of the store. Fortunately for Wilma, most frustrated people simply grumbled and tried to do their best with their stamps.

In addition to food, clothing, shoes, gasoline, tires, and fuel oil also were rationed. In the case of gasoline, there were four classifications. An "A" classification entitled the holder to four gallons per week. A "B" classification was worth eight gallons per week, and it was made available to workers in essential industries such as the oil refineries. Walter Rankin, who worked at the Shell Oil refinery seven miles away in Martinez, was eligible for this level. A "B" was posted on a stamp that was placed in the corner of his windshield. Walter and other men who worked at the refinery and lived in Port Chicago shared rides, thus leaving them all some gasoline left over. In Walter's case, he was often able to drive to Oakland to visit his brothers and their families, as well as his mother, who lived with one of his brothers. There were other classifications: "C" with more gasoline for doctors, "X" or unlimited gasoline for politicians and other important people, and "T" for trucks and tractors.

Finally, as a contribution to the war effort, most people developed victory gardens in which they grew vegetables and various kinds of beans. One of Johnny's jobs was to weed and water the family garden. Sometimes whole families would go to farms to pick fruit and vegetables and then bring them home to can them for year-round use.

Johnny began to notice girls when he was eleven and in the seventh grade, just before the war began. He had sneaked a kiss from a classmate a couple of years earlier, but that didn't amount to anything. His first serious encounter was with a neighbor girl, Gloria Grumman, who was two years younger than him. She was a pretty blond girl with bobbed hair. She was very talkative and quite bright. She was also a tomboy. Earlier, Gloria and Johnny had often played and roller-skated together, along with Gloria's younger brother, Dennis. One day the two of them were playing hide-and-go-seek. Johnny was *it* and had to find Gloria. After hunting all over the neighborhood, he went out into the lot across the street from his house where the eucalyptus grove was. Beyond the trees was an open field with tall grass.

Johnny walked into the tall grass and, lo and behold, there was Gloria. He tagged her, and they began to push and pull at each other, giggling all the time. Finally, things got a bit more serious, and the game turned to one of "you show me yours, and I'll show you mine." For several months the two children kept up their sexual explorations, but nothing serious ever came to pass, and their parents never learned about it.

Johnny was twelve years old when he entered eighth grade. Because he'd skipped fifth grade, he was younger than most of his classmates. He also was smaller than most of them, and although he no longer wore overalls, his clothes were plain and often mended. Being brighter than most of his classmates didn't win him any popularity contests. He usually was one of the last children chosen when teams were being formed to play games, and he often was picked on by older, bigger boys. In the fall of his eighth-grade year, there was an election for student body officers. Traditionally, it was eighth-graders who won these elections. Johnny was nominated for the office of vice president. However, there was a well-organized campaign to elect one of the popular sixth-grade boys rather than

Johnny. The sixth-grader won, and Johnny was devastated. One of his friends tried to make him feel better. "It was very close, Johnny. You shouldn't feel bad."

Though he didn't mean it, Johnny responded, "I didn't want it anyway."

For the first time, in the eighth grade, Johnny fell in love. Elisa Mercurio had flashing dark eyes, short dark hair, and a ready smile. She was very popular with her classmates and had been elected secretary of the student body. Johnny was in awe of her.

The girls of the eighth grade organized several parties, which many of the seventh- and eighth-grade students attended. The favorite game at these parties was spin the bottle. At one party, Johnny tried very hard to spin the bottle so that it pointed at Elisa. He finally was successful, and the couple went into the adjoining bedroom to kiss. They then returned to the front room and sat in the circle where the bottle was spun. The next time Elisa spun the bottle, it pointed at Johnny. When he spun again, it pointed at Elisa. This went on for several turns until Johnny got up the nerve to ask, "Can't we just stay here by ourselves instead of going in and out of the front room?"

Elisa blushed and answered, "That sounds like a good idea." With that, she kissed Johnny again.

Johnny asked Elisa if he could walk her home. She agreed. The walk began in silence. Both of them were thinking about what had happened. Finally, Johnny said, "I really like you, Elisa. Would you be my girlfriend?"

Elisa responded, "I like you, too, Johnny, but I don't think my father would allow it. You aren't Catholic, and my father has made it clear that I should marry a Catholic who has promise of being rich. We can be friends, though."

Johnny was very disappointed, but he had no options. On the verge of tears, he said, "Yes, we can be good friends."

At the eighth-grade graduation ceremony, Johnny received

an award as the outstanding boy scholar, sponsored by the Royal Neighbors, an all-female service organization. Interestingly, Wilma Chapman, Johnny's aunt, was the president of the organization. Elisa received the award as the outstanding girl scholar. As they stood side by side on the stage, Elisa whispered to Johnny, "We did it! I'm proud of you."

⟨∞⟩

In 1943, as Johnny began his four years of high school, the war was rapidly turning in favor of the Allies. British and American planes were regularly bombing German cities, particularly those like Stuttgart, which was a major site for the production of wartime goods. The Germans were sending civilians out of Berlin because of the bombing. The Allied troops had driven the Germans out of North Africa, had taken Sicily, and had landed in Italy. Before the end of the year, Italy surrendered to the Allies.

On the eastern front, the Soviets, who had been provided with a great deal of war material by the United States, were driving the Germans back toward the western border of the Soviet Union.

In the Pacific, the British had run the Japanese out of Burma. The Americans and Australians had taken New Guinea, and the Americans were beginning their island hopping on the way to Japan. Also, a good deal of damage had been done to the Japanese fleet.

⟨∞⟩

To get to Mt. Diablo High School in Concord, Johnny and other students from Port Chicago no longer rode a train. They went in a bus. Boys who stayed after school for sports or other activities had to hitchhike home. Fortunately, this was a safe practice in those days—in most cases, they were picked up by neighbors.

Johnny was enrolled in the college preparation track. Most of the girls, including Elisa, took classes in the commercial track, being prepared as secretaries or office workers. There also was a general track that offered low-level academic classes as well as shop and home economics classes. In 1943 there were no black students at the high school, and most Mexican students had dropped out of school after eighth grade. They found jobs, which were plentiful because of the need for labor while so many young men were in the service.

As a freshman, Johnny at first attempted to have lunch with the "in crowd," consisting of mostly popular athletes, including Aldo Contavalli. They gathered at one of the long stairways, and there was a pecking order. The most popular sat at the top, and the less popular were arrayed in order down the stairway. Johnny found himself relegated to the bottom stair. As the year went on, however, he began to make friends with others in his college prep classes, and by November he was eating lunch with them instead.

Johnny did well in all of his classes with the exception of algebra. He started off fine, but fell behind as the class moved on. His work was good in his other classes, which included English, PE, Spanish, a required freshman orientation class, study hall, and shop. College prep students had one semester of wood shop and one semester of metal shop. In wood shop, Johnny managed to plane a board to almost nothing. In metal shop he made a sort of crooked sugar scoop and a well-hammered metal ashtray for his parents.

Johnny still admired Elisa, but because of their different tracks, they hardly ever saw each other except when they rode the bus to and from school. However, in his orientation class, a new girl, Margaret Charles, enrolled during the second week. Because she was a sophomore transfer and two years older than him, she seemed very poised. With her long brown hair, beautiful face, and outgoing personality, Johnny found her enchanting and tried hard to make her acquaintance. They also were enrolled in the same Spanish class and became good friends for the next three years. During that time she was very popular, and in her senior year she became the girlfriend of the football quarterback, who was her own age.

Johnny frequently went alone to dances at the high school. He would join the other boys, watching the dancers and eyeing the girls who had come alone and gathered with other girls. Occasionally he would ask a girl to dance, but not very often. The boys would be dressed in clean jeans, their shoes would be shined, their hair would be neatly combed, and they often would have on shaving lotion. The girls wore their best dresses, which were cut just below the knees as a means of saving cloth for the war. They also had their hair done neatly, and, unlike during school hours, they would wear a hint of rouge and lipstick. The teacher chaperones would make sure that the dancers kept each other at arm's length.

Much of the music at dances focused on the war. For example, one popular song sung by Vera Lynn, "I'll Be Seeing You," was frequently played at dances:

> *I'll be seeing you in all the old familiar places*
> *That this heart of mine embraces all day through—*
> *In that small café, the park across the way,*
> *The children's carousel, the chestnut trees, the wishing well.*
> *I'll be seeing you in every lovely summer's day,*
> *In everything that's light and gay.*
> *I'll always think of you that way.*
> *I'll find you in the morning sun*
> *And when the night is new.*
> *I'll be looking at the moon, but I'll be seeing you.*

As another part of the war effort, students were organized into groups and sent to local farms to help harvest crops. Johnny's group made trips to pick tomatoes on three separate days. On their own,

Johnny and his friend Nikos Kostupolous knocked, picked, and husked walnuts in the many groves of the area. In the beginning, Johnny observed, "Nikos, you're taller than me, so you should use the long pole to knock the walnuts down. I'll pick them up and husk them. If you get too many on the ground, you can help me husk." Nikos agreed to this arrangement, and between them they were paid fifty cents for each full large burlap bag. This was good money for young boys at that time.

Sports were still a major activity of the boys of the town. Without intending to do so, the navy enhanced the playing of baseball and football by taking the dirt dug from the hills south of the town and using it to fill in the marshy area at the point of the bay. This digging left large dug-out areas that the boys converted to athletic fields. Initially, they took shovels, spades, and rakes to the hills and leveled off the fields. They even found chalk to line the fields. There was a natural cutoff line on a cliff that served as a fence. When a baseball was hit above the line, it was considered a home run.

In local sports, the greatest rivalry was that between the boys who lived on the hill side of town versus the boys who lived on the bay side of the town. Often the boys would taunt each other with such comments as, "You guys are really dumb. You're so dumb, even your parents make you wear a dunce cap." Finally, the bayside boys, tired of the taunts, challenged the hill-side boys to a football game on the area that had been dug out by the navy. Boys from both sides went to the site and prepared it for the big game. In addition to raking and lining the field, they built goalposts.

When the time came for the game, many people of the town— young and old, men and women—came to watch. The game went on for three and a half quarters, and the score was nothing to nothing. Off in the distance a train went by and blew its whistle. The bay-side boys thought the game was over, so they ran off the field.

Three plays later the hill-side boys scored a touchdown. Which group proved to be the dumbest?

⌘

The navy base grew rapidly in 1942 and 1943. In addition to the civilian housing at Knox Park, there was a great deal of construction at the tidal area as well as at the inland storage area. At the tidal area there were barracks for enlisted men; bachelor officer quarters for officers; separate mess facilities for enlisted men and officers; and recreation facilities for enlisted men, officers, and civilians that included an auditorium, movie theater, gymnasium, swimming pool, pool room, bowling alleys, exercise room, soda fountain, and store. There were a number of other buildings, including offices, wood and metal shops, a firehouse, a laundry, and storage buildings. At the waterfront there were three piers with two berthing spaces each for deep-draught vessels, a barge pier, and additional mooring facilities for six barges.

The naval enlisted men made a mark on the town. Two nightclubs catered to Negro sailors, and young black girls came from nearby towns to dance and drink with them. The white sailors, stationed at the base or off ships that were loading, went to three bars in the town. Some of these young men were lucky enough to find girls from the town to date. There were mixed feelings about these young men, particularly if they became intoxicated and behaved badly. One could hear arguments among men of the town, with statements such as, "The navy should keep these sailors on the base. We shouldn't have to put up with their drunkenness and bad behavior." Sometimes there would be agreement, but often someone would come back with a statement such as, "We should treat these boys as well as we would our own sons. After all, our boys are stationed somewhere, and we would want them to be treated well, wouldn't we?" The arguments went on and on, but in the main, the townspeople were tolerant of the sailors. Some families even invited sailors to an occasional dinner at their homes.

With the war going better for the Allies, positive attitudes were on the rise in the town of Port Chicago, along with a sense of pride. People were working hard and coping well with the hardships of war. What no one could have foreseen was a catastrophe that, once again, would put great stress on the people at the point of the bay.

CHAPTER 17

THE PORT CHICAGO
EXPLOSION

On the night of July 17, 1944, Johnny left the house after dinner
and walked to what was usually an empty lot near the Bay Point
Elementary School. On this night the lot was not empty: a traveling
carnival with rides and booths had been set up that morning. There
also was a circus-like big top with clowns, some wild animals, and
a few acts. There Johnny met a number of his friends, including
Nikos, Eric Johnson, Marco Contavalli, and Bart Cox. A contest
ensued at the booth where the boys threw baseballs at clay bottles
painted silver. "Look at that," yelped Marco. "I got three bottles."
"Throw again," said Johnny. "Two more and you get a prize."
Marco did throw again, and he did get two more. He received
a small stuffed doll. "What am I going to do with this?" he
grumbled.

"Give it to your sweetheart," answered Nikos with a big laugh.
Straightening his shoulders, Marco responded gruffly, "I don't have
a girlfriend."

The boys moved on to the "high striker," a contest of strength
in which a player uses a long hammer to hit a block that rises to
ring a bell at the top of a tower. Once again Marco proved to be the
best. To the surprise of the other boys, Johnny was a close second
because, while he was not really very strong, he did know how to
swing the hammer at the correct angle to send the block toward the
top. Bart's response to all of this was, "You two are just lucky. It
doesn't take any brains to hit a block."

Johnny responded, "Oh, yes, it does. You have to know *how* to hit the block." Once again, the boys moved along. They walked by the carousel, and that was when Johnny saw Elisa Mercurio with her cousin Tina Bianci. They were each riding a horse. Johnny stopped to watch the two girls. After the ride, he went over to them and asked if they would like some cotton candy. Tina answered, "That would be lovely." Elisa agreed.

Marco heard this exchange. "Maybe you should have gotten the prize so you could give it to Elisa," he said, walking on with Nikos, Eric, and Bart.

Johnny blushed and walked over with the girls to the cotton candy machine. Together the trio strolled around the carnival, taking in the Ferris wheel and the house of mirrors. At that point, to Johnny's dismay, the girls indicated that they had to leave for home. Johnny was torn. He would have liked to walk with them, but he also wanted to stay with his friends because they had not yet gone to the event they all wanted to see—the "hootchy" show.

After saying good-night to the girls, Johnny caught up with his friends, and they continued around the carnival, going on the cyclone ride, watching the fire-eating man, and then finally getting up the nerve to try to get into the hootchy show. When they tried to buy tickets, the man at the door laughed. "No tickets for you, boys. Come back in a few years after you've grown up."

They begged the man to let them in, and he finally agreed. He took their money and when no one was looking shooed them in. The boys were wide-eyed as two older women, slightly the worse for wear and somewhat overweight, did a sort of dance around a small stage and quickly removed their upper garments, exposing their breasts for a few seconds at a time. For the boys, this was a big deal, something to brag about!

At about 9:30, the boys split up. Nikos, Marco, and Johnny decided to go home, while Eric and Bart chose to go to the late movie at the local movie house to see the war film *China,* starring Loretta Young, Alan Ladd, and William Bendix.

_ ᏎᏫᏪᎤ _

The liberty ship *E. A. Bryan* had been moored at the Port Chicago Naval Base for four days, being loaded with ammunition and explosives night and day. By 10:00 p.m. on the night of the carnival, the ship had taken on 4,600 tons of munitions and 1,780 tons of high explosives. Sixteen rail cars loaded with 430 more tons of high explosives were on the pier alongside the ship.

A second ship, the *Quinault Victory*, was on the other side of the pier. It was brand-new and preparing for its maiden voyage. It had moored at about 6:00 p.m. and was being prepared for loading beginning at midnight. Railroad cars carrying ammunition and bombs were waiting on the pier alongside.

The pier was very congested with men, equipment, a locomotive, sixteen railroad boxcars, and tons of bombs and projectiles ready to be loaded. About one hundred black sailors who had recently arrived at the base were busy rigging the ships in preparation for the loading. Many of them were afraid and often asked if the job was safe. "There is no danger that the bombs will explode, because they have no detonators," the officers in charge would assure them.

Clearly they were wrong. The *Quinault Victory* exploded first at 10:18:47 p.m., followed in a few seconds by the explosion of the fully loaded *E. A. Bryan,* which went off like an enormous bomb and sent a column of fire and smoke more than twelve thousand feet into the air.

The University of California seismograph, fifty miles away in Berkeley, shuddered for three full minutes and recorded an impact equivalent to a 3.4 magnitude earthquake. An Army Air Force C-47 cargo plane flying at about nine thousand feet above the blast saw a white flash with a large smoke ring about three miles wide. The pilot described pieces of white-hot metal, some as large as a house, flying straight up past the plane. The copilot reported a "fireworks display" that lasted about a minute.

All 319 of the men on the pier and aboard the two ships were instantly killed. Two hundred of them were black enlisted men.

It was never determined what caused the explosions. However, it was known that officers and men assigned to the task of loading the ships had no training or experience handling cargo, let alone munitions or explosives. Furthermore, competition was encouraged: average loading rates were posted for each group of men loading, and incentives were awarded for high performance. It also was known that officers often bet on the results. In none of this was safety of the highest concern.

Johnny got home at about 10:00 p.m. and found his mother and stepfather sitting at the kitchen table having a snack and coffee while they played a game of cribbage. Walter was on the graveyard shift so would be going to work in about forty-five minutes.

Martha put her cards down and got up to clear away the coffee cups. The night was hot, and her old blue dress hung limply from her thin shoulders. "How was it?" she asked with a smile, wishing she could have gone to the carnival herself, perhaps with her friend Gizela Zaworski.

"It was great," Johnny answered enthusiastically. "We had a lot of fun. I didn't want to go to the movie, so came home early." He looked to his right as he moved through the kitchen. His brother, Hugh, was asleep in the little bedroom. Johnny went into the front room, where he found the couch already made into a bed by his mother. He put on his pajamas and turned the light on so that he could read *Tarzan of the Apes.*

Johnny read for about ten minutes and then put the book down and turned off the light. He had barely closed his eyes when the first explosion rocked the house and the kitchen light went out. The second, much larger explosion followed. The sky lit up, and Martha began screaming. Walter had been knocked off his chair and had landed in a box of plums that they had picked earlier that day for canning. Things seemed to move in slow motion during the flash as Martha saw Walter in a mess of red on the floor. Her first thought was that he was hurt badly and bloodied. She screamed again.

"Martha, stop hollering. I'm fine—just covered with plum juice … see?" Walter got a small candle and lit it so she could see that he really wasn't hurt. "Why don't you start cleaning up in here, and I'll go check on the boys." But Martha was frozen at the broken window, looking north in the direction of the burning piers.

Walter speculated, "I wonder if we have been attacked by the Japanese." He dashed into Hugh's tiny bedroom and found his five-year-old son huddled way down under the covers, still sound asleep. "Geez Louise," he muttered to himself. "That kid sure can sleep!" He pushed open the curtains covering the window at the foot of Hugh's bed, and that's when he saw that the windowpane had shattered in the blast. Bits of glass were all over Hugh's pillow.

Martha appeared in the doorway with a candle just moments later and found her husband carefully picking pieces of glass off the pillow. "Shh, kiddo. He's still asleep, and he's fine. Let's try not to wake him up yet. Here, you work on this," he said, handing her the wastebasket he was using to collect the glass. "I'll go and see about Johnny."

Johnny, not yet asleep, was up and at the front door with the first blast and on the steps when the second blast occurred. "Dad, Dad! Can I get dressed and go see what happened?" he begged when Walter stepped to the door.

"Definitely not," Walter answered, taking the boy's arm. "It's too dangerous. There may be more explosions. Get back inside!"

Johnny went back to his bed, but, too excited to sleep, he quietly crept back to the door and opened it a crack. His father was outside talking to their neighbor Kent Grumman, Gloria Grumman's father. Johnny couldn't hear what they were saying, but when Walter came back into the house, Johnny overheard him tell his mother, "Seems two ships blew up at the navy base. There's a lot of damage at the base and in town. Kent talked with a county sheriff's deputy who told him that even though martial law would be maintained for several days to prevent looting, we'll be able to go to work tomorrow."

Martha and Walter swept up the broken glass in Hugh's room, the kitchen, the bathroom, and their bedroom by candlelight. Shortly after they finished cleaning up the glass, there was a knock on the door. Walter opened it to find two representatives of the Salvation Army. Walter, a bit nonplussed, asked, "How may I help you, gentlemen?"

One of the men responded, "We're from the Salvation Army, and we are going from door to door to see if there is anything at all that we can do for you. We have blankets, food, medical supplies, and even some clothing. Can we be of any help to you?"

Walter said, "No, I think we're okay, but thanks for asking." The men moved on to the next house. Walter learned later that the Red Cross also offered help. They set up an office at the elementary school, and people wanting help had to go there, fill out paperwork, and hope to get the help they needed. They also set up a canteen at the school prepared to feed anyone who came for a meal. The Red Cross also solicited contributions from those who went to the school.

Johnny went out the next morning and walked to Nikos's house. As far as he could see, all of the windows in the houses he passed were blown out. He saw chunks of steel in a field and in the road, and it looked like one had gone through the roof of a house. A couple of houses had doors off their hinges, and some eaves were hanging down from the roofs. The Kostupolous house was no exception. All the windows were gone, and the roof on a shed in the back was caved in. However, all of the broken glass had been cleaned up.

Nikos answered the door, and Johnny asked, "Can you come out? Let's walk around the town and see what's happened."

"I have to bring in some wood for the stove. After that, I can go with you. Just wait a minute."

Soon the boys were walking toward the downtown area. They first came to the movie theater on Main Street. The glass from the ticket booth was all over the sidewalk, and the north side of the theater facing the navy base was blown in.

Next they turned north on Main Street toward the busiest part of town. On the way they saw a large piece of metal in the middle of the street. When they got to the center of town, they found a crowd of people milling around looking at the damage. There was not a window in place, and many building fronts and walls were caved in. The justice of the peace's office was open in the front, and the inside was in shambles, with big pieces of plaster fallen from the ceiling and furniture and shelving strewn all around. All of the businesses were closed, and some, including the post office, were boarded up.

Johnny and Nikos were joined by their friends Eric Johnson and Bart Cox, who had been in the theater the night before. Eric described the scene inside the theater. "Just as the explosion went off, there was a bombing scene in the movie. The theater shook a lot, and it seemed to be the most real movie we'd ever seen. But then the side of the theater blew in, and we knew that it was more than the movie. Everyone ran out to see what had happened."

Bart added, "All the girls were screaming, but I don't think anyone was hurt in the theater. Maybe there were a few scratches."

The four boys, now joined by Marco Contavalli and his brother

Guilio, kept moving north from the main part of town toward the navy base. On the way they came upon a small crowd watching something in the street. The boys tried to push forward to get a better look, but they were kept back by soldiers.

Johnny turned to the sailor standing next to him and asked, "What's going on? Those men in the street are all dressed up like something out of a *Flash Gordon* movie." They were dressed in heavy, padded suits.

The sailor explained, "That's an army bomb squad. They're disarming a live bomb that landed here after the explosion."

The boys walked way around the crowd and continued north toward the navy base until they came to the Southern Pacific Railroad station, where they found the roof caved in, the whole northern wall gone, all of the windows blown out, and everything inside in a jumble. Later, the depot agent, who lived with his family above the station, recalled the night of the explosion. "I looked down at the port, and it was lit up like daytime. I was standing at the window, and the glass blew out into my face." Luckily, he had only a few scratches, and none of the glass went into his eyes.

The boys walked back through the town and headed for the hills just to the south to get a better view. On the way up the hill, Guilio shouted, "Stop! Look at that. What is it?" The boys crowded around, and Bart let out a gasp. "It looks like part of a leg with a piece of pants over it. Do you see the toes?"

Nikos chimed in, "Look over here. This is an arm, but the hand is gone."

The boys kept searching the area and found more pieces of bodies. Eric asked, "Do you think we should pick the pieces up and take them to one of the soldiers in town?"

Johnny responded, "No, I think we should find some of the soldiers and tell them what we have found. They can take care of things themselves."

With that, the group returned to town and eventually split up. Johnny headed for home. On the way he decided to stop at the house of his aunt and uncle, Wilma and Frank Chapman. They were home, as were his six-year-old cousin, Marni, and Carol, the baby. Only one window on the west side of the house was intact; all of the others had been blown out. Marni took Johnny into her little sister's room to show him what had happened there during the explosion. One of the six-pound solid iron weights from a nearby window had come loose and with its pulley had flown across the room and wrapped itself around the corner of the baby's crib. It had come very close to hitting Carol. This was just one of many close calls resulting from the explosion in the 660 houses of the town. Fortunately, though, no one in the town itself had been killed. There were some 109 injuries, most of them minor.

During the night and early morning of July 18, the injured at the navy base were removed to hospitals, and many of the uninjured were sent to other military locations. By midmorning all of the fires had been put out. Many of the uninjured sailors volunteered for cleanup duty. The cleanup detail began early in the morning to dig into the wreckage of the pier and tear out the damaged portions. Some men were assigned to pick up corpses and body parts. It was gruesome work: a shoe with a foot in it, a head floating in the water, an arm. Of the 319 dead, only 51 were identifiable.

Rebuilding began almost immediately. Telephone service was restored within three hours after the explosion. By the third day all essential utilities were working. By July 19 contracts were let for immediate reconstruction of magazine facilities, buildings on the base, and the pier. On July 20 the navy moved a contingent of Seabees and their equipment to the base.

The navy asked Congress to give each victim's family $5,000. Representative John Rankin of Mississippi insisted on reducing that amount to $2,000 when he learned that most of the dead were black men. Congress settled on $3,000.

Despite the explosion, by the end of July the navy announced a plan to greatly expand the base at Port Chicago into one of the country's largest supply bases. A budget of approximately $20 million was drawn up for the expansion.

By late July the navy had set up a claims board to assess the total amount of damage to the town. Almost 90 percent of the homes had sustained damage. Townspeople worried about who would pay for property damage. Johnny overheard Walter, Kent Grumman, and another neighbor, Luigi Amato, discussing payment for repairs they wanted to make.

Amato said, "I think the navy should buy the whole town for a good price. Then they can use it for living space for the base when it is expanded. Their civilian employees would be happy, they wouldn't have to worry about other civilians getting hurt, and most important, we would get a fair amount for our property and not even have to repair it."

Grumman scratched his wiry beard, stroked his mustache, and responded, "I think we should stay put, get our repairs paid for, and, in addition, get paid for mental and physical damage. This damned thing has been very stressful for all of us, and we deserve to get compensated for that."

Walter was the most realistic of the three. "I don't think the navy is ready to pay the whole town a lot of money for its property. Neither do I think we will get money for physical damage, and we sure as hell won't get money for mental stress. What we need to do is accept payment for the actual costs of repairs. That means we need to keep careful records of what materials we buy and what we pay people who do the work for us."

The three discussed the matter for a good while longer, and, as it turned out, the three ideas were debated for some time by many of the townspeople.

What did happen was that the government provided a number of carpenters to aid with repairs, and the Red Cross provided a great deal of building material. The US government set up a panel to review claims for damages. Nearly ten thousand claims were filed, and over 90 percent were for property damage. The rest were personal injury claims. Within six months nearly all of the houses and businesses in the town had been reconstructed.

During these rebuilding months, the navy organized special programs for the children of the town. On several occasions they took large groups to Marsh Creek for swimming, games, and picnics. The children who participated loved the excursions, but they remained totally unaware of other events that were unfolding at the navy base.

⊙෴෴෴⊙

The invasion of German-occupied Western Europe had begun on the beaches of Normandy one month before the explosion in Port Chicago. By August, Paris was freed, and by September, the Allies entered Germany. By the end of December, US troops captured Bastogne in the Battle of the Bulge, thus overcoming the last-ditch stand of the Germans. Nightly and daytime air raids were carried out, destroying much of the German war machine and bringing mass destruction to German cities.

In Eastern Europe at the time of the Port Chicago explosion, German forces had mostly been driven out of the Soviet Union, and the Soviets were moving into the Baltic countries. By the end of the year they were moving across much of Eastern Europe. Romania switched sides and joined the Allies, Hungary and Yugoslavia were invaded, and Poland was occupied.

In the Pacific, US troops took Japanese-held islands one by one, including Saipan, Tinian, Guam, and other islands in the Marianas group. Leyte island in the Philippines was invaded, US planes began to bomb Okinawa, and in late November twenty four B-29s bombed the Nakajima aircraft factory near Tokyo.

On the home front, people had settled into their wartime routines. There was little complaining about sacrifices that had to be made. Patriotism was the dominant feeling in the land, including in Port Chicago. These feelings were promoted by the movies of the day, as well as by the songs that filled the airwaves. One such song was "Till Then."

Till then, my darling, please wait for me.
Till then, no matter when it may be.
One day I know I'll be home again.
Please wait till then ...

ᐊᗡᗡᗡᓷ

Back in school in his sophomore year, Johnny enjoyed all of his sophomore classes, particularly geometry and biology. The geometry teacher was an older man who seemed distracted a great deal of the time. Johnny made a new friend in the class, Bob Newman, who always seemed to be joking and, at times, annoyed the teacher. In one memorable class session, the lesson was about circles, and Bob described a "circumcised circle." The teacher either missed the mistake or decided not to acknowledge it. Only a few of the students noticed it, and the best they could do was give a slight snicker.

Johnny's homework load was heavier than it had been in his freshman year. He participated in far fewer ball games in Port Chicago, since a number of his friends had become involved in sports at the high school. After the town built two new pool halls, he and his friends began to play a good deal of pool. Johnny and his friend Bart also liked to go to the roller-skating rink in Martinez. Because he had roller-skated a good deal on the sidewalk in front of his house, he was pretty good at it. The rink also was a great place to meet girls.

At fourteen years of age, Johnny attended services at the Congregational church almost every Sunday, although no one else in his family did. The Congregational church was kitty-corner to the local Catholic church. Services at the Catholic church were from 9:00 a.m. to 10:00 a.m. Those at the Congregational church were from 10:00 a.m. to 11:00 a.m. Almost every Sunday, Johnny would stand on the corner until the last minute before going into church, hoping to see Elisa Mercurio as she came out of the Catholic church. Most Sundays the two would briefly acknowledge each other across the street.

In the late summer of 1944, after most of the damage to the town had been repaired, Johnny took a part-time job as a cleanup boy in a butcher shop for fifty cents per hour—a good deal of money for a boy in those days. He worked every Friday from 4:00 p.m. until 6:00 p.m.; on Saturdays from 9:00 a.m. until 6:00 p.m., with an hour's break for lunch, which he took at home; and two hours on Sunday, when he washed the insides of all of the meat counters. One of the advantages of the job was that he was able to bring home some meat for the family's table. The main advantage, however, was that he, like many of the young people who worked, had money of his own to spend.

In the fall of 1944, Walter and Martha bought a newly renovated house across the street from the elementary school, which cost them $5,500. The house had running hot water, a well-equipped kitchen, a gas floor heater, and much more space than the old house. He and his brother, Hugh, now six, shared a bedroom. The family, like many others in the town, had "moved up."

The people of Port Chicago were aware of the fact that the navy was considering creating a buffer zone that might eventually necessitate the destruction of the town. What they were not aware of was that the navy was in the process of punishing the black sailors who had survived the explosion.

CHAPTER 18

THE AFTERMATH

On August 9, 1944, Earl Thomas Hughes, seaman second class, and Willie Lee Battle, seaman first class, were part of the Fourth Division, which was ordered to fall in for work. The black sailors who loaded ships were organized into divisions of approximately 120 men. Each division was headed by a white lieutenant and had black petty officers as foremen. After the explosion, the division had been transferred from Port Chicago to the Mare Island Naval Station across Suisun Bay.

The men hadn't been told where they were going. They thought they would be going to the parade ground which was on the right. However, the lieutenant ordered, "Column left." Hughes gasped and asked no one in particular, "Where we goin'?"

Battle, who was marching next to Hughes, responded, "Those SOBs are taking us to load that ship the *San Gay*." All the men stopped. They were afraid and they simply froze.

The lieutenant gave the order again. "Column left." No one moved. Not knowing what else to do, he turned and walked to the administration building and reported to the captain. "Sir, the men have refused to load the *San Gay*. They're too afraid."

The captain slammed his fist on his desk and strode over to the window. "Shit, those black bastards are chicken. They won't get away with it. If they don't load, I'll see that they get punished."

A number of attempts were made to convince or threaten the men in order to get them to load munitions. Some men did agree, but most continued to refuse. Subsequently, they were ordered to the recreation building, where they were individually interviewed about their willingness to work. At the same time, officers of two other divisions were told to order their men to work. In the end, most of the men refused. Of 328 men in the three divisions, 258 refused and were imprisoned on a barge.

On the first night of the imprisonment, Seaman Battle, Seaman Hughes, and Petty Officer Jethro Ross Smith, also of the Fourth Division, had bunks near each other in one corner of a very crowded room on the barge. They found themselves talking about the events of the day and about what had happened over the past three weeks to bring them to this point. The three men had quite different backgrounds, but found themselves thrown together by the circumstances surrounding the explosion of July 17.

Smith was from Newark, New Jersey, and in his early twenties. His family had come to Newark from a small town in southern Georgia in 1927. His parents valued education and had made Jethro attend high school; then they encouraged him to go on to a trade school for two more years, where he learned carpentry and welding, along with academic skills. He joined the navy in 1942, right after the bombing of Pearl Harbor, and he expected to be able to use his skills. He was immediately sent to Camp Barry at the Great Lakes Naval Training Center just north of Chicago. His training included general naval procedures, and had nothing to do either with his skills or with the loading of munitions. After Camp Barry, he was assigned to the Mare Island Naval Station, and later, in the spring of 1943, he was transferred to Port Chicago as petty officer second class. In early 1944, he was promoted to petty officer first class. He was bright, hardworking, and respected by both the black sailors and white officers with whom he worked.

Willie Lee Battle was from Chicago. Like Smith's family, the Battles had migrated from the South to the North, specifically from Natchez, Mississippi, to Chicago, in the late thirties. He was twenty and had a high school education, and he also had been trained at Camp Barry. Like Smith, he had no training in ordnance.

Earl Thomas Hughes was different. He came from a small town in Alabama, had dropped out of high school, and had not been trained at Camp Barry. He had come to Port Chicago at the age of eighteen in June 1944. Essentially, he was being trained on the job.

"How'd we get here?" asked the frightened Hughes. "I didn' do nothin' bad. I just don't want to load no more ammunition. It's too dangerous. Why can't we be sent overseas to fight the Germans or the Japs?"

"We refused to load any more ammunition," Smith explained. "They say that's mutiny. That's why they put us here. If we don't change our minds, they're going to put us on trial, and some say that if they find us guilty of mutiny, they're going to shoot us. As far as going overseas to fight, they don't think we're smart enough to do that. They want to keep us separate and work us like slaves."

Willie Lee chimed in, "How can they call what we done mutiny? We didn't try to take anything over. I thought mutiny meant that sailors try to take over a ship and tie up the officers. We didn' do nothin' like that."

"That's true," said Smith. "However, they say this is wartime, and that's why it's mutiny. It looks like we have a choice. We either go back to loading ammunition and get punished for what we done, maybe lose some pay, get demoted, or something like that; or we continue to refuse to load and maybe get shot."

"That's no choice," said Hughes. "It seems to me that either way, we goin' to die."

At that point, the three men heard a loud noise coming from across the room. They got off their bunks and walked over to see what was going on. What they found was a small group of men fighting each other. Smith asked a sailor standing next to him, "What's goin' on?"

"Those two on the left said they want to go back to loading. The other three jumped 'em and started poundin' on 'em an' yellin', "You yellow bellies are going to make us all have to go back, and we're goin' to get killed.""

The fighting went on for a brief while until a couple of petty officers broke it up. The quarters were very crowded, tempers were hot, and a number of such fights broke out during the next three days.

"One last thing," said Willie Lee when they got back to their bunks. "I heard some of our boys asked for a thirty-day survivor's leave, which usually goes to men who have suffered some real problem during wartime. Why didn' any of us get that kind of time off?"

"I think," answered Smith, "that they didn't want to admit that we deserved any leave, because they wanted to be able to blame us for the explosion. It's that simple: they want us to get the blame." In fact, some white officers had been granted leave.

Willie Lee said, "I think I'll go back to loadin'. What you going to do, Chief?"

Smith took a long time to respond. "I think that each man has the right to make his own decision. But I also think that if we stick together and refuse to go back to loading, they won't be able to accuse us of mutiny. Like I said, they can demote us, take away some pay, or even give us a dishonorable discharge. That's what I think."

Willie Lee spoke up. "We never got trained with no ordnance. It's real dangerous. Also, the officers put pressure on us to go fast. I heard that they'd bet on which group would load the most ammo in the shortest time. They didn' give a damn about safety."

Smith said, "You're right, but they'll deny the betting and the pressure. They don't want any responsibility for what happened. They want it blamed on us." The fact was that in April the captain in charge of the Port Chicago Navy Base had initiated the practice of posting daily averages of loading for each division of sailors.

At fifty-three years of age the captain was very fit, jogging every day at dawn and working out in the gym each evening. He was an imposing figure, and he had little sympathy for those who didn't work up to his expectations. He had a negative attitude toward the black sailors and had been heard to say, "I have never felt that it would be possible to maintain a satisfactory loading rate with the type of enlisted personnel assigned to Port Chicago. The officers need to keep on top of these men." His constant pressure on subordinate officers created an atmosphere of competition that caused the men to hurry when they loaded.

A court of inquiry was convened by the navy on July 21, four days after the blast. The charge to the court was to determine what had happened to cause the explosion. Ordnance experts, officers, and civilians at the base were called as witnesses. Almost no black sailors were called.

Officers who were questioned, including the captain, appeared to be busy trying to avoid responsibility for the explosion. The issue of competition came up at the inquiry. The captain insisted that it had no negative impact on loading, and he also stated, "Anyone who says it did, don't know what he's talking about."

The issue of safety was hotly argued. The fueling of the ships, possible sabotage, problems with equipment, and defects in the ammunition also were examined but were ultimately dismissed by the court. This left the question of the role of the black sailors who loaded the ammunition. It was stated that they were not temperamentally or intellectually capable of handling high explosives. White witnesses testified that there was rough and careless handling of the explosives being loaded at Port Chicago.

Rear Admiral Carleton "Bosco" Wright had graduated from Annapolis in 1912. He specialized in ordnance and during World War I had duty assembling mines to be used in the North Sea. At the outbreak of World War II, he was the captain of the US cruiser *Augusta*. He was promoted to rear admiral in May 1942 and led a task force of five cruisers and four destroyers against a Japanese force of eight destroyers in November of that year. In this encounter, the Battle of Tassafaronga, Wright's ships sank one Japanese destroyer, but one of his cruisers was sunk and three other cruisers were badly damaged and out of commission for several months. The battle was one of the worst defeats suffered by the US Navy in the war. Wright was awarded the Navy Cross for his performance, but was reassigned to shore duty. Ultimately, he became commander of the Twelfth Naval District in San Francisco, and Port Chicago was under his command at the time of the disaster. Wright was a stern officer who had no sympathy for the black sailors at Port Chicago and believed that they were an inferior lot.

On August 11, the men from the barge were marched to the baseball diamond at Mare Island and placed under heavy guard. Admiral Wright arrived and told the assembled men, "They tell me that some of you men want to go to sea. I believe that's a goddamn lie! I don't believe any of you have enough guts to go to sea. I handled ammunition for thirty years, and I'm still here. I have a healthy respect for ammunition; anybody who doesn't is crazy. But I want to remind you men that mutinous conduct in time of war carries the death sentence, and the hazards of facing a firing squad are far greater than the hazards of handling ammunition."

The men were stunned. They now seemed to have a choice between possible death working with ammunition or sure death for refusing, as Jethro Smith had predicted three weeks earlier. After the admiral left, the men were ordered to fall into two groups—those willing to work and those not willing. The men were confused. Some went back and forth between the two groups, unsure of what to do. Some men wept.

In the end, all but forty-four of the men chose to return to work. The forty-four were taken away under guard. The next day six other men who had indicated they were willing to work but who failed to show up for duty joined the forty-four. After that, things moved quickly.

The fifty men were sent to the army base Camp Shoemaker, thirty-three miles south of Port Chicago and just north of San Jose. The 208 men who had indicated that they were willing to work also were sent to the camp for interrogation and summary courts-martial. All were questioned without counsel present. Again, there were efforts to cajole, convince, and threaten the men. The interrogators made special efforts to identify those whom they thought might be ringleaders of the effort to balk at loading.

A written statement was drafted for each of the fifty men based upon what he had told the interrogators, and each man was required to sign. Some of the men tried to get out of signing by saying that the statements were not their own words and were not what they had said. A few men refused to sign, but most did because they thought they had no option.

Once they were formally charged, the trial of the fifty men began on August 14, just three days after Admiral Wright's ultimatum. The prosecution completed its case in only eight days, concluding that there was a conspiracy among the enlisted men to refuse to obey orders to load ammunition.

The defense responded that not all the men were given the order to load; therefore there could not have been a conspiracy. It also argued against the use of the written reports of the interrogations as evidence because of the way they had been obtained. The defense position was that the men were afraid; they did not conspire; and no direct orders were given. However, and even though most of the prosecution evidence was ambiguous and based upon hearsay, the court clearly leaned toward a guilty decision.

On October 9, Thurgood Marshall, chief counsel of the National Association for the Advancement of Colored People (NAACP), came to Camp Shoemaker. After sitting through several days of the trial, on October 16 he called for a formal investigation by the government of the circumstances that led to the work stoppage. He pointed to three things that required attention: First, the policy of the Twelfth Naval District was to restrict the use of Negro seamen, regardless of their training and qualifications, to duty as laborers in segregated units. Second, ammunition loading at Port Chicago was inefficient and unsafe prior to the explosion, and the Negroes working on it were given no instruction or training in the proper handling of it. Finally, the fifty men accused of mutiny were singled out for trial in a haphazard and unfair manner.

The mutiny trial lasted ten weeks. On October 24, after only eighty minutes of deliberation—including lunch—all fifty of the defendants were found guilty of mutiny. The court, subject to review by higher military authority, sentenced all of the men to fifteen years in prison, except for one very young sailor who was given clemency.

The court's findings were sent to Admiral Wright for review. On November 15 he reduced sentences to twelve years for twenty-four of the men. Another eleven had their sentences reduced to ten years. The five youngest men had their sentences reduced to eight years of imprisonment. The fifteen-year sentences were maintained for the rest, those who had been identified as leaders. The other 208 men who had joined the work stoppage were given summary courts-martial, bad conduct discharges, and three months' forfeiture of pay. None of the officers who were actually responsible for the conditions at Port Chicago were ever accused of negligence or wrongdoing.

By September 1945, the severe sentences no longer seemed necessary. The atomic bombs dropped on Hiroshima and Nagasaki, which effectively ended the war in the Pacific, had been shipped from Port Chicago. For that reason, as well as due to the growing pressure to desegregate the armed forces, the sentences were reduced to two years for men with good conduct records and three years for the others, with credit for time served. In a larger sense, the sailors involved could take credit for significantly contributing to the desegregation of the military as well as to the cause of racial equality in the nation as a whole.

⊙∭⊙

In January 1945, US troops had taken the city of Bastogne, giving them a victory in the Battle of the Bulge and leaving Germany open for Allied troops. Axis forces in Greece surrendered. In the East, Soviet forces had entered East Prussia, taken Warsaw in Poland, liberated the Auschwitz and Birkenau concentration camps, and were moving through other countries in Eastern Europe. In the Far East, Japan was retreating in China, and US troops had landed on Luzon island in the Philippines.

By the end of March, Allied forces had captured Cologne in western Germany and were relentlessly bombing German cities. The Soviets had captured Danzig and were moving on Berlin. In the Far East, Burma had been freed from the Japanese, and US fire-bombing of Tokyo had taken about eighty-five thousand Japanese lives.

In April, President Roosevelt died of a cerebral hemorrhage at the age of sixty-three, German troops trapped on the Ruhr river surrendered, US and Soviet troops met at the Elbe river in Germany, the final Allied offensive in northern Italy began, Benito Mussolini was captured by anti-fascists and executed, Adolf Hitler and Eva Braun committed suicide in a Berlin bunker, Soviet troops reached Berlin, and Okinawa was invaded by US troops. On May 7, Germany surrendered. On June 21, US troops captured Okinawa and used the island as a base for bombing flights. On August 6, an American atomic bomb was dropped on Hiroshima, Japan, killing approximately 140,000 people. On August 8, the USSR declared war on Japan and invaded Japanese-held Manchuria. On August 9, a second atomic bomb was dropped, killing approximately 70,000 people in

Nagasaki. Five days later Japan surrendered unconditionally, and on September 2 it signed the formal surrender agreement on board the USS *Missouri* in Tokyo Bay. World War II was over. In California, the Port Chicago mutiny trial was just getting started.

⚭

In the spring of 1945, as the tide of the war was rapidly turning, Johnny was enrolled in a typing class, which, while he didn't realize it at the time, prepared him well for college. The only problem he faced in the class came about because of an accident while he was working at the butcher shop one Saturday at the beginning of the semester.

When he arrived at work, Carlos, his boss, said, "Here, Johnny, trim these bones and grind up the bits of meat for hamburger."

"Sure," said Johnny as he tied on his apron. He went into the walk-in box and brought the tub of scraps and bones with meat on them out to the grinder. After he finished trimming the bones and cutting up the meat, he began to stuff the pieces into the grinder.

"Oooh!" came a loud scream. There was blood all over. Johnny had put the middle finger of his right hand into the grinder.

Johnny didn't lose the finger, but he did have several stitches put in, and a very large bandage protected the finger for several weeks. The typing teacher was an understanding woman and somewhat creative. She had Johnny do his practice work on a paper keyboard. In the end, he was able to type fifty-five words per minute.

In the fall of 1945, in his junior year at Mt. Diablo High School, Johnny continued on the academic track. He was enrolled in English literature, Spanish III, chemistry, PE, and mechanical drawing. Interestingly, although Johnny didn't realized it at the time, his Spanish teacher was Ruth Galindo, the last living descendent of Francisco Galindo, the son-in-law of Don Salvio Pacheco, founder of the original Rancho Monte del Diablo.

Johnny's elective was drama. His drama teacher liked him and one day asked him, "Johnny, would you like to do something very important in this class?"

Johnny saw a chance to impress the teacher and guarantee himself an A in the course. "Yes, Miss Brimley. What would you like me to do?"

She continued, "November 11 is Armistice Day. This year, because the war has ended, it is a particularly important Armistice Day. You do a good job of speaking with emphasis. I would like you to recite the poem 'In Flanders Fields' at the town square in celebration of the day." Johnny readily agreed to the recitation and immediately began practicing.

In Flanders fields the poppies blow
Between the crosses, row on row,
That mark our place; and in the sky
The larks, still bravely singing, fly
Scarce heard amid the guns below.

We are the dead, short days ago;
We lived, felt dawn, saw sunset glow,
Loved and were loved, and now we lie
In Flanders fields.

Take up our quarrel with the foe:
To you from failing hands we throw
The torch; be yours to hold it high.
If ye break faith with us who die,
We shall not sleep, though poppies grow
In Flanders fields.

As with the typing class, Johnny didn't realize at the time how he would use this experience in the future. Later, as a junior high school teacher of English and social studies himself, he would often have his classes perform choral verse programs to celebrate Armistice Day. The program invariably included this poem and others, such as Rudyard Kipling's "Boots."

Johnny also acted in school plays. In *Pride and Prejudice*, by Jane Austen, for example, he played the role of the priggish Mr. Collins.

It was not until his senior year that he was actually able to participate in interschool athletics. Because of his small size he was on the "B" track and basketball teams. He did well in track, being the lead low hurdler and broad jumper.

Often, he and his best friend in high school, Ed Freire, would use the lunch hour to walk to the small downtown area of Concord. They would eat a quick lunch and talk about events at school and about their dreams of the future. Johnny was clear about what he wanted to do. He would always say, "I want to be a teacher. I think I would enjoy it and be good at it."

When Ed asked him what he wanted to teach, he was less sure. Sometimes he would say, "I want to teach history." Other times it was, "I want to be a PE teacher." More and more frequently the response became, "I think I want be an elementary school teacher so I can teach all subjects."

Ed was unsure. His father was a farmer, but that was not what he wanted to be. He thought about having his own business. He thought about teaching. He thought about a lot of possible jobs.

Little did the boys know then that they both would have jobs that provided the opportunity to travel the world; nor did they realize at the time that these noontime discussions would, in some measure, help them to decide what their future lives would be like.

After the war, dances were held for teenagers every other week at the Port Chicago Legion Hall. Johnny would go to most of them and use them as an opportunity to ask Elisa Mercurio to dance. She would dance one dance with him and then return to sit with her cousin Tina Bianci.

During his high school years, his stepfather, Walter Rankin, never allowed Johnny to drive the family car. He would always say, "The car is too valuable, and I need it for work. You'll have to wait until you can get your own car."

As the end of the final semester of his senior year came near, Johnny worked hard to get a friend who was allowed to drive a family car to transport him and a date to the senior ball. He got up the nerve to ask Elisa if she would go with him. Her answer was very painful for Johnny. She said, "Johnny, you know that I care for you, but I will be going to the ball with my future husband, who has been chosen by my father. His name is Oscar Mueller. He is a lawyer and is very handsome. We are to get married in July, after I graduate from high school."

Johnny took another girl to the ball, but spent most of the time watching Elisa dance with her older partner and future husband.

In the months before his graduation from high school, everything seemed set for Johnny to move on to college. The final event that made that decision a sure one was his conversation with his boss, Carlos Lopez, at the butcher shop where he had worked part time on and off throughout his high school years. One day, Carlos asked Johnny to step to the back of the butcher shop. After wiping his hands on a clean towel and easing his thin body into a chair, he said, "Johnny, I know you are thinking about what to do next year. If you want, I'll give you a full-time job and you can become a journeyman butcher. The money is pretty good, and it would be a secure job. On the other hand, you can go on to college. If you do, I will keep you on part time for as long as you wish. Also, if you need any extra financial help, I can give that to you. I think you should go to college."

Johnny grinned. "Wow, thanks a lot, Carlos! I do think I will go to college. I really appreciate your offer, and I probably will come home on weekends and would like to keep working."

Johnny went to his graduation by himself, hitchhiking there and back. He never really understood why his parents didn't attend. The high point of the graduation was when a very surprised Johnny received a $140 scholarship to be used when he went on to college.

After graduation, Johnny had the good fortune to get a summer job at the nearby Shell Oil Company refinery. He was put to work on what was called the "labor gang." Each day he would report to a certain place and be assigned to a foreman who would take him and other young men to where they would perform some kind of labor. Most frequently it would be cutting weeds around the large storage tanks or digging ditches for laying pipelines. On one occasion, his gang was cutting weeds. Some of the other members of the labor gang were lolling around, avoiding work. Some of them began to tease Johnny. "Look at that kid work. He does so much that we don't have to do a thing," said one older boy.

"He's bucking for a promotion to head weed cutter," added another. The whole gang laughed.

At that point, the foreman called Johnny over to him. He was a kindly man, so Johnny wasn't sure what he had done wrong. "Johnny, you need to slow down. You're going too fast. If you keep this up, there will be no work for the rest of us to do. Just go slower." Johnny had learned his lesson. He now knew how to pace himself at his work.

The main outcome of the summer job at the Shell refinery was that Johnny was able to open a savings account with about $250 for his first year of college. Many of the companies along the south shore of Suisun Bay hired college students for summer jobs. Johnny, for example, came home from college in San Francisco every June and worked one more summer at the Shell refinery, one summer at the Tidewater Associated Oil refinery, and one summer at the US

Steel factory in nearby Pittsburg. These jobs, along with working part time in San Francisco as a theater usher, butcher's helper, and/ or janitor, allowed him to pay his way through college.

During their frequent walks to town in their senior year of high school, Johnny and Ed had talked a lot about where they would go to college. Both of them really wanted to go to UC Berkeley. In the end, Johnny decided upon San Francisco State College, because he had heard that it offered a very good progressive teacher training program. Ed decided to work for a year and then go to college.

Thus, Johnny's future was set. He graduated from Mt. Diablo High School and went on to San Francisco State College for his four-year bachelor's degree and elementary teaching credential.

⌘

In 1951, John Rankin, at the age of twenty-one, graduated from San Francisco State with a BA degree in elementary education. He took a teaching job in the Mt. Diablo Unified School District and was assigned to a fourth-grade class at Ambrose Elementary School, five miles east of Port Chicago.

Before he began that assignment, which paid $300 per month for ten months, he worked one more summer at the Tidewater Associated Oil Company refinery as a "C" operator. That meant that he worked shift work—one week of days from 8:00 a.m. to 4:00 p.m., a second week of nights from 12:00 a.m. to 8:00 a.m., and a third week of afternoons from 4:00 p.m. to midnight—just as his stepfather, Walter Rankin, had done. His job was to make the rounds of the catalytic cracking unit every two hours, checking gauges that recorded the flow of oil and levels of heat throughout the cracking process. This involved the application of various levels of heat to crude oil, causing it to separate into a number of products, such as butane, propane, ethane, gasoline, kerosene, diesel fuel, light oils, heavy oils, and asphalt. Each round of checking gauges took John about forty-five minutes, leaving him a good deal of time to talk with the three senior operators who shared his shift.

John lived at home with his parents and his younger brother, Hugh, who was entering eighth grade at Bay Point Elementary School. He once again shared a bedroom with Hugh, and he paid his parents eighty dollars per month for room and board. Once he started teaching in the fall, he also went to work again on weekends for Carlos Lopez in the Port Chicago butcher shop. This arrangement lasted a year. In his second year of teaching, he moved out of his parents' home and shared an apartment with a fellow teacher.

In the fall of his first year of teaching, John was called up for military service. The Korean War had started the year before, and the draft again was in full swing. He felt conflicted as he reported for the physical examination. On the one hand, he wanted to serve. On the other, he wanted to begin his career. The issue was decided by the physical exam. Everything went well for a while. He moved from station to station: his eyesight was checked, his lungs were listened to, he was checked for hernias, and so forth. He was passed at all stations, including the ear exam. He did not tell the doctor who checked him about the chronic mastoid infection, which would never quite go away. At the end of his checkup, he met with the final doctor, who went over the results of the exam with him. The doctor asked his final question. "Mr. Rankin, is there anything else I should know about your physical condition?"

John sighed. "I do have a chronic mastoid condition, but I don't think it should make any difference."

The doctor was not pleased. "I'll be the judge of that." He examined the ear and then exclaimed, "You do not pass the physical exam." With that, John was classified as 4F. His career as a teacher was not interrupted by military service.

☙

The Korean War began on June 24, 1950, when North Korean troops crossed the thirty-eighth parallel, which arbitrarily separated North and South Korea. By the following day, North Korean tanks reached the outskirts of Seoul, the capital of South Korea. By the June 30, a UN resolution was passed condemning the aggression, and US naval, air, and army divisions were committed to Korea under the command of General Douglas MacArthur.

By September 15, US, UN, and Republic of Korea (ROK) forces had been pushed back to nearly the southern end of the Korean peninsula, and MacArthur launched a surprise amphibious attack at Inchon, on the west coast just south of the thirty-eighth parallel. From there US/UN/ROK forces drove north, captured Pyongyang, the North Korean capital, and began to push north toward the Chinese border.

China entered the war on October 25 on the side of the North, pushed south, and inflicted heavy damage on US/UN/ROK troops. On January 4, 1951, Seoul fell to the Chinese and North Koreans. It was not until March 15 that Seoul was retaken by US/UN/ROK forces. For the following four months the tide of the battle moved back and forth, until on May 30 the southern allied forces began a major offensive that drove Chinese and North Korean troops out of South Korea.

Battles continued until July 27, 1953, when a peace treaty was signed and the thirty-eighth parallel was reset as the boundary between North and South Korea. General Mark Clark declared, "I have the unenviable distinction of being the first US commander to sign an armistice without victory."

PART SEVEN

THE TOWN IS DEMOLISHED

CHAPTER 19

YEARS OF TENSION: 1954–67

June 1954 was an unusually hot month. The outside temperatures were in the high nineties. Inside Giovanni's Barbershop, even with two fans working, it was just a few degrees cooler. At 10:00 a.m. on a Saturday, local rancher Greg Daniels came in for his monthly haircut and shave. Easing his hardened frame into the barber's chair, he greeted Walter Rankin, who had come in just behind him.

Daniels asked, "So what are people in town saying about the House Armed Services Committee decision the other day to drop the weapons storage expansion money from its appropriations bill?" Giovanni tied a large towel around Daniels's neck, preparing him for a haircut and a shave. Daniels continued, "I heard about it on the radio, but living outside of town on the ranch like I do, there's probably a lot I don't hear."

Rankin, choosing a chair near one of the fans, picked up an old copy of the *Saturday Evening Post* and fanned himself. "I think we have Congressman Baldwin to thank for getting the money out of the bill. It was nothing but a navy land grab."

Andy Zaworski had come into the shop as Rankin was speaking. As he sat near the second fan, he interjected, "As commander of the American Legion Post, I can say that fifty of our sixty-one members are opposed to a navy takeover. The majority of our veterans want the navy to leave."

Rankin added, "I heard that the local navy officers have questioned our patriotism because most of us oppose a takeover."

Zaworski responded, "That's true, Walter. Personally, I think that since the Korean War is over and there seems to be a lessening of world tensions, perhaps there should be a reduction of such installations instead of expansion."

All of the men nodded. Then Greg Daniels spoke again. "At this point I and others interested in selling part or all of our property can't get good prices because of the announcement of the expansion plans."

Giovanni, an excitable type, waved his razor around. "I rent this place, but I have valuable equipment, and I have built up a lot of goodwill in the past twenty-five years I've been here. They won't pay me for any of that. How am I going to start over someplace else?"

Daniels, with his hair cut and his face shaved, got up out of the chair, paid Giovanni, snapped his suspenders, and moved toward the door. As he started to open it, another customer, Aldo Contavalli, greeted him. "How are you, Greg? I haven't seen you in a while."

Daniels replied, "I'm okay. We've been talking about the navy's attempt to take more land."

Contavalli snorted. "Don't get me started. I'm really ticked off about what's going on. The navy needs to move the base somewhere else. There's no question about it."

Contavalli's comment summarized the feelings of most of the people of Port Chicago. Little did they know at this point the trouble they would see over the next several years.

⁘

By late July, a House-Senate committee proposed a bill to purchase land on the north shore of Suisun Bay and move the Port Chicago Naval Base there. However, at a public hearing of a subcommittee of the House Armed Services Committee in late August in Martinez, the capital of Contra Costa County, the navy surprised everyone by changing its plans and announcing it still wanted to buy the homes and businesses inside the two-mile buffer zone. Several Port Chicago leaders were in attendance at the meeting and had the opportunity to testify. Judge Oscar Litchfield, who had been the justice of the peace in Port Chicago for sixteen years, was dressed in a dark suit and was soft-spoken, but he projected a commanding presence. He testified first and made it brief. "We had a town meeting last night to discuss the idea of the navy's expansion. At the end of the meeting we took a vote. The result was 64 to 1 to ask the navy to move rather than buy the town."

Andy Zaworski reported on the opposition of American Legion members to the purchase of Port Chicago. He also complained, "The navy is unfairly questioning the patriotism of anyone who opposes their position on the issue. That's unfair. The members of the Legion have all served their country well and deserve better."

Eric Johnson, a real estate agent, added in a booming voice, "The navy's presence at Port Chicago makes the town undesirable for residential and commercial development. Getting loans for building is almost impossible now."

Aldo Contavalli was the youngest to testify and the most articulate. "Port Chicago represents all that is good in America. Many of its older citizens are immigrants from other countries. Others are refugees from the dust bowl states of Oklahoma, Arkansas, and Texas. Of late, we also have seen growth in the Negro population. All of these people get along well. The town is safe. There is a volunteer fire department and a local constable. We have very little crime. People often don't even lock their doors. Most young men served their country well during war, and several gave their lives. And now our own government is denying the people of the town the right to keep their homes. This is not fair. The navy should consider moving the base to another place." At this, many of the people in the crowd applauded loudly.

❦

Around this time, a group of men from the town started meeting at the Main Street Bar on Tuesday evenings after work and before going home for dinner. They would order a couple of pitchers of beer and talk about what was going on in the town. On one Tuesday in February 1956, Andy Zaworski, Frank Chapman, Kent Grumman, Ron Smith, Bart Cox, and Walter Rankin were sitting at their usual table. Grumman returned from the bar with a pitcher of beer. "What do you all think about the navy's attempt to open a real estate office here in town?" He sat down hard, looking around for a response.

Some of the men chuckled; others grimaced. Finally Cox, the owner of a car dealership in nearby Pittsburg, responded, "Yeah, the navy asked Congress for nearly $24 million to buy the land, buildings, and businesses in the two-mile zone. They sure were confident. Without even asking anyone, they opened a real estate office here in town, right on Main Street, just down from the theater."

Chapman, a master carpenter at the chemical company in nearby Nichols, chuckled again and said, "When Congressman Baldwin got wind of that move, he raised a ruckus, and within three days the navy closed the office. Good for him."

Zaworski chipped in, "The navy justified the office by saying that two hundred property owners asked for information and appraisals of their property. I think that's bull. No way there were two hundred people doing that."

Rankin, who had been quiet, now joined the conversation. "We know that there are people who are running scared and have asked for appraisals. We also know that Greg Daniels and his wife are now in favor of selling."

Grumman spoke again. "I've heard that Daniels and some others have formed what they call the Committee of Twelve. They support the navy and want to sell their property. They seem to think that there's no point in fighting the inevitable."

At that moment Greg Daniels; Luigi Amato, who owned a small

local trucking company; and Harold Martinson, a local businessman, entered the bar. They sat at a table not far from the larger group.

Ron Smith, the fire chief, turned to the newcomers and said, "We've just been talking about you and your Committee of Twelve. Frankly, we all think you're a bunch of sellouts. How can you do this to your neighbors?"

Martinson, with a flash of anger, answered, "You folks live in a dream world. The navy will never move out. We believe they will get what they want, and they want Port Chicago."

Amato added, "It will be better if residents sell their land to the navy and move out of the danger zone. I'm confident the navy will pay fair prices. Personally, I don't want to stay here as the town falls apart. I want out!"

Zaworski countered, "There will be another battle before the Senate Armed Services Committee, and until the navy is actually moved out, we will not let down our guard. Personally, I will go east if necessary to fight the navy takeover."

Rankin had the last word. "I want you to know, Luigi and Harold, that although we have been friends for a long time, from now on none of us will do any business with you. You will suffer a boycott for being traitors to the town."

At that moment, the door to the bar opened and two young men walked in. Walter Rankin got up from the table and went over to the young men. "What are you doing in here?" he asked his son Hugh.

In a low voice the boy responded, "Fred came home for a few days from college at Santa Clara. Baseball season is starting soon, and he won't be able to get away to come home and see his mom for a while." He braced himself and went on, seeming to dare his father to give him an order. "Me and him are going to have a beer."

"Oh, no, you're not," responded Walter. "You're only seventeen and too young to drink in a bar. Get out of here!"

Hugh grumbled, and Fred hung his head. They walked out the

door. Then Walter walked over to the owner of the bar and asked, "Why are you selling liquor to minors? Do you want me to report you to the constable and get your license taken away?"

The owner responded, "I didn't know he was so young. I won't serve him anymore."

"You'd better not." Rankin held his eyes locked on Barney for a minute before he walked back to the table, where the group was getting ready to leave. They paid the bill and left the bar. From this point on the town became polarized, with people no longer speaking to old friends and boycotting businesses whose owners sided with the navy.

⟨∞⟩

At seventeen years of age in 1955, Hugh Rankin attended Mt. Diablo High School in nearby Concord like his older brother and mother had done before him. He was enrolled in the general education track and was an average student. His broad smile, good looks, and reputation as being somewhat of a tough guy made him popular with many of his fellow students, particularly those who didn't want to go on to college. He was taller than his brother, Johnny, and more muscular. He participated in sports and was particularly good at the pole vault. In his younger years, Hugh had been very involved in scouting activities. His mother, Martha Rankin, was a Cub Scout den mother, and it was in the scouts that Hugh learned lessons of honesty, cleanliness, and respect, as well as how to do simple tasks such boiling eggs and setting the table. Later he was very active in the Boy Scouts, where he learned a number of crafts and developed a sense of responsibility.

As with all boys growing up in Port Chicago, Hugh participated in athletics year-round. Ron Malden, one of the leading citizens of the town, organized athletic programs for boys, and those teams were good. They played baseball and basketball games against teams from nearby towns and usually won. The eighth-grade basketball team, on which Hugh played, was so good that it defeated the Mt. Diablo High School junior varsity.

Like his older brother, Johnny, Hugh was a hard, reliable worker who earned his own money. He cut weeds for neighbors and did errands for his mother. Of particular note was his work for Eugenia Van Horn, the grande dame of Port Chicago. Mrs. Van Horn had no children of her own and was quite taken with Hugh, who until he was eight years old had lived a few blocks down from her and her stately home and grounds up toward the hillside. He cut weeds for her, fed her animals, helped with her garden, and swept and did other cleanup work. At fourteen years of age he had gone to work for Carlos Lopez in the butcher shop, as his brother had done. He stayed with that job for several years and ultimately became a journeyman butcher as his life's work.

Hugh's only real problem was his relationship with his father, Walter Rankin. Because Hugh was on the rowdy side, Walter tried to control his behavior. This, of course, caused Hugh to resent his father and to act out even more. They constantly found themselves disagreeing about things. The worst part of this behavior was its effect on Martha Rankin. She tried, often unsuccessfully, to be the arbiter.

Hugh left high school in his senior year and enlisted in the US Army, where he continued his butcher work and received his General Equivalency Diploma (GED).

⟬∞⟭

It wasn't just the men who were concerned about a possible buyout. Many of the women of Port Chicago had lived there a long time and had deep roots and strong friendships. The Royal Neighbors, a women's charitable group, met once a month to do things for the town. They gave scholarships to graduates of the elementary school, organized food drives for the poor, and sponsored cleanup campaigns. In June 1958, the monthly Thursday evening meeting of the board of officers was held at the home of Wilma Chapman, who was a past president and who had been a member since 1942. Other members present were the current president, Ramona Cabrita; the vice president, Nancy Caudell; the secretary, Tina Contavalli; and the treasurer, Betty Johnson. The women were casually dressed but very neatly made up. A couple even wore slacks. They had invited a special guest for the evening, Eugenia Van Horn.

After the minutes were read and approved and the treasurer's report was given, the meeting turned to a discussion of the latest news about the navy and its buyout plan. Ramona Cabrita opened the discussion. "Well, we know that two years ago the Arthur D. Little Company was given a contract to study our situation, and they recommended that the navy be given $17.1 million to buy Port Chicago."

Tina Contavalli followed by saying, "Yes, but we also know that last year Congressman Baldwin introduced a bill opposing the buyout, and the bill is not to be considered until next year. Here we are again at a stalemate." She took a cookie from the plate being passed around.

As she moved around the room with a pitcher of lemonade, Wilma Chapman commented, "Selling the town will uproot and bring financial hardship to the older home owners and business-people. I really don't think they'd be adequately reimbursed."

Her usually calm voice sounding a bit panicky, Betty Johnson said, "Eric tells me that real estate values are depressed 15 to 20 percent. My next-door neighbor's house has been on the market for three years. Real estate people are reluctant to take listings. My cousin Larry Herman has good credit, but he was denied a real estate loan to make repairs to his property."

Ramona spoke again, trying to calm the group. "The navy

still doesn't have the money to buy us out. Until they get it from Congress, they can't move us. The only way we can stop them is through the power of public opinion. The town meetings need to be continued, and the results need to get into the press."

Tina followed up. "Aldo was pleased with the Port Chicago Improvement Association meeting the other night. More than fifty people were there, and they all agreed that they want to stay. That's getting into the papers."

Nancy Caudell finally entered the conversation. "This is all very sad, though. The town is torn apart on the issue of the buyout. We're no longer speaking to some of those who favor it. We've lost both Maria Grazia Amato and Donna Martinson as members of the Royal Neighbors because they are on the navy's side. It's just too bad; they were good friends of mine."

Wilma Chapman turned to Eugenia Van Horn and asked, "What do you think about all of this, Mrs. Van Horn?"

As the leading businesswoman of Port Chicago, Eugenia Van Horn commanded the respect of her fellow citizens. She sat erect, and with her well-coiffed gray hair and smoothly tailored suit, she gave an impression of authority. She rose from her chair with the assistance of her cane, stood, and spoke firmly. "We do know that the navy didn't get an appropriation this year. It looks to me like they are just trying to keep things in a state of turmoil to get us all discouraged and move us toward wanting to sell. The town is still making progress. If and when the navy gets its money, then it will be time to worry. Right now, we just need to hold on."

There was a strong feeling of frustration in the group, so at that point they turned to the business of planning the next food drive.

〇෴๑

Things continued to drag on in Port Chicago. But by 1961, American involvement in Vietnam was on the rise, adding to the importance of the naval magazine.

The French had left Vietnam in 1956, and the United States had taken over the role of training the South Vietnamese forces. In 1957, communist insurgent activity in South Vietnam began. Guerillas assassinated more than four hundred South Vietnamese officials. Thirteen American trainers were wounded in a bomb attack in Saigon. In 1959, North Vietnamese forces began infiltrating South Vietnam via the Ho Chi Minh Trail. The first American servicemen were killed by guerilla forces at Bien Hoa. In 1960, Hanoi formed the National Liberation Front of South Vietnam. The South Vietnamese named these forces the Vietcong.

In 1961 Vice President Lyndon Johnson visited Saigon, the capital of South Vietnam, assuring South Vietnamese leaders that the United States was firmly behind them in their struggle against the communist forces. In 1962 the US Air Force began using Agent Orange, a defoliant that came in orange containers, to expose roads and trails used by Vietcong forces. In 1963, the Vietcong defeated the South Vietnamese army in the battle of Ap Bac.

President Kennedy was assassinated on November 22 of that year, and the problem of Vietnam became Lyndon Johnson's. On August 2, 1964, three North Vietnamese patrol boats allegedly fired torpedoes at the US destroyer *Maddox*. Five days later the Gulf of Tonkin Resolution was approved by Congress, authorizing President Johnson to take all necessary measures to repel any armed attack against American forces. In 1965, the United States began bombing raids on North Vietnam, and the US troop level exceeded two hundred thousand. The practice of protesting American involvement in the war by holding teach-ins at colleges became widespread.

Feelings between the navy and the majority of the people of Port
Chicago continued to run high. In the summer of 1964, the hard
feelings sometimes turned violent. There often were fights between
sailors and young men of the town.

On occasion, some of the younger sailors would attend the popular dances held at the legion hall. Often, they would have too much
to drink and would try to dance with some of the young women of
the town. On one particular night, one sailor kept trying to dance
with JoAnne Rankin, Hugh Rankin's attractive new wife.

Finally Hugh, himself a bit inebriated, told the sailor to quit
bothering JoAnne. The sailor responded with a challenge to step
outside and fight. JoAnne tried to get Hugh to ignore the sailor, but
he wouldn't back down. They went outside, and Hugh, tough as he
was, gave the sailor a good thrashing.

Two weeks later, the sailor and two of his buddies came looking
for Hugh. They found him at the Main Street Bar. However, he was
not alone. Several of his friends were with him. The three sailors
attempted to jump Hugh, but when his friends joined the fray, all of
the sailors were pretty badly hurt.

As a result Barney, the owner of the bar, told Hugh and his
friends to leave. He was angry with the young men from the town
because he was afraid that sailors would stay away from the bar,
thus hurting his business.

As it turned out, the bar owner was right. The recurring violence
against sailors caused the Navy to put the town off-limits, and the gates
at the base were closed at 5:00 p.m. Navy officials met with Judge
Litchfield. As a result, he asked for more police protection in the town.
The undersheriff in attendance responded, "We have asked our units to
spend more time in the town, particularly on the weekends."

The navy restrictions lasted for a few weeks and hurt town merchants, particularly the owners of bars and restaurants. One restaurant owner said, "The fights aren't enough of a reason for the navy

to close the gates. It's just a way for the navy to shut the town down. Sheriff's records have shown that most of the trouble is caused by guys from out of town, as well as the sailors. In the last five years, there have been three times as many attacks by navy people on civilians than vice versa. Even some of the marines have come into town looking for trouble, and they really hurt people!"

Congressman John Baldwin passed away on March 9, 1965, and was replaced by Jerome Waldie. He, too, opposed the buyout, but he did not have the seniority in Congress that Baldwin had. He immediately met with a group of the town leaders: Aldo Contavalli, Bart Cox, and Hugh Rankin's friend Fred Cabrita, now a pro baseball player with the San Francisco Giants after his graduation from Santa Clara University.

Cabrita was somewhat of a town hero and was quite outspoken about the navy. He told Waldie, "The amount proposed by the navy is not enough. I believe the property owners are entitled to a premium over the fair market value."

Cox added, "That's right. Over the years the value of the land has been depressed due to the navy's threat to purchase it."

Contavalli had the final word. "Congressman, you've got to do whatever it takes to get the navy to move. Short of that, they need to pay fair prices for homes and businesses."

Antiwar demonstrations began at the ammunition depot gates on July 4, 1966. The protests grew for two years, eventually involving more than four hundred protestors. Captain T. R. Eddy, commanding officer of the depot, responded to questions about the protests. "I am retaining my poise about the protests. The demonstrators do irritate us, but so far have not interfered with the basic supply mission of the station."

In March 1967, the Bureau of the Budget finally approved $19.8 million to allow the navy to buy the town and the area around it. The navy estimated that the town itself would cost $9.5 million, including $300,000 for demolition of the buildings. This was the navy's sixth buyout attempt.

When the buyout budget was approved, the media arrived in town, and most newspapers supported the navy position. Many condemned the opponents as antiwar and even as traitors. Some articles painted a picture of the town as shabby and run-down. One article in a county paper reported on its "random" survey, claiming that the townspeople had mixed feelings. It did not report that only two of those surveyed approved the buyout.

Three Port Chicago leaders flew to Washington on August 21 to try to save the town: Jim Edwards, retired army colonel; David Hansen, mechanical engineer; and Aldo Contavalli. The trip was paid for by donations from the townspeople. In Washington, the group met with several individuals and small groups of legislators.

On their return, the trio held a community meeting at the legion hall. Contavalli, acting as spokesperson for the group, gave an upbeat report. "They showed great interest in our fight to prevent the navy's purchase of the town. Each meeting was to last fifteen minutes, but all of them went longer, up to two hours. I think we were heard. We'll soon find out."

On August 28, nearly seventy senior citizens from the town boarded three chartered buses early in the morning and headed to Sacramento for a fifteen-minute meeting with Governor Ronald Reagan. They laid out their case, but received no commitment from him. He briefly told the group, "I'll look into the matter."

A week later, Reagan met with a Contra Costa County supervisor; an assistant to the assemblyman from Contra Costa County; and town representatives Aldo Contavalli, Bart Cox, and Eric Johnson. They too made the case against a buyout. Reagan responded, "I will forward your information to my office in Washington, and I will look into the matter in greater depth." No one heard from him again. On their way out of the meeting, the group passed the famous clown Emmett Kelly on his way in for a meeting with the governor.

The House Armed Services Committee met again on October 19 and reaffirmed the decision to authorize the buyout money. However, they required the Defense Department to complete an "exhaustive" study as soon as possible to look at an alternative to the buyout.

The navy immediately proposed a one-month time limit for the study. Arguments involving navy officials on one side, and Congressman Waldie and citizens of the town on the other, grew increasingly heated. One newspaper in the area characterized the navy position as follows: "This appears to be a situation in which a bull-dogged, insistent navy is dead set on acquiring the town, justifying both the intensity of its efforts as well as the speed of a study with the myth of safety. The navy is hell-bent on 'protecting' 3,400 people in Port Chicago, but it continues to ignore the safety of its own workers on the piers, that of employees in the nearby chemical firm, which will be allowed to remain because there is not enough money to buy it, and the safety of thousands of other people in nearby towns."

On December 8, 1967, President Johnson signed a bill authorizing the buyout money. Three days later, the appraisers arrived in town. To go with the downcast mood in Port Chicago, the most popular tune of the time was "Bridge over Troubled Water," by Simon and Garfunkel:

When you're weary, feeling small,
When tears are in your eyes, I'll dry them all ...

Like a bridge over troubled water,
I will lay me down ...

CHAPTER 20

THE DEATH OF THE TOWN

Wanda Sykes, a waitress at Walt's Inn, the old Bayview Inn, stood up, her back straight, her hair neatly combed, and her eyes flashing. She was angry. The setting was a meeting of the Save Port Chicago Committee. When she was acknowledged by Chairman Bart Cox, she said, "I overheard a conversation between members of the Committee of Twelve, including Greg Daniels, Harold Martinson, and my boss, Marsha Humphrey. They were meeting with Captain Eddy and some of his officers. Eddy guaranteed members of the committee special consideration in the sale of their properties. He told them that they would receive a larger payment than other people because they supported the navy." Wanda took a deep breath and added, "I'd be willing to bet that some people in the community who heard about this deal will go to the navy hoping for a bigger payoff for their property."

That didn't happen, but the issue remained a talking point for the rest of the battle between the navy and the townspeople who opposed the buyout.

Everyone, including the navy, knew that the "exhaustive study" was a sham. The navy was confident that its buyout plan would eventually be put into action. They contracted private firms to do the appraisal work and claimed that this was part of the study, a way of gathering necessary data.

⚬𝍕𝍕⚬

By this time the Tuesday night after-work meetings had continued for twelve years, but they weren't held every week as in the past. The membership had changed over the years, and the venue had moved from the Main Street Bar because of the problems with fighting between sailors and young men of the town. The meeting was now held at the Downtown Cafe, where the group took over a large table in the back. Still attending were Andy Zaworski, Eric Johnson, and Bart Cox. On occasion, Walter Rankin and Ron Smith, the fire chief, would attend. At the meeting in November 1967, newer members of the group included Aldo Contavalli; Mel Stout, the new chairman of the Save Port Chicago Committee; and Fred Cabrita, who was home because it was off-season for the San Francisco Giants. He was running, exercising, and pumping iron to keep in shape.

After coffee and soft drinks were served, Stout opened the conversation. "I guess we have some breathing room. The navy has said that the 'exhaustive study' will include a study of alternatives to a buyout of the town. They say that it will take them at least five months of work before the results can be released."

Contavalli noted, "They say that the result of the appraisals will be included in the report, and Eddy says the report will have no recommendations."

Cabrita, who always had trouble controlling his temper when talking about the navy, spoke loudly. "This is just bullshit! They already have their minds made up, and they're just going through the paces to please Congress. You wait and see—they'll recommend the buyout."

"I agree with Fred," said Smith. "Seven hundred letters were sent to property owners last month. I've heard that if owners don't cooperate, nothing will be done. However, if Congress approves the purchase, they might take people to court. If we don't cooperate and allow the appraisals, the appraisers can simply send an opinion based upon how the property looks from the outside. That *is* bullshit!"

Johnson joined the conversation. "This is just harassment on the part of the navy. Congress hasn't authorized the money. Also, I think the navy will take cooperation as a sign that people are willing to sell. That isn't true. People may cooperate in order to get the matter settled, but that doesn't mean they want to sell."

Cabrita, still angry, spoke about Captain Eddy, the commander of the base. "He's a liar. He said that only a few people oppose the buyout, and the appraisals will show what the situation is. He also claimed that people backing the navy aren't speaking up because they're afraid of reprisals."

Contavalli followed up. "There is absolutely no truth to those claims about reprisals. The navy is just trying to put the majority of us in a bad light."

"Congressman Waldie says that the study can't be completed without the appraisals," said Rankin. "He also accuses the navy of ignoring the congressional order to conduct an exhaustive study, and he predicts that they'll recommend their original plan, the removal of Port Chicago."

"The navy hopes that an approval of the appraisal process will dispute the independent survey by Supervisor Langley," interjected Smith. "It showed that more than 75 percent said that they did not want to sell their homes to the navy."

Zaworski added firmly, "We should *not* let the appraisers into our homes!"

All the men nodded their agreement, and Contavalli volunteered to prepare a statement that citizens could give to the appraisers: "I decline to permit you to come onto my property on the grounds that what you request is not proper at this time."

The entire group approved the statement and contributed to the costs of mimeographing and distributing it to the townspeople.

$\backsim$

On December 19, 1967, it was announced that the "exhaustive study" was finished. The majority of the townspeople were shocked. The study had taken less than two months, and everyone had thought that it would take at least five or six months.

Two months later, Aldo Contavalli and Eric Johnson flew to Washington to once more make the town's case against the buyout. Mrs. Van Horn paid for the trip, and they were joined by County Supervisor Langley. They met with the House Real Estate Subcommittee and other individuals. Johnson reported that he had the feeling that the navy had prompted those they visited to ask common questions such as, "Aren't you pleased that the people in the town will be out of danger after the navy takes over the town?" Johnson also reported that after the meetings he was told that the subcommittee had already made its decision before the meeting.

Contavalli returned from Washington still not convinced that the navy would win. He told a crowd at a meeting of the Save Port Chicago Committee, "Before we went to Washington, I felt that Port Chicago was dead. Now I feel that there is still some hope."

Late in February 1968, the navy real estate agent reported, "Appraisals are going well, and about one-third of the parcels have been done. Enough will be done by April to begin negotiations with those people whose property has already been appraised. After that, we will continue the appraisals, and negotiations will be finished, we think, by September."

In March, he added, "Negotiations will be done in a fair and helpful manner. Our experience has shown us that less than 1 percent of these cases go to trial. Navy policy is to reimburse for the cost of moving personal property. In early 1969, a condemnation auction will be held, and property owners will be able to buy back their homes and other buildings if they wish to move them to other locations. The purchase price will be deducted from the original amount paid by the navy." Clearly the navy felt that they had won and that the buyout was going ahead.

At this point, the media had a field day, painting the town as a run-down, dilapidated, dirty, and undesirable place to live. Often, they used such remarks to make the case that the navy was being more than fair in its payment for such property.

୧ୠୠ୨

In September 1968, it again was off-season for Fred Cabrita, and he was able to spend time in Port Chicago with his family. By that time, about two-thirds of the townspeople had agreed to sell. Cabrita and Hugh Rankin occasionally spent time together. On one particular day they agreed to walk around the town to look at what was going on.

They met at Cabrita's house, the old Cunningham home, which was spacious enough for his growing family, and which was located just across the street from Humphrey's Inn. Cabrita opened the door when Rankin knocked. "Fred, where would you like to walk?"

"Let's go downtown. I'd like to walk by my mother's old house on the way. Also, maybe we can go by the legion hall and the school to see what's happened to them." He pulled on his Giants cap and shut the screen door behind them.

"Good," said Hugh as they reached the sidewalk. "Then we can see what's happened to my folks' place. They really were unhappy about having to move. They got about $12,000 for the property, and that was not enough to buy anything decent nearby. My dad wanted to be near a Kaiser medical facility and also to be able to buy a replacement home outright. He looked all around and settled on a three-bedroom used tract home in the Sacramento area. I think JoAnne and I will move up that way, too. My parents are getting old, and I should be near them. My brother, John, is in Los Angeles finishing his doctorate at UCLA, and he gets up this way only once in a while."

While they were walking toward his mother's old house, Fred said, "I was on my way home after church last Sunday, so I drove by my mom's house. We have moved her in with us, but a lot of her furniture and things are still in her old house. As Marni and I were driving by, we saw the garage door was open. I pulled up and got out of the car, and there were a couple of teenagers trying to steal anything they could. I confronted them and told them that if they didn't leave things alone and get off the property, I was going to beat the shit out of them. I guess I scared them. They jumped in their car and drove off. I think I'm going to start carrying one of my hunting rifles and shoot some of these thieving bastards."

As they walked by the house, things seemed to be okay. Fred commented, "Look at this place. All the plants are dead or dying, the lawn is gone, the windows are dirty … it looks like hell. I guess all the abandoned houses look like this."

Just across the street, Hugh and Fred saw two large piles of garbage. Fred commented, "People from out of town come here to dump their garbage. They're too damned cheap to have the garbage-man pick it up."

They continued on, walking past the fire station. At this point Hugh, with a shaky voice, said, "My dad was the fire commissioner for years. This was a volunteer fire department, and the men used to love to come here, have a beer, and play cards. Not anymore."

They passed the legion hall and came to the Bay Point Elementary School. Once again, Fred spoke. "Next week they're going to close the school. I've heard that they are going to bus the 150 or so remaining students to schools in other towns. The navy is going to keep the firehouse, legion hall, and school to use for their own purposes."

Across the street from the school was a whole block of unoccupied houses. Most had windows boarded up; a few had broken windows from rocks thrown by youngsters. When they came to the Rankin house, Hugh's anger showed. "The goddamned navy. My parents loved this house. So did I. Look at it now. The fishpond is full of scum, the plants are all dying, and someone has stolen the picket fence." They walked around the side of the house into the backyard. Once again, they saw dead plants and weeds. Also, to their surprise, they found that Walter's workshop, which he had built with his own hands, had been torn down and the wood hauled away by looters.

They walked back out of the yard and continued on toward Main Street. In the first block they came to, they saw the theater. On the marquee of the closed building was the message, "LBJ Let Us Down—Crucified Port Chicago." Farther on the two young men spied a banner hanging across Main Street that read, "Freedom Was Born in the USA and Died in Port Chicago—Wake Up, America."

As they proceeded north on Main Street toward what had been the busiest part of the business district, Cabrita began reminiscing. "I remember the Easter parades we used to have every year. I guess the one this past April was the last. They always started after lunch, at Humphrey's Inn, across the street from my house. In the morning there was an Easter egg hunt for the kids. Kids who marched in the parade received prizes for their costumes, decorated pets and bicycles, and other things. It seemed that every kid got a prize. The fire department always led the parades, members of the American Legion were color guards, and the Lions Club had a queen's float. At night there always was an Easter dance. What a great town!"

When the pair got to the main block of the downtown area, they found that most of the businesses were boarded up. Only one grocery store, two bars, the post office, two restaurants, and the drugstore were still open. However, they, too, were destined to be closed. With his face frozen in an angry expression, Fred muttered, "We have to shop in Concord for most of what we need, but damn it, we're not leaving until they come and drag us out."

GOMMG

The navy set February 1, 1969, as the date by which the entire town would be vacated. By the end of November a steady stream of property owners were leaving Port Chicago, and the house movers and wreckers were at work clearing the houses away. The navy was preparing eviction notices for the remaining residents.

Early in December, Fred Cabrita posted a sign in front of his house. It said, "No trespassing. Unauthorized violators will be shot." On December 6, the navy served eviction notices to 165 residents who had refused to leave. Cabrita was alerted to the fact that he was to get one.

A car pulled up at the Cabrita house on the sixth, and two men in suits, broad-brimmed hats, and dark glasses got out of the car and came to the front door. Cabrita stepped out of the house onto the screened-in porch. He had a 30-aught-6 rifle with him.

The men did not identify themselves. One of them said, "We have something for you."

Cabrita knew that they were going to serve him with an eviction notice. He said, "Get off my property."

The second one said, "We have something for you. You shouldn't act like this. What's wrong with you?"

Cabrita raised his voice. "Get off my property, or I'll shoot!"

The first one responded angrily, "We are marshals, and we have an eviction notice to give you." The second man went back to the car and opened the trunk. He started to pull a gun out.

By that time Cabrita was really furious. He had his gun pointed directly at the man standing by the car. The yard was not very deep, so Cabrita was fairly close to him. He laughed and then, in a loud voice, said, "You'd better do a good job on your first try, fella. If I were you, I wouldn't take that son of a bitch out of the trunk."

The men glanced at each other and then, without another word, got back in their car and drove away. Fred had won the skirmish that day, but not the war. He continued the fight in the courts and finally had to settle with the navy for his several properties in Port Chicago. Ultimately, charges against him for pointing a gun at the marshal were dropped. The Cabritas moved to Concord.

The navy did not meet its goal of removing all of the property owners by February 1, 1969. In early March, fifty homes were still occupied, plus there were 150 families in two trailer parks who had been given extra time to move. Mrs. Van Horn opened a small store to provide food supplies for those who remained. It was not until December 1969 that the last family left Port Chicago.

⚬⚭⚬

In 1966, American B-52s began bombing North Vietnam, and South Vietnamese troops successfully took Hue and Da Nang from the Vietcong. In 1967, a major ground war effort called Operation Cedar Falls, involving 16,000 US and 14,000 South Vietnamese troops, set out to destroy Vietcong operations near Saigon. They discovered a large system of tunnels that allowed the Vietcong to move around undetected. In January 1968, the North Vietnamese and Vietcong caught the United States off guard. They swept down upon several key cities and provinces, including Saigon. General Westmoreland requested over two hundred thousand more troops.

The My Lai massacre took place on March 6. The victims were mostly elderly men, women, and children, all noncombatants. Many were tortured, sexually assaulted, or mutilated. The official death toll according to the US government was 347, but the North Vietnamese set the number at over 500. When the news of this event became public knowledge, it sent shock waves throughout the United States, giving significant fodder to the antiwar movement. Later in March, President Johnson announced that he would not be a candidate for reelection. In May, peace talks began in Paris. The war continued, but massive antiwar demonstrations took place.

The war did not officially end until 1973, but by early 1969 it became clear that it would soon be over. On August 11, 1969, the navy gave termination notices to over 260 civilian workers at the Port Chicago Naval Base, even though just a year before, the navy had declared that they would never close it down. The navy shipped 98,000 tons of munitions in May and only 60,000 tons in August. Shipments were to be reduced to 20,000 tons, which meant that there would be a need for just one pier. Also, it turned out that it was cheaper to ship munitions to Vietnam from the East Coast through the Panama Canal. The navy had been holding back the truth the whole time.

At this time, there were no songs or verse at the point of the bay. An eerie silence, broken only by the noise of the wind or the occasional whistle of a train moving ammunition to the pier, was all that could be heard.

But the weapons station at the tidal area did not go away. Over several more years it alternately contracted and expanded, standing in the way of the development of a new set of dreams for the point of the bay.

PART EIGHT

UNCERTAINTY ABOUT THE FUTURE

MAP EIGHT: CLOSURE OF INLAND PORTION OF CONCORD NAVAL WEAPONS
STATION IN 2005

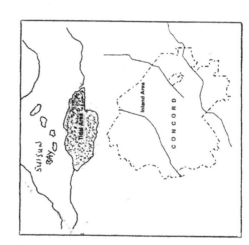

CHAPTER 21

TO BE OR NOT TO BE

Fred Cabrita and Hugh Rankin remained friends. Cabrita had retired from his successful baseball career in 1969 after several injuries and had opened a business of his own. Rankin moved with his family to Auburn in the foothills of the Sierra Nevada mountains, where he continued his career as a journeyman butcher. One day in June 1973, Fred called Hugh on the phone. "Hey, buddy, I haven't seen you in a long time. I have an idea for some fun and want to know if you'd like to join me. I have a friend who has a motorboat that he will loan me. What I'd like to do is borrow it and take a spin by the naval weapons station to see what's going on."

Hugh was quiet for a while and then asked, "Doesn't the Coast Guard patrol those waters? Can we get into trouble? The last thing I want to do is to get arrested!"

Fred laughed. "Hell, we'll be in and out of there so fast that they won't even know we've been there."

Hugh thought about this. He *was* curious. "I think I'd like to do it, but I have one condition: you don't bring your damned shotgun. If we got stopped, that would be a real problem."

"Come on, you know I'm smarter than that. What say you come down to my house a week from Tuesday in the morning? It shouldn't take you much more than an hour. Then we can go to Martinez and get the boat."

"Fine, I'll call you the night before to confirm. It should be fun." After sharing information about their growing families, they agreed once again to meet.

Hugh got to Fred's house at 9:00 a.m. on the designated day. He had gotten up early and left his house at 7:00, only to find a good deal of traffic. When he arrived at the Cabrita house, he was greeted by Fred's wife, Marni. After some small talk, she told him that Fred was in the garage, working on something. She wasn't sure what.

Hugh walked around the side of the house to the garage, where he found Fred working on some fishing gear. Fred, seeing Hugh, let out a loud laugh. "Ha! If the Coast Guard pulls us over, they'll think we're fishermen. We won't have any trouble."

The two set out in Fred's car for the marina in Martinez, seven miles away. Fred was excited. "Bob's boat is a brand-new fiberglass Glastron 150 Bowrider Tri Hull. It's fifteen feet long and is rigged for fishing for bass, sturgeon, and salmon. It has a fifty-horsepower two-stroke engine that can get up to thirty-five miles per hour. It has a tiller, but we can control it with the steering wheel. The gas tank will be full. We also have a radio on board in case anyone wants to contact us, including the Coast Guard."

Hugh was impressed. "I hope you'll let me drive it some of the time. I've never done that before."

"Of course," said Fred. "We'll share and share alike on this trip."

The friends found Bob's motorboat at the marina, and with the key he had given to Fred they were able to start the engine and take it out into the bay. They headed east and soon went past the Avon refinery, where they saw a tanker unloading crude oil. They moved on until they reached what was now called the Concord Naval Weapons Station. They were about a half mile from the coast. Fred stopped the boat, and he and Hugh got out the fishing gear. Fred handed his line to Hugh and took out his binoculars. He pointed them to the station.

"What do you see?" Hugh was really curious.

"The pier where the ships blew up is smashed up, and there is a piece of the hull of one of the ships that blew up sticking up in the water. Farther east there are three other piers that look to be in good shape." Fred added, "There is only one ship tied up at the last pier to the east. None of the piers seem to be busy."

"Well, there was a cease-fire in Vietnam last January. There isn't much need to ship munitions right now. Maybe the place will close," Hugh said in a hopeful voice.

"I don't think so," Fred said with certainty. "My neighbor works in the inland area, and he told me that since the cease-fire, a lot of missiles and other ammunition are coming back here from Vietnam for checking, necessary repairs, and storage."

Fred handed Hugh the binoculars. As he looked beyond the piers, Hugh began to describe what he saw. "I see a train with a few cars coming into the area and heading toward the piers. There also are a number of cars sitting on sidings. A number of buildings look as if they have gotten new paint jobs, and there are quite a few people, both naval personnel and civilians, walking from one place to another. It's still busy here. Off in the distance, the legion hall, Bay Point Elementary School, and the firehouse are still there. So are the two eucalyptus groves. As you know, I lived near the farthest grove until my parents moved us across the street from the elementary school."

Fred added, "You can drive into the town and see where everything used to be. It's *spooky*." Just then the two young men heard the radio crackle. This was followed by a strong voice. "This is the Coast Guard. You are in protected waters. Either leave the area right now, or we will come to tow you ashore. If we have to do that, you will be arrested and fined."

Fred immediately took the wheel while Hugh started the engine. The bow of the fiberglass boat lifted out of the water as Fred spun it around and headed back for the Martinez Marina.

The two men tied the motorboat up to the dock when they got back to the marina and covered it with a tarp. After they were finished with the mooring tasks, they got into Fred's car and drove toward Concord.

As they were driving, Hugh spoke about their experience in the motorboat. "I really enjoyed myself today. I wouldn't mind doing it again, or even going a bit farther up the bay. We probably should wait awhile before we try to view the weapons station again, though they may have taken note of our boat. Perhaps we should even rent another one."

Fred nodded. "Speaking of fun, are you and JoAnne going to attend the annual Port Chicago reunion at Ambrose Park on the last Saturday in July? The park isn't far from the school where your brother used to teach. This will be the fourth annual reunion. The kids sure have a great time. It's like the Port Chicago Easter celebration. There are prizes for every kid. There are games for people of all ages, as well as a barbecue. The park has a swimming pool, basketball courts, horseshoe pits, shaded picnic tables, and lots of room in shaded areas for people to move around and greet old friends. Last year we put together T-shirt and hat sales, door prizes, raffles, food, games, and dancing."

Hugh responded, "I'll bet it's fun, but I can't get away from work on Saturdays. It's the busiest day of the week for a butcher shop. If it was on Sunday, we'd go."

They arrived at Fred's house, and Hugh went to his car for the drive home. His parting words to Fred were, "Let's figure out a way to get into the weapons station and get a really good look at what's going on. Of course, we have to do it without getting into trouble."

"I'll think about it and ask my neighbors who work at the station if there is a way. I'll give you a call. Take care on the way home."

⊙〜〜〜◯

The 1980s were calm. There was no war. While there was less shipping of weapons and ammunition, several ships were assigned permanently to the base. Often such ships did training or humanitarian work as well move ordnance out and in. The station maintained its personnel levels, and repairs were made to a number of buildings. Security was increased, making adventures like another motorboat incursion by Fred Cabrita and Hugh Rankin unlikely. A number of ideas were developed for expansion, which did not really come to fruition until later years.

One thing that did draw headlines was the increase of protests and protestors. There had been protests in the 1970s, but there were far more in the 1980s. This increase, at least in part, was probably due to the suspicion that the Concord Naval Weapons Station was now responsible for the movement of nuclear weapons. There had been much speculation all the way back to the end of World War II suggesting that components of the two atomic bombs dropped on Japan at Hiroshima and Nagasaki had been shipped through the base. The navy neither denied nor confirmed this rumour.

The protests usually took place at the gate of the inland area, right where the railroad tracks crossed the highway and transported ordnance from the inland area to the tidal area. Some of the protests involved big names from the entertainment industry, such as Joan Baez and Ed Asner.

The most publicized event occurred on September 1, 1987. A Vietnam veteran named Brian Wilson, along with two other veterans, sat down on the railroad tracks at the inland gate of the Concord Naval Weapons Station in front of an oncoming train full of munitions. The three were part of a crowd engaged in a nonviolent protest of US government munitions being sent to the right-wing Nicaragua military government's war against the left-wing militia known as the Contras.

The train didn't stop. Wilson suffered several broken bones and a fractured skull, and he lost both his legs. His two friends were barely able to get off the tracks in time to avoid being hit as well.

At the time, the train was accelerating to over fifteen miles per hour in the five-miles-per-hour zone. The train crew had been ordered to stop the train, but they didn't.

A week later nine thousand people went to the site, tore up three hundred feet of the tracks, and stacked them up, making an interesting sculpture. Even after the tracks were replaced, from that day on, for over two years, there was a permanent, around-the-clock occupation of the tracks with up to two hundred people. Hundreds of people were arrested. Now the trains did stop, because they had to wait for the many arrests.

പ്പു

As the 1980s drew to a close, it was quiet at the Concord Naval Weapons Station. In fact, there was much speculation that the station would be closed in the 1990s. However, that did not happen. On July 15, 1990, Iraq accused Kuwait of stealing oil from Iraq's Ramalia oil field near the Iraq-Kuwait border and threatened military action. On August 2, a little over one hundred thousand Iraqi troops invaded Kuwait, and by August 4, Iraq declared victory. On August 7, after the UN Security Council imposed a trade embargo on Iraq, the United States launched Operation Desert Shield, and troops were sent to Saudi Arabia. By August 12, there was a naval blockade of Iraq, but it was not until November 29 that the UN Security Council passed a resolution setting a deadline January 15, 1991, for Iraq to withdraw from Kuwait, or Iraq would face military action.

On January 12, 1991, the US Congress passed a resolution authorizing the use of military force to drive Iraq from Kuwait. On January 18 Iraq launched Scud missiles toward Israel, and on January 22, Iraqi troops began to blow up Kuwaiti oil fields. On January 29, Iraqi forces invaded Saudi Arabia, but by February 1, they were driven out by Saudi, Qatari, and US forces. On February 22, US President George H. W. Bush issued a twenty-four-hour ultimatum: Iraq must withdraw from Kuwait to avoid the beginning of a ground war. Two days later the US-led Coalition forces invaded Iraq and Kuwait. On

February 27, US Marines and Saudi Arabian troops entered Kuwait City, and the US Army engaged the Iraqi Republican Guards in tank battles on Iraqi soil. Finally, on March 3, Iraq accepted the terms of a cease-fire from the UN Security Council.

During all this time, the Concord Naval Weapons Station was handling weapons requests. The number of stevedore teams expanded from six to sixteen. These teams loaded up to one thousand tons of munitions per day. Following the end of the Gulf War, the station returned to the readiness exercises and humanitarian aid operations of the 1980s.

During the Gulf War the number of ammunition ships stationed at the Concord Naval Weapons Station held at six. Beginning in 1994 one ship after another was decommissioned until there were none left by the end of the decade.

⌘

Fred Cabrita and Hugh Rankin had kept in touch over the years, but they did not see each other very often. One day in late 1998, Fred called Hugh. "Hugh, do you know that the navy closed the roads three years ago into and out of what used to be Port Chicago? We can't even drive through there now."

Hugh knew. "I've gone through there a couple of times in the past. The last time was in 1992, I think."

Fred made a proposal. "Are you still interested in what's going on there? If so, why don't you come down to our house some evening later this month. I'll invite three of my neighbors who work at the tidal area. They can tell us what's happening and if it looks like the base will close anytime in the near future."

Hugh was interested. "That would be great. How about next Tuesday evening? Also, can I bring JoAnne? She'd like to see Marni and the kids."

Hugh and JoAnne arrived at the Cabrita house at 7:30 p.m. on the following Tuesday. They all went into the living room, where the other three men were visiting. Marni got coffee and cake for the group, and after introductions Fred spoke to Warner, who was sitting across the room from him on the couch. "Warner, you have been at the base for the longest. There always has been a lot of speculation about whether nuclear weapons have passed through the base. Do you know anything about that?"

Warner flushed a bit before he answered. "I'm not really sure about that. The navy policy always has been to neither deny nor confirm the presence of nuclear weapons. I never saw any. However, I did hear that more than three hundred tactical nuclear weapons were in storage at the naval weapons station as of 1991, but I've also heard that all of those were removed before 1996."

Marni spoke up angrily. "So without admitting it, it is probable that the navy put all of our lives at risk. That fits with what they did to Port Chicago. They just can't be trusted."

Fred said, "Honey, there's no use getting mad now. Like the Beatles say, 'Let It Be.' What we really want is to know the truth. Warner, I've also heard that the navy has been bringing in highly enriched spent fuel from other countries to stop them from building their own nuclear weapons. Can you tell us about that?"

Warner once again responded, only this time with certainty. "There's a long history to this. It dates back to 1954 when President Eisenhower initiated the Atoms for Peace Program. The United States offered to provide assistance to countries that wished to pursue peaceful application of nuclear technologies and pledged not to develop nuclear weapons. This included those countries sending their spent fuel rods to the United States for destruction. In recent years the navy agreed to resume having spent fuel shipped through the base and then on to other storage places. It's brought in by ship and immediately transferred to trains to be taken for storage elsewhere."

Warner's colleague, Richard, had something to add. "A lot of people are afraid that there could be leakage, but it really is safe. The spent rods are enclosed in steel casks, and there's been no trouble so far."

JoAnne spoke up. "Yeah, but things happen. Way back in the seventies there were explosions near us in Roseville. Railroad cars loaded with bombs blew up. Nobody was killed, but a lot of people were hurt. You can't tell me it's always safe!"

Hugh threw out a question without directing it specifically to any one person. "Are the legion hall, the school, and the firehouse in Port Chicago still being used? When I was a kid, I lived across the street from the school, and my dad was the fire commissioner."

The third guest, Grady, answered, "The legion hall and the school were taken down last year, I think. I'm not sure about the firehouse, but I do know there's a relatively new firehouse in the tidal area."

Fred addressed another question to Grady. "A few weeks ago you were telling me about your work. It sounded interesting. Why don't you tell the Rankins what you do?"

"Sure," said Grady. "I work in what's called the Weapons Quality Engineering Center. We are responsible for testing various kinds of ordnance, including missile guidance systems, ammunition, bombs, and other things. We use computers and do metallurgical, spectroscopic, radiographic, and other kinds of tests. In the end, we decide whether to keep, repair, or destroy the items being tested. It's highly technical work and quite safe."

Richard seemed anxious to make a comment. "There's always a lot of talk about the base closing. However, a lot of money is being spent for repairs and new equipment. Also, they are moving to use containers to load on the ships. Containers can be transferred directly from trucks and trains to the ship or vice versa. It doesn't feel like they're thinking of closing the base anytime soon." He went on, "We hear that the tidal area will be turned over to the army next year. What that means, I don't know."

The conversation went on for a long time until finally JoAnne suggested that it was getting late and that she and Hugh should start for home. The evening was a success, because both the Rankins and the Cabritas felt that they had learned a lot about the base. However, the bitterness about losing their town was not lessened. Even so, after the guests left, Fred found himself singing, "Let It Be":

When I find myself in times of trouble,
Mother Mary comes to me,
Speaking words of wisdom, let it be ...

Let it be, let it be ...

⊙ɯɯɕ

In March 2000 an Amtrak train was on its way east from Richmond to Stockton along the south shore of Suisun Bay. It passed through Martinez and the Avon oil refinery. The engineer was Roger Axelrod. He had with him in the engine a trainee, Mark Cinnamond. After passing by Avon, Roger gave Mark some instructions about speed limits for the train. He then said, "In a minute we will cross through what is now called the Military Ocean Terminal Concord, run by the US Army. We usually come through here at night and pass under a bridge on the base. If you pay attention, you can see some of the work going on at the base. Just look north."

"Wow!" Mark was impressed. "Out there by the water I see two enormous cranes loading containers on ships at two different piers. The whole area is lit up like a Christmas tree, and there are a lot of men moving around on the piers. What's in those containers?"

Roger chuckled. "Those cranes *are* enormous. They're also new this year. I hear they can now load up to six hundred containers per day and that the cranes cost more than $20 million. I guess they're loading all kinds of ammunition onto the ships, maybe even nukes. I don't think our passengers really understand the possible danger there is on this ride!"

⁋

In early 2004, Fred and Hugh were thinking of borrowing the same motorboat they had used before, in 1973. They were curious to see the cranes and the work at the piers. Fred called his friend Bob to ask him whether or not he thought it would be safe.

Bob laughed. "It's okay, if you want to go to jail. Last December the Coast Guard established a security zone in the waters around the Military Ocean Terminal Concord because of the danger of terrorism. The security zone will prohibit all people and vessels from entering the zone without permission of the captain of the port. You'd better believe you won't get permission. Maybe if you have a strong spyglass or binoculars, you could walk up into the hills south of the terminal and see the cranes and piers. I'm not really sure."

In the end, Fred and Hugh didn't think it was worth the effort.

⁋

On May 13, 1995, Secretary of Defense Donald Rumsfeld recommended that the inland portion of the base be closed and that the tidal area be turned over to the US Army. In late 1999, the inland ammunition magazines were emptied, and the station's remaining functions were relocated to the Naval Weapons Station Seal Beach in Southern California.

Ten years later, Congress authorized the closure of the inland portion of the Concord Naval Weapons Station. This portion included 5,170 acres and was entirely within the city of Concord. The

Concord City Council was designated as the Local Reuse Authority (LRA). The business and government leaders of Concord, unlike in a number of cities facing base closures, asked the navy to close the entire base so that it could be used for private development. Needless to say, the tidal area was not closed, and the point of the bay remained off-limits to ordinary civilians.

⚭

Marni Cabrita had two very close friends in Clyde, the little town just three miles from Port Chicago that was right next to the inland area that had been the Concord Naval Weapons Station.

A year after the closure of the inland portion of the base, she went to visit the two friends, with whom she had gone to Mt. Diablo High School in Concord. She drove to Mabel Weston's house to meet Mabel and her other friend, Priscilla Duncan.

Mabel's house was in the old part of town, and the backyard faced west toward the old Port Chicago Highway, which had been closed eleven years before. The view also included the fenced-off road and train tracks that went from the inland area to the tidal area.

At first, the trio talked about their families and current activities. After a while, Marni commented, "It must be nice not having all the traffic from the inland area of the old base to the tidal area that is still operating."

Mabel frowned and put down her coffee cup. "Weapons, including nuclear weapons, used to be stored here in the bunkers just to the south of us. We have been told all the bunkers have been emptied and all the ammunition is gone."

Priscilla added, "But there are still trucks and trains coming in and out with explosives signs on their sides. The military has blocked off the view into the area where the bunkers were, *or still are*. Personally, I think the weapons are still flowing."

Marni was puzzled. "How can they do that if this part of the base is supposed to be closed and supposedly has been turned over to the City of Concord?"

Mabel picked up the conversation. "The army commander of the Military Ocean Terminal Concord on the bay said a while ago at a public forum in Concord that military weapons *are* still being shipped through here. He said there are no more nuclear weapons passing through the base, though what comes in doesn't stay very long. The munitions come in by ship and go out by rail and vice versa." She stopped for a moment and then continued. "He said that when the cargo moves, it goes west to Martinez, across the Benicia Bridge, and north to Sacramento and beyond. Other trains go east to Pittsburg and then to Stockton. According to him, it's all very safe."

"Who loads the ships?" asked Marni.

"We do know that sailors don't do it anymore. They have long-shoremen who are hired whenever there is loading to do, and they load containers with huge cranes," answered Priscilla.

Marni asked the other women, "Do you both feel safe? I think I'd be worried. I remember the explosion in 1944. I was six years old, and it still scares me."

"We know there is danger." Mabel shrugged her shoulders. "Amtrak trains run through there. If terrorists wanted to, they could stop a train and set off explosives. That could cause a lot of damage, including here in Clyde and where you live, Marni, in Concord."

Marni frowned. "This seems dangerous to me. No one really seems to be accountable. I just wish the military was truthful with us, instead of leaving us wondering what is going on."

"The one good thing we do know is that they are doing a lot of cleanup work," added Priscilla. "A lot of waste has been deposited in the marshes of the tidal area over the years. Some of it is poisonous, like DDT and mercury. We hear they have long-term plans to complete cleaning up the whole area. It will cost a lot. But if the military leaves, then it will be better for private business to move in. That, of course, is what the movers and shakers of Concord hope for."

EPILOGUE

In May 2013, John Rankin and his wife, Heather, visited the Port Chicago Naval Magazine National Memorial, operated by the National Park Service. It was dedicated in 1994 in honor of the lives lost in the Port Chicago explosion and was upgraded to a national park in 2002.

The Rankins and three other visitors were taken in a small bus from the inland area headquarters to the memorial on Suisun Bay, located at the remains of one of the destroyed piers.

The experience was a bit eerie for John. In the midseventies, he had driven through the empty streets of the abandoned town, past the locations of the two houses where he had lived as he was growing up. He had seen the legion hall and the Bay Point Elementary School (which he had attended), both of which had been kept by the navy for administrative offices; and the firehouse which had been turned over to the US Coast Guard. These buildings were now gone. The three highway entrances to Port Chicago had been fenced off, stopping all public traffic from entering the place where the town had been.

The park ranger who was driving the bus described the explosion, the mutiny, and the closure of the town. The visitors could view the remains of one pier, an empty ammunition revetment, and part of the hull of one of the two ships that had exploded on July 17, 1944. Except for a few whitewashed sheds and, off in a distance, two giant cranes, there was no evidence of human activity.

The eerie part, for John, was looking south to see the two eucalyptus groves that had been planted in 1907 by the Cunningham family, early settlers of Bay Point. The house he had lived in as a child had been across the street from the smaller of the groves. The larger grove had belonged to Greg Daniels. Johnny, as a youth, had played "capture the flag" there with his Boy Scout troop. The moment brought back a flood of long-forgotten memories.

As John and Heather looked at the memorial and viewed the tidal area, they thought of the stories about the city officials and business leaders of Concord who longed to develop the area. As he turned to leave, John realized that the point of the bay would probably be settled once again, as it had been so many times since the original Chupcan people lived there centuries before.

POEMS, SONGS, DANCES, AND LETTERS

The Coyote Creation Story from www.native-language. org/ohlonestory.htm

"Thou Art a Girl No More" from Margolin, M. (Ed.) (1993). *The Way We Lived: California Indian Stories, Songs, & Reminiscences.* Berkeley: Heydey Books, p. 22.

"My Heart Goes to the Bay Waters" from Margolin, M. (Ed.) (1993) *The Way We Lived: California Indian Stories, Songs, & Reminiscences.* Berkeley: Heyday Books, p. 81.

Native American War Dance & Song adapted from http://groups.yahoo.com/group/indigenous_peoples_literature/message/34853

Catholic Chant from www.catholicchant.com

"The Heavens Wept that February," unpublished poem, courtesy of Dean McLeod, scholar of Chupcan life.

Choral Reading from the Sacrament from http://www. catholictradition.org/Classics/imitation4-6.htm

Victory Song adapted from Fletcher, A.C. (1994) Indian Games and Dances with Native Songs. Lincoln, Nebraska, pp. 128–131.

Secularization Letter sent by Father Soria at Mission San Jose in1840 to Father Jose Gonzales Rubio, who presided over the secularization of the California missions from 1836 to 1842. A copy was found on a wall of the museum of Mission San Jose.

"El Fandango" from Nunis, D. B. (1994). *Tales of Mexican California: Cosas de California*. Santa Barbara, California, p. 88.

"Arruru mi Niño" from http://www.tsl.state.tx.us/ld/projects/Niños/songsrhymes.html

"La Bamba" from www.johntoddjr.com/143%20Bamba.bamba.htm

"Oh Susanna" from http://www.lyricsmode.com/lyrics/s/stephen_foster/oh_susana.html

"Oh My Darling Clementine" from http://www.metrolyrics.com/oh-my-darling-clementine-lyrics-traditional.html

The Bachelor Song" from http://pdmusic.org/1800s/49tbs.txt

Black Bart Versifying from http://comspark.com/chronicles/famous.htm

"We'll Never Say Goodbye" from http://hymns.me.uk/well-never-say-goodye-funeral-hymn.htm

"The Stars and Stripes Forever" from http://en.wikipedia.org/wiki/The_Stars_and_Stripes_Forever

"The Charleston" from http://www.kidsongs.com/lyrics/charleston.html

"The Beer Barrel Polka" from http://www.lyricsmode.com/lyrics/b/bobby_vinton/beer_barrel_polka.html

"I'll Be Seeing You" from http://solosong.net/seeingyou/seeingyou.html

"Till Then" from http://www.oldielyrics.com/lyrics/the_classics/till_then.html

"In Flanders Fields" from http://www.elyrics.net/read/j/john-mccrae-lyrics/in-flanders-fields-lyrics.html

"Bridge over Troubled Water" from http://www.azlyrics.com/lyrics/leanrimes/bridgeovertroubledwaters.html

"Let It Be" from http://allspirit.co.uk/let.html

KEY RESOURCES

Allen, Robert L. *The Port Chicago Mutiny: The Story of the Largest Mass Mutiny Trial in U.S. Naval History.* New York: Amistad Press, Inc., 1993.

Gutierrez, Ramon A., and Orsi, Richard L. (eds.). *Contested Eden: California Before the Gold Rush.* Berkeley, California: University of California Press, 1998.

John Marsh. http://www.theschoolbell.com/history/early/marsh.html

Keibel, John A. *Behind the Barbed Wire: History of Naval Weapons Station Concord.* Concord, California: John A. Keibel Publisher, 2009

Kroeber, A. L. *Handbook of the Indians of California.* Mineola, New York: Dover Publications, 1976.

Margolin, Malcolm. *The Ohlone Way: Indian Life in the San Francisco-Monterey Bay Area.* Berkeley, California: Heyday Books, 1978.

McLeod, Dean L. *Images of America: Bay Point.* San Francisco, California: Arcadia Publishing, 2005.

McLeod, Dean L. *Images of America: Port Chicago.* San Francisco, California: Arcadia Publishing, 2007.

Milliken, Randell. *A Time of Little Choice: The Disintegration of Tribal Culture in the San Francisco Bay Area, 1769–1810.* Menlo Park, California: Ballena Press, 1995.

Nunis, Doyce B., Jr. (ed.). *Tales of Mexican California.* Santa Barbara, California: Bellerophon Books, 1994.

CPSIA information can be obtained at www.ICGtesting.com
Printed in the USA
LVOW13s1625140713

342772LV00004B/223/P

Pitt, Leonard. *The Decline of the Californios: A Social History of the Spanish-Speaking Californians, 1846–1890*. Berkeley, California: University of California Press, 1966.

Port Chicago Disaster. http://en.wikipedia.org/wiki/Port_Chicago_disaster

Rancho Monte del Diablo. http://en.wikipedia.org/wiki/Rancho_Monte_del_Diablo

Rand, Ken. *Port Chicago Isn't There Anymore: But We Still Call It Home*. West Jordan, Utah: Media Man! Productions, 2008.

Starr, Kevin. *Americans and the California Dream, 1850–1915*. New York: Oxford University Press, 1973.